"*The White Rose Resists* is that rare and powerful story that rips your heart apart at the same time that it inspires you to live for something greater. With a lyrical and skillful voice, Amanda Barratt tells the amazing true story of the German students who dared to use their voices in a culture of oppression. This novel will have readers turning pages late into the night; it will have their blood surging and boiling with a need for justice. Most of all, it will remind them of what is truly important. A beautiful masterpiece of a novel!"

Heidi Chiavaroli, Carol Award–winning author of *Freedom's Ring* and *The Tea Chest*

"Woven with bittersweet delicacy, Barratt's intimate voice holds you so closely you are surprised at an outcome history already taught you. A monument to courage and conviction, *The White Rose Resists* blends Barratt's hallmark of immersive research with poetic resonance. This staggering portrait of love, danger, treachery, and unfathomable bravery in a time of sheer evil leaves us, in Barratt's intelligent care, with the most potent sense of shimmering hope. This book deserves to be on every shelf, at the center of every book club conversation, and on the tip of every reader's tongue for years to come."

Rachel McMillan, author of *The London Restoration*

"Young, daring, faith-filled, in love with life, yet committed without reservation—this is the White Rose, a close-knit group of university students determined to defy Hitler and rouse the German people from their egocentricity and complacency, no matter the cost. With meticulous research and beautiful, brilliant writing, Amanda Barratt weaves tension, suspense, love, and loss with a skillful hand. A stirring reminder that courage should never be relegated only to the pages of history, *The White Rose Resists* kept me turning pages as fast as my eyes could read."

Cathy Gohlke, Christy Award–winning author of *The Medallion*

"In *The White Rose Resists*, Amanda Barratt cherishes the past and honors true lives while inspiring this present generation to courage. Her storytelling deftly moves between perspectives of characters both real and fictional, portraying radiant hope against a backdrop of darkness. Painstakingly researched and masterfully rendered, this account deserves space in every mind and heart."

Amanda Dykes, author of *Whose Waves These Are* and *Set the Stars Alight*

T0051670

"Amanda Barratt masterfully brings history to life, honoring the unforgettable stories of those who lived before us. In *The White Rose Resists*, Amanda draws the reader into the heart of World War II Germany and introduces us to brave men and women who put their lives on the line because they were compelled to do the right thing. Their story is challenging, beautifully told, and carefully researched. I was entrenched from beginning to end and won't soon forget their sacrifice."

Kelli Stuart, author of the award-winning *Like a River from Its Course* and *A Silver Willow by the Shore*

THE WHITE ROSE RESISTS

THE WHITE ROSE RESISTS

A Novel of the German Students
Who Defied Hitler

AMANDA BARRATT

KREGEL
PUBLICATIONS

The White Rose Resists: A Novel of the German Students Who Defied Hitler
© 2020 by Amanda Barratt

Published by Kregel Publications, a division of Kregel Inc., 2450 Oak Industrial Dr. NE, Grand Rapids, MI 49505.

All rights reserved. No part of this book may be reproduced, stored in a retrieval system, or transmitted in any form or by any means—electronic, mechanical, photocopy, recording, or otherwise—without written permission of the publisher, except for brief quotations in reviews.

Distribution of digital editions of this book in any format via the internet or any other means without the publisher's written permission or by license agreement is a violation of copyright law and is subject to substantial fines and penalties. Thank you for supporting the author's rights by purchasing only authorized editions.

This is a work of fiction. Apart from the central characters in the book and certain historical facts and public figures, the persons and events portrayed in this work are the creations of the author, and any resemblance to persons living or dead is purely coincidental.

Scripture quotations are from the King James Version.

Library of Congress Cataloging-in-Publication Data
Names: Barratt, Amanda, 1996- author.
Title: The white rose resists : a novel of the German students who defied
   Hitler / Amanda Barratt.
Description: Grand Rapids, MI : Kregel Publications, [2020]
Identifiers: LCCN 2020002152
Subjects: LCSH: Weisse Rose (Resistance group)—Fiction. | Scholl, Sophie,
   1921–1943—Fiction. | World War, 1939–1945—Underground
   movements—Fiction. | Anti-Nazi movement—German—Fiction. | GSAFD:
   Historical fiction.
Classification: LCC PS3602.A777463 W48 2020 | DDC 813/.6—dc23
LC record available at https://lccn.loc.gov/2020002152

ISBN 978-0-8254-4648-1, print
ISBN 978-0-8254-7661-7, epub

Printed in the United States of America
20 21 22 23 24 25 26 27 28 29 / 5 4 3 2 1

Somebody, after all, had to make a start.
—Sophie Scholl

A man's moral worth is established only at the point
where he is ready to give up his life
in defense of his convictions.
—Henning von Tresckow (1901–44)

⤍

To the White Rose—
brave men and women who raised their voices
while their world fell silent.
We remember your sacrifice.
And to all whose hearts beat with a refrain for truth.
May we strive to be White Roses in our world.

Soli Deo Gloria.

CHARACTER LIST

The Scholl Family

Sophie Scholl—A twenty-one-year-old biology and philosophy student in her first semester at Ludwig Maximilian University.

Hans Scholl—Sophie's twenty-three-year-old brother. A medical student at Ludwig Maximilian University.

Robert Scholl—Sophie's father.

Magdalena Scholl—Sophie's mother.

Inge Scholl—Sophie's twenty-five-year-old sister.

Elisabeth "Lisl" Scholl—Sophie's twenty-two-year-old sister.

Werner Scholl—Sophie's twenty-year-old brother.

The Brandt Family

Annalise Brandt—A twenty-one-year-old art student in her first semester at Ludwig Maximilian University.

Standartenführer Horst Brandt—Annalise's father.

Marta Brandt—Annalise's mother.

Horst Brandt—Annalise's twenty-year-old brother.

Heinz Brandt—Annalise's fifteen-year-old brother.

Albert Brandt—Annalise's thirteen-year-old brother.

The Hoffmann Family

Kirk Hoffmann—A twenty-three-year-old medical student at Ludwig Maximilian University.

Pastor Paul Hoffmann—Kirk's father.

Emilie Hoffmann—Kirk's mother.

The Student Resistance

Alexander "Alex" Schmorell—A twenty-four-year-old medical student at Ludwig Maximilian University. Alex is sometimes called by his Russian nickname "Shurik."

Christoph "Christl" Probst—A twenty-two-year-old medical student at Ludwig Maximilian University. Husband of Herta Probst and father of Michael, Vincent, and, later, Katja.

Wilhelm "Willi" Graf—A twenty-four-year-old medical student at Ludwig Maximilian University.

Traute Lafrenz—Hans's girlfriend and a student at Ludwig Maximilian University.

Other Characters

Leutnant Fritz Hartnagel—Sophie's fiancé.

Professor Kurt Huber—Professor of philosophy at Ludwig Maximilian University.

Gisela Schertling—Acquaintance of Sophie.

Katharina Schüddekopf—Friend of the Scholls.

Manfred Eickemeyer—Architect friend of Hans Scholl.

Falk Harnack—Member of the Berlin resistance.

Else Gebel—Inmate at the Wittelsbacher Palace.

Inspector Mohr—Gestapo interrogator.

Judge Roland Freisler—Infamous People's Court judge.

Dr. Friedrich Voigt—Physician at Stadelheim Prison.

Katrin Voigt—Friedrich's wife.

CHAPTER ONE

Sophie
May 1, 1942
Munich, Germany

MY FUTURE IS WAITING, a spark in the distance burning steadily brighter as the train approaches the city.

Scrunched into a window seat near the back, I fix my gaze on the smudged glass, my reflection an overlay. To some, the outskirts of Munich aren't what could be called beautiful, but to me they are. Perhaps it's simply because they're new. New, after so many months of bleak sameness.

As we near the Hauptbahnhof, the sprawling patchwork of the city comes into view, the skyline dominated by ancient churches with spires seeming to pierce the skies, the twin cupolas of the Frauenkirche soaring high above them all.

But even now, as the train carries me toward my new life, longing twinges through me for Ulm, the city of my childhood.

On the rack above rests my suitcase and, beside that, a satchel packed by Mutter last evening. Her face flashes before me, graying hair piled into a wispy bun, apron wrapping her waist, and eyes intent on her task. I came into the tiny kitchen and found her adding a large *kuchen* to the bag on the counter.

"Where?" Since the outbreak of war, such confections are a rare treat.

She turned with a smile I could tell was bittersweet. "I've been saving rations for weeks. You only turn twenty-one once. And I want you to have the best of birthdays, my dear daughter."

I hugged her. A goodbye embrace. Not only to her, but to the last vestiges of childhood. She smelled like fresh bread and soap. Frail though she is, she hugged me back with surprising fierceness. As if something innate tells her we will not see each other again for some time, and that when we do, much will have changed in me.

"Danke, Mutti," I whispered against the soft cotton of her blouse.

The memory fades. Smoke belches from the train, the whistle blows. I scan the blur of forms and faces on the platform as the train pulls into the immense brick station. Hoping, *knowing* Hans will be waiting for me.

The train jolts to a stop. I stand on legs that shake from the motion of the train and, I admit, a touch of giddiness. I grasp my well-worn suitcase in one hand, satchel in the other, and join the queue of passengers waiting to disembark. The narrow corridor is rife with the scents of too many bodies packed together—sweat, stale cigarettes, and someone's cheap perfume.

I descend the train steps, feet shod in sensible brown lace-up shoes, and draw in a breath of warm, slightly smoke-hazed air.

The station is flooded with light, echoing with conductors calling out departure times, the brisk footsteps of travelers. An officer in crisp Wehrmacht gray catches sight of a young woman expectantly scanning the crowd and hastens toward her. A cry of delight. A kiss. A trio of soldiers stride toward the exit, duffel bags slung over their shoulders.

I stand off to the side near a board listing train fares and schedules, everyone certain of their destination, it seems, but me. The daisy in my hair, fresh this morning, faded now, droops lower, petals tickling my ear. The weight of my suitcase sends an ache through my arm. I swallow, glance both ways.

He'll come. Of course he'll come.

Then it all fades. Hans strides jauntily through the crowd. No longer does the vast city seem to gulp me in and swallow me whole. Hans is here.

With him, Munich is, will be, home.

I drop my bags and throw my arms around him. My brother, so dashing, so tall, hugs me back, then puts me from him, his warm, strong hands still in mine.

"You've arrived at last." He grins down at me, brown eyes twinkling. "It's taken long enough."

It isn't the train he refers to. I've wanted to attend Ludwig Maximilian University with Hans since passing my *Abitur*. But first I had to do my duty for Führer and Fatherland and complete a term of labor service, which ended up turning into a two-year ordeal before I was pronounced able to start my studies. Hans has been privy to my frustrations from the beginning, and the twinkle in his gaze seems to say: *It's all behind us. The future is ours.*

He grabs my suitcase and satchel. It's then I notice Traute Lafrenz lingering in the background. My brother's girlfriend watches us with a half smile. Everything, from her stylish gray suit to the jet-black curls brushing her shoulders, suggests a cosmopolitan elegance I could never hope to attain.

"Welcome to Munich, Sophie." Traute smiles and embraces me warmly.

"It's good to see you again." Her Hamburg-accented voice is rich and slightly husky, not in a seductive way, but like a girl who isn't afraid to laugh often or cheer her lungs out at a sporting event.

"And you," I reply. "You look well."

Hans turns to us with a broad grin. Curling strands of dark hair fall over his forehead. "Ready, ladies?"

We nod and he falls into step between us, one arm looped through mine, the other through Traute's, our threesome leaving the station behind, merging into the crowd. For a glorious instant, I'm here with my beloved brother on the cusp of the world, and I forget about the grueling years of labor service, about my anxiety for Fritz, even about the war. Warm air stirs my hair against my cheeks. Munich bustles with streetcars, pedestrians, buildings of stucco and stone rising high.

A flash of red catches my eye. Flags hang at intervals from buildings along the street. Reality floods back, smacking me like a storm-tossed wave. In Munich, I'll never have the chance to forget.

The sea of black and scarlet will always be near to remind me.

Gruesome spiders drenched in blood.

Hans's flat is, putting it kindly, what one would expect of a bachelor who doesn't have his mutter around to pick up after him. Books and papers piled onto a round table probably meant to be used for dining. Unemptied ashtrays. A coat with worn-in elbows tossed over the back of the lumpy sofa. Even Hans's prized modern artwork hangs crooked on the walls, prints by artists like Franz Marc, Emil Nolde, Wassily Kandinsky—bursts of color in the otherwise dingy student apartment.

The Nazis are firm in their insistence such artists are degenerate. Whatever doesn't suit the Führer is always dubbed by that term. Degenerate art. Degenerate swing music, books, authors. Degenerate humans—Jews, Poles, the mentally handicapped. A familiar knot twists my stomach.

Settled on the sagging sofa, I cross my legs and watch Hans and Traute rummage through my satchel. We've spent the past hour chatting, sharing family news, and catching up. Hans and Traute kept their arms around each other the whole time. I'm happy for my brother. Traute is lively and intelligent, a medical student like Hans. Though with his record of past girlfriends, I can't help but wonder how long this one will last.

Traute pulls out the bottle of wine, brandishing it aloft. "Tell me, Hans, do any of your other sisters want to celebrate a birthday in Munich?"

Hans laughs, holding up the *kuchen* and inhaling its rich, buttery scent.

Seeing them together makes me long for Fritz. Leutnant Fritz Hartnagel, my fiancé. We exchange letters, as do so many couples separated by war. But pen and paper aren't the same as sitting in some sun-drenched spot in midsummer, his whisper in my ear, and my head against his shoulder. There's no denying that.

"The rest of the party will be here soon." Hans ambles over and sits on the edge of the armchair.

"Party?" I ask.

"Of course." Hans grins. "I wouldn't dream of marking this momentous occasion without a party for your birthday. I invited some friends, the ones I've told you about."

I gasp. "You mean Alex and Christl and Kirk?"

Hans nods, looking pleased. "I can't wait for you to meet them."

"You won't have to wait long," Traute calls. "I hear them coming up the stairs."

Instinctively, I tuck my hair behind my ear (I've since plucked out the faded daisy) and smooth my navy dress. I've never put much stock in my appearance, save to bob my hair in a daringly boyish cut during my teens. But I might start if I spend much time around the pulled-together Traute. Like all proper German girls, her face is bare of cosmetics, but her fine cheekbones and dark eyes need no accentuation.

A knock sounds on the door, and Hans rises to open it. In an instant, the room is bursting with three young men, all exchanging hearty handshakes and greetings with Hans and Traute. I stay where I am, on the sofa, watching the scene. The three arrivals fill the room with their broad shoulders and deep voices, an unmistakably masculine presence. I've missed being around young men. Much of the past two years have been spent in the company of dimwitted girls my own age or kindergarten students and fellow female teachers.

"Come here, Sophie." Hans motions me forward. Their gazes fix on me. *So this is Hans's little sister*, they must be thinking.

I cross the room and stand next to Hans.

"Sophie, meet Alex Schmorell, Christl Probst, and Kirk Hoffmann. Everyone, my sister, Sophie, arrived in Munich at last."

Lanky, blond-haired Christl is the first to step forward. His smile is gentle and warm, as is the handclasp he gives me.

"We're so happy you've joined us, Fräulein Scholl."

"Please, call me Sophie." My smile is easy.

"Very glad to meet you. Hans says you're enrolled at LMU for the summer semester." Brown-haired and broad-shouldered, Kirk has the look of one who makes feminine pulses flutter while being oblivious to it. His welcoming grin and strong handshake endear him to me instantly.

"*Ja*, and I can't wait to get started."

"At long last we meet the famous Sophie." Alex takes my hand, but he doesn't shake it. Instead, he bows low, reddish-blond hair falling into his eyes, lips grazing my skin. When he looks up, there's a twinkle in his blue-gray gaze.

"I feel as if we already know each other, Hans talks about you so often."

"All good things, I hope." His mouth tilts in a sideways grin.

Unlike the others, who wear suits, a coffee-brown turtleneck sweater encases Alex's shoulders. His voice has a cultured quality, with intonations that mark him as not altogether German. Hans has told me of Alex's Russian heritage; he's the son of a German vater and Russian mutter, the latter who died before Alex's second birthday. Alex lived in Russia until he was four, when his vater took him and a Russian nursemaid back to Germany. Yet Russia remains the land of Alex's heart, and he was never more grieved than when our country invaded his.

"There's another grand thing about Sophie. Along with her lovely self, look what she brought us. Wine and a birthday *kuchen*." Traute brings the *kuchen* from the table, Hans, the wine. They place both, along with plates and glasses, on the low table in front of the sofa. Traute claps her hands. "Gather 'round, everyone."

The young men waste no time. Traute settles on the sofa, along with Hans. Christl takes the armchair, and the rest, the floor, sitting cross-legged on the carpet near the table. The casual atmosphere loosens the tension between my shoulders, almost unrelenting since the day I started labor service.

"Do the honors, Sophie." Hans slips his arm around Traute, and she leans her curly, dark head against his shoulder.

"Your birthday is soon?" Christl asks, as I move to cut the *kuchen*.

"*Ja*, my twenty-first. On the ninth." I cut and plate generous slices of the brown, sweet-smelling confection.

Once everyone has been served, Hans lifts his glass.

"Everyone, a toast. To Sophie. May she have the happiest of birthdays, enjoy her time in Munich to the fullest, and get high marks on every exam." He winks at me.

"To Sophie," the group choruses with lifted glasses.

"Danke." I smile, sipping the fruity, earthy wine. I settle on the floor beside Kirk, smoothing my skirt over my knees.

"Mmm. Wonderful." Traute dabs the corners of her mouth with a hand-kerchief. "You must take a piece home to Herta, Christl." To me, she adds. "Herta is Christl's wife. They have the two sweetest little boys."

"I actually can't stay long. I haven't seen them much lately and promised to tuck them in." Christl sets his glass on the table, a look of deep fondness in his eyes. As if, even now, he's not with us, but in some lamp-lit bedroom, kissing his little sons' fresh-from-the-bath hair and reading them a bedtime tale.

"I hope I have the chance to meet them sometime." The *kuchen* is sub-lime, buttery and rich. I savor another bite.

"You will." Christl smiles, his words as genuine as if it's already done.

"So what do you think of Munich, Sophie?" Kirk turns to me.

I hesitate. Honesty is not a virtue in the Germany in which we live. Unless one's honest opinions align with the Führer's, of course. But these are Hans's friends. I trust him enough to know he would never add some-one to his close circle who didn't share our beliefs.

Plate balanced on his knee, Alex swirls the wine around in his glass. The reddish liquid reminds me suddenly, uncannily, of swastikas rippling bloodred in the wind.

How long has it been since I've been able to give free vent to my feelings, trusting that no ideology-tuned ears are within range? Too long.

"Red and black everywhere." I meet Kirk's eyes, sensing the gazes of everyone upon me—these bright young university men. "There's not a great building in the city that isn't plastered with one of Hitler's symbols. It's disgusting, scars on our beautiful architecture. Of course, Ulm isn't much different."

"I wonder how long before it becomes our symbol of defeat, instead of victory?" Alex sets aside his half-finished plate as if he no longer has an appetite.

"That"—Kirk's tone is quiet, but distinct—"depends on the people."

Alex's eyes, twinkling moments ago, now blaze with inner fire. Looking into them makes me start. Embodied in their depths is a passion the whole army of Hitler's goose-stepping minions, puffed up with propaganda, can't match, much less quench.

I cannot tear my gaze away.

"It's our fault, you know." Our casual circle seems to shrink, until we're leaning forward, hanging on Hans's words. "We've allowed ourselves to be governed without resistance by an irresponsible faction ruled by dark instincts. Worse than children. Children, at least, sometimes question their parents' decisions. But have we questioned? Nein, we've let ourselves be led like dogs on a leash, panting after Goebbels's every speech, *Sieg Heiling* like trained monkeys." My brother spits out the words.

Christl nods. "Yet some have spoken out. Bishop von Galen, for example."

"Who's reading him?" Darkness creeps through the window, a shadow falling on Alex's features. Soon, it will be time to draw the blackout curtains. "He preached three sermons, which a few brave souls dared to duplicate, resulting in a few hundred copies, likely little more. That's not enough. Germany has been allowed to nap in the middle of carnage. It's time to wake up, for this country to rub its eyes and look around and see the truth."

Christl glances up. He's no longer the gentle family man, smiling at the mention of his little ones, but a revolutionary with a fervor Goebbels, no matter how many stupid speeches he gives, could never emulate. His hands draw into fists. "It's not just 'this country.' It's *our* country. When this madness has ended, those who are left will be judged by the world, no matter what they thought amongst themselves. It's action that will stand the test. Only action provides absolution."

The words remain in my mind long after the men leave for their lodgings. I stand at the window, peering through a crack in the stifling blackout curtain, the evening chill soaking into my bones.

"Only action provides absolution."

CHAPTER TWO

Annalise
May 3, 1942
Berlin, Germany

BERLIN IS A PRISON. My vater, my jailor.

I'm leaving—escaping both—today.

I descend the stairs, case in hand. My new low-heeled black shoes make little sound against the carpet of our family's Berlin mansion. Before Hitler claimed power, we knew nothing of such riches. We lived in a cramped apartment in a low-rent district of the city, where the faucet leaked and the queue for the communal bathroom snaked down the corridor.

Now our residence boasts suites for each member of the family. Now I have new clothes to wear at university, a real leather suitcase.

But at what price do these luxuries come?

They wait for me near the front door. Mutter, the model German *hausfrau*, dressed in a serviceable gray dress. Wide hipped, big boned, blond haired. Once she may have been pretty, but birthing four Aryan children has left her worn and faded. At twenty-one, I'm the oldest, the only girl followed by a string of boys.

Vater stands beside her. On two weeks leave from the eastern front, he isn't in uniform today, though one wouldn't know it by his posture. Shoulders square, back straight as a broom-handle, hands behind his back. Angular face, steel-blue eyes. Ever the standartenführer. With his blond hair, he's far more the model German than the Führer. Hitler is squat and dark, and his mustache makes him appear cartoonishly absurd.

I've already said "Auf Wiedersehen" to my brothers who are off to school for the day. My twenty-year-old brother, Horst, I haven't seen since Christmas. He's away, doing the duty of an able-bodied German son, serving the Fatherland in the Wehrmacht. Offering himself like the sacrificial lamb to be shot, blown up, or destroyed in whatever method our enemies are making use of at the moment.

"You're ready, dear?" Mutter's eyes are two wide question marks in her round face. This parting is not easy for her. I hate to cause her pain, but cause it I must.

I *will* break free of this cage.

I nod. I set down my suitcase and wrap my arms around her. She hugs me back, doughy arms clinging as a child's would, as if she wishes she could stop time and keep us frozen in this moment forever. A rebel knot nooses my throat, though I've already vowed not to cry. Without me, Mutter will be lost, the only woman in a house of Nazi-crazed men and of boys pushing to become Nazi-crazed men.

She'll survive, I tell myself. She'll find strength.

"You'll write and tell me everything?"

"I'll write. And call. You'll hear from me so often, you'll forget I'm even away." I kiss her gently on her smooth cheek. Her skin smells like faded lavender.

Mutter nods. Her chin quivers, but no sobs escape. Vater says only the weak shed tears. Weak, meaning those not of the Aryan race. Poles, Jews, and the mentally ill are always termed weak. It's one of Vater's most scathing epithets. I suspect it's why my littlest brother, Albert, no longer cries. Not even when he fell down the stairs and broke his arm last year. He only lay there, gritting his teeth. So brave it was almost eerie.

Off to the side, Vater views our parting without emotion. I retrieve my suitcase and let its weight strengthen me.

"Auf Wiedersehen, Vater." We could be two associates bidding goodbye after a business meeting. The coal of anger in my stomach gathers tinder. How little he cares for me.

How foolish I am to even want him to.

"Auf Wiedersehen, Annalise." He looks me up and down, as if I'm one of his troops on review. I hold my breath, skeptical I'll pass inspection. My blue skirt suit is new, a rarity in these days of rationed clothes. Upon Vater's return from the front, Mutter happened to broach the subject at dinner about my getting some new things for university. A couple of days later, a box appeared on my bed with the suit, two skirts, two dresses, a blouse, and a sweater. All exceptional quality and just my size. Mutter purchased the matching hat atop my short curls—short because I hacked off my reddish-blond braids with the kitchen shears when no one was around. German girls are supposed to wear their hair braided or in a simple bun, though I can't see why. I like my chin-length hair. It makes me feel confident, like a film star, though my skin is bare of cosmetics.

Right now, I do not feel confident. In front of Vater, I shrivel.

"You'll study for a year." Our agreement issues from his lips, a reminder. I need none. Agreeing to our arrangement is the only way I've convinced him to allow me to attend university. I'm to get my fill of "whatever it is I'm going to school for" and return to Berlin after a year's time to perform the real task of an Aryan woman. Vater will choose a marriage candidate. I'm to submit, my body given over to childbearing like a good broodmare for the Reich.

"A year." I hesitate, looking up into his iron gaze. What am I waiting for? A hug? A handshake?

Nothing. I'm waiting for nothing.

He doesn't even touch me. Just stares, no doubt counting the seconds until he can return to his study and dwell on military maneuvers for the Fatherland. I won't embarrass myself by waiting any longer. He doesn't need to see the hurt I strive so desperately to hide. He isn't worth it.

I flash Mutter a smile. She returns it faintly. I stride toward the door, turn the knob, cool metal pressing into my damp palm.

Vater's black Mercedes waits at the curb to drive me to the train station. I clatter down the steps in my new shoes, the warm May air soothing my skin. The driver takes my suitcase and opens the door. I climb in, settling onto the smooth leather seat. The door closes with a firm bang. I sit straight, fingers clenched in my lap as the driver stows my suitcase. My breath comes easier now. I relax my hands, flattening them against my skirt.

A rumble as the engine starts.

Just before we turn down the street, I glance once at the house, the stately brick, manicured shrubs, and mullioned windows. How do prisoners regard the bars that once kept them captive? Loathing? Triumph?

A mix of both stirs through me as the house disappears from view. I do not call it home. Home, if any place in my life could be termed such, is the little apartment in the low-rent district where we lived before the National Socialist German Workers' Party sank its teeth into our family. Vater smiled there sometimes. Mutter spoke louder, more freely, her laughter honey warm.

Munich, my destination, will be home. There, art and study will encompass my life. I intend to drown in it, soaking in hue and texture before my world becomes a black-and-white landscape of a husband I do not love and childbirth and the endlessness of doing my duty.

But not yet.

"I will be free," I whisper. The driver glances over his shoulder, but I doubt he catches my words. I say them again, a smile blooming on my lips.

"I will be free."

CHAPTER THREE

Kirk
May 6, 1942
Munich

WHAT IS THE MEASURE of my life if I stand by and do nothing? Does the blood of Jews stain my hands any less because mine did not pull the trigger? How can I go on, day after ceaseless day, occupied with study, friends, concerts, lectures?

How can any honest German continue with life as usual while our country sinks deeper into the mire of dehumanization?

I remember the moment these thoughts first turned through my mind as clearly as if it were yesterday. November 10, 1938. My life is two parts—divided down the middle in a sweeping, chilling slice. The tenth of November is that slice.

Sitting at the desk in my apartment, staring at a blank page on which I'm supposed to be writing a research paper, I see their faces, burned into my soul with searing clarity. Their eyes . . .

Their eyes haunt me.

It was after midnight when it began. I was nineteen, home after completing my term of National Labor Service—six months of manual labor building the new autobahns. I did not intend to remain home long and would soon begin the next round of required service, this time in the Wehrmacht. My parents' way of life—their piety, their distrust of Hitler's Reich—dug beneath my skin like splinters I couldn't pluck out.

I'd never denounce them. Nor did I agree with them, a state of affairs that led to years of arguments and tense silences. Including that night. I had escaped at ten p.m., slamming the front door, leaving my mutter standing in the hallway, arms folded against her sweater-clad chest, pain etched upon her features. I ended up at a nearby *bierhalle*, planted on a stool, nursing my second drink, the yeasty scent heavy in the air, its taste in my mouth. Smoke hazed the dim-lit room, familiar raucous laughter sounding at the other end. The source of that laughter stumped across the room, carrying an empty tray. Herr Koch.

He leaned burly arms on the bar, smelling like he'd just eaten a keg of sauerkraut. Sweat shone on his apple-cheeked face. No matter the weather, the man always seemed to glisten with perspiration.

"Keeping yourself scarce around here lately, Hoffmann."

"I've been away," I muttered into my drink, fingers clenched around its handle.

Herr Koch said something else, likely starting in on a joke, and I stood, knowing the only way to escape him was to leave. I plunked a few coins down on the bar's grooved wooden surface. As I headed toward the door, I sensed Herr Koch's gaze on me. Once, I'd enjoyed nothing better than swapping stories with him, one of the few times I felt like more than the Lutheran pastor's son. But tonight, I was riled. Angry at Vater for his refusal to embrace National Socalism. Angry at myself for the words I'd flung at him. *Traitor. Disgrace. Ashamed to have you as my vater.*

I pushed through the door, its hinges groaning. Cold air slapped my face. I pulled up the collar of my coat, shoving my hands in my pockets. The wool of my collar chafed my skin as I walked, long strides eating up the distance, alone with my simmering thoughts.

I glanced up. The moon glimmered, a silver oyster in the sky. A strange glow emanated in the distance. It gave the inky sky an orange tinge. A gust of wind bore the faint, acrid scent of smoke.

Something was on fire.

Footsteps pounded the cobblestones, rushing past me. I walked doggedly on as a group of men jogged down the street, rounding the corner. I kept walking, turning the opposite way, headed toward my parents' house.

A crash, like the contents of a china cabinet smashing. I started. It came from somewhere nearby, perhaps the next street over. A shout followed.

Light gleamed from a nearby two-story business—Wollheim's Fine Furniture. A greenish-gray van sat parked next to the building. Instinctively, I slipped into the shadows, pressing myself flush against the clammy brick of a building across the street.

The windows. I'd traveled this route dozens of times, always noting the shop's stylish window displays. This night, a spider web of cracks pockmarked the glass, punctuated with gaping fang-like holes. Crystal shards littered the ground.

But not only the windows. Broken and battered furnishings lay in front of the shop like debris after a storm. A chair with one leg. A lampshade. An end table.

Had they been vandalized? My heart beat faster. I should get the police.

Figures emerged from within the shop, forms vaguely illuminated. Two women, a man between them grasping one arm each. Both women wore kerchiefs over their hair and bulky coats.

I took the risk of getting closer. My curiosity had vanished. I don't know what replaced it. Maybe it wasn't my mind that forced my feet to move nearer to the group across the street, but a divine hand.

An elderly man walked behind the two women, also held by force, his left arm gripped by a uniformed Brownshirt. Behind him, the only member unescorted, toddled a little boy. The child looked hastily awakened from dreamland. A tiny nightcap sat crooked on his head, his shoulders covered by a coat several sizes too large. In one hand, he clutched a toy bear.

The Wollheim family. And three SA, swastika armbands reddish smears on their biceps.

Each breath seemed to squeeze my lungs as I bore silent witness to the scene.

Dear God, what is going on? Not a prayer so much as a plea.

"*Schnell*!" barked the man carrying a flashlight. "Out, *Juden*. Out!"

Juden? These people were Jews? My brain hadn't made the connection until that moment. My stomach knotted.

One of the women stumbled, tripping over something. Her skirt? The curb? The man with the flashlight noticed. He marched over.

Fear is an odor, rank and ugly. It crouched here in the air, radiating from the young woman. Her breath clouded in short puffs. Surprisingly, she didn't shrink back or cower as the man loomed in front of her. Just stood there, face pale in the white beam of light, regarding him. Resignedly? Defiantly?

He leaned in, face pressed toward hers. "When I say *schnell* I mean it. You filthy Jew whore."

The elderly man behind her balled the hand loose at his side into a fist. But he uttered no protest. Only his eyes marked unspent anger.

The SA man noticed. "What are *you* looking at?" But he didn't hit the old man. I expected him to, could see it coming.

Instead, he turned, raised a fist, and struck the girl in the midsection. She cried out, doubled over, and crumpled to the ground. The older woman pulled the little boy to her side. The SA man laughed. Much as Herr Koch had only an hour ago.

Thinking back, their laughter blurs in my mind. Herr Koch, face beet red and chuckling; these men, their visages contorted in a display of hate; until they become one and the same. The laughter of November 10, 1938.

The laughter of Kristallnacht.

"Get up." He kicked her huddled form with the toe of his boot. "Onto the truck."

The old man bent to help her. The Brownshirt pushed him away. The other SA watched, arms folded, gazes approving.

"The whore can get up by herself."

Slowly, the woman rose, pressing her hands against the cobblestones and standing. A streak of dirt marked her pale cheek.

They herded the three adults into the back of the van. The little boy stood behind them, clutching his toy, looking up at the grown-ups. He didn't seem afraid, waiting as patiently as if standing in line for his turn on a carousel.

What possessed me to stand there, shadows shrouding me, and do nothing? Was it the rhetoric inbred from my years in the Hitler Youth that the Jews had evil running through their veins like blood? Nein. If any emotion could be named, it was fear. Fear at the unfolding horror, at what would happen if the men unleashed their anger on me.

Coward is too kind a word for what I was then. What I am still.

The man climbed in with little help, as did the younger woman. But the other struggled, clambering in her long skirt. One of the SA pushed her hard in the rear. Not a helping hand, but a weighty shove that sent her floundering. A thud, as she landed in the van.

Even cattle, on the way to the slaughterhouse, were given more courtesy.

The tallest SA, the one who'd struck the young woman, reached down and picked up the little boy, hefting him into his arms like a sack of flour. The motion jarred the teddy bear from the child's grip. It fell to the ground. The boy let out a wail, chubby arms and legs flailing.

"*Teddybär!*" he screamed, hysterical. "*Teeeddybär!*"

The man threw him into the back and slammed the doors. The others followed, climbing into the front, talking and laughing. The engine started and the van trundled down the street, turning the corner and disappearing from sight. Leaving the street barren, save me, the sole witness to one of hundreds of crimes that would take place that night in Munich and across Germany.

Finally I could move, and I did, emerging from the shadows and crossing the street to stand in front of the shop. A home and a business, now empty, their occupants stolen away in the middle of the night like criminals. Criminals whose only crime was to have been born God's chosen people. I stared at the building, fighting to breathe, hands clenched at my sides. *Why?* Why did these people deserve this while my own parents were allowed to sleep in their warm bed, undisturbed?

Growing up, I'd witnessed mild injustices—stronger schoolmates pranking on the weaker, an angry man kicking a mangy dog. Compared to this, I'd been sheltered. This made my breath seize in my lungs as if frozen by shards of ice. This . . . changed me.

There on the damp ground, surrounded by fractured glass, lay the toy bear, empty eyes staring up at me. I picked it up, holding it in both hands. Its fur was matted and worn, smelling of clean sheets and little-boy kisses.

I never discovered the fate that befell its owner.

That night, as I wandered further through Munich, I witnessed more horrors. Burning synagogues, bearded men forced to dance like schoolchildren while crowds pointed and laughed. The Star of David painted in ugly smears across buildings. Women screaming hysterically as their men were hauled away.

Glass. Thousands of shards strewn across the cobblestones, diamonds of desecration.

That night, I went into my parents' room, and wept great, wracking sobs, begging their forgiveness for my blindness. I'd been caught up in the banners and marching and songs of the Nazi Party, eyes closed to the brewing evil. All along, they'd known the truth, and tried to make me see it. It had taken Kristallnacht to rip the scales from my eyes and force me into the light of day.

A week later, before leaving for the Wehrmacht, I bowed my heart and surrendered my life to a God greater than Adolf Hitler.

The years passed. Kristallnacht was only the beginning. The war began in 1939, our triumphant army trampling Poland in a month. After completing basic training, I'd joined the Wehrmacht as a medic in the hope it would enable me to mend, instead of destroy. In 1940, during the invasion of France, I witnessed Germany's suppression of a rich and beautiful country while tending to hundreds of our wounded. In France, I met Hans Scholl. In the following years, my request to study at university was granted, and I was assigned to Ludwig Maximilian University's Second Student Medical Company.

But what did I do? Was it a coincidence I was there that November night?

I stare at my blank paper, the faces of those lost receding. At university, I'd made friends, reunited with Hans Scholl, and been introduced to Alexander Schmorell and Christl Probst. Young officers and medical students like myself. They grappled with the same questions, all of us unwilling to remain part and parcel with criminals by our complicity. So far, all we'd done was talk at cafés or late-night conferences in Hans's apartment and the Schmorells' villa.

Christl is right. Only action offers any hope of absolution.

But I hadn't acted. I'd witnessed the horrors of November 10 and done nothing as a result of what I'd seen.

No longer. I won't spend another day going through the motions of life while others journey through hell itself. I will rise up and fight, not for, but against Hitler's regime.

I will, I must act.

God help us, we will resist.

CHAPTER FOUR

Annalise
May 12, 1942

I AM FREE.

But I am also alone. A little island in the great sea that is Munich. It's a strange sensation, this aloneness, when in reality I'm surrounded by people. Each day, I walk from the rooms I rent from a perpetually scowling landlady to Ludwig Maximilian University. During these early morning walks, I take in the city, its lofty architecture smothered by swastikas and signs directing one to the nearest air-raid shelter. I study the faces, men with heads bowed low and newspapers under their arms, weary-faced women trekking to stand in long market lines in the hopes of getting something for their ration coupons.

And the students, heading to classes as I am. I say little to them, this morning no different than the others. I've always been shy, or perhaps simply unaccustomed to the camaraderie of friends my own age. In my early teens, the girls in the Bund Deutscher Mädel—League of German Girls—never singled me out or welcomed me in, nor did I rise to leadership among their ranks. I've kept to myself, and my exchanges with fellow classmates, both then and now, are short and awkward.

I lift my hand in a wave to the girl who sits behind me in mathematics. She smiles, nods, as if expecting more from me. But I can't bring my mouth to open, my tongue to form words of introduction or greeting. She disappears, joining a group of other students, leaving me standing on the sidewalk. Watching them and cursing myself for my stupidity. My inability to reach out and connect.

I'm cold. Like Vater. I know it and I hate myself for it.

I force the ugly thoughts aside as I cross the bustling cobblestoned Ludwigstraße on the way to an art class. One can't be overwhelmed with anger and expect to create a work of beauty. That is my dream. To create something beautiful. Even now, my fingers ache for the feel of a brush in my hand, a blank canvas. To lose myself in color and texture.

Maybe even to find myself, my true self, in those very things.

A foursome hurries down the street, going the opposite way. Sunlight turns the sky a milky shade of cloudless blue, the warm light framing the majestic pale stone university buildings. What colors would I employ to capture the scene? I mentally envision my palette.

And find my gaze caught instead by a man with eyes the deepest shade of amber, so intense they snatch my breath.

I'm struck by him. He's handsome. It's not a phrase I use often—for goodness' sake, everyone calls the Führer the most handsome man in Germany—and I scarcely dare think it now, but the young man is indisputably so. His face is strong, but not like Vater's. Vater's strength is fueled by anger and discipline. This young man's strength, as if it flows from something deep within. His hair is the color of spilled molasses, parted in the middle and curling ever so slightly over his forehead. Tall of stature, strong of chin, broad of shoulders. He wears a beige suit, a satchel in one hand, a book beneath his other arm. His steps slow. Mine do too.

Seconds pass as we regard each other, gazes locked in a stare that whittles the meters between us down to centimeters. A smile curves his lips, an expression that sends warmth pooling through me, down to my toes.

I return his smile with a hesitant one of my own. His deepens as he nods, his figure framed by sunlight and the university building in the background. My fingers burn for a sketchbook and my pencils, though I scarcely trust myself to capture such an image and do it justice. It would be worth trying though, to render his features on paper to set before my eyes at will.

One of his friends calls for him to keep up. He turns, our contact broken.

My eyes fall closed as aching loneliness swells through me, sharper than before.

I do not know the man Vater will choose for me in a year's time. I know what my duty will be with him, and loathing fills me at the realization that duty is all it will be. Vater could never be so human as to select someone who could actually feel the emotion of love.

Powerfully, my heart goes out to him-with-the-amber-eyes-and-magical-smile. I walk in the direction of class, giving myself a mental shake.

I'm here for art, not idle daydreams. The course of my life has already been set.

And the hands that put it in motion brook no room for alteration.

Kirk
May 13, 1942

We're supposed to be studying. Instead, we linger in Manfred Eickemeyer's studio, gripped by the man and his words.

The studio isn't much to look at—a dingy basement cluttered with sculptures and sketches, smelling of old plaster and cheap cigarettes, low ceilinged and shadowed. Nor is Eickemeyer. He's awkwardly tall, balding, and too thin, rumpled suit hanging on his scarecrow frame.

But his voice fills the room with desperation's echo. It is that we listen to and understand.

"I spent several months in occupied Poland. Kraków, mostly. Apparently my architectural gifts are useful to the Fatherland." He gives a slight ironic smile. "Though of late, our Führer seems to enjoy the act of destruction more than anything else."

Beside me, Alex's lips twist wryly. He's smoking; pipe an extension of his fingers, curling gray tendrils of smoke filling the air with pungent vanilla. Hans sits nearest to Eickemeyer, leaning slightly forward, elbows on his knees. It's on Hans's invitation that Alex and I are here—"we must hear his experiences." I recall Hans's whispered words as we walked to Eickemeyer's. "He's seen things."

"I also did a good deal of traveling in the occupied territories. Have any of you heard of the SS-Einsatzgruppen?" He looks to each of us in turn. I shake my head. Something curls within me, like a worm unfurling in my stomach.

"Nein?" Eickemeyer shakes his head. "I didn't think so. The Nazis don't like to air things like that out in the open, even if the crimes are against Jews. Muddies the morale."

"We never had any morale to be muddied, Herr Eickemeyer," Hans says.

"All the better for you." Eickemeyer clears his throat. "I'd been sent to a village in Poland to meet with a Sturmbannführer Braunn. When I arrived, the sturmbannführer wasn't in his quarters. So I decided to take a walk." Eickemeyer stands and paces, leaving a trail of footprints in the plaster dust. "Get some fresh air for a few hours, stretch my legs. The village was quiet. Strangely so, I thought. It was March and the ground was muddy. I still remember how my boots squelched in the mud. They were new boots, and I was annoyed with myself for getting them dirty."

Alex taps away pipe ash and sighs, as if suppressing his irritation at Eickemeyer's tangent. Hans's brow creases. I shift in my seat. Not from impatience, but from a sick sense of dread.

"I walked, wind in my face, the tall grasses scratching against my trousers. I crested a hill and stopped to catch my breath." He draws a jagged inhale. "This . . . this is difficult for me to remember. When I remember, I am there again."

Hans gives a nod of understanding. "Please, Herr Eickemeyer," he says quietly. "Continue whenever you're ready."

Eickemeyer picks up a half-filled glass of amber liquid resting on the table behind him. Flicks his wrist and tosses back the barest amount, just enough to wet his lips. Returns the glass to the paper-strewn tabletop with a faint clink. "Standing there at the top of the hill, I heard a tramping, like my own feet had made, only magnified a thousand times. Curious, I waited." Somewhere outside, a car trundles past. Eickemeyer listens, silent until it is gone. "And then they came.

"They came in lines that curved like snakes without end. Men. Women. Children. Working men, carrying sacks bulging with their families' worldly goods. Men in suits, with cases of leather, their wives in furs and velvet. Children, clutching vaters' hands, babes in the arms of their mutters. Humanity. Humanity herded by soldiers in pressed uniforms and shining insignias." Eickemeyer's voice shakes.

The worm spreads in my middle. I cannot tear my gaze away from Eickemeyer's face. Nor can I stop my ears from hearing his next words.

"They were ordered to undress and leave their clothes in piles. Those that didn't comply were instantly shot . . . right there, in front of their children. There was no decency, no separation of the sexes. It was then most realized what would happen to them. I watched the moment it came over their faces. For some, dull resignation. For others, silent tears. Few made any outward protest. It's like they *knew* they were powerless. Those with children tried to calm them. One family started to quietly sing. Not a hymn, but a song about springtime and birds. I can still hear the high voices of those little ones, carried by the wind." Eickemeyer's hands tremble. He fumbles for a cigarette. A quiet click as he lights the narrow cylinder, the scent of sulfur.

I glance at Alex. His face is gray, like dirty cotton. Hans sits motionless.

"Their identity left with their garments. In their nakedness, they were no longer the businessman, the baker's wife. They were bodies. And to the soldiers who ordered them to stand at the edge of the ditch, they were targets.

"I wish I could tell you they died proudly, with some grand display to sear the hearts of their murderers." Eickemeyer's throat convulses. "How I wish I could tell you that. But they just . . . died. Mowed down by machine guns." His voice is choked. "One on top of the other, on top of the other.

Round upon round, falling into the pit. After the first volley, I vomited into the grass, while below the shots went on." He stares down at the ground. A sigh shudders his shoulders. "And then I left."

Silence falls over the room. The hanging lightbulb flickers above the table. I stare at my hands, remembering the little boy hugging his toy bear moments before the truck took him away. Did that family, that child, meet their end in such a ditch?

Eickemeyer turns away from us, bracing both hands on the table. His shoulders stoop.

There are no utterances to fill the void following words like Eickemeyer's. Had it been a tale of human cruelty, perhaps some platitude could be conjured.

But what Eickemeyer had witnessed hadn't been human cruelty. There are not strong enough syllables in mortal vocabulary to answer what he described.

"Herr Eickemeyer." Hans breaks the silence, voice strong, but with a shaken edge. "Your studio?"

Eickemeyer turns. Sweat clings to the meager strands of hair atop his shining head. He stares at Hans. "My studio?"

"Can we use it?"

Alex glances at me. We both understand. The three of us look to Eickemeyer, the man who has gone to hell and back to tell us what he witnessed. Not so we can listen and do nothing, but so we can act. The three of us have debated often about the various forms of resistance. We've rejected the idea of active opposition like making bombs and other types of sabotage, returning time and again to the idea of putting our thoughts down on paper and producing leaflets.

Doers of the Word, and not hearers only. One of my vater's favorite verses.

There is not a tendril of flesh inside me that wants to remain a hearer only.

"Of course." Eickemeyer's nod comes without hesitation. "It's yours for whatever you need. I'll see to it spare keys are made."

"Danke." A faint smile creases Hans's lips. He stands and rests a hand on Eickemeyer's shoulder. "We'll make good use of it." He faces Alex and me. "Mark my words."

We say our farewells to Eickemeyer and leave the studio in silence. The street is ink. A few stars puncture the sky overhead. Though the air is balmy, a chill wraps around me.

My friends are shadowy figures beside me as we walk, footfalls brisk on the cobblestones. Though the mandatory blackout has long since fallen, were it any other evening, we'd laugh and trade whisper-jokes that poke fun at Hitler.

Tonight, the men on either side of me stare straight ahead, each lost in his own thoughts. If they at all mirror mine, I do not envy them the restless hours ahead.

In minutes, we reach the street where we are to part ways. A peeling poster plastered across the brick of a nearby building declares: "With the help of all Germans, total victory will be ours."

If what Eickemeyer told us is victory, then I welcome defeat.

"Good night." Alex grips my hand.

"Night," I reply, turning to Hans.

"Danke for coming." Hans's face is murky in the darkness.

"Hans, Eickemeyer's studio?"

"Our base of operations." Hans's tone is smooth. "We'll need one, you know. Good night, Kirk." He nods to Alex, then walks away, steps firm and even.

I hurry through the familiar streets toward my apartment, passing few others. The buildings crouch in their places, windows hidden by swaths of black. I shove my hands into the pockets of my trousers and walk faster. Eickemeyer's voice echoes in my ears.

"Women. Children. One on top of the other, on top of the other. Round upon round, falling into the pit."

I will not sleep this night.

CHAPTER FIVE

Sophie
May 15, 1942

THE PROFESSOR'S VOICE ECHOES through the crowded lecture hall. I shift in my seat in the back row, notebook resting on the desk, pencil in hand. I fix my gaze by rote on the man behind the podium, pretending to listen. In reality, I couldn't be more disinterested.

Volk and Race is among my list of course requirements, a hackneyed conglomeration of ideological rhetoric, as if the professor recycled the scraps from a dozen Hitler Youth meetings. Across the hall, a row of young men in tan uniforms—members of the National Socialist Student Association sit military-straight, listening intently.

"Purity." The professor lifts one hand. "That is what we seek as an Aryan people. A pure, united Germany rising up as one against the taint of Bolshevism . . ."

Applause ripples through the room, which I don't echo. Someone coughs.

Fingertips resting on the paper of my notebook, I glance at the girl sitting next to me. She looks straight ahead, chin propped in one hand. Daringly cropped reddish-gold curls brush her jawbone, and she wears a fitted cream blouse and burgundy pleated skirt—more fashionable than most female students.

I look away, focusing my eyes on the professor, letting my mind drift. Thankfully, not all my lectures are like this. There are a few who dare to speak truth. Professor Kurt Huber is one of them. He lectures on philosophy twice a week to a packed hall of students. Rarely have I met someone with a less likely persona. He's short, balding, and limps, more than walks, to the podium. His tone is at first husky and garbled, as if from an injury to his larynx. But when he gains his voice, it strengthens, and I'm caught up in his words and ideas, his rendering of the thoughts of philosophers such as Kant and Leibniz.

The dry remarks he occasionally interjects barely veil his contempt of current ideas. Speaking of a seventeenth-century philosopher, he recently said with a half smile, "Take care when you read his work, students. As a Jew, he may contaminate your minds."

His lectures have me counting the days until the next, striving for excellence in my notes and assignments.

A rustling sounds to my left. I steal a glance. The girl with the reddish curls is no longer looking at the podium.

Instead, she's reading, head bent, hand shielding the volume concealed between the covers of her notebook.

For several minutes, I alternate between pretending to focus on the professor and watching her. She's completely engrossed, softly turning pages, fingers cupped around the top of the book in an effort to conceal it. In an instant, I'm taken back to my time at the Fröbel Seminar, where I trained as a kindergarten teacher in a vain attempt to avoid the labor service. One evening, chafing at being required to listen to a speech by Hitler on the radio, I brought a book along. Seated in a shadowy corner, I did just as this girl is now, until our teacher noticed and motioned for me to put the book away. I was fortunate in her latitude. I could have been expelled.

I risked for Thomas Mann's *The Magic Mountain*. What is this girl reading?

The professor's guttural voice fills the hall, as he pontificates on the greatness of the Aryan race. I glance around, scanning the other students in our vicinity. They're taking notes or looking at the professor. Carefully, I lean over. The girl reads on.

I catch a glimpse of the spine. Heinrich Heine's *Book of Songs*.

The girl looks up. Her eyes widen. Her exhale stills.

We stare at each other, gazes locked. My heart drums. Heine was a nineteenth-century poet.

He was also Jewish. Today his books are banned.

The girl is the first to look away. She stuffs the book into the satchel at her feet, then stares straight ahead.

The remainder of the lecture is completely lost on me. As the professor drones on, I'm keenly aware of the girl beside me, who dared to read a forbidden book during a lecture on Volk and Race.

Heine is one of my favorite poets. I even spoke up once during a BDM meeting, proposing a discussion of Heine's poetry. My suggestion was met with aghast faces all around, as the leader replied in a cool tone that we only discussed true Aryan authors.

I can hear my reply, muttered under my breath, but still audible. "Whoever doesn't know Heine, does not know German literature."

To read Heine—or any banned author—is to go against the tide. To read it in a class populated by National Socialist Student Association members is audacious.

Finally, the lecture ends. Footsteps and voices fill the hall, as students gather their things and disperse out the double doors. A few linger behind to speak to the professor. I slide my notebook and pencil into my satchel.

When I look up, the girl is watching me. Her satchel hangs from one hand, and she stands near the middle of the row. Her gaze flickers with uncertainty.

She's afraid I'm going to report her.

I move closer, until we're standing a step apart. Impulsively, I whisper a stanza by Heine.

> "I at first was near despairing;
> Never hoped to endure as now,
> And at length the whole I'm bearing;
> Only, do not ask me how."

Faint color brushes her pale cheeks. "You saw," she whispers. "That was stupid of me." She shakes her head. "I shouldn't have been reading."

"I like him too." I smile. "His *Book of Songs* is one of my favorites."

The girl visibly relaxes. "Really?" Her forehead creases. "But isn't he—?"

"Degenerate?" I finish. "What great writer isn't?"

"I found it at a used bookshop the other day, wedged way in the back." She gives a hesitant smile. "As a child, I was captivated by his poems. I'm glad to have a copy again."

"I wouldn't bring it to the university though. Especially not during this lecture. You'll likely not have it, or your place here, long if you do."

She nods. "I won't." Then she holds out her hand. "I'm Annalise Brandt."

"Sophie Scholl." We shake hands. A smudge of paint mars her forefinger. "Are you an art student?"

She gives a rueful glance at her hand. "*Ja.* It's my major. What are you studying?"

"Biology and philosophy," I reply.

My gaze lands on my simple wristwatch. Almost one. I'm to meet Hans in front of the fountain near the university entrance at one.

"I have to go. I'm late to meet my brother." I grab my satchel from the seat.

"Of course." She gives a shy smile. "Danke."

"It was nice meeting you." I return the smile, and Annalise's deepens. "Auf Wiedersehen."

"Wiedersehen." Annalise moves down the row, and I follow behind as we exit the lecture hall. I flit through the corridors of the university building, passing students hurrying to and fro. The sweet summer air beckons as I let myself out the double doors.

The sun pierces through the clouds; wind stirs my hair around my cheeks as I stride across the grounds. Hans will . . . well, knowing Hans, he's probably late too. Caught up in a discussion with one of his friends or finishing his shift at the hospital where he interns.

My steps quicken as I reach the fountain. Water splays in delicate arcs, catching the sunlight in glittering dance and play. I move closer, tilting my face and letting the mist fan my flushed cheeks.

I perch on the sun-warmed stone edge, satchel propped beside me, face tipped toward the sun. In my time at university, other than Hans's circle, I've kept mostly to myself. Traute has been welcoming and helpful, and Alex, Kirk, and Christl already seem like old and dear friends.

Still, I find myself hoping this won't be my last encounter with the girl who studies art and reads Heine's poetry.

Hair falling into my eyes, I check my watch again. A quarter past one. By now, the back of my navy cotton dress clings to my skin, dampened by the fountain's spray.

The hand on my watch ticks forward. I wait.

And still Hans does not arrive.

The streetcar lets me off not far from Hans's rooms on Mandlstraße. Linden and chestnut trees bloom in neat rows. Their fragrance perfumes the air, its sweetness one of the few pleasures not rationed.

Walking briskly, I scan the shops and apartments, their stucco exteriors painted in shades of dusky rose, buttercream, and pale blue, roofs shingled in brown. Soon, Hans's rooms will become mine, while Hans moves to Lindwurmstraße to be closer to the university's medical school. For now, I'm staying with an elderly professor who is Hans's good friend.

Reaching the apartment building, I push open the door and hurry into the entry hall and up the spiral staircase, until I reach Hans's door on the second landing. I knock once. Twice. No answer. I sigh and shift my satchel beneath my arm, fumbling for the key in my dress pocket.

My key is newly cut and sticks as I jiggle it in the lock. Hair falls into my eyes.

Finally, the door opens.

The front room is in its usual state of chaos. Books on every table and chair. Cigarette ashes on the rug. Dirty tea things and crumbs scattered across the table. I pause to admire a new French impressionist print on the wall beside the window. A lake scene done in a blur of vivid green and startling blue, a flash of orange depicting a sunset sky.

Bad housekeeping notwithstanding, I do admire my brother's taste in art.

I tidy up and wash the tea things, glancing toward the door every few minutes, expecting to hear Hans's step on the stair and his key in the lock.

I rub a cloth across the kitchen counter. It's nearing six.

In the two weeks since I've arrived in Munich, my brother has been kind and attentive, helping me find my bearings around the city, introducing me to acquaintances. He's also been distant. Preoccupied, as evidenced by this afternoon, when he apparently forgot about me.

I move to the front room and pick up a pile of books to move them somewhere other than the overcrowded table. My shin slams into the sharp table corner. Pain splinters my leg. I stumble, the volumes clattering around me with a terrific thud.

Rubbing my throbbing shin, I bend to pick up the scattered books. A wayward piece of paper catches my eye. I snatch it up. Hans's scrawl fills the page.

Nothing is more unworthy of a civilized nation than to let itself be "governed" without resistance by an irresponsible faction ruled by dark instincts. Is it not true that every honest German today is ashamed of his government?

The words wrest the breath from my lungs. I stare down, the paper like a live coal in my shaking hands. It's frayed around the edges, several lines crossed out with thick, diagonal slashes, notes scribbled in the margins. But I can't stop reading. Parts are incoherent, scraps of thought pulled together piecemeal. My brother's voice reverberates in my mind, snippets of conversations we've had over the years woven through the text.

Not since Bishop von Galen's sermons on euthanasia have I read such bold words on paper.

I clutch the page against myself, hands shaking, my heart a wild thing inside my chest.

If the Gestapo searched this apartment, like they did our home in 1937, the consequences for Hans would be dire. Worse than before, even.

What does my brother intend to do with this? I skim the page. On the front, near the top right corner, two words catch my gaze.

Leaflet One

Bile fills the back of my throat. I well remember how the discovery of a leaflet in our mailbox containing Bishop von Galen's statements on the murder of the ill and the degradation of our country shook our family last year. Hans's eyes glowed as he grasped my shoulders.

"What we really ought to have is a duplicating machine of our own."

I shake my head, standing in the front room surrounded by clutter and scattered books. There's something of self-preservation inside each of us, no matter how brazenly we fling our words, how lofty our ideals. It's there, innate, like trying to catch oneself from falling.

Vater, facing trial in the coming months for remarks about Hitler overheard by his secretary. Hans, still in his teens, spending weeks in prison because of his membership in a group not conforming to Hitler Youth ideals. It doesn't matter if Vater's words were true—of course, every one of them was. Nor if the purpose of Hans's group was to give young men an outlet beyond endless marching and propaganda speeches.

What matters is what happens to those who take chances.

What matters is what will happen to my brother, to our family, if he is discovered.

Steps sound in the corridor. My heart hammers as I stand frozen. Hans's light whistling, the fumbling sound of his key in the lock. The door opens.

"Hey, Sophie." He smiles offhandedly, tossing his satchel on the sofa. He's in uniform, likely fresh from duty at the hospital, cap atilt atop his hair.

I say nothing as he closes the door. Not one word. He crosses the room, eyebrows raised. "What's the matter?"

I hand him the paper. He takes it, skims the lines as if seeing them for the first time.

He looks up. "What of it?"

My hands ball into fists. "What are you thinking?" The low words emerge from between gritted teeth.

His expression changes, the smile falling, something dark and serious taking its place. "I really have no idea what you're talking about."

I snatch the paper from him, jabbing the top corner. "Don't play games with me. *Leaflet One.* You're writing leaflets. Do you have a duplicating machine? Do you?"

He doesn't answer.

My fingertips dig into the paper's edge, crinkling it. "You don't deny it then?"

Slowly, he shakes his head.

For a moment, my eyes fall closed. It's true. My fears realized.

"How long have you been planning this?" I ask softly.

"Practically, only a couple of weeks. Mentally . . . years, I guess." He gives a half smile.

"And if you're discovered? There will be a price to pay for all of us. It's not just your life, Hans. It's Mutter, Vater, Inge. Every one of us."

He nods. Swallows. "I know. If you think I haven't considered that, you're wrong. But I can't continue to do nothing. Not anymore. Not after what my friend Eickemeyer told us about what's happening in Poland. People—good, innocent people—murdered by our soldiers. Little children, Sophie, shot in cold blood." His gaze flares. "Here it isn't much better. They're taking away Jews, hauling them to camps, while the rest of us are being drugged by lack of knowledge. It's got to stop."

"Are you doing this by yourself?" My voice is dull. Hollow.

He shakes his head. "Kirk and Alex are helping. They've accepted the risk, same as me."

Of course Alex, daring and fearless, a Russian heart beating beneath his Wehrmacht tunic, would be first in line to join such a cause. And Kirk, with his ties to the Confessing Church and passionate desire to see wrongs made right, wouldn't hesitate to accept the cost.

I walk over to the sofa and sink down on the sagging edge, clasping my hands in my lap.

Hans joins me, sitting on the other side. He scrubs a hand over his eyes, shoulders lifting in a sigh. His Adam's apple bobs as he swallows.

"Why didn't you tell me?" I whisper. "After all the talks we've had, the views we've always shared . . . you kept this from me."

"I'm sorry." His gaze meets mine. "I thought I could protect you."

"So now I need protecting?" Pain leaks into my voice, in spite of myself. I thought we were equals. It stings that Hans concealed something this important.

"From this, *ja*." He blows out a breath. "Please, Sophie. Forget you saw anything."

"I can't do that."

He slams a fist into his palm. "I *won't* let you become involved. It's one thing to sacrifice my neck, but I'll be dashed if I let you risk yours."

"Why?" My voice escalates, anger rising inside, hot and sudden. "Because I'm a woman?"

He doesn't answer.

I can't take anymore. Not tonight.

Grabbing my satchel, I head for the door. I look at him, still sitting on the sofa, hands limp, watching me in the dimness. "I thought you knew me better. But if you think I'll stand by and watch you take risks alone, Hans Scholl, then you don't know me at all."

I slam the door, the forceful jolt releasing some of the pressure inside. I clatter down the steps and out of the building.

The sky is the gray of used dishwater. Sticky air clings to my skin. I move slowly down the street, remembering.

On a grim November day in 1937, the Gestapo burst in on our family and arrested Inge, Werner, and me. Hans, away at basic training, was picked up at his base. Though the rest of us were released within a week—myself within hours—Hans languished in a cold cell throughout the Christmas holidays, while the Gestapo drilled him about his involvement in a dissident youth group: the Deutsche Jungenschaft vom 1.11.1929, known as d.j.1.11.

Mutter, wringing her hands. Kneeling by the bed in a swath of lamplight, praying for her son. Vater, swearing and vowing to go to Berlin and murder every last one of them if they harmed his children.

That was before the war. Before things became much worse.

I rest a hand against the nearest building, eyes closed, swallowing the cloying taste of memory. I disliked National Socialism before. After Hans's brutal confinement, I loathed it.

If Hans's arrest taught me anything, it is this. The Reich punishes rebels, no matter their age, nationality, or sex.

And printing subversive material is no mild offense.

It's treason.

CHAPTER SIX

Sophie
May 16, 1942

LEAVING THE BEDSHEETS IN a tangle, I cross the worn floorboards and pull back the blackout curtain. Dawn streaks the sky, cresting over the pitched brown rooftops in shades of peach and gold. Barefoot, I stand looking out, hidden in the shadows, clad in a worn cotton nightshift.

Sleep was an absent visitor. All night, I tossed and turned, thought and prayed.

Gazing out at a wakening Munich, I draw in a shuddering breath. The words of Hans's leaflet haven't stopped haunting me.

If everyone waits for others to begin, Nemesis's avenging messengers will move closer and closer, and then the last victim, too, will be thrown in vain into the jaws of the insatiable demon . . .

Hans, Alex, and Kirk. What they are doing is not born of a moment's decision. They're giving truth its rightful voice, even if it means risking discovery. Their very lives.

I press my hand to my fast-beating heart, the warmth of my body penetrating my palm.

I'm ashamed of the fearful thoughts crowding in, eclipsing all else. If I give into my fear, I'll be no better than the rest. Buckling beneath the oppressing hand of the Reich out of cowardice. How often have I flung words forth with my brother, Fritz, Vater. How easy it is to trumpet truth, scorn the blinded. But when action presents itself, what do I do?

Cringe away. Oh, perhaps not outwardly, but my inward feebleness longs for nothing more than a safe and simple life. My life—my family's lives—will be neither of those things if I join Hans in his work.

I turn away from the window, the blackout curtain falling into place. A desk and chair is wedged against the opposite wall, nearly bumping the footboard of the double bed.

I settle onto the chair and pick up a small, worn volume. St. Augustine's

Confessions. I've carried it from place to place during the years of labor service, reading with a flashlight under the covers while the rest of the girls slumbered. The earnest words, as if the writer would prefer to tear his heart from his body rather than forsake God, were penned by a man who understood what it means to know the weight of one's own emptiness.

Perhaps today I can find comfort, some answer in these pages. I turn them slowly, gaze falling on familiar lines:

> But now my years are but sighs. You, O Lord, are my only solace.
> You, my Father, are eternal. But I am divided between time gone by
> and time to come, and its course is a mystery to me. My thoughts,
> the intimate life of my soul, are torn this way and that in the havoc
> of change. And so it will be until I am purified and melted by the
> fire of Your love and fused into one with You.

I pause, caught by the words as if reading them for the first time: "Divided between time gone by and time to come, and its course is a mystery to me." I recall the past, wonder about the future, and stand in the middle of both, betwixt and between.

"Show me what to do," I whisper, eyes closed, hands clasped beneath my chin. "You, O Lord, are my only solace." I continue praying, resting my bent head on my arms, leaning my cheek against the page I just read. I'm weary. So weary . . .

A crash from downstairs. I wake with a start, gingerly raising my head, neck stiff and aching. I must have fallen asleep. I stand, hair tangled around my face, walk to the window, and pull back the curtain. The sky is full morning, blazing with a radiant sun. The rays, spreading as if by a heavenly hand, mingle with the cloud-scattered blue. My breath catches.

Freedom looks like this sunshine. Freedom to live without fear, to speak one's beliefs without first glancing around and behind.

Hans and his friends fight for that freedom, the written word their weapon.

I will join them. I told Hans as much last night, but then, the decision brought with it no peace. Only anger and shock.

A quiet certainty settles within me now. I'm still afraid, but something stronger pushes beyond the fear. As if everything I've read and done and believed up until now culminates in this decision.

I don't expect Hans to be pleased, but he'll come around. He and his friends will see the logic of having another person, particularly a woman, involved.

I turn away from the sunlit window. A swirl of dust motes float in the air.

I feel no rush of excitement, no heady thrill, as one might expect at such a venture. Only calm decision. I'm thankful for that. I can enter into this levelheaded without the sentiment of a firebrand, fully aware of who I am, what I will be doing. And what I risk.

I move to wash and dress, purpose in my steps, trading the nightshift for my navy dress. I stand in front of the cracked oval mirror in the bathroom down the hall, brushing my straight, bobbed hair and pinning back one side. Brown eyes against a pale face stare back at me. I'm not pretty like Traute. Nor dashing like Alex and Hans. I'm ordinary. A girl from a middle-class family.

I swallow, straightening my shoulders and inhaling a long breath.

What little I have to offer, I will give. It's prayer and benediction both. *No matter the cost.*

That evening, I stand in front of Hans's apartment door, prepared for a struggle. I raise my fist and knock. Footsteps sound from inside.

My brother opens the door. He's wearing his uniform trousers and a half-buttoned white cotton shirt. His gaze meets mine, and I sense his unspoken reproach. I can't say I blame him, after I ran out last night.

"May I come in?"

He opens the door wider. I duck inside. Alex and Kirk sit in the front room, on either end of the sofa. They, too, are wearing half their uniforms, coats shucked on the back of the sofa. Alex takes his pipe from his lips and inclines his head in an almost courtly bow. Kirk gives me a quick smile.

I'm invading a man's abode (never mind the man is my own brother). Though their looks are friendly enough, I sense they note the invasion. Hans must have told them.

Sophie is all right to be friends with, but to join in our work . . .

I can almost hear their thoughts.

"Hello, Kirk, Alex." I set down my satchel.

"It's good to see you, Sophie." Kirk stands. "Here, have my seat."

We exchange a smile as I walk past him and sit beside Alex. Kirk takes the armchair. Hans stands opposite him, thumbs looped in the belt holes of his trousers.

The three men regard me in silence. I swallow.

"These leaflets you're working on. Do you have a production plan?" My tone is matter-of-fact. Hans will get no more hysterics from me.

Hans sighs, shaking his head. A forelock of hair falls boyishly into his eyes.

"You don't need to know all this, Sophie." Alex leans toward me, whelming me in the fragrant odor of tobacco. His tone is kind, despite the pinch of his words.

Let them see I'm more than just a girl.

"I can be useful, you know." I direct my gaze toward Hans. "For the purchasing of supplies, the distribution of leaflets. No one would suspect a woman. We're expected to be anonymous, so we blend in better. Tell me, who do you think will attract more suspicion? One of you soldierly types? Or a slip of a girl?"

"All right. Suppose you're mailing leaflets and you're stopped and questioned. What would you do?" Hans folds his arms, gaze appraising. As if this is some kind of test.

If it is, I'm not about to fail it.

"Remember what I told you Mutter did when the Gestapo showed up at our house? She didn't cower or flinch. She just grabbed all the d.j.1.11 papers you'd left in your room and stuffed them in her market basket. Then she marched right past the officers and said she had to hurry to the baker's. They let her go because she was a woman, and it was her quick action that day that saved you from greater incrimination later."

Am I mistaken, or has the stubborn refusal in his eyes been replaced by reluctance?

"We do need help buying paper and stamps," Kirk says. Alex nods, smoking thoughtfully.

"There. I can do that." I'm on my feet, looking into Hans's eyes, grateful for my height which allows me to meet him eye to eye with a lift of my chin. My brother. My childhood playmate. Always I've been the tagalong sister, trying to keep up with him in everything. Striving to run the fastest, get the best marks in mathematics.

Now, I want him to see me as an equal. Realize I can do more than participate in intellectual debates.

I can join this resistance.

I *will* join it.

"If we're caught," Alex says quietly, "they'll treat her as a girl."

Hans looks past my shoulder to Alex. "In the occupied countries, women are already receiving the same punishments as men for resistance and sabotage." He turns to me, placing both hands on my shoulders. His touch is warm, his gaze piercing mine. His chest lifts with a weighty breath. "You can't forget then?" His tone is almost pleading.

I shake my head. "I've felt powerless for too long." My heart races, though my tone remains calm. "I know the risks. They're worth it to me. If I'm not willing to pay the price, then who am I to expect others to do so? If I do not fight against, aren't I as good as fighting for?"

"Then you feel as we do." He looks as if he wants to pull me close, wrap me in his arms, and remain my protective older brother, but instead he nods. I return the nod. Our relationship will change from here on out. We'll be comrades fighting on the same battle lines. He won't be able to shelter me like he's always tried to do.

I turn to the others. Alex rises and holds out his hand. "*Za pravdu i pravo.*"

"What?" I smile.

"It's Russian. It means 'for truth and right.'" He winks at me.

"*Za pravdu i pravo.*" I repeat, annihilating the pronunciation.

Alex laughs and we all join him, becoming, if only for a few seconds, simply four young people enjoying a joke.

I settle into my seat beside Alex and turn to Hans. "Now, will you answer my questions?"

"If you're wise, you won't ask many. I'll tell you what you need to know."

"Fair enough." What one doesn't know one cannot repeat under interrogation. Knowledge equates guilt.

"The three of us are writing a leaflet. Alex is getting ahold of a typewriter. That's the extent of our accomplishments. Other than a great deal of discussion."

"No duplicating machine?"

"They're hard to come by, not to mention expensive." Alex leans back against the sofa, propping his hands behind his head. "You need an order stamped to get a new one. Only officers and Party officials can get the stamp."

A little burst of excitement ricochets through me. Fritz will be in Munich on leave. If I have the order made out, perhaps he could get his commanding officer to stamp it. Surely I could make up some pretext.

"My fiancé, Leutnant Fritz Hartnagel, is stopping in Munich on leave. He might be able to help us."

Kirk's brow furrows. "What are his political views?"

I pause, taking time to form my words. Sometimes I marvel at the irony. Out of all the men to fall in love with, I chose one who loves me, cares for my family . . . and believes in loyalty to the Wehrmacht.

I hadn't chosen Fritz though, not really. He chose me. I let myself be chosen, and loved him for it, despite the complexities of our relationship.

"He believes in duty to the oath he took. But he's beginning to change." I think of the letters we've exchanged. I've argued and reasoned. He's listened, countered, and begun to see truth, the senselessness of the war angering him. "Now his greatest wish after the war is to have a farm and keep chickens." I smile. "I won't tell him what we need the machine for. I'll say we want to increase the circulation of *Storm Lantern*."

"*Storm Lantern* is a little publication we've circulated among family and friends for a few years," Hans says to Kirk and Alex. "A lot of theological and philosophical stuff."

"Might be worth a try," Alex says. "I'm still working on finding something used."

"When are you meeting Fritz?" Hans asks.

"On the twentieth. He only has a few hours. He wants to visit his family too."

"Don't tell him anything. If he even begins to suspect, drop the subject." Hans's gaze is serious. He knows Fritz, likes him even. But friends have been known to turn in friends for no other reason than it was their so-called duty. Even the secretary who denounced Vater had no grudge against him, just his politics.

I'll be venturing into dangerous territory by even broaching the subject.

But I trust Fritz. He wouldn't betray our family.

I sit up straighter and try to look confident beneath the gazes of the three men. "Leave it to me."

CHAPTER SEVEN

Sophie
May 20, 1942

THE KNOCK HAS BARELY sounded on the front door, before I'm flying into the hall, skidding a bit on the newly polished floor. I pause, gathering my breath, smoothing a hand down the front of my navy dress. My pulse hammers in the hollow of my throat.

I open the door, peering into the afternoon sunlight. Fritz stands on the stoop.

"Sophie," is all he says. Then I'm in his arms.

There are times when words become the least important things, and this is one of them. I press my cheek against his chest, the warmth of him radiating through the scratchy fabric of his uniform coat. His strong arms hold me tight, almost crushing. He smells of musk and travel dust, his face buried in my hair. Our lips meet in a kiss born of longing and need.

It's what I've dreamed about for months. Him, alive and well, clinging to me as if to life itself. In moments of physical oneness, the distance between us ceases to exist. Or maybe, ceases to matter.

When he lets go, I'm filled with an almost tangible ache. I take in the sight of him. He's thinner, the uniform once a perfect fit, hanging on his frame, his angular cheekbones more pronounced. I've changed too. My hair, once cropped short as a boy's, has grown longer, almost brushing my shoulders, and I've had to take in my skirts due to the rationing.

Such differences are only outward. They matter little. What matters is everything inward. That's what we've always shared.

"Missed me, have you?" A grin stretches his mouth.

"Oh, Fritz." I smile. "Come in. We've tea and *kuchen*."

A regretful look replaces his grin. "I wish I could. But I don't have long. Can we go somewhere, just the two of us?"

"Of course." My answer is automatic.

I haven't seen him in months, and all he can give me is hours. War steals everything. Even time.

But voicing such reproaches would do neither of us good. I shut the door. My skirt brushes my thigh, and I feel the piece of paper in my pocket, the one containing the order for the duplicating machine. I ignore it. For now.

He smiles at me, his gray hat with its black brim tilted at just the right angle atop his dark hair. "Where should we go?"

Home. I want to say. *To Ulm and the banks of the Danube and the world before the war.*

Instead, I return his smile. "Shall we take the streetcar to the Englischer Garten?"

A stroll through the bustling Marienplatz wouldn't seem right when we only have a few hours together. Our romance has deepened among nature, holidays mostly—swimming in the North Sea then lying on its banks to sun ourselves dry, skiing the Austrian Alps all day and dining by firelight in a quiet restaurant, holding hands across the table, deliciously exhausted.

It's foolishness to try and recapture our former closeness through a location. This seeking to capture happiness is yet another sign of my own weakness.

"If you like." Fritz offers his arm.

I slip mine through his, and we stroll down the street. The fragrance of the chestnut trees lining the sidewalk perfumes the air, and the sky is unadulterated blue. An afternoon for lovers.

If only the texture of our love could be as simple as the weather.

"How's your family?"

I relay the latest news—Mutter's health is still poorly, Werner's somewhere in Russia, Vater still awaiting trial, Inge keeping busy at home, Lisl with tutoring.

"And what about Sophia Magdalena?" He looks down at me, blue-eyed gaze half teasing, half searching. "How is she?"

Lonely. Confused. Preparing to mount a campaign against the cause he's fighting for.

But I say none of those things.

"She's here." I lean my head against his shoulder, needing his closeness. "That's enough."

After a half-hour streetcar ride and a short walk, we reach the Englischer Garten. The rolling parkland dotted with trees and woven with small graveled paths isn't the woods around Ulm, and the Kleinhesseloher Lake isn't the River Danube, but it will suit our purposes.

Arm in arm, we move down a wooded pathway. In the distance, children sail wooden boats on the lake's sun-brushed surface. A breeze fans my cheeks.

A bench sits in an alcove of trees. We settle onto the wrought-iron seat. I smooth my skirt over my knees. Fritz pulls his cap from his head and places it in his lap. I turn to him.

"Tell me about your friend, that young corporal you wrote about. How is he?" Fritz had written several amusing anecdotes about him in his letters. Perhaps he'd tell another, and we'd laugh until our sides ached, as we used to do.

Fritz glances away, down at his hands. Slowly, he begins to twist the cap, working the stiff fabric. "He's . . . he died, Sophie. Killed by an exploding shell."

I draw in a breath. "I'm sorry." I reach for his hand, place mine over his, stilling it.

He looks up at me. "I watched him die, you know. I've watched lots of men die. A good many more than I've written you about. It's a horrible thing, to see a man once hale and hearty with half his body blown to bloody shreds. Horrible."

"And you still think this war is a worthy thing?" My words are fast, my tone much too sharp.

After a long pause, Fritz shakes his head. "I don't know what I think anymore."

We sit in silence for several minutes. Fritz plucks a piece of bark from the tree behind us, turning it over in his strong hands. "Do you remember what you once told me you wanted to be?" A hint of a smile fills his words.

Memories. Sometimes they seem the only safe things to smile about.

"What?"

"A piece of bark. You said you wanted to be one with the trees. For in nature, there is freedom. Nature doesn't judge. It exists for our good pleasure."

I grin. "It's true."

"I can't tell you how many times I've thought about that. When everything around me is dirty men and smoke and the sound of shots, I remember nature and you." He slips an arm around my waist.

Before, I might have argued with him, said that while nature can be enjoyed, one cannot live in a state of perpetual escape. We must face the realities of our lives.

But our time is too short, and I don't want to waste it arguing.

In the end, much between us is left unsaid. We spend the hours sitting on that little iron bench, my head on his shoulder, his arm around my waist.

I don't speak of the late-night discussions in Hans's apartment, the plans we're putting in place. Fritz avoids the war. We exchange the Englischer Garten for a crowded café nearby, where we order *kaffee* and sit at a corner table, holding hands across the space between us.

I don't need to check my watch to know our time is running out. Cloth napkins and *kaffee* cups with nothing left but brown residue clutter the scarred wood.

Taking a deep breath, I pull the piece of paper from my pocket. Our knees bump under the table. Fritz's large frame is hunched in the small chair.

"Would you do me a favor?" I hold out the paper to him, keeping my tone offhand. "Could you get this stamped and submitted? I have it all filled out, see."

Fritz takes the paper, scans it. His brow furrows. Beneath the table, I clench and unclench my fingers.

"This is an order for a duplicating machine," he says quietly.

I nod. "*Ja.* It's for *Storm Lantern.* We're hoping to increase circulation."

Fritz glances back at the order, running his fingertip along the lines. "Those are hard to get. I'm not sure it's possible. Why . . . why do you care about increasing circulation of *Storm Lantern*? Don't you have better things to do?"

I swallow. "Why not?" My words falter. "It seems like the perfect time. Our writing encourages truth. People need to be woken up, the sooner the better. Our . . . publication may not do much, but at least it's something."

He nods slowly, gauging me. Then he leans across the table. His gaze reaches into me, as if he can see everything. His face is taut. "I don't know what you're doing, Sophie. I'm not sure I want to know." He casts a furtive glance around the restaurant. Pots and pans clatter in the background. A couple exits through the swinging door, the bell jangling in their wake. He looks back at me. His voice lowers. "But are you aware this could cost you your life?"

I meet his eyes, looking into his handsome, earnest face. Fritz, my fiancé and friend, who wishes nothing but good things for me. There have been few people outside of my family to whom I've shown my true self. Fritz is one of the few. In the past years, almost the only one.

"I know," I say simply.

His face pales. Quickly, he takes the order and stuffs it in his pocket. I don't ask him what he intends to do with it. He exhales a shuddering breath, reaches across the table, and brushes his fingers over my cheek. I lean into his touch.

"Be safe, Sophie. For afterward." There's a catch in his voice. "When this is all over, we're going to find ourselves a little church and get married. I'm counting on it."

I nod, swallowing back the lump in my throat. Only minutes remain. Then he'll get up and walk away and go back to his duty. Leaving me to return to mine. I reach up and place my hand over his. I smile, but it trembles at the edges. "*Ja*, Fritz. Me too."

Annalise
May 25, 1942

The weekend before I met Sophie Scholl, loneliness prompted me to leave my apartment and walk to a used bookshop. I spent hours wending my way among the shelves, elated to discover a copy of Heinrich Heine's *Book of Songs*, the thin volume wedged between a dictionary and a cookbook on the bottom shelf. As a child, Heine's poetry seemed to me art in written form, and I spent hours curled up on the sofa, immersing myself in every word. One evening when I was twelve, Vater strode into the room and plucked the book from my hands. He glanced at the spine.

"Heine," he muttered. "Degenerate Jewish trash."

I watched, dumbstruck, as he crossed to the fireplace and tossed the volume into the crackling blaze. "The Fatherland must be cleansed of un-German literature." In those days, his hardness had not been fully formed, and he returned to where I sat, gazing down at me. "If you like to read, we'll go to a bookshop on Saturday. We'll get you something better, *ja*?" He gave my shoulder an awkward pat, as if to console me.

I didn't look at him, riveted on my beloved book, pages blackening in the flames. My heart thudded, hot and cold drenching my body. Suddenly, I jumped to my feet, facing him.

"Heine says 'Where they have burned books, they will end in burning human beings,'" I shouted, angry tears filling my eyes. I tried to storm past him, but he grabbed my arm with a bruising grip.

The crack of his hand against my cheek reverberates through me, even now. I stared up at him, vision blurred, a chill soaking through me at the anger in his gaze. In Munich, finding and buying Heine had seemed like another way to affirm my independence, but reading it during the dull lecture had been nothing less than stupid. Had I been caught by someone else . . .

I shudder.

Since that day, I've seen Sophie several times at the university, greeting each other as we passed in the halls. On Friday, after mutually enduring another Volk and Race lecture, she suggested we meet today and walk to the Bodega, one of her favorite cafés.

I hurry across the cobblestones, plaid skirt bouncing against my knees. Sophie stands by the fountain, in the midst of a circle of young men. She tilts her head, listening, then addresses one of the group. A breeze stirs the bottom of her navy dress and a satchel hangs from her hand. The three young men around her carry books or have their hands in their pockets. All of them wear Wehrmacht uniforms. Another girl, tall and stylish in an olive suit that accentuates her curly dark hair, is also a part of the circle.

I hesitate to join them, shyness taking hold and halting my steps.

One of the young men turns, angles slightly toward Sophie.

My heart falters.

It's him. The man whose smile so captivated me. He doesn't see me—just one of many students taking advantage of the break between classes. Fingers wrapped around the spine of the notebook clutched to my chest, I watch him as the crowd circulates around me. He gestures as he speaks, stance easy without any of that soldierly stiffness common among young men these days.

I wait, almost breathless, willing him to smile.

He does. And I'm lost in its warmth, awash in its half-crooked brilliance. The desire to draw closer flits through my mind. What would I say if I stood near him, that smile upon me?

Involuntarily, I take a few steps closer. My bobbed curls brush my cheek. Sunlight winks from the sky. A couple walks past, blocking my view.

Sophie glances in my direction. She waves and bids farewell to her companions, hurrying toward me.

"I'm sorry." The words rush out. "I didn't mean to take you from your friends. You did say after morning classes?"

She smiles. "No need to apologize. You're just in time." We fall into step, but not before I steal a glance over my shoulder, to see if the young man is watching us.

He isn't.

It shouldn't send a pang through me. I don't even know him.

"How were your morning classes?"

I slide my notebook into my satchel, hesitating. Two of my three art teachers are cut from the same mold as Vater. True art, they insist, is that which glorifies the Führer—beaming blond women surrounded by a horde of children, a parade of storm troopers marching in tandem. The old masters are presented, but only those the Führer hasn't ousted from the galleries. We students are advised to emulate the pieces showcased in the House of German Art—a gallery of some nine hundred works selected by the president of the Reich Chamber of Visual Arts. I've already been, when it first opened, with Vater. It's not worth a return visit.

Despite our shared love of Heine, I pause. I don't know Sophie's feelings on the Führer and his regulated systems. Honestly, do I even know my own?

"All right," is all I say.

Her brow creases in a quick, puzzled frown. We pass through the *Siegestor*—the stone victory arch on the outskirts of the university. I scramble for something to say. "Tell me about where you're from, your family." Isn't this what normal girls with normal friendships talk about? Families?

Her answering smile is warm. "I'm from Ulm."

"The cathedral there is beautiful, I hear."

"We take walks by the Danube at twilight." Her tone becomes wistful, as if she's transported far away from the bustle of pedestrians and shop windows. "Hans, Vater, and me. Sometimes Inge comes too. Inge's the oldest. Then there's Hans. You haven't met my brother, have you?" She pauses beneath the awning of a pharmacy. Our reflections stare back at us in the front window.

I shake my head, while inside, my heart jumps. Her brother . . .

Could he be the man whose smile fills me with hummingbird wings?

"He's on duty at the hospital today, or I would've introduced you. You'd like him. It's impossible to meet Hans without falling under his spell. He has a way about him." She grins, flashing slightly uneven teeth. We move down the street. "After Hans, there's Elisabeth—Lisl, we call her—and then me. Werner's the youngest." She says something else about Werner, but I'm processing the fact that the man I've been watching is not Sophie's brother.

"And your parents?" I ask, trying to hold up my end of the conversation.

"My vater used to be the mayor of Forchtenberg. Now he manages a business and tax consulting firm. I've only seen my family off and on the past few years. Labor service, you know."

I nod. Do I ever. Though I rather enjoyed the compulsory stint of farm labor (particularly the stolen moments sketching nature), Vater's shadow followed me, even there. As Standartenführer Brandt's daughter, I lived under a magnifying glass.

"Didn't care for it?" We approach the café.

I shake my head. "Not really."

Sophie laughs. "Neither did I."

Our conversation lapses as we enter the low-beamed room. Oak-paneled walls match square tables and wooden chairs. It's sparsely populated with working men and soldiers, a few women. Their voices mingle with the scents of greasy food and cigarette smoke.

The waitress greets Sophie with a smile and leads us to our seats. Placing worn parchment-paper menus in front of us, she takes our drink orders and bustles away.

I skim the selection and prices. Though Vater's allowance is generous, it has to last. As do my ration coupons.

"Tell me about your family." Sophie folds her hands atop the table.

My throat goes dry. I will not lie. I will not.

"My vater is a standartenführer in the SS." My breath webs inside my chest. I can already tell she's not one of those swooning, Führer-infatuated girls. Her eyes hold too much intelligence.

The waitress returns with our cups of ersatz *kaffee*, leaning over the table to place them in front of us, her ample bosom obscuring Sophie's face from view. We order bowls of bean and pea soup.

When the waitress leaves again, Sophie turns to me. "And your mutter?"

No comment? No adoration? Just a question about my mutter, who would, by her own admission, call herself the most ordinary woman in Germany.

"She's a wonderful person. A kind and loving woman." I pause. "But in my vater's shadow . . . she's diminished, somehow."

"A woman's place though, isn't it? To be diminished?" Sophie's tone is slow, almost testing. Her keen eyes fix upon me.

"I don't think so. Just because a woman is married doesn't mean she should become her husband's mirror. She's still her own person, worth more than *Kinder, Küche, Kirche*." Children, kitchen, church—one of the Führer's pet phrases about the realm of the ideal woman. "Those things are important. But they're not the sole reason for her existence."

What have I just said? If Vater heard me, I'd be on the next train home, promise or no promise.

Sophie nods, eyes sparking. "Women are more than the vehicle by which future generations are propagated."

Her words are soft, but their impact strikes me like a shout. Never have I dared to utter my unvoiced thoughts. But they are true.

More so because that is who I will become in a year's time. The vehicle by which future generations for the Fatherland are propagated. Just thinking about it makes me nauseous.

"What does your vater think of your views?" That quizzical frown wrinkles her brow again.

"He doesn't know. We're not close." I lower my gaze to my clasped hands. I didn't want to speak of him today. Why must he follow me everywhere, even on this first chance at real friendship I've had in years?

Something warm brushes my hand. I look up. Sophie's fingers rest against mine. Her brown eyes radiate understanding. "His loss," she says simply, then takes her hand away.

CHAPTER EIGHT

Sophie
May 28, 1942

IF I HAVE LEARNED anything in these years under Hitler's rule, it is that every person we meet represents a choice. To trust. To conceal. To let in. To shut out.

To do otherwise, especially if one's opinions don't align with the political consensus, means devastating risks for oneself and one's family.

Annalise—the girl who risks reading Heine and chafes against *Kinder, Küche, Kirche*—is the daughter of an SS standartenführer. He would not have ascended to such a position if his views did not conform to the Führer's in every respect.

I should be wary of Annalise, and in a way, I am. But our own family situation is proof that offspring don't always choose the same side as their parents. My own vater opposed Hitler from the beginning, but as adolescents, Hans, Inge, and I proudly rose to leadership in our local branches of the Hitler Youth and BDM. Hans was even chosen to be flag bearer for the Hitler Youth contingent from Ulm during the 1935 Nuremburg Rally. He returned home distant and disillusioned, the breaking point of his growing disgust at the Hitler Youth's attempt to regulate and control every aspect of the lives of its members, reaching to the books they read, the music they listened to, and the friends they chose.

Werner finally became so repulsed he walked out, right in the middle of a meeting. His insubordination cost him the opportunity to attend university, thus making certain he was drafted straight into the Wehrmacht. He responded by scaling a statue outside the Ulm courthouse in the middle of the night and wrapping a swastika flag over the eyes of the figure holding the scales of justice. I was furious when I found out he'd done something so dangerous, but also secretly proud.

My musings carry me outside, past the entrance of the Lichthof—the immense glass-ceilinged great hall of the university. I pass a trio of brown-shirted National Socialist Student Association members, their proud step and swastika armbands marking them as rabid devotees. They mar the university landscape, sitting in on lectures to ferret out any speck of sedition uttered by the professors.

I catch sight of Annalise, sitting on an iron bench beneath a spreading tree, head bent over a sheet of paper held in both hands.

Should I speak to her? It's safest, especially in light of our work on the leaflets, to be civil in passing, but nothing more.

I'm about to pass by, when Annalise looks up. Her face breaks into a smile and she waves as if to beckon me over. It would be rude to ignore her now, so I wave back and cross the grass.

"Hello."

"*Grüß Gott*," she replies. "See, I'm trying to become a true Bavarian."

"You're doing well." The difference in dialects between Berlin and Bavarian Munich would be an adjustment for some, but Annalise seems to be handling it admirably, only the slightest crisp Berliner flavor making its way into her pronunciation. At first, that's the main thing I notice. Then I realize she greeted me with the formerly popular Bavarian *Grüß Gott*—may God bless you—instead of the standard, almost mandatory Heil Hitler. I duck using the latter as often as possible. No man deserves to be Heiled. It's just another method of controlling us, turning our everyday greetings into one-on-one Nazi Party rallies. But an SS officer's daughter would surely use the correct greeting.

Annalise Brandt is an enigma.

"I'm trying. I muddle a few words here and there, but it's getting easier." She scoots to make room for me on the bench. "Please, sit down."

I sit, placing my satchel on the grass beside the bench, and smooth my skirt over my knees.

"You've spoken Bavarian dialect before, I take it?"

Annalise nods. "I've wanted to study at Ludwig Maximilian University since I was a girl. I had a cousin who was enrolled here in the mid-thirties." A fond smile touches her lips. "She used to write me letters about the things she was learning, the friends she made. I saw her on holidays, and we always spoke Bavarian dialect together."

"So that's why you chose LMU over the University of Berlin?"

"I didn't want to stay in Berlin. I thought if I could just have a little freedom . . . it would be enough." She looks down at her hands, a wisp of a sigh falling from her lips.

"Enough for what?"

She glances up, into my eyes. "I'm not going to graduate from LMU, at least not with a degree. I'm only going to be here less than a year."

My brow furrows. Though a degree is the least of the reasons I came here to study, it makes no sense why someone would leave after only a year. "Are you transferring to a different university?"

She shakes her head. "I'm . . . I'm getting married."

"Congratulations." I say it quickly, by rote, not sure if it's the right thing. No glow lights her eyes, no smile frames her mouth.

"You don't need to say that." She fiddles with a button on her sweater. "It's not what you think. When I approached my vater about the possibility of studying here, he refused, though I got high marks on my *Abitur*. My place was to complete labor service and find a husband. Good, strong offspring for the Reich, you know." Her smile is brittle. "But I persisted, more than I've ever dared before. Eventually, we struck a bargain. I'd marry whom he wished after two semesters of university. I'm counting it a triumph to have made it this far."

For a moment, I stare at her. She's to be married off, just like that, as if she were no more than a machine put into service for its rightful use.

Annalise ducks her head, almost as if she's ashamed. My heart goes out to her; how trapped she must feel.

"Do you know your intended?"

"Nein. Vater hasn't decided. He's on the eastern front, likely taking applications." She gives a broken laugh. "Come to think of it, it sounds almost medieval. The bravest knight wins the prize of the king's daughter."

"Have you thought about refusing? Telling him you won't marry unless you meet someone you actually want to be with?"

"You don't know my vater, Sophie." Annalise's tone is maddeningly calm. I suddenly want to shake her. "We've made a bargain."

"Even when, by keeping it, it's your future that will suffer the consequences?"

She nods, looking regretful, yet resigned. "*Ja*. Even then."

We lapse into silence, gazes straight ahead. The air carries the scent of fresh-trimmed grass and the voices of students hurrying across the grounds. Annalise turns to me.

"I'm sorry if you think badly of me now. I shouldn't have brought it up. It's just . . . I don't know what to do."

I don't have much patience for weak-willed people. I've never been one myself. But Annalise isn't weak-willed; she's simply trapped. As we all are. These days, we have little power over so many decisions, making those we do have a say in all the more important.

"It's not my place to judge you, Annalise."

"Danke." She gives a grateful smile, but her gaze is still troubled.

"But"—my voice lowers—"in the end, it comes down to the worth you ascribe to freedom. What price you're willing to pay."

She presses her lips together as if letting the statement sink in. Then she straightens, putting on a smile. "What about you? Are you seeing anyone?"

"I'm engaged to an officer in the Wehrmacht. I saw him a few days ago, for the first time in months."

I'm not accustomed to sharing personal details. In my years of labor service, I managed to get by without letting my comrades see my true self.

Yet Annalise has been open with me. She sits quietly now, head tilted, not rushing to fill the silence. If she had, I would have left it at that.

"Perhaps it would have been easier had we not seen each other at all. Then there would be no parting to look back on."

Annalise's eyes radiate understanding. "It's never easy to part from those we love." Sunlight gilds the reddish strands of her hair. "We're always thinking back, wondering how the time went by so fast, if we said the right things, marveling at how many details we've already forgotten."

Unexpected tightness rises in the back of my throat. Since Fritz left, I've had every one of those thoughts and so many more.

I swallow, sucking in a shallow breath.

This time, it's Annalise who reaches out and places her hand over mine.

CHAPTER NINE

Annalise
May 29, 1942

"IN THE END, IT comes down to the worth you ascribe to freedom. What price you're willing to pay."

I stare up at the ceiling, humid darkness coating the room. Shifting onto my side, I punch the flattened pillow with a sigh.

If only I could chalk up my sleeplessness to the heat.

I sit up and flick on the bedside lamp. Sheets tangled around my legs, I snatch my pillow and hug it close. Doubtless it's after one in the morning.

Since my conversation with Sophie, I've been unable to think of little else. I've never spoken about my bargain with Vater to anyone. It's just been there—a marker at the end of one road pointing to another.

Then comes Sophie Scholl. Right away, I sensed she was different, with her love of Heine and later her talk of women's roles. Impulsively, I told her. Maybe because deep down I wanted to hear what she had to say.

She questioned me, made me want to entertain the possibility of something different. To rip out the marker and chart a new path.

I press my fingers into my temples with a groan. Here I am, with my grand independence, thinking myself so brave and bold to have defied Vater enough to attend university. Sophie's words stripped away my independence, like a hard scrubbing revealing rotting wood beneath a polished veneer.

An illusion. That's all it's been.

Since the Führer came to power, the world has changed. Again and again, we've been told Germany can become a great nation again if every citizen gives their all. The "all" women are to give is their bodies to bear healthy Aryan children and their lives to running a home on the principles taught by the Führer. Vater often quotes from Hitler's Nuremberg speeches when admonishing my brothers.

"German youth are to be swift as greyhounds, tough as leather, and hard as Krupp steel."

No longer do I hear Vater's voice, but the Führer's. Sharp. Impassioned. Hypnotic.

"Youth, glorious youth, is the future. A new generation of strong, proud young people."

"The catch of it is," I whisper, "we're not to be all of those things to better ourselves, but to be used for whatever purpose the Thousand-Year Reich proposes." My hands fist around the pillowslip.

It's astonishing how we've all believed and fought for and trumpeted these ideals, thinking they're for our good. When, in reality, they only serve to further the aims of those in power.

Vater is no different. He wants me to marry and bear children. Why? Not for me, but for himself. So he can boast to his SS comrades about the fine baby boy his good Aryan daughter delivered.

It's wrong. The fight for supremacy, the talk of Germany becoming not just a great nation but "a nation to surpass all others." Instinctively, I've known for a long time. But rarely have things fitted together in my mind with such eye-opening clarity.

What price am I willing to pay for freedom? Not just for myself, but for the freedom of those around me also mired in the swamp of delusion?

I rub a hand across my eyes and lean my forehead into my palms.

I won't do as Vater asks. I don't know how I'll manage it, but I won't marry the man he chooses. I won't raise innocent children on a foundation of lies.

Just thinking such defiance terrifies me deep down. I'm under no illusions as to what it will mean. If I take a stand, I'll lose my family. They're flawed, perhaps, but they're still the only family I've ever had. Even now, I can see the pain in Mutter's eyes, the confusion in the faces of my younger brothers. The condemnation in Vater's.

I lift my gaze, jaw firming.

There may be days I regret my decision. Many of them, perhaps.

But I won't let myself be swept along on the tide of National Socialism another day, blindly clinging to the coattails of those supposedly wiser than I.

I, Annalise Brandt, will be different.

Voices and footsteps echo off the glass-domed ceiling of the Lichthof. In repose, the room must be a thing to behold—an airy atrium of marble flooded with sunlight by day, carpeted with shadows at dusk.

Today the space is crowded with students and faculty hurrying to and from lectures.

In the sea of bobbing heads and swinging satchels, I glimpse Sophie coming down the staircase, one hand trailing the banister.

I weave through the crowd and reach Sophie just as she descends the last step. She stops at the bottom of the staircase.

"*Grüß Gott*," I whisper, conscious of the students around us.

One corner of her mouth tilts upward. "*Grüß Gott*."

I swallow, fingers growing damp around the handle of my satchel. "Sophie . . . can I, can we talk?"

She nods, giving me a curious look. "Of course."

We make our way through the crowd to the front doors. Outside, the air is sticky and a faint drizzle mists from the sky, the clouds bulging with unspent rain. Without speaking, we walk, as if by one consent, toward the bench we occupied yesterday.

We sit, the moist metal chilling my legs through my light skirt. I tuck my hair behind my ear. Sophie sits, ankles crossed, wordless.

I look down at my clasped fingers, gathering my thoughts. Then raise my gaze to hers.

"You're right, you know." My voice is soft. "My vater has been commanding, ever since I can remember. Becoming involved in National Socialism only served to hone his belief in power. It became his sole purpose. That and molding his offspring into the perfect image of a National Socialist family. Including my marriage to some rising officer colleague of his." I pause.

Sophie's expression says little about her feelings, her forehead creased in that peculiar frown. Misting rain sprinkles down, dampening our clothes.

Courage gaining, I continue. "I don't want it. Have never wanted any of it. It's like you said. What worth do you ascribe to freedom?"

"Freedom," she whispers, tilting her face toward the rain, eyes closed. "What a word."

"What you said yesterday made me think. I thought about it all last night, and I'm not going to do what my vater wants." The words rush over each other, coming fast from my lips.

"What will you do?" Sophie glances up as a trio of brown-uniformed students march past. They turn smartly down the path, tempo unaltered by the weather.

"I don't know." I sigh. "Making a determination is one thing. Fulfilling it, another matter altogether. But I'll stay my course."

For a long moment, Sophie looks lost in thought. "You should meet my brother and his friends. We're planning a little party for Sunday, the seventh. You ought to come. You'd enjoy getting to know them."

"Would my vater?" I ask, somewhat mischievously.

"I don't think so." Sophie grins.

The camaraderie lauded in the BDM is just an attempt to keep everyone marching in tandem. Of course, friendships arose, but never for me. The thought of a group who challenges and questions and chooses their own path sends excitement swirling through me. "Then I'll be there."

CHAPTER TEN

Kirk
June 7, 1942

"WE MISSED YOU AT church, Son." Vater rests his warm hand on my shoulder. I lean against the entrance to the dining room. The round table is set with Mutter's linen tablecloth and scalloped china. A yawn fights to escape. Blast it all, I'm tired. Hans, Alex, and I didn't break up until after midnight. Our talk of leaflets and plans for duplication had the effect of a strong cup of *kaffee*. The fatigue only hit when I got back to my apartment. As a result, I'd overslept and broken my promise to join my family at church.

I look up, meeting his gaze. His eyes are the same brownish-gold as mine, the fine creases wrinkling the corners evidence of his fifty-eight years. My parents married late, and I followed two years after their wedding day, to the date. I've grown up an only child, the sole son of Paul and Emilie Hoffmann.

"I'm sorry." I blink and yawn, covering my mouth with my closed fist. "I was out late last night." I straighten my shoulders. "I promise to try harder to make it next time."

"With friends, were you?"

My vater is one of the few Confessing Church pastors remaining—a dwindling group of dissidents who refuse to bend to Reich Church policies. A crucifix, rather than a portrait of Hitler hangs on the chapel wall, a Bible, not a copy of *Mein Kampf*, rests on the altar in the run-down building Vater rents for services. Vater's rate of attendance declines, rather than increases, pews emptying as young men leave for the front and many parishioners bow to the pressure and quit attending altogether.

He's already putting himself in enough danger, what with all that's happened to Pastor Niemöller, imprisoned in Dachau for his outspoken protests and other so-called treasonous activities. And Niemöller isn't the only Confessing Church pastor serving a sentence. Vater must not discover our leaflet operation.

Even if it means I must lower myself in his opinion.

"*Ja*. With friends." It's all I will tell him. "You know how it is. Roll call at the barracks, classes, shifts at the hospital. Sometimes we just need an evening off."

Vater looks at me soberly. In a much-mended suit, gazing down at me from his slightly stooped height, he's again the pastor-parent I rebelled against for so many years. If only I hadn't wasted so much time. "As long as they're the right kind of friends, Kirk. These days one can't be too careful."

"Oh, they are. Don't worry about that." I try for a confident grin.

Mutter bustles into the dining room, apron wrapped around her trim waist, a steaming platter in both hands.

"Smells amazing." I move to help with the platter, inhaling the tantalizing scents of beef and cabbage. My mouth waters. Sunday dinner at the Hoffmann house is an occasion, even with the increase in rationing that took effect this spring. Usually, we have guests, either parishioners or the needy Vater brings in off the street—whoever needs a warm meal and a listening ear. Today it's just the three of us.

We slide into our usual seats—Vater at the head, Mutter on his right, me on the left. My stomach rumbles at the sight of the beef, a small slab perhaps, but thick and juicy on its bed of cabbage. Sunlight streams through the spotless windows, the blackout curtains drawn back. Little rays dance across the table, catching the reflection of the silverware.

We bow our heads.

"Merciful God, we thank You for the bounty before us and for Your many acts of provision. We ask that You surround all those suffering during this time of war with Your comfort. Be with those who are in prisons or camps and with Pastor Niemöller and his family. Watch over the Jews, Lord, Your chosen people. Be with the men fighting on the front, and the families they have left behind. Put an end to this terrible war and bring repentance and peace to the inhabitants of our land. Guide me and my wife. Guide my son, Kirk, in all his ways. He needs Your strength, Lord."

I sneak a glance up. Vater's graying head is bent, his hand wrapped around Mutter's. Her eyes are closed, her lips moving in silent agreement. It's not the first time I've been included in family prayers. In adolescence, I usually ignored Vater's words and swung my legs, counting the minutes until it was over.

Today my throat tightens. If Vater only knew the truth. How I need the strength that comes from God, now more than ever.

Vater's closing words are lost in my musings, and I echo my *amen* half a beat later than the others. Neither of my parents seem to notice as Mutter fills our plates with cabbage and beef, knives clinking against china.

Mutter passes me my plate and settles into her seat. "How are things at the barracks?"

I chew slowly, savoring the seasoned meat, then lower my fork. "The usual. Drilling and speeches, always threatening us with the front."

Vater wipes his mouth with a napkin. "Is there any substance to what they're saying?"

I shrug. "Some. Hans thinks we'll be shipped to the eastern front after the summer semester. But nothing's definite yet." We've all seen prior service. Hans and I in France as medics, and Alex in Austria, Czechoslovakia, and France. None of us are eager to be sent out again, but we accept it as a probable eventuality.

Mutter's delicate brow creases, but she says nothing.

I change the subject, another leftover habit from my rebellious days. "I'm going to a party tonight. Hans's sister Sophie is hosting a get-together at Hans's apartment. You'd like Sophie, Vater. She's a biology student at the university."

"Is she single?" Mutter's eyes light with a teasing spark.

I smile, shaking my head. "Engaged to an officer on the eastern front."

"How unfortunate." Mutter sets down her water glass.

"Besides, even if she were, I don't have time for that right now. Hans struggles to find enough hours to spend with Traute. You'll have to be content with a bachelor for a son, Mutter. For now, at any rate." I grin. "At least since the Wehrmacht has taught me to mend, you no longer need to worry about patching my clothes."

"There's a lot more to finding a good woman than simply someone to do your mending." Vater places his hand atop Mutter's. They share a warm smile. "Friendship. Unity of mind. Love." He chuckles. "This fine beef and cabbage."

"Oh, stop, you!" Mutter laughs, giving his hand a playful slap. "You men and your food."

Our shared laughter binds the cracks between us. I let it reach inside and warm me.

The only sure thing about these moments of togetherness is that they are fleeting.

Annalise
June 7, 1942

You are going to meet Sophie's brother and friends. Your stomach will steady. You will be brave.

Standing outside Lindwurmstraße 13, twilight brushing the city, I repeat the mantra over and over in my mind. Outwardly, I'm a girl in a burgundy dress, hair pin-curled, a swipe of just-purchased cherry lipstick contrasting with my fair skin. Inwardly, I'm a tumble of nerves, the build-up of a lifetime's uncertainties conglomerating in this moment.

What if they dislike me? What if I'll always remain the girl outside the circle, never invited in? What if—

I must move past these emotions. If I don't, nothing will ever change.

I try the front door. It's open, so I let myself in. The entryway is still and dark. The narrow stairs creak as I climb to the second floor. A single door waits to the right. I straighten my shoulders and push my hair behind my ear. Then give a firm knock and step back, clasping my hands at my waist.

The door opens.

It's him.

For a long moment, we simply stare at each other. My heart thuds. He's even more arresting up close. Tall, dark-haired, the slightest of smiles curving his strong jawline. He wears a button-down shirt and gray trousers, hair curling over his forehead. With one hand, he holds the door open, revealing echoing laughter and soft lamplight.

"Good evening." I utter the words with a calm I don't feel.

"Hello." He holds out his other hand. "You must be Sophie's friend, Annalise. I'm Kirk Hoffmann." His fingers twine with mine. His grip is firm, but not unduly strong. He smiles, the half moon of a dimple appearing in his cheek. It's a smile unlike any I've ever seen. Genuinely, achingly kind.

Kirk.

"*Ja.* I'm Annalise." Our fingers part. My hand falls into the folds of my skirt, suddenly bereft.

"Come in." He holds the door wider. I step past him, senses caught in a wash of clean soap and something masculine and spicy. Standing on the threshold, I take it all in. Three men and two women sit in a circle of sorts in the apartment's front room, laughing, talking.

Conversation breaks off, and five sets of eyes look up. Sophie jumps from her perch on a lumpy sofa and rushes to greet me.

"Annalise! You're here." She clasps my hand in a quick squeeze and faces the group. "Everyone, this is my friend, Annalise Brandt. Annalise, this is Alex, Traute, Christl, and Hans." She points to each in turn.

"Hello." My smile is uncertain.

"And you've already met Kirk." Sophie glances at Kirk, standing behind my shoulder. He smiles, gives a quick nod.

"Come and sit down." Sophie leads the way to the sofa. "Alex, give Annalise your seat."

A striking young man with reddish-blond hair rises. "Gladly." He takes my hand and lifts it to his lips with a slight bow. His hair falls into his eyes as he looks up. "Alexander Schmorell, at your service, Fräulein Brandt." He grins, roguish, disarming.

"Please, call me Annalise." I flush at his chivalry.

Hans crosses the room and shakes my hand. "Welcome, Annalise." He and Kirk could be brothers, same brown hair and handsome looks. But Kirk is taller, and in appearance Hans seems the older of the two.

"It's a pleasure to meet you. All of you."

The other young man—Christl—ambles over. "We don't stand on ceremony. If Herta and the children were here, they'd be climbing all over you in an instant. The children that is, not my wife." Christl takes a pipe from his mouth with one hand and reaches to shake mine with the other. His handclasp is brief and friendly, his broad smile radiating warmth.

"I wouldn't mind. I love children. In their innocence, they embody everything that's right with the world." I clamp my lips shut, hearing Vater's words: *What are you trying to do? Sound like a philosopher?*

"I couldn't agree more. My boys are my pride and joy."

"How lovely." I smile.

After a few more pleasantries to me, Christl turns to Alex, and the two move toward the other side of the room, heads bent in conversation. Voices drift from the adjoining room, and Sophie, Hans, and Traute are nowhere in sight. A painting on the wall across from the sofa catches my eye, and I cross the room to get a closer look. A print of Franz Marc's Blue Horses. Standing before it, I drink in the colors and textures.

"It's remarkable, his use of color." A voice sounds behind me. I turn. Kirk stands at my side, so close our fingers almost brush.

"He paints boldly," I say, voice soft. "As if he's trying to say 'I'm not ashamed. I'm free.'"

"Are you an artist, or simply a good judge of character?"

A smile tugs my lips. "Hopefully, both. But *ja*, I'm a student of art. This is my first semester at the university."

"That's it," he says, almost under his breath.

"That's what?" I look away from the painting and into his face.

"I knew I'd seen you somewhere before." His eyes crinkle when he smiles, the dimple flashing again.

My cheeks flush. I don't dare admit I've seen *him* before, watched him, wondering. Dreaming.

He braces one hand on the wall, body turned toward me. Again, that heady mix of fragrances fills my senses. "How do you like your studies?"

I bite my lip. If I reply with my true feelings, they could be construed as disloyal to National Socialism. If I answer with something trite, I'll despise myself later.

The voices of the others reverberate in the background, Sophie's laughter mingling with Alex's. This is a group marked by oneness of mind. These people couldn't meet so freely if they didn't share the same feelings.

"Art, I love unreservedly. But the way it's presented at the university leaves me cold and disappointed." I look at the painting again, the mingled blues and reds. The majesty, magic, and at the same time humanness of the painted animal. "Art is supposed to be expression, but there it's . . . empty. How can one be creative if one is told how to create?"

His gaze holds mine. I've never been looked at like this before. Not merely studied, but seen. "Aptly spoken, Annalise Brandt."

CHAPTER ELEVEN

Kirk
June 7, 1942

I NEVER HEARD HER name before tonight.

In less than an hour, she has captivated me more than anyone I have ever met. From the moment I opened the door and saw her standing in the shadows—a vision in a dark red dress, a faint smile on her lips, gaze hesitant. When I took her hand, I suddenly, inexplicably, never wanted to let go.

We stand in front of Hans's cheaply framed Franz Marc print, her words lingering in the air.

"How can one be creative if one is told how to create?"

It's a statement as startling as it is true. Her eyes darkened, her voice brimming with passion. She isn't speaking out of mere intellect, but as if every word is pulled from some hidden, precious place inside her.

"What are you studying?" Her reddish-gold curls brush her jawline as she looks up at me.

"Medicine. I hope to become a doctor, but it's taking a long time. My studies keep being delayed, the semesters shortened."

"I doubt there's ever been a generation of young people who've had to exercise more patience than we." She gives a wry smile.

I chuckle. "You're probably right." Delay after delay as we're told to put the interests of the Reich above our own. We don't matter, as long as our country succeeds. I'm all for selflessness, but I can see very little of it in Hitler's plans for Germany.

"Why medicine?" she asks, head tilted.

I pause. It's not a question I've often been asked; why one path over another. In truth, I chose medicine because I knew I couldn't be responsible for shedding blood in this war of aggression. "I like helping people. Mending things that are broken. Making right what needs to be."

Her lips soften in a smile. "I like that. Making right what needs to be.

There's so much broken in the world, it's good to know someone's still trying." Lamplight frames her in a butterscotch glow.

"The way I look at it, we should all be trying. We may not be able to change the universe, but if we can be a force for good in our corner of it, at least that's something, right?"

She turns her face away and looks back at the painting, expression almost . . . troubled.

Great job, Hoffmann. Five minutes with a pretty . . . nein, beautiful girl, and what do you do? Sermonize. Very smooth.

"I'm sorry." I rub the back of my neck with a sheepish grin. "I'm not usually so philosophical with people I've just met."

She turns, the troubled look erased from her eyes. A smile tugs at the corners of her lips—lips tinted a distracting shade of red. "I started it, remember? Of course, we *could* talk about the weather. If you wanted to." Her tone is teasing.

"It's been unseasonably warm for this time of year," I say, deadpan.

"Unseasonably." She gives a vigorous nod, a laugh escaping. "There. We've gotten that out of the way. Feel better?"

"Very."

"Admiring Hans's painting?" Sophie's voice breaks into our laughter. I like Hans's sister. Really, I do. But couldn't she have picked another conversation to interrupt?

Annalise nods. "It's a favorite of mine."

Sophie looks between us. "We're about to have tea and strudel. Care to join us?"

I motion for Annalise to precede me. We cross the room and join the others. I settle onto the floor next to Alex and Sophie, and Annalise joins Hans and Traute on the sofa.

Christl passes out plates, as Traute fills them with thin slices of strudel. Hans's low table is looking more battered by the day, cluttered with books, the strudel platter, a teapot, and cups. I spy a piece of paper covered in his scrawl poking out from the corner of one book. A draft for our leaflet?

And it's there. The secret, hanging in the air. Concealed by our gaiety, lingering regardless. Christl knows what we're doing, though he's not involved in the practical aspects. Hans hasn't told Traute. We're keeping them out of it for their own good, though they share the same views. What we're planning is dangerous, the fewer involved, the better.

What of Annalise? What are her views? Laughter spills from her lips as Christl regales the room with a story about his boys. The sweet sound threads inside me, settling in a place I didn't know was empty.

Our gazes meet. Remnants of laughter linger at the corners of her mouth, in the form of a gentle smile. Her eyes sparkle, as if she too senses whatever sudden, powerful thing is between us.

I lose myself in her eyes, in the warm lamplight, the friendship all around me. In Christl's story, Hans and Traute with their arms around each other, Alex's laughter, Sophie's deep brown eyes crinkling at the corners. Annalise, a newcomer, yet sitting in our midst as if she belonged.

It's enough.

Tonight, it's all enough.

CHAPTER TWELVE

Kirk
June 15, 1942

"COMING?" I LEAN OVER the stair railing, as Alex and Hans trundle up the steep steps, boots making scuffing sounds. Each of them carries one end of a wooden crate.

"It's not the lightest thing in the world to haul around, you know." Alex's face is red from exertion. Hans goes backward up the narrow staircase.

"Careful," he cautions as they turn a corner. "Careful . . . Alex!"

I help them once they reach the top. We gain Alex's apartment—third door down—and set the crate in the middle of the room. I shut the door. Alex and Hans flex their fingers. Blackout curtains drape the room in shadows.

Like a child at Christmas, I kneel beside the crate. Alex heads into the next room, returning with a butter knife. I raise a brow.

"I don't have a crowbar," he says, handing it to me.

I work the knife around the edge of the crate, prying the top off, revealing layers of wood shavings. Hans crouches beside me. Together, we reach inside. My fingers touch cool metal. We lift . . . and there.

Gleaming black and shining silver. A simple crank handle.

A duplicating machine.

Ours.

I stare at it. Silence fills the room. We're all riveted: Alex from where he's seated on his sofa and Hans and I kneeling on the floor, surrounded by scattered wood shavings. A weight settles inside me. Even the ownership of such an item could bring us under suspicion.

We've taken our first steps. Today those steps have led us to the edge of the Rubicon. With the distribution of our first leaflet, we'll cross it.

Then there will be no going back.

"Von Galen's sermons must have been printed on a machine just like this." I rest a hand on its edge, the metal smooth beneath my fingertips.

"We should have gotten one long before now," Hans says. "The very day we read that first sermon."

All of us remember when we were introduced to the words of Clemens von Galen. Last summer, the Scholls discovered a leaflet in their mailbox, which Hans later showed to me. I wish I could meet the brave soul who dared to copy and anonymously mail Bishop von Galen's bold words denouncing the Reich's euthanasia program. I don't know the total number of copies distributed. But each represents a person no longer denied truth.

Please duplicate and pass on—the plea at the end of von Galen's leaflet. Finally, in our own way, we're answering that plea.

"How does it work?" Alex stands. After making discreet inquiries, Alex purchased the duplicating machine, donating thirty-two marks from his allowance for the purpose. Fritz was unable to fulfill Sophie's request for an official stamp, so we bought our machine second-hand.

"You feed the paper through here." Hans gestures like a university lecturer. "And turn the handle. The papers come out there. It's quite simple, really." He gives the handle a turn. He's shucked his jacket and rolled up his shirtsleeves.

"Simple, huh?"

"It's very well designed."

Alex leans down, running his fingers along its edge. "Nothing is ever simple, Hans." He looks up, brow furrowed. Hair falls over his high forehead. A beat passes.

Hans nods. Swallows.

Alex isn't talking about the machine.

We undertake more than merely printing words on paper and passing them around. We undertake resistance against a regime that has taken down armies with the ease of leveling dominoes. We've thought about it, talked about it, and now the tangible evidence sits before us. A duplicating machine. Metal and silver. Ink and treason.

"But simple things aren't worth doing, anyway." Alex's face eases into a grin. "Isn't there a Goethe quote about that, Hans?"

"Not Goethe, I don't think." I stand and brush the shavings from my hands. The springs of Alex's sofa groan as I sit.

"Definitely not Goethe." Hans stands and pulls up Alex's desk chair. Books and papers clutter the surface of his desk. Along with a few love letters, I suspect. Alex exists as the center of an orbit of female admirers.

I shift positions and cross my legs. "So what of these leaflets? Do we have a name?"

"Not yet." Hans pulls the chain of Alex's desk lamp. Light filters into the room. "Any suggestions?"

"It has to be something memorable." Alex paces back and forth, tunneling a hand through his hair. Wood curlings sprinkle his gray trousers. "Some kind of symbol. A knight, maybe?"

"Nein." Hans shakes his head. "Nothing military."

"We want to represent truth. Truth is the opposite of darkness. It's light." I'm thinking out loud. "Truth is . . ."

Hans picks up something from Alex's desk. A faded flower. The remnants of a white rose.

I expect him to make a crack about which one of Alex's girlfriends bestowed this upon him, but instead he holds it by the stem. Turns it in his fingers. The petals are wrinkled and aged with time. White has faded to cream. Yet the unspoiled purity of the rose remains.

"Truth is a white rose." As he finishes my sentence, a light enters Hans's eyes. "The White Rose."

Alex grins. "I can't think of a more apt name. Remember that book, Hans? The one by that author with the pen name of Traven? It was also called *The White Rose*."

"Peasants fighting against exploitation. *Ja*, I remember."

"Leaflets of the White Rose." It slides off my tongue. Fitting. Fragile purity against blackness.

A simple symbol to fight a complicated battle.

Alex disappears into the adjoining room, returning a moment later with a single bottle. "Cheap *bier*, I know, and warm at that." He opens the bottle. The sharp, yeasty scent fills the air. "But I think this moment deserves a toast. To the White Rose." He swigs from the bottle, passes it to Hans.

Hans holds up the bottle. "To truth." He drinks and hands it to me.

"To freedom." The daring words mingle with the bitter taste of alcohol. We exchange glances, the ensuing silence almost sacred. We've thrown our lots in together. Together, we'll work and sacrifice and risk. Come what may.

"It's a start." Hans slaps his hands against his knees. "But our work has only begun. The text of the leaflet needs to be finalized. Distribution planned. We'll need paper and ink and stamps. All of these must be bought at separate locations. Purchasing vast quantities in one place will only arouse suspicion. Particularly, stamps. Sophie can help us."

"Your mental lists are endless." Alex takes another drink.

"My mental lists are necessary." Hans snatches the bottle. I watch them, my friends, drinking and talking, purpose beneath every word, even the joking ones.

Years from now, will we look back upon this afternoon in June as the beginning of something great? Only time will answer us. I smile faintly, grab the bottle from Hans, and remember the child with the teddy bear who opened my eyes to the truth of my own complacency.

We, a humble group of students, cannot hope to change the tide of history. But we can leave our stamp upon it.

We may not achieve greatness. We may not even change much of anything. But we will look back and know one thing.

We were not silent.

⟀

Sophie
June 16, 1942

I pin a swastika button to the lapel of my jacket before leaving the apartment. It stands out against the brown fabric, a miniature crooked cross surrounded by bloody red.

I pick up my satchel and hurry out, locking the door behind me. I take the stairs quickly, hand trailing the banister, footsteps echoing in the silence.

Outside, the sky is steel gray. Rain splatters down in fat drops, giving the facades of buildings a washed-out hue, darkening the limp swastika flags. Coated figures waste no time in scurrying toward their destinations, boots slapping against the forming puddles. Black umbrellas bob up and down.

I walk, head down, heedless of the rain pelting my face and hair.

We have a duplicating machine. I haven't seen it yet. But with the machine in our—or rather Alex's possession—everything is moving at full speed.

And finally, finally Hans has given me something to do. I'm to purchase fifty stamps from a nearby post office. Then walk to another and do the same.

A mix of fear and anticipation stirs inside my chest.

Ignoring people when they give the Hitler salute, reading banned books beneath the covers during labor service, listening to BBC broadcasts with Vater . . . all of these are dangerous.

But none as dangerous as this.

A sleek motorcar drives past, windshield wipers squeaking at full speed against the glass. I glimpse men with grim faces and gray uniforms. Momentarily, I still. Muddy water splashes onto my shoes and stockings.

The car drives on. I keep walking, scanning street signs. Water soaks through a hole in the sole of my shoe.

At last (or is it too soon?), I reach the post office. A shawl-wrapped woman bumps into me as she exits, hurrying past without muttering so much as an apology.

My heart quickens as I stare at the brick building. If I fail, Hans will lose what little faith he has in me. I'll be trapped again, trapped by doing nothing.

God, please . . .

The beveled glass window bearing the words *Post Office* is smeared with tracks of rain. Inside, a queue stretches from desk to door.

I let myself in and take my place at the end of the line. The air is damp and musty, and the coat of the elderly man in front of me reeks of stale cigarette smoke. I fix my gaze on my hands, knuckles white around the handle of my satchel, running my cover story over and over in my mind.

You are a grieving sister. Your brother has died on the front. You need stamps to send letters to family and friends informing them of his death.

The line inches forward. Those exiting the post office bump and jostle me as they pass. Out of the corner of my eye, I size up the clerk behind the tall counter. A bristly mustache bisects his round face.

My stomach churns as the elderly man in front of me requests ten twelve-pfennig stamps. The clerk opens a drawer, rips off the requested quantity, and passes them over the counter. The customer hands over some coins. He turns and hobbles away from the counter.

Time seems to stop. My surroundings blur. All except the man behind the counter.

I walk with steps neither too fast nor too slow.

"*Ja?*" Sunken patches of flab sag beneath the man's eyes. He looks bored. Tired.

"Fifty eight-pfennig stamps, please." I don't look directly at him, but I don't avoid his gaze. After all, I'm a grieving sister. Not a traitor.

He moves to open the drawer. Then he stops. His eyes flicker over me. "Fifty? So many?"

"My brother has fallen on the front." I keep my voice soft and sad. "We need to send letters to our family and friends, letting them know the news." I give a little tug at the lapel of my jacket, hopefully drawing the man's attention to my swastika pin.

The clerk looks me over once more. I meet his gaze evenly, hoping all he will see is a pale girl in a brown coat. That he won't notice my shallow breath or hear my pounding heart.

With a grunt, he opens the drawer, muttering as he counts out fifty stamps. I pull coins from my jacket pocket, sliding them across the counter as he passes me the sheets of stamps. He opens another drawer and fumbles for my change. I hold out my palm. His fat fingers brush mine as he places the cold metal discs in my hand.

"Danke," I murmur. My fingers close around the coins, and I slip them into my pocket, whisking the sheets of stamps into my satchel.

Head down, I turn and walk out of the post office. No one looks up as I pass. The door shuts behind me. Raindrops sting my cheeks.

I turn the corner, pent-up breath coming out in a whoosh. My legs go suddenly weak, but I force them to keep moving.

No longer am I a helpless bystander. By handing these stamps to Hans, I'll show him I can be useful, that he can trust me, the same as he trusts Kirk and Alex. Affixing these square miniatures of Hitler's face to envelopes means our words will be delivered. Read by people who desperately need to be woken up.

I smile, as I walk through the rain, steps lighter than they've been all day. *This is only the beginning.*

My smile vanishes with the realization, leaving me suddenly sapped of energy. It's foolish to be giddy over one success. Countless more must follow for there to be any real progress.

Countless acts.

Unknown risks.

CHAPTER THIRTEEN

Kirk
June 18, 1942

WE BEGIN TONIGHT.

I walk to Eickemeyer's studio, steps fast, keenly aware of the approaching blackout and lack of other travelers. The air is dank and humid, weighted with anticipation. Or so it seems to me.

A man strolls down the sidewalk, an umbrella swinging at his side. I force myself to slow as I stride past. Speed is a cue for one to take notice.

We need no notice this night.

I reach the studio, a pale, stucco-sided building set back from the street. Not so much as a flicker of light glimmers from the blackout-covered windows. Sliding my hand into my pocket, I pull out a key—the three of us each have one. It turns smoothly. I glance behind—just once—to make sure no one is watching, then close and lock the door behind me in the darkness. I don't bother with a light, groping my way through the blackness until I reach the door to the basement. I descend the narrow, creaking steps with light footfalls.

"Hans?" I know better than to not announce my presence.

The door opens. Hans appears in the crack. "Kirk." He grins. "You're just in time. Alex is already here."

"Is Sophie coming?"

"Not tonight. She had a bad headache. I told her to stay home and rest. She gave me stamps though. A hundred of them. She said she got them without a problem."

"You should be proud of your sister."

The studio looks much the same as when we visited it when Eickemeyer was in Munich. Dingy and spacious, sprinkled with sculptures and crated artwork belonging to an artist friend of Eickemeyer's.

Except for two additional items resting on now-cleared tables. A Remington typewriter. And our duplicating machine.

What would Eickemeyer say if he knew what we planned to do in his studio? I suspect he guesses it isn't to drill like good little Hitlerites, but we're keeping him in the dark as to particulars. It's better this way. For all parties concerned.

Alex sits in a chair pulled near the typewriter. "Hey, Shurik." I clap a hand to his shoulder, greeting him by his Russian nickname.

He turns. "Finally decided to join the party, did you?"

I laugh and pull up a vacant chair. Sheets covered in Hans's scrawl, and a few in Alex's and mine, are already scattered on the table.

Shirtsleeves rolled to his forearms, collar open, the dim light casting smoky shadows on his rumpled hair, Hans takes a seat in front of the typewriter. He meets our gazes.

"Let's get to work." His eyes are alight with energy, despite the late hour. "I've read each of our drafts." Hans picks up one of the papers and holds it up to the light. "There's good material in each. I propose we blend them together."

Alex and I nod.

"Once we're in agreement a paragraph should be included in the leaflet, we'll type it out. I've already disconnected the typewriter ribbon." He carefully lifts a precious sheet of wax stencil paper and inserts it into the typewriter.

I get up from my chair and move to stand behind Hans's shoulder. He settles his fingertips on the keys. The typewriter clacks. Inked letters march across the sheet, impressing themselves into the stencil paper.

Leaflets of the White Rose

It sounds so . . . organized. Like we're more than three university students in a basement. Like the words we risk our lives to pen could actually make a difference.

Hans takes up a page covered in his loping handwriting. He clears his throat.

"'Nothing is more unworthy of a civilized nation than to let itself be "governed" without resistance by an irresponsible faction ruled by dark instincts. Is it not true that every honest German today is ashamed of his government?'" He looks up.

I let the words settle inside, take root. How many times have similar thoughts crossed my mind? Once, we could lay claim to a civilized nation. Even after the Great War. Now who among us who knows the truth can do so? Not a one.

Alex nods. "I like it. It's forceful."

"And true," I add.

"Good." A little grin creeps over Hans's face. "Because I labored over an hour on that paragraph." He turns to me, forehead creased. "Kirk, are you good with a typewriter?"

I shrug. "I've used one before."

Hans stands and gestures to the chair. "It'll be faster if I dictate and you type. That way I can self-edit as I go."

My heart pounds as I take the still-warm seat. My fingers hover over the keys, poised and ready. Hans rereads the paragraph, slower this time, as I type.

Pencil can be erased, forgotten. Ink is finality.

Nothing is more unworthy . . .

"The next part's yours, Shurik." Hans rounds the table and points to a place on one of Alex's papers. "Except you used the word *evils*. I suggest *crimes*. Crime implies something that's legally wrong. It's more concrete."

"That makes sense. But other than that, you agree with what I've written?"

Hans nods, resting one hand on the back of Alex's chair. "One hundred percent." He reads aloud. "'Who among us can guess the extent of the shame that will come upon us and our children when someday the veil has fallen from our eyes, and crimes of a most atrocious nature, infinitely exceeding all measure, will come to light?'"

My fingers fly over the keys, as I strive to keep up.

Hours pass. Alex packs and lights his pipe, whelming the air with aromatic smoke. My shoulders begin to ache. Hans presses his finger to his upper lip, forehead creased. We work on. Most of the words are Hans's, with a few insertions from Alex and me.

If everyone waits for others to begin, Nemesis's avenging messengers will move closer and closer, and then the last victim, too, will be thrown in vain into the jaws of the insatiable demon.

For so long, we've been guilty of doing nothing. Now, we're taking action. I feel little fear. Trepidation, perhaps. And urgency. Deep, soul-throbbing urgency.

Offer passive resistance—RESISTANCE—wherever you may be. Prevent the continuation of this atheistic war machine before it is too late, before the last cities, like Cologne, lie in ruins, before the nation's last youth has bled to death in battle for the hubris of a subhuman.

We close with a quotation from Goethe:

Now I meet my brave ones,
Who convene at night

To remain silent, not to sleep,
And the beautiful word of freedom
Is being whispered and stammered,
Until in strange newness,
At our temple's steps,
Delighted we call out anew:
Freedom! Freedom! Freedom!

Hans lowers the paper. The Goethe, read in his baritone voice, rich with passion, has lured us all into a kind of trance, even me at the typewriter.

His voice is hoarse, perhaps with the strain of dictating, perhaps with some deeper emotion, as he adds a sentence from memory. "We ask you to make as many copies of this sheet as possible and to redistribute it."

The keys clack as I type the final words. It's a call to action. The answer to those who read the leaflet and ask: what now?

Distribute and pass on. Spread the word. Don't be silent.

I snatch the sheet of stencil paper from the machine and push back my chair.

"That's it then." My eyelids are heavy, weightier still because I must report for duty at the hospital at 8:00 a.m. tomorrow.

But . . . we have a leaflet.

"We'll reconvene to begin mimeographing within the next few days." Hans stands, takes the stencil paper from me, and stares down at it.

"Then we'll distribute the leaflets?" A curl of smoke rises above Alex's head. Alex, who longs for the garb of a Russian peasant but is forced to wear that of a Wehrmacht officer. Alex, who fits into the life of the carefree artist, but studies medicine to please his vater. Alex, who I'm proud to call my friend.

Hans nods. "Then we'll distribute the leaflets."

⟶

Annalise
June 19, 1942

Since the party, Kirk and I have seen each other in passing at the university. Each time, we stop and chat, ordinary niceties about the day and our classes.

Is there more beneath the surface, or is my hopeful mind conjuring things that don't exist? Is the smile that creases the corners of his eyes when he looks at me something special, meant for me alone, or how he looks at everyone?

With all the might inside me, I hope it's not my imagination. That when he asked if I'd meet him for an evening walk through the Englischer Garten, it's because he genuinely wants to get to know me, not because he feels sorry for Sophie's lonely friend in Munich.

We've arranged to meet in front of the Seehaus restaurant, located on the banks of the Kleinhesseloher Lake. Wind stirs the hem of my red, polka dot summer dress, the breeze prickling my arms. I clutch my handbag and scan for Kirk. My shiny low-heeled shoes pinch my toes. I can't deny I made an effort to look nice for him, setting my unruly hair in pin curls last night, brushing on a layer of lipstick.

Finally, I spot him striding across the grass toward me. He waves. I wave back and brush a curl behind my ear. My heart speeds up at the sight of him. He's wearing a light brown suit, shrugging on the jacket as he walks. Wind riffles his hair.

"Sorry I'm late." He smiles apologetically. His tie is askew. I resist the sudden urge to straighten it for him.

"You're not late. I'm early."

"Shall we?" He offers his arm. The gesture warms my cheeks. Not that I haven't experienced male chivalry before. The young officers Vater invites to dinner have it honed to a science. With them, though, it always seems forced, their compliments as wooden as their marching. With Kirk, nothing seems more natural, though his smile suggests a touch of shyness.

I rest my hand on his arm—not just my fingertips—and together we move away from the restaurant and begin a slow circuit around the lake. Being on the arm of a man I actually like is an entirely new experience, and not an unpleasant one. The warmth of him, the swell of muscles in his forearm make me want to lean closer, instead of draw away.

"Beautiful." I look out at the lake, the shadows of sunset turning its surface to flame.

He nods, and we walk in comfortable silence. The sweet crispness of the evening air, like biting into a freshly picked apple, brings a smile to my lips. I steal a glance at him. He catches me watching him and grins.

"We're not saying much, are we? What must you be thinking? 'He sure is a nice fellow. Invites me out, and then ignores me.'"

I smile. "Nein. Anyone can chatter endlessly. Silence is something special."

"That it is." He nods. "But I think we can break it for a while, don't you?"

Laughter escapes my lips. "I think so."

"Hans always says the lake reminds him of home. You?"

I shake my head. "Nein, home . . . home is in Berlin. We've lived there since I was little."

"Who does 'we' include?"

He asks the question in a light tone, but it sends a skitter through me nonetheless. My family is part of my life, like it or not. If only I were Sophie, with her tax-consultant vater and sprawling family in Ulm. If only Hans were my brother, not Horst.

I shove the thoughts aside, ashamed.

"I have three brothers. Horst, a year younger than me, is in the Wehrmacht. Heinz is fifteen, and Albert is two years younger. They're still in school." Which Heinz gives the barest amount of attention to, consumed with rising in the Hitler Youth, while Albert struggles to get even passing marks.

"All brothers then." He grins. "Poor you. Were you always getting dragged into ball games?"

I shake my head. "Never dragged. I liked playing with them." For as long as it lasted.

"And your vater? What does he do?" Again, a casual question.

With a complicated answer.

I swallow, looking straight ahead as we turn down a wooded path, high-reaching elm branches creating a shaded shelter above. How easy it was at the party to simply be an ordinary university student, instead of the daughter of an SS officer.

But if I hope to have any kind of relationship with Kirk, even friendship, I must tell him the truth.

Our eyes meet. "What does *your* vater do, Kirk?"

A guarded look enters Kirk's gaze, the same kind my own must hold. Neither of us trusts the other completely, despite the attraction between us.

"I've always been a pastor's son," Kirk says slowly. "When I was young, my vater pastored a Lutheran congregation in Munich. During the church struggle, he broke away and is now employed, if you can call it that, by the Confessing Church."

My mind reels. I stifle the urge to laugh out of shock. Of all the young men at university, I, the daughter of a man who claims God doesn't exist and our salvation rests in Hitler, find myself attracted to the son of a pastor. Not just any pastor, mind you, but one who broke away from the Reich Church to join what Vater calls "a group of lunatics and rebels who need the teaching of Dachau to straighten them up."

"A pastor." I mutter the word to myself, my hand falling from his arm and down to my side.

"Why? Are you surprised?"

I have to tell him. I shake my head. "My vater is . . . he's an SS stan-dartenführer. Personally acquainted with the Führer, a guest at the Berghof more than once, and a favorite dinner companion of the Goebbels." I stop, the false bravado in my words little masking the misery beneath.

Kirk regards me, something sharp and guarded in his eyes. "I see."

I clutch my handbag with both hands. With that look in his eyes, I'm fifteen again, ignored by the other girls, the darling of the teachers, but the friend of none but those who seek my acquaintance for advancement. It's not that way with Kirk. He's not interested in rising in the ranks of the SS, but he sees me now in a different light.

I'm Standartenführer Brandt's daughter. Not Annalise.

"I should be getting back." I try and shield the hurt from my tone, but some of it escapes anyway. "I have studying to do."

He nods, shifting, hands in his pockets.

I give a brief nod in return. "Auf Wiedersehen, Kirk." I turn, walking away with my shoulders straight and my head high, the crush of gravel beneath my heels. Not once do I look back.

I leave the Englischer Garten with its grassy parklands and sunset lake. My feet begin to ache, courtesy of the heels. Wearing them was a stupid idea.

Accepting his invitation was even more so.

The streets are drowsy with the approach of nightfall. A group of ado-lescent boys kick a ball across the cobblestones amid rowdy laughter. A uniformed officer strolls with his sweetheart, putting an arm around her waist with the abandon of a man on three-days leave.

I want nothing more than to go home, brew a strong cup of tea, and rest my feet. The bobby pins pulling my sculpted curls back from my face dig into my scalp. Kirk's taut face fills my mind.

Why, oh, why did I let myself like him?

Stubborn tears press against my eyes. To let them fall would be childish and stupid. My pace quickens.

"Annalise? Annalise Brandt?"

Startled, I turn, swiping my eyes with the back of my hand. A man walks toward me, the door of a *bierhalle* swinging in his wake. He wears a crisp gray-green uniform, a matching black-brimmed cap marked with the SS insignia. His face breaks into a grin, revealing crooked front teeth.

"Can it really be you? Annalise Brandt?"

I frown, confused. I'm a stranger in Munich, and I don't recognize this man, though he apparently knows who I am. "I'm sorry. Do I know you?"

"Herbert Mayer." His grin broadens. "Don't you remember?"

Recognition slowly dawns as I take in his blue eyes, the faint white scar on his chin, his face an older version of the boy I remember.

If I'd ever had a childhood playmate, it was Herbert Mayer. When we were eleven, we discovered we both shared a love of art. Sitting at Herbert's kitchen table, we talked of someday being famous artists and stained our fingers with cheap paint. Four months later, Herbert moved away, his parting token of our friendship a sketch he'd done of Alpine roses—my favorite flower. Mutter had thrown away the painting while spring cleaning my room, and with its absence, I'd almost forgotten Herbert.

"Herbert! I don't believe it." I reach out and clasp his hands, smiling. "How long has it been?"

"It was 1932, wasn't it?"

"Oh, that seems ages ago. Do you remember what we did that summer?"

"Remember?" He laughs. "How could I forget?"

"That mural we painted in your room." I grin. "Was your mutter ever cross when she saw it."

He shakes his head ruefully. "Don't remind me. I was the one who had to use the money I'd been saving for a pair of ski boots to repaint it. But look at you now. All grown-up."

"How did you recognize me?" I notice the freckles on his nose, only added in number since we last met.

"Your hair. I've never forgotten that shade of gold and red. You're wearing it differently."

I nod, its strands brushing my jawline. "A recent alteration."

"It suits you." A streetcar speeds by a distance away, its silhouette cutting through the fading light. "Why are you in Munich?"

"I'm a student at the university."

"Let me guess? Art?"

"*Ja.*"

"Marvelous." He tilts his head. "What are you doing tonight? I'm staying at a hotel not far from here. A chat about old times would be just the thing to brighten up a lonely evening. What do you think?"

Had it been anyone but Herbert, I'd have emphatically refused. It's been a long day, and the memory of my exchange with Kirk still stings. But Herbert looks at me so hopefully, I can't bring myself to decline. Herbert, in his innocent youth, never flattered or snubbed me. All he cared about was that I brought my box of new paints and liked sneaking *kuchen* from the icebox as much as he did.

"I'd love to." The answer falls from my lips.

"Excellent," he says, and we make our way down the street.

Half an hour later, I'm seated in an easy chair in Herbert's hotel room. Blackout curtains cover the windows, muted light from a desk lamp illuminating the space. Herbert sits on the edge of the double bed, boots planted on the thick rug. His cap rests beside him, green and black against the cream coverlet. In one hand, he holds a full tumbler poured from a brandy bottle on the bedside table. He offered me some, but I refused. I didn't eat much before going out with Kirk, and the emptiness in my stomach makes it unsteady. Herbert is already on his second glass.

We spent the walk here reminiscing, the past overruling the present in our dialogue. I didn't ask why Herbert wears an SS uniform. Its cut and insignias, marking him with the rank of untersturmführer, suddenly brings back the twist of unease that always tightened through me in Berlin, where similarly garbed officers and my vater populated the landscape of my male world.

"Remind me again, what type of mural we wanted to paint?" Herbert takes a swallow, the golden liquid now halved in his glass.

"You wanted to paint the Alps, so you could look at them every morning when you woke. I don't know how I got roped into being the assistant to your Michelangelo."

He chuckles. "Sistine Chapel, it was not. And if I were to judge between us, I would say you were the Michelangelo, and I your obedient serf. You always had lots of opinions about art."

I arch a brow. "And you didn't?"

"But you . . . you always won our arguments." His voice slurs. He reaches for the bottle and refills his glass.

On our walk, I noticed the scent of *bier* pervading him, but we were laughing and talking so I didn't think much of it. Now that I'm here, and he's continuing to drink, I'm starting to regret coming to the hotel. I suppose that ought to be a lesson for me in how people change. I'm not the little girl I was then, and Herbert isn't the same boy.

I cross my ankles, hands in my lap. "What do you do now?"

"Currently, I'm on leave. I visited my sister in the country for the first two days, and I've been in Munich for the second two." His syllables blend into each other. "I've got to go back tomorrow." The liquid swirls as he puts the glass to his lips. Alarm cuts through me.

"To Russia?"

He looks up, hunched forward on the bed. "Nein." A shadow crosses his face, making him look older, almost hardened.

"Do you still paint?"

He shakes his head and gulps another drink. "Nein . . . no time for things like that."

I should go. Herbert seemed so sober when we met, despite the waft of *bier* on his breath. Though I guess I wouldn't know. Vater has many faults, but like the Führer, he doesn't imbibe.

"Art is fine for women and children." Herbert's words slur. "But I have no time for childish pursuits. I'm engaged in . . . important work for the Fatherland." His hand wavers, the drink slopping onto his hand, the sleeve of his uniform coat.

I rise. That's it. I'm leaving. "Herbert." My voice is firm.

He looks at me, gaze unfocused. "SS Untersturmführer Herbert Mayer. Pretty good for a butcher's son, eh? A valuable asset to the Führer. Someone has to wipe out the parasites invading the Fatherland's *lebensraum*. The diseased limb." He makes a chopping motion with the hand not holding the glass. "We must cut it off before gangrene infects the healthy body."

I've heard such rhetoric before, mostly from Vater. In Herbert Mayer's slurred tone it isn't anything but repellent. I grab my handbag, shoving it beneath my armpit, and stride toward the door.

"If only . . . if only they didn't tempt me. The Poles are a very convincing lot, you know. Making you believe they're human."

I still, turning.

"When you shoot them, they die like anyone else. Their blood looks the same. But it isn't. We must always remember that. To pity is to weaken and to weaken is to stab our Führer in the back." He stares directly at me, but it's as if he doesn't see me. "There's this village, near where I was stationed. Some partisans thought they'd be clever and blow up our supply trains. What a mistake." He chuckles.

I stare at him, frozen.

"We caught them . . . in the act. My men went into the village and the forests, rounded up the whole town. It was crawling with partisans, mostly Jews." He coughs and drains more liquor from his glass. Wipes his mouth with the back of his hand. "Not anymore. I ordered them to cleanse the area. When I have a problem, it's dealt with thoroughly. But it takes the right kind of man to handle it. That day, one of the men on the firing squad was new. Fresh from training. He shot the men, but the girl . . . He stood there, holding the gun, shaking like a leaf. Just couldn't do it." He shakes his head with a chuckle. "What weaklings new recruits can be."

My throat goes dry. The heat in the room (or perhaps it's not heat, but my imagination) stifles me. The rank odor of my sweat mingles with the scent of the alcohol.

"I taught him a lesson though. Cut him down to size. The girl he wouldn't shoot . . . I did the job. I grabbed her, pulled her away from the wall. She was so small . . ." He rubs a hand across his jaw. "I'm ashamed to admit it, but for an instant . . . she tempted me too. She had . . . brown curls and blue eyes, like my sister's child. She had a doll, a little rag of a thing. She was crying for her mutter. Her screaming . . . I didn't like that. So I raised my pistol. A click." He looks up. "The screaming stopped. It's astonishing how easy it is to die. One minute screaming, the next . . . nothing. But I can still hear it. It's in my head." His gaze darts wildly. "Her ghost is haunting me."

My legs shake. The room spins. Herbert's red face blurs, his wavering hand bringing the glass to his lips, the insignias on his collar gleaming in the light. My stomach churns. I'm going to be sick.

I whirl around. My hand shakes as I open the door. Herbert is still talking as I slam it, cutting him off from view. The narrow corridors and steep staircase pass in a haze. I fling open the door to the hotel, heedless of the gaze of the clerk behind the counter. Blessedly cool air fans my cheeks, the street clothed in semi-darkness

My stomach cramps, and I bend double, vomiting onto the cobblestones. Heaving shudders convulse my body.

After a few minutes, I stand, bile acrid in my mouth. Numb, I turn toward home. I force myself to concentrate enough to follow street signs, reach my apartment, unlock the door, and relock it behind me.

Fully clothed, I climb on top of my bed, curling into a ball, hands fisted beneath my chin. I squeeze my eyes shut, but Herbert's face, his words, follow me still.

"Cleanse the area . . . dealt with thoroughly . . . she was so small . . . crying for her mutter . . . a click . . . the screaming stopped."

These are my countrymen. Men like Herbert, who was once my playmate, men like my own brother murdering hundreds, thousands. Not only military executions or killing in warfare, but a ruthless extermination of those who have committed no crime.

I want to scream at the top of my lungs, yell down curses at the lot of them, tear them apart with my bare hands. This is what blindly following our Führer has reduced us to. Murdering as if those killed are no more than the parasites Herbert spoke of. The lust for dominance has poisoned us, made us believe we have the power to decide who lives and who dies.

No one has that power over an innocent human being. No one.

I blink, my eyes dry. This is not something to cry over. Tears would render it among that which is human. Which it is not.

Something hot and fierce rises inside of me as I lie huddled on my coverlet in the darkness.

The Germany we've become is mine no longer.

And neither it, nor I, will ever be the same again.

CHAPTER FOURTEEN

Kirk
June 20, 1942

OUR FIRST EFFORTS ARE fumbling, but soon, typed sheets roll from the duplicating machine one after the other, in perfect harmony. Hans feeds the blank pages. I crank the handle and pull out the freshly inked leaflets, adding them to the growing stack. Alex sits at the rickety table, hunched over the typewriter, a pile of envelopes at his elbow, typing addresses. Opposite Alex, Sophie takes the printed pages, folding and sealing them into addressed envelopes. The clacking of the keys and the pungent scent of ink become my world.

After an hour, my muscles ache. Perspiration trails down my back, my cotton shirt sticking to my skin.

I glimpse a typed sentence, the ink still glistening.

Offer passive resistance—RESISTANCE—wherever you may be.

I ignore the ache and keep turning the handle. Hans feeds a sheet of paper. Crank. The sheet slides free, imprinted with words we've labored over.

Hans works with single-minded concentration, feeding the sheets, urging us to work faster. Sweat stands out on his forehead.

It's after nine at night. We three men have pulled long shifts at the hospital, finishing only a couple of hours ago. Another round of casualties came in from the front, with bloody stumps and gangrenous wounds and silent pain on every face.

"There's another twenty," Hans announces. "How are the addresses coming, Shurik?"

Alex holds up a pile of envelopes.

"Good." Hans takes a moment to rest, kneading the muscles in the back of his neck. "Doing all right, Sophie?"

She looks up, dark hair brushing her cheek. She hasn't left her seat except to fetch new stacks of pages fresh from the duplicating machine.

"*Ja.*" She nods with a hint of a smile.

"Then let's keep at it. The night is young, and so are we." He flashes a smile full of derring-do.

Hans and I trade places. Feeding sheets is easier than cranking the machine, and things regain speed. Alex's fingers fly across the typewriter, as his gaze darts between the keys and the list of addresses. Some at random from a telephone directory, some targeted at acquaintances and professors at the university, some to proprietors of local restaurants in the hopes they'll spread the word to their patrons. Sophie seals envelopes with a little brush dipped in water.

The bulb above our worktable flickers. Alex lights his pipe and continues typing with it in his mouth. The room is shadows and leftover plaster dust, haphazard stacks of artwork and architectural diagrams affixed to the wall with little brass tacks.

And the four of us, working with single-minded fervor.

Alex breaks the silence. "It seems strange to be doing this without Christl. After all the discussions we've had together . . ."

Hans looks up, as does Sophie. "You know he can't get involved, Shurik. He's got a wife. Children. More to lose than the rest of us." As if that's the end of the matter, he resumes cranking. His breath comes fast. Our gazes meet over the duplicating machine, and I sense the ache in his. Hans cares for Christl as we all do—his noble heart, his gentle soul. He seeks only to protect our friend.

My thoughts drift to Annalise. The wounded look in her eyes. When we met, I'd no idea who she was. Sophie just said she was a friend. I never expected a Scholl to befriend someone whose vater was SS.

How right the deepening of our friendship seemed. Not once did she hint at anything like allegiance to the Reich. Being on the side that's not only unpopular, but treasonous, makes one attuned to the loyalties of others. It's a fostered habit, like taking care while crossing a particularly dangerous intersection. Usually with new acquaintances, I keep my guard up.

With Annalise, I let it down. Not only did I reveal my loyalties (not outwardly perhaps, but by omission), I hurt her. Her face rises up, wind-teased curls, sparkling eyes, the curve of her smile. Her beauty tugged at me, but it was more than that. The directness with which she asked a question, and the honesty with which she answered one. Even about her vater, she was honest.

I wouldn't blame her if she never spoke to me again. I behaved like a cad when I let her walk away.

We finish just after midnight, both pages of our leaflet duplicated. A hundred copies, two hundred sheets.

"That's it then." Alex lays the last envelope on the pile. "The last of them."

Sophie takes the envelope, folds a leaflet inside, and seals the flap with a dab of water and a press of her fingertips.

Hans cranks off a few more leaflets. Finally, the machine rests. Silence fills the room for the first time in hours. My ears still ring with the reverberations of typewriter keys and Hans's labored breathing.

We work quickly to stash our supplies, storing the duplicating machine under a drape cloth, the typewriter in its case. My mind is fuzzy, my limbs heavy. I could fall asleep standing up.

"We'll reconvene for delivery within the next few days. In mailboxes, telephone booths, over propaganda signs."

Alex and I nod.

Hans grips my hand. Both of our fingers are streaked with ink. "Good work tonight." He claps Alex on the back. "Moving forward, Shurik."

Hans says something to Sophie about walking her home. She nods, smiles up at him. He slips an arm around her shoulders and gives a quick squeeze.

Alex and Hans exit the room followed by Sophie, going single-file up the narrow staircase. I give one last glance at the empty studio, then flick off the light and follow the others into the night.

↙

Annalise
June 24, 1942

Every night, I lie amid tangled sheets, fighting to stay awake.

Failing to escape the nightmares.

Since that night, whenever I've slept, I've dreamt the scene again. Men, women, children lined up against a brick building, armed SS facing them in a solid wall, barrels raised. A little girl at the end of the line clutches a doll against her chest. Herbert strides forward, the command issuing from his lips. "Ready." The little girl looks up. Soft curls frame her round face. I try to cry out, to move, but my lips are immobile, my limbs as if mired in quicksand. "Aim." Her innocent eyes gaze into mine, pleading, begging, as if to say: *Why? Why won't you do something?* Everything in me wants to move, to act, but I'm frozen. Slowly, she turns her face away, as if in resignation. A burst of gunfire rings out.

I wake then, pillow wet with sweat and tears.

After another night of fitful sleep, I rise and dress, body as weary as if I hadn't gone to bed at all. Standing in front of the mirror, I run a brush through my hair, smoothing the curls. Bruised circles stand out beneath my eyes, evidence of my sleepless nights.

I wish I could talk to someone. Give vent to the emotions shredding me from the inside.

But who? Though Kirk's rejection has faded in comparison to what happened afterward, I'm still raw from the way he looked at me when I told him who Vater was.

According to the Führer, Vater has chosen the path every man should aspire to. High military rank. Leadership.

While my interactions with those I feel drawn to have been hindered by those very things. Were I the daughter of a grocer or even a low-ranking corporal, everything would be easier.

I can't do this alone. Maybe someone braver, better would be able to, but I'm not that person.

Sophie.

Could I confide in her? She's challenged my thinking before. Could I ask her for counsel now? Would she look at me in disbelief, think I've concocted the story from imagination? After my initial horror wore off, I doubted whether or not Herbert spoke the truth. I soon dismissed that though. His drunken, boastful rambling was a recounting of experiences. Doubtless he has no memory of the incident, seeing as he was so drunk. Whereas I cannot erase it.

I brace both hands against the sink, hair falling into my face, head bent.

I have to tell someone.

That evening, a knock sounds on the door.

I cross the room and open it. Sophie stands outside. I managed to catch her this afternoon at the university and asked if she'd like to come for tea. She agreed.

"I'm glad you found it all right." I smile.

"It wasn't difficult." She steps inside, taking in my apartment. It differs little from her brother's, a four-room affair containing a living-dining space, a tiny kitchen, and a narrow hall leading to bedroom and bathroom. I've tacked up a couple of pieces of my artwork—one my attempt to copy Franz Marc's Blue Horses, the other a sketch of a lake at sunset.

"Nice place."

"Danke." I smile self-consciously. "I've only just cleaned it up today. I haven't been feeling well lately."

Sophie's expression sobers. "You've been ill?"

I move toward the pot of tea, which I've arranged on the low table next to the sofa. I pour the steaming liquid into cups. "In a manner of speaking. Please, sit."

She crosses the room and sits on one end of the sofa. I hand her the cup. For several minutes, we drink tea and make small talk, most of which I barely hear above the thrum in my chest.

My cup clinks as I set it down on its saucer. I place both on the table. Having something as formal as a teacup in hand doesn't seem appropriate for what I'm about to say.

"A few evenings ago, I ran into an old friend."

"Oh?"

"We knew each other as children. He was visiting the city on leave and invited me to his hotel room."

Sophie tucks her hair behind her ear. Usually, she keeps one side pinned back with a bobby pin. Today the bobby pin is absent. Her gaze fixes on me, and I realize she must be thinking this story is about to head in a very different direction.

"I don't mean it like it sounds," I hasten. "We were just friends, and there was nothing in his manner that suggested he wanted us to be otherwise. It was nice, at first. But once we were in his room, he started to drink. A lot."

I swallow, meeting Sophie's gaze. Retelling is reliving, and I'm there again, in that cloistered room, Herbert's face reddening, amber swirling in his glass, his voice filling my ears.

A chill crawls up the back of my neck. "I've never been around some-one who drank like that, so I wasn't sure what to do." I draw in a jagged breath, gathering my next words. "He started to talk. He's SS, stationed somewhere in Poland. They're murdering people. Innocent people, because they're Jewish or partisans or God knows what else." My voice cracks. "Herbert, this man who was once my friend, *boasted* about it. He shot a child because an underling wouldn't do it. A little girl." I squeeze my eyes shut, shaking my head. "It's . . . I can't believe the things he said."

I open my eyes. Sophie sits motionless, the tea forgotten. Her lips are pressed in a tight line.

"I couldn't listen after that. I ran out." I glance down at my hands. My knuckles are white from clenching my fists. "What kind of world are we living in?" My voice rises. "What has Germany become? Why has no one raised their voices and declared, *Enough*!"

"Our instincts for evil have been nurtured. Once, acts of violence were condemned. Now, they're condoned. As long as one targets those deemed deserving." Sophie's voice is quiet.

I stand and start to pace. "I don't know what to think. I'm so angry. At my vater, for being one of them. At the Führer, for feeding us lies, leading us into this mad fight for dominance." My words are treasonous. But right now, I don't care. If it's treasonous to be angry at injustice, the injustice of innocent lives being taken, then I'd rather be a traitor than in concord with those in power.

"What are you going to do about it?"

I stop pacing, gaze on Sophie. I wanted answers, not questions. Rarely have I seen such a direct stare as the one she gives me now. As if she's telling me only I can be the answer. Only I can make the decision to change and be different.

"Something. I don't know what. I don't know what I *can* do. I'm nobody. If I told my vater, he'd say I was insane. Or that the Poles deserved it. It's not as if I can barge into the Führer's office and declare the truth."

"Perhaps if enough people had, it would've been stopped before it went this far."

"Perhaps."

"But you're wrong about one thing, Annalise." Sophie gives a slight smile. "You're not nobody. Each of us has been given one life. It's ours to spend as we will. Every voice matters. If they arise as one, change can happen. But first, one has to rise. There has to be a beginning."

Her words soak through me, lingering long after she goes home, our conversation ended without my receiving any concrete answers. That night, lying in bed, waiting for the dreams to claim me, I turn onto my side, facing the blackout-curtained window, whispering over and over, "There has to be a beginning."

CHAPTER FIFTEEN

Kirk
June 26, 1942

FROM THIS MOMENT FORWARD, there will be no turning back. After two hours fueled by *kaffee*, debating the wording of our next leaflet, the three of us venture into the darkness. Each of us carries rucksacks containing the pages we've toiled over.

Three different mailboxes. Three parts of town.

Three chances of discovery.

I don't acknowledge the others, not even looking at them as we separate. Compared to some of the packs I've carried, the rucksack on my back is light.

Yet its weight seems to buckle me, mire my feet in quicksand.

It's eerily quiet. The air is cool and still, the darkness murky. Were it not for the luminous paint on curbs to aid pedestrians in the blackout, and the gleam of moonlight, I'd be walking blind.

My footsteps on the cobblestones are too loud. My heart drums inside my ears.

What if I'm stopped? Searched? They'll read the words we've written to rouse our deaf countrymen and call it sedition.

It will mean arrest. Imprisonment.

I can't think beyond that. If I do, I might stop walking altogether.

Stars scatter the sky overhead. Are angels looking through these pin-pricks of heaven, down upon the three of us?

My heart breathes a silent petition, and I pray it is so.

A car passes in a blur of sleek black. I don't turn to see who is within. I walk on, fighting the urge to look back. Dressed in a dark overcoat, I blend into the landscape. Hopefully.

Every sinew is on alert, my senses sharpened by the *kaffee* I drank less than an hour ago. I don't let my thoughts drift, wander to Annalise as they have for the past week.

I near the street where the mailbox is located.

Footsteps sound, a set other than mine. I taste the tang of fear, bitter in my throat. Straighten my shoulders and keep my head high. The stranger walks at a brisk pace, bulky frame garbed in a long overcoat. My gaze centers on his left bicep, noosed in a swastika armband.

Sweat breaks out on my forehead.

Like two dogs sniffing, testing, we approach each other. The man looks me over, gaze hooded.

My right arm flashes out. "Heil Hitler!" It's the salute of a fanatic, not like the limp gestures I usually try to get away with.

He returns the greeting, his own salute perfunctory. "Heil Hitler."

I deign to nod. If Hitler has taught me anything, it's that power will win a situation better than anything else. With one last glance, I stride past him with the swagger of a Party faithful. *I will not be detained*, my bearing seems to say. *I'm a loyal citizen of the Reich, and my business is for the Führer.*

It's for the Führer all right.

I don't look back, rerouting my steps until I'm certain the man is out of view. The mailbox is paces away. I approach, glancing both ways, then cross the street. It gleams in the darkness, the slot a gaping mouth of metal.

My hands shake as I swing the rucksack from my shoulders and fumble with the buckles. The quicker I tell myself to work, the slower my movements seem to be. Finally, I loosen the buckles. I reach inside and pull out a handful of envelopes.

I let go. They fall into the box, out of sight, with a fluttering rustle. I dive back into the rucksack and repeat the process twice more. Each time, I glance both ways, scanning the empty street.

I sling the empty rucksack over my shoulders and walk away.

Tomorrow, a hundred German citizens will leaf through their stack of mail. In the midst of bills, newspapers, and letters, they'll discover one of our envelopes, their name on the front in neat black type. What will their reaction be when they read our proclamations?

Nothing is more unworthy of a civilized nation . . .

No doubt many will promptly turn them in to the Gestapo out of self-preservation, the ever-present fear of being informed on. What of the rest? Will they heed our call?

Action. The word fills my mind like a prayer with every step I take.

Let them take action.

Sophie
June 30, 1942

Weariness fogs my senses like steam over a mirror. Tension draws a thick line through the steam, clearing my mind enough to focus on typing addresses. The keys clack as I type, glancing from the typewriter to the list, then back again. Hans and Alex run the duplicating machine. Across from me, Kirk folds leaflets, seals them into envelopes, affixes stamps.

Last night, we stayed up until 3:00 a.m., composing and finalizing the second leaflet. I managed to sleep from four until eight, when I had to get ready for classes.

Now, night blanketing Munich, we're back at the studio. I blink, stifling a yawn with my ink-smudged hand. What I wouldn't give for real *kaffee*, rich with sugar and milky with cream. The ersatz stuff does little to alleviate fatigue. But the men used up what rations remained the night they delivered the first batch of leaflets.

In spite of my exhaustion, the risk of discovery, the nagging anxiety, I wouldn't go back to doing nothing. Pain is better than emptiness.

My gaze falls on the stack of printed leaflets.

Here we see the most terrible crime against human dignity, a crime unparalleled in the history of mankind. The Jews, too, are human beings . . .

Listening to Alex and Hans dictate that passage, interjecting and interrupting each other, on fire with passion, thrilled me like nothing has in years. Truth. Finally truth.

I move down the list, inserting a fresh envelope into the typewriter.

"Hey, Sophie."

I look up at Hans's voice. He's wearing only an undershirt, sweat glistening on his face and shoulders. The air in the studio is unseasonably warm, scented with ink and must.

"Switch with me. My arm's tired."

Excitement surges through me. I've never been asked to run the duplicating machine.

I stand. Hans and Alex are set up on a table beneath a hanging lightbulb. The duplicating machine sits in the middle, completed and fresh stacks of paper on either side.

"Show her how to use it, Shurik." Hans crosses the room to take my place at the typewriter.

Alex stands behind me. "The paper goes in here." He demonstrates feeding paper into the machine. "I do that. All you do is crank the handle. Think you can manage it?"

I nod, turning my head to smile at him. His half-crooked grin flashes, a look of shared exhilaration. Disagreements may come, but for now, our four hearts beat with unity. Over and over, I crank the handle. Alex works beside me, moving in synchrony. The fluid, even movements remind me of dancing.

How I once loved to dance. Spin and twirl, abandoning myself to the music. I haven't done that in years, can barely remember dancing since the war began. The first time we met, Fritz and I danced together. He walked across the room, right up to me, tall and dashing, a smile on his lips, and asked me to dance. I was sixteen, half girl, half woman, my hair cropped short, momentarily shy in the presence of this attractive stranger. It was an evening of simple joy and easy laughter, the sensation of being held in strong arms, turning in three-quarter time to a waltz. How long ago that seems.

If we danced now, would either of us remember the steps?

We work in silence. My arm begins to ache. I pause to rub the sore muscles, then keep cranking the handle. Paper, envelopes, stamps, and ink are becoming costly. I asked, and Fritz loaned me a hundred marks. I didn't tell him what it was for. Would he have given it to me if he knew?

"Liven up, everyone. Let's keep things moving." Hans strides over to us, clapping his hands together.

"It's after one in the morning," Alex gives a mock yawn.

"*Jawohl*, Herr Kommandant." Kirk salutes, grinning.

"Requesting permission to sing." Alex turns to me. "Sophie, why don't you pick something?"

I know instantly what to choose. "Thoughts Are Free."

"Not exactly in the Hitler Youth songbook, but it'll do." Alex winks at me.

Alex's voice rises onto the air, melodic and rich. I join in, and soon the four of us are singing in soft chorus, the words blending with the clacking of the typewriter and the sleek sound of the duplicating machine.

Thoughts are free,
Who can guess them?
They fly by
Like shadows in the night;
No one can know them,
No hunter can shoot them
With powder and lead,
Thoughts are free.

The song revitalizes us. It's not *kaffee*, but the words speak to what we all feel. I tuck my hair behind my ear and look up, hand steadily cranking the machine. Hans, pencil behind his ear, striking the keys. Kirk, folding leaflets, features swathed in meager light. Alex, working alongside me, music spilling from his lips as if poured from his soul.

As we wrap up our work, I wonder what Annalise is doing tonight. Is she lying awake, robbed of sleep by haunting thoughts? The horror she spoke of is not news to me, but to hear the anguish in her voice as she told of it . . .

An idea dawns. I drop the handle, the last newly inked sheet sliding out. I pick up a stack of freshly mimeographed leaflets and carry them to the table. Hans and Kirk stand next to a crate of artwork, heads bent in discussion.

If I delay, I'll change my mind. Each leaflet represents a danger, not only to us, but to its recipient.

I seize the opportunity and slip into the chair, taking up a fresh envelope. I slide it into the typewriter. Fingers poised, I wait only a moment before making my decision.

Quickly, I type Annalise's name and address onto the envelope. I snatch up a nearby leaflet, and fold and stuff it inside. A completed stack of envelopes sits off to one side, and I slip Annalise's in the middle of the pile. I stand before Hans notices me and begin to clear the table. My gaze lands on the rectangles of white waiting to be mailed.

Annalise wants answers.

On behalf of the White Rose, I will give her some.

CHAPTER SIXTEEN

Annalise
July 2, 1942

A KNOCK SOUNDS AS I'm finishing breakfast—ersatz *kaffee* and toast with a thin layer of marmalade. I leave the table, brushing crumbs from my hands, and open the door.

"Morning mail, Fräulein Brandt." My landlady hands me two envelopes. As always, she's wearing trodden-down slippers, graying hair in curling papers. She looks past my shoulder, into the apartment (what a snoop!).

"Danke." I nod and shut the door, taking the letters back to the table. I take a sip of *kaffee* and dab my lips with a napkin, before picking up the first envelope. My name is written across the envelope in my eldest brother's scrawl. I slit the envelope with my fingernail and skim the lines—his upcoming promotion to the rank of hauptmann, his talk about the girl he hopes to marry, his brief questions about my time at the university.

I fold the letter and set it down amid white china dishes and toast crumbs. Ah, Horst. What would he have become if not for National Socialism? As a boy, he was always building things, while I followed behind to help as much as little sisters are allowed. He would have made a fine architect, but like Vater, Horst's mind is warped by Nazi greatness, a piece of raw wood left too long in the downpour of *Germany above all else.*

I pick up the next envelope. My name and address is typed across the front. I don't know anyone who uses a typewriter for correspondence. Maybe it's some kind of notice from the university.

The envelope tears as I slit it. I pull out two sheets of paper, small type filling both. Smoothing my hand across the creases, I read.

One cannot grapple with National Socialism intellectually because it is not intellectual . . .

My breath catches. Heat surges through my fingertips. I glance over my shoulder—once, twice.

Drawn by an insatiable curiosity, I read on. It criticizes *Mein Kampf* (the author declares it's comprised of the worst German they have ever read and quotes Hitler as having written that one must betray a people, in order to rule them). It speaks of how three hundred thousand Jews have been murdered in Poland, the annihilation of Polish aristocratic youth, and the forced prostitution of Polish young women in SS brothels. The author demands an answer to the question of why the German people have remained apathetic in the face of these abominable crimes. Declares that everyone in Germany is *guilty* of them, repeating guilty thrice like a cry.

It ends with:

We ask you to make as many copies of this sheet as possible and to redistribute it.

I set down the pages. My hands shake. I stare at the words.

Someone has dared to risk the consequences of writing and circulating this leaflet.

Why was I chosen to receive it? An uncanny feeling crawls up my spine, as if I'm being watched. As if someone has read my mind and the unrest brewing there.

It's true. Every word. The paragraph about the atrocities against Jews and Poles makes my stomach clench. Not only because they're printed here, but because I've heard of them firsthand. Even now, the dreams, the fragments of Herbert's words, fill me.

What can I do? It's not as if I can change the outcome of the war, the treatment of those in Poland. I have no voice, at least not an acknowledged one.

My gaze falls on the last line, the plea to copy the leaflet and redistribute it.

How many in Germany are aware of the truth? Know instinctively, yet deny it because it hasn't been laid out for them in black and white?

Could I, somehow, show them by copying and distributing this leaflet?

I press the heels of my palms into my eyes. I don't deny the fear shaking inside me. This is a far greater step than refusing to marry the candidate of Vater's choosing. Defying the Third Reich, even in something as innocuous as distributing pieces of paper, could cost me everything.

Everything.

It would be easier to crumple the leaflet, throw it in the wastebin, and continue like everyone around me. Going about daily life as much as they're able, living beneath the shadow of what Germany has become, yet taking no action against it.

I press my lips together, gazing at the typed words of the leaflet. Whoever the author is, they're taking risks. Resisting the government because to do so has become a moral necessity.

Some things, you can't wait to do until you're strong enough.
Some things, you just have to do afraid.

⟋

Kirk
July 2, 1942

I lean against a pillar of the Schmorells' veranda. Conversation and laughter buzzes around me. Hans decided to take the evening off from our frenetic pace of producing leaflets—we're working on the third now, and Alex invited everyone to a party at his family's villa. He's hosted many of these gatherings over the years, and I've always enjoyed his parents' hospitality.

I look out at the grassy lawn, the elegant garden in full bloom, its floral fragrance a subtle perfume. The Schmorells' are part of that group of people fortunate to have both money and taste. If Alex weren't so sincere and considerate of others, looking at his house, one would think him spoiled.

Three figures make their way up the graveled path leading to the villa. Hans, arm in arm with Traute, alongside a middle-aged man familiar from the university. Professor Huber. He walks with his arms behind his back, shoulders slightly stooped, head tilted as he listens to something Hans is saying.

I quick-walk down the steps to greet them. I've only met Professor Huber in passing, though I regularly attend his lectures. Hans is curious about the older man's views on our leaflets, and I suspect his decision to take the night off has more to do with feeling out Huber than giving us a break.

"*Grüß Gott*, Hans, Traute." I shake Hans's hand and make a slight bow in Traute's direction. She returns the greeting with a smile, one hand resting elegantly on Hans's arm, a picture in a trim gray suit, curls swept back from her face.

"Herr Professor, you remember Kirk Hoffmann?" Hans gestures to me. "He's a great admirer of your lectures."

"It's a pleasure to see you, sir." I hold out my hand, and Professor Huber returns the handclasp with a surprisingly strong grip. "Your lectures on Leibniz have inspired me to deepen my study of his work."

"I'm glad to hear it." Professor Huber speaks in the same halting way due to his speech impairment, yet his tone is more reserved than when he's behind the podium.

"Come, Herr Professor. There are some people I'd like you to meet."

Hans disengages his arm from Traute's, leaving her standing there, as he escorts the professor up the steps. She watches them, hands clasped at her waist.

"He's always on the hunt for a rousing discussion." She gives a faint, accepting smile.

I nod. "That's Hans for you."

She leans closer. Her wide, almond gaze meets mine, her thick lashes blinking. "I know about the leaflets. Finally, Hans told me. I want to help. Hans says we need all the paper and stamps we can get, and I have friends in Hamburg who would be greatly interested in what we're doing. He says Sophie already knows."

"We all trust you implicitly." I place my hand on her arm. "Hans is lucky to have you."

"Is he?" Traute turns her gaze toward the veranda, where Hans makes introductions. "I wonder if he knows it," she says softly.

I don't know how to answer her. It's true, Hans thinks of nothing but the leaflets. Especially with the recent announcement that the Second Student Medical Company will be sent to Russia later this month. I still haven't told my parents, delaying the inevitable as long as I can.

Traute lifts her chin. She'll stand by Hans and his leaflets, no matter their personal relationship (or lack thereof). Like Sophie, she believes in what we're fighting for, and her level-mindedness will serve our group well.

"Come." I offer her my arm. "Let's join the others."

She slips her hand in the crook of my elbow with a grateful smile, as we ascend the veranda steps. Hans doesn't even notice as she walks past him toward Frau Schmorell.

"Hello, Willi." I greet the tall, blond man whom Christl recently introduced to Hans, Alex, and me. A fellow officer in the Second Student Medical Company, he'll be shipping out with us later this month.

"Kirk." Willi Graf gives a slight smile. "Good to see you again." His words are quiet, as if he's unaccustomed to meting them out often. I don't know him well, but I sense he's the type of person who wouldn't say "good to see you," unless he really meant it.

For several minutes, we chat about the Bach concert where Christl introduced us.

"Have you seen prior service in Russia?" I ask. Willi looks to be several years older than Hans and me. Or perhaps his thinning hair, the serious cast to his features make him appear so.

"In '41." Willi's face tightens, at variance to the laughter drifting from the other side of the veranda. "You?"

"I've been to France, but not Russia."

"Russia." Willi pauses. "Russia is a world far removed. The dimensions of war found there . . ." He stares across the lawn and says no more. Yet the undertone of misery in his gaze is unmistakable.

As the sky turns to milky twilight, the group moves into the Schmorells' parlor, settling themselves on damask-upholstered settees and plush armchairs or standing around the fireplace. A gilded mirror hangs above the mantel, and a sleek grand piano shines in a corner of the room. Willi's gaze is instantly drawn to it.

Alex bounds toward us, grinning. Despite the warm weather, he's dressed in a cream-colored turtleneck sweater and tan suit jacket, completely at ease in his elegant surroundings. "You're more than welcome to use the piano, Graf."

"You don't mind?"

"We'd be delighted."

Willi needs no further invitation. Soon he's coaxing the strains of a Beethoven sonata from the instrument, his large frame at variance to the slight piano bench, yet completely at home upon it.

Professor Huber sits on the settee, in conversation with Hans and another student whom I've seen briefly around the university.

"I recently received an interesting piece of printed matter," the young man remarks. "A leaflet by a group calling themselves the White Rose. Have you heard of it, Herr Professor?"

"*Ja*," Professor Huber says slowly. "I've heard of it. I received a leaflet myself, actually."

I tense. Hans leans forward. Sophie, standing by the piano next to Willi, turns slightly.

"The White Rose?" Traute's friend Katharina props her elbow on the arm of her chair. "What's that?"

Hans turns to her with a look of surprise. "You don't mean to say you haven't heard of the White Rose?"

Be careful, Hans.

Katharina shakes her head. Willi finishes the piece and stops playing, glancing in the direction of the conversation.

"I've got one of their leaflets here." Hans reaches into the pocket of his suit coat. "I received two of them. Have a look, if you care to."

Katharina takes the leaflet and unfolds it.

"So you got one too, Herr Professor?" Hans's voice is as casual as if he's inquiring whether or not Professor Huber read the day's newspaper, yet I catch the undertone of expectancy. "What did you think of it?"

Professor Huber pauses, his bearing stiff and uncomfortable. His forehead creases, as if he's pondering a difficult subject from the lecture podium. "I'm not certain the leaflet's impact will be worth the terrible risk incurred by its author. It was well-written, I suppose."

"I thought it made some good points," is all Hans says in reply. "When you're finished, Katharina, I'd like it back."

Katharina nods, blond head bent over the paper. Willi turns back to the piano, soft music unfurling through the room.

Hans's expression remains unchanged, but I can tell he's disappointed. He admires Huber, and his veiled protests against National Socialism disguised as philosophical commentary. With enough encouragement, Hans would likely ask the professor for his intellectual support of our endeavors.

I glance at Alex standing beside me, the mirror a backdrop behind him. "I guess we can't expect any support from him," he mutters.

"Professor Huber doesn't know any of us well." I keep my voice low. "It's understandable he'd be guarded around strangers. He'd be a fool if he weren't."

Alex shrugs. "Not that it matters much. We'll soon be in Russia. We can't exactly continue printing leaflets from there."

"Russia." I clap my hand against his shoulder. "Your homeland, Shurik."

He flashes a smile almost childlike in its anticipation. "Perhaps the Wehrmacht will be doing us a favor, sending us there."

I see the pain on my mutter's face as I tell her, the added hours to my vater's evening prayers. They'll trust and pray, but not even my pastor vater and his wife are immune to fear. I hate causing them that.

I force a smile for Alex's benefit. "Perhaps."

Annalise
July 3, 1942

There's only one person I trust enough to show the leaflet to.

Sophie.

During the streetcar ride, I'm acutely aware of the pieces of paper in my satchel. As I descend the steps behind a mustached man wearing a Party armband, my heartbeat trips over itself. The air is sticky, and sweat slides down my back, my dress clinging to my skin as I walk through Schwabing, toward Sophie's apartment on Mandlstraße. I'm weary after a long day of classes, pretending to be interested in a lecture on the Führer's favorite painters, while the words of the leaflet ran through my mind like a newsreel on repeat.

I reach the apartment building and ring the bell. I glance behind me as I wait. A *hausfrau* stands on the stoop across the street, beating rugs. Dust clouds around her. Two boys in knee socks push a hoop, quarreling loudly over whose turn it is.

The door opens. A woman stands inside.

"*Ja?*" She wipes reddened hands on a dishtowel.

"I'm here to see Sophie Scholl."

"Second door at the top of the stairs."

"Danke." I ascend the creaking staircase and knock when I reach Sophie's door.

A minute passes. Maybe two. The door opens.

"Annalise." Sophie greets me with a smile. "Come in." She opens the door. Schoolbooks lay scattered across the sofa. "I'm in the process of being a good student, but you're welcome to have a seat wherever you can find a place." She piles the books on the floor, then settles onto the sofa, stockinged feet tucked beneath her.

I join her, though I don't sit with such casual abandon. Old habits die hard.

"I'm sorry. I should have called first."

"You're welcome here," she says. "I'm low on practically everything, or I'd offer you something to drink."

"I didn't come for refreshments." I reach into the satchel I'd propped against the sofa. "I came to show you something." I rummage for the leaflet. "I got this in the mail and wanted to know if you'd seen one." I retrieve the papers and pass them to her.

She takes them, smoothing the creased sheets with her palm. Slowly, she scans the words. I wait, sitting stiffly upright. A clock ticks. I try to read her features, but they remain blank.

Several minutes pass. She hands the pages back to me. I keep the leaflet in my lap, the paper brushing my clasped hands.

"What do you think of it?" Her gaze meets mine.

I take a deep breath. My life over these past months has been a series of crossroads. Taking paths different than those others would choose for me. It started the day I cut off my braids and told Vater I intended to study at university.

Now I'm faced with another, more defined fork in the road.

I've already made my decision. It's time I voiced it.

"If you don't agree with me, will you promise to forget we ever had this conversation?" In spite of myself, my voice falters.

Sophie nods. Belief is a dangerous thing. I might regret trusting her. But I'll regret it more if I don't.

"This leaflet is the truest thing I've ever read. Our country has been lied to again and again. These words are honest. Powerful. I wish every German could read them."

"They are honest." Sophie tilts her head, eyes on me as if taking my measure. "I've read the other leaflet, and it's equally so."

"There are more?" My breath catches. More clarifying truth printed on cheap paper. The prospect makes me almost giddy.

"One, I think. Hans showed it to me."

I pause, drawing in both breath and courage. "Do you think truth is worth taking risks?"

"What do you mean?"

"Let's say someone wanted to do as it says: copy and redistribute the leaflet. Would a person be justified in risking to get pamphlets into the hands of their fellow citizens?" My heart pounds in my ears. A breeze from Sophie's half-open window—blackout curtains pulled aside—dries the sweat beneath my arms.

Sophie rises and crosses to the window. I watch her from my seat on the sofa. What is she thinking? Was I too impulsive?

I shouldn't have done this. If anything comes of my plan, and I get caught, I don't want her incriminated. I hate second-guessing myself. Yet I sense this is something I cannot do alone

Time passes while she stands facing the window. The few minutes seem like hours.

Finally, she turns and looks directly at me. Her bobbed hair brushes her cheek, and she stands in the center of a dying puddle of sunlight. "I think if someone was set on doing as you said, they would have to have a solid plan in place. And they'd have to be certain they were willing to risk the consequences. Absolutely certain."

"But you believe it's worth it?" Why am I looking to this girl to be my moral compass? Because I'm scared? Because I have no one else?

Sophie nods. A strange half smile edges her lips. "*Ja*, Annalise. Truth is worth everything."

CHAPTER SEVENTEEN

Sophie
July 4, 1942

"SHE *WHAT?*" TO MY surprise, it's Kirk, not Hans, who rounds on me first.

"She asked if I would consider helping her duplicate the leaflets of the White Rose." I sit sideways on a slat-backed chair in Eickemeyer's studio. Hans and Alex mailed the third leaflet last night, and we're already drafting a fourth. Kirk stands next to the typewriter, hands fisted at his sides. His jaw tightens.

Alex chuckles, shaking his head. "We're making waves." He blows a plume of pipe smoke into the air.

"Annalise Brandt is the daughter of an SS officer." Hans steeples his fingers atop the table. "And she wants to distribute leaflets? Just how does she plan to do that?"

I shrug. "She didn't say. She only asked if I'd be willing to incur the risk along with her. I told her I'd have to think about it."

"How did she find out about the leaflets?" Alex fingers his pipe.

My stomach tightens. "I sent her one."

"What possessed you to do that?" Kirk's voice rises.

"Because she heard about what's going on in Poland, the mass killings of partisans and innocent civilians. I wanted her to have answers. Isn't that our aim? To give people answers? To open their eyes?"

Kirk rakes a hand through his hair. "You have to discourage her. Tell her it's a stupid idea, and she'd be better off forgetting about it."

"I won't do that." I bolt from my chair, taking a step toward Kirk. "To lie to keep her safe would mean going against everything we stand for. Annalise has just as much right to resistance as any of us."

"So what do you propose?" Hans levels his gaze on me.

I swallow. "I propose she join us. She's going to do it anyway. It will be safer with us, where we can control her activities."

"Absolutely not!" Kirk slams his fist on the table. Stray papers flutter to the floor. "I won't have her involved."

"Hans?" I turn to my brother.

"It's dangerous enough as it is, Sophie. The more people who know, the more chances we have of getting caught. Having her involved would put all of us at risk."

"I can't believe you're saying this! You're the ones who produced the leaflets. Who wrote the lines 'we ask you to make as many copies of this sheet as possible and to redistribute it'? Now that someone wants to answer your call, you're refusing her? Do you, or do you not, believe in what you've written?" I cross my arms.

"You're being needlessly obtuse." Hans's tone is firm. "Everyone we've invited to join us: Shurik, Kirk, you, Traute, even Christl, I've known for years. How long have you known this girl? A couple of weeks? A month? Who's to say she isn't her vater's spy? Maybe he heard about the leaflets and asked his daughter to keep an eye out."

"She despises her vater. He cuts her down at every opportunity and wants to marry her off to a high-ranking officer to increase his own standing."

Kirk pales. A muscle twitches beneath his eye.

"Even so, how can we be sure she'll keep her word? Anyone can have a moment of passionate fanaticism. Who's to say she won't back down at the first setback, after we've already revealed our identity? All of us have been against the regime for a long time." Hans pushes his chair back from the table and stands.

I shake my head. "That's not entirely true. Remember when you returned from the Nuremberg Rally? All of us expected you to be elated at the honor of being a flag bearer in a procession for the Führer. But you weren't elated. You were disillusioned. The way Annalise is right now."

Hans gives a grudging nod. He blows out a sigh. "I'm sorry. But we're not running a debate club. We're not a haven for every passerby disillusioned by Hitler and his war. We're risking our own lives as it is. I won't gamble with someone else's."

I press my lips together.

"I'll talk to her." Kirk speaks up. "We've . . . spoken a few times. I'll tell her Sophie confided in me about her plans to duplicate leaflets. I'll convince her it isn't a good idea."

"She won't be that easily convinced." I pick up a cigarette lying on the edge of the table, roll it between my fingers. "We spent a long time talking. She's utterly serious when she says she wants to do something. If she doesn't help us, she'll get her own duplicating machine."

"I said I'd talk to her." Kirk turns away. "We're wasting time with this discussion. Let's get back to doing what we came here to do."

I've never seen Kirk act this way. He's always been kind and considerate, even when sleep-deprived and frustrated when stencils ripped or the duplicating machine stalled.

A weighted silence fills the room. Hans resumes his seat, chair legs scraping against the floor as he pushes up to the typewriter. Kirk joins him on the other side. Alex gives me a sympathetic glance.

"Want a light?" He gestures to my cigarette.

I shake my head and shove the cigarette back into the packet. In many ways, Hans is right. Asking Annalise to join us would be risky. But we shouldn't discourage her. If she was moved by our words, how many others might be? If Kirk tells her to choose safety and do nothing, isn't that the very complacency we're fighting against? Resistance means sacrifice. Who are we to discourage someone willing to pay the price?

Annalise isn't daft. Impetuous, perhaps, but not stupid. I know she'd follow orders and give her all. She may not fully know the measure of what that *all* may entail, but then, do any of us? Yet must we not act anyway? Now before more time is lost?

"It's only getting worse, Shurik." I meet Alex's gaze, voice soft. "Fritz wrote me. He says . . . he says his commander talks about killing all the Jews in Russia."

Alex pales, a comma of hair falling over his forehead. He's wearing a loose-fitting blue shirt belted at the waist, brown trousers. With his simple clothes and tumbled hair, he looks like the Russian peasants he shares such an affinity with. "Oh, Sophie." He shakes his head, voice hoarse. "Sometimes . . . I'm ashamed to call myself a German."

I nod, a sigh falling from my lips. I well understand such shame. "I know."

"Shall we continue?" Hans looks between the two of us from behind the typewriter. Kirk still wears a scowl and avoids my gaze.

We move toward the table.

"Would you read the next paragraph, Kirk?"

Kirk clears his throat. In one hand, he holds the rough draft of our fourth leaflet. "'In this struggle for the preservation of your highest good, I ask you, as a Christian: Is there any hesitation, any toying with conspiracies, any postponement of the decision in the hope that someone else will raise arms to defend you? Did not God Himself give you the strength and the courage to fight?'" He pauses. "'We have to engage evil precisely where it is most powerful, and it is most powerful in the power of Hitler.'"

The typewriter clacks as Hans jabs the keys.

Kirk meets my gaze, face shadowed in the golden light. All traces of anger have left his eyes.

In their place . . . is fear.

⟋

Kirk
July 5, 1942

I have to try. If I don't and something happens to her, I'll never be able to forgive myself. It's one thing for the rest of us to risk our lives—Hans, Alex, and the others. But Annalise is different. An SS officer's daughter. An artist. A woman who wears her heart in her eyes.

I have little hope this will go well. We've not spoken since that evening in the Englischer Garten. In that moment, I found myself astonished and ashamed by the stirring inside me. For me to fall for the daughter of a man at the center of the regime I'm fighting against seems the height of irony and impossibility. Nonetheless, I shouldn't have let her walk away, and I need to apologize for my behavior.

I'll go to her as a friend. No more and no less.

I'm about to raise my fist to knock, when the door to her apartment building opens. I step back. Annalise closes the door behind her, backing out, bumping a bicycle down the steps. She turns, fingers wrapped around the handlebars.

For a long moment, we regard each other. A breeze stirs her loose curls, fluttering them around her face. Her eyes are guarded.

"Hello." I try for a smile as I descend the steps and stand near the front of the bicycle.

"Hello." Her tone is flat.

"Nice bicycle." I study the shiny metal, the new-looking tires. I haven't seen a new bicycle in years.

"My mutter sent it to me."

"Should save you a lot of money on streetcars."

She nods.

I pause, shove my hand into my trouser pocket, looking from the bicycle back to her.

She sighs. "Why are you here, Kirk?"

I swallow. "To apologize. I acted like a cad, and I came to tell you I'm sorry."

Her eyes soften a fraction.

"And I wanted to talk to you."

"What is there to say?" She lowers her voice, chin jutted forward. "You're the son of a Confessing Church pastor. I'm the daughter of Standartenführer Brandt. In your eyes, we've nothing in common."

"There's more to both of us than that. Walk with me?" I place my hand on the handlebars, brushing hers. She doesn't pull away. "As friends. Can we not still be friends?"

She presses her lips together, looking out into the street. I force myself not to linger on the curve of her jaw, the contours of her finely boned face. *Just friends.*

She sighs. "I was about to take this for a ride, but I suppose it can wait. Give me a moment, and I'll put it inside." She hauls the bicycle back up the steps and into the apartment. I wait on the sidewalk, wondering if she'll decide not to come out again at all.

A few moments later, she emerges, shutting the door behind her.

We move down the street, walking far enough apart that there's no chance our shoulders might brush. We fill the silence with polite conversation about our various classes, the weather, her new bicycle. Those topics take us from her apartment to the Englischer Garten.

"Do you mind?" I glance at her as we meander through the park. The slopes and paths are dotted sparsely with people—men in uniform with their sweethearts likely on their way to the Chinese Tower *biergarten*, a mutter with three children in tow. In the distance, the Kleinhesseloher Lake glitters in the setting sun.

"Nein." Our footsteps make crunching sounds on the gravel. "It's a nice evening."

We move down a deserted path, sheltered on both sides by leafy elms. I slow my pace, watching her out of the corner of my eye. "There have been some leaflets circulating throughout the city. Leaflets of the White Rose. Have you heard of them?"

She turns her head slowly, meeting my gaze. "In passing, perhaps."

"The stuff written in them is dangerous. I hope you didn't linger on them long."

"Why ever would I?"

Her voice and eyes remain cool and composed. For the first time it actually occurs to me that she might have the backbone to join us. I stop in the path. We're alone, surrounded by trees and an ever-darkening sky. She faces me.

"Sophie told me what you asked of her," I say quietly.

A trace of fear flashes through her eyes. "I don't know what you're talking about."

"She said you intend to distribute the leaflets of the White Rose. She spoke to me purely in confidence. I must advise you to use caution—"

"Caution? That's the last thing I expected to hear from you." She arches a brow. "It's well-known those of the Confessing Church are dissenters. Being a member is practically illegal."

"I'm not questioning what's in the leaflets. I'm questioning your involvement with them. It's dangerous to even consider taking part in their distribution, and if I have my way, I'd like to talk you out of it."

Silence hangs between us. I try to read her expression, but she averts her face from me.

A serrated breath escapes her lips. "Then I'm sorry you've wasted your evening."

"What?"

She hugs her arms over her chest, turning away. "We shouldn't be having this conversation. I don't want to discuss it."

"You're still going to follow through with your plans?"

She whirls to face me. Her eyes burn. "I refuse to do nothing." Her voice is a choked whisper. "There. Have I answered your question? When I read one of the leaflets, it was like it spoke directly to me. People are dying, Kirk. Polish children. Jews whose only crime is their heritage. German boys who are forced to fight in a war of insanity. I'm through with turning my back on what our world is coming to. And if you think I'm a stupid woman who isn't aware of what she's getting herself into, well, maybe I am. But I have considered the consequences."

The way she looks at me . . . we need people like her. Those with enough passion to push aside the status quo and take risks for truth. Who her family is matters, but is it really enough to douse the fire inside of her?

It scares me, the thought of her going forward alone.

God, if I'm about to do something I'll regret, show me, please.

Hans will be angry if I tell him she's joining us, but what if she proves herself beforehand? I take her measure. A girl with an innocent face in a schoolgirl blouse and skirt. So young. We all are, though we've been aged by the war. Altered by it.

Maybe our youth makes us ideal to be at the forefront of resistance. Hitler always says young people are the future. We'll be the future to show Germany a different one. It sounds idealistic, and maybe it is, but I've vowed to walk a different path, no matter where it will lead me. If Annalise is determined to walk that path too, why not alongside us?

I draw in a deep breath.

"I know the people who wrote the leaflets."

Her eyes widen. Otherwise, she makes no movement or sound.

"Actually, I work with them." I push out the words. Annalise sucks in a breath. A shudder passes through me. I've just committed one of the cardinal sins of resistance—revealing my identity.

Might as well say the next part. "Perhaps you should join us."

"You'd have me?" Her voice is a whisper of disbelief.

"It's not that simple. The person in charge is careful about newcomers. For him to accept you . . ." We walk up the secluded path, back into the open parkland.

"I'll do anything." She sounds pathetically eager. The way I sounded when Hans first told me his plans: "Just tell me what to do."

A man strides across the grass. Instinctively, I place my hand on her elbow. Anyone who saw us walking would think we're a pair of sweethearts out for an evening stroll.

I wait until he passes before turning to her. "We need paper, envelopes, and stamps. But we're running short on funds."

Annalise doesn't hesitate. "I can get those. Just give me a few days."

It's happening so fast. I was supposed to use my powers of persuasion to convince her to forget the idea. Now, I've revealed our identities, told her our needs, as good as sent her on a mission. What if I've made a mistake? What if she endangers herself? What if—

"Danke, Kirk," Annalise's soft voice pulls me from my thoughts.

"For what?"

"I know you're probably wondering if you've made a mistake." She gives a little smile, likely at my bewildered expression—*how did she know what I was thinking?* "I wish I could tell you with all certainty you haven't, but we don't know the future." In the fading light, her features are pale and resolute. "But I do know one thing. You've given me a chance for action, and I'll do all in my power not to let you down."

In her power? We leave the Englischer Garten, and I walk her home while dusk fades to darkness.

So little of life is, Annalise.

CHAPTER EIGHTEEN

Annalise
July 6, 1942

FOR THE FIRST TIME in weeks, I slept without nightmares. I wake, instantly alert, mind thrumming. Paper, envelopes, and stamps. I have twenty marks for emergencies stashed in a rolled up pair of stockings.

This qualifies.

Clad in my nightdress, the bedroom darkened by blackout curtains, I push past the few dresses hanging in the small armoire to the shelf in the back. My fingers brush the silk stockings—my only pair. I unroll them, and the cylinder of bills falls to the floor.

I bend to pick it up, a bit breathless. Its papery weight resting in my palm, I take in the enormity of last night's revelation.

Kirk is one of the leaflet writers. I never would have imagined it. He seems so clean-cut, a handsome university student and physician in training. Not a man behind words that smack of subversion and echo with intrepid truth.

If Kirk is one, who are the others?

"Sophie told me what you asked of her."

I was so shocked, bent on maintaining my bluff, then furious he'd lecture me about caution, and then awed and thrilled when he revealed he knew the authors of the leaflets, I didn't put two and two together.

If Sophie told Kirk, then Sophie knows Kirk is involved. And if Sophie knows, could she be part of the group herself?

Kirk. Sophie. Are there others?

A chill seeps through my body. This information is dangerous. Doubtless, the Gestapo are aware of the leaflets and on the lookout for the perpetrators. If they're traced in any way back to the authors, it could mean severe consequences. The weight of responsibility makes my legs tremble. I'm not the only one at stake here.

A simple shopping trip for paper, envelopes, and stamps is no longer simple.

"No fear," I whisper, the words a command. "No fear."

Kirk
July 10, 1942

For almost a week, I've counted Annalise as one of us. Ever since she phoned me, voice breathless on the crackling line: "I've got a present for you. Come over to my place tonight and pick it up." I did as instructed, and she invited me up to her apartment in the manner of an old friend, while her landlady shot us looks of matronly disapproval as we climbed the stairs. Splayed across Annalise's table were stacks and stacks of pristine white paper, envelopes, and stamps. My breath hitched at the sheer quantity. "I went to four shops in different parts of town," she said. "Will it do?"

"It'll more than do," I replied. She grinned, and we bundled it all up in my briefcase and satchel. I left with a promise to be in contact soon and delivered the supplies to Hans and Alex. After another lengthy debate, they agreed to allow Annalise to come to the studio.

Today, in the crowded Lichthof, I passed her a folded slip of paper: *Leopoldstraße 38. 9:00 p.m.*

I reach the studio a half hour early. Hans, the basement's only occupant, is setting up the typewriter.

I toss my satchel on the table and spread out the stamps I've purchased. Combined with what the girls bought, it should be enough for the distribution of 120 copies of our fourth leaflet.

Hans straddles the chair beside the typewriter. His face is drawn, the light casting haggard shadows over his eyes. He blows out a breath.

"Everything all right?" I pull up my own chair, its legs scraping the floor.

Hans looks up, pain in his gaze. "Traute broke up with me." His tone is dull. "She still wants to help with the leaflets. It's me she's through with."

"Oh." Judging from my conversation with her at the Schmorells', I'm not surprised. "I'm sorry, Hans."

He clears his throat. "I'll get over it. There's too much to do to let myself wallow. I really cared about her though. She's always been special, not like other girls. She's so determined to take our leaflets to Hamburg, start her own revolution there. She's stubborn and bright . . . and . . . if we'd only had more time. More time . . ." He scrubs a hand across his face. "But we don't." He glances at me, as if just now realizing he's been talking out loud. "That's life, I guess." His smile is off-kilter, like a tie he's put on crooked. "Let's get started. The others will be here soon."

We work in silence. I sense Hans doesn't want my sympathy any more than an adolescent boy would want his mutter fussing over a scraped knee. Hans has fallen in and out of love before. I only hope he resists the temptation next time, for both his sake and the girl's. Our work is complicated enough without bringing in personal angst.

We're finishing preparing the duplicating machine when Alex arrives, followed by Sophie. She pierces her brother with a look, as if she knows what happened between him and Traute. He ignores her. Sophie moves to add her pile of stamps to mine.

Alex and Hans have already finalized the draft and typed the stencil. Extra shifts at the hospital have left me low on spare time, so I had little to do with the composition of this one, though I wish I had. It's our most powerful yet, every word ringing with the call to take action.

"I'll wait upstairs."

"Why?" Alex rolls up his shirtsleeves.

"For Annalise," I say, before turning away and heading up the stairs.

I lean against the wall in the darkness of the entryway, listening for footsteps. I don't have long to wait. Two raps sound. I open the door, and Annalise slips inside, dragging her bicycle along with her. She's wearing a black coat and kerchief, face pale against the charcoal fabric. I help her prop the bicycle against the wall.

"They're all downstairs."

She tugs off the kerchief, reddish-gold curls clouding around her cheeks. "Let's go then." She stuffs the kerchief into the pocket of her coat and follows me down the steps.

As we reach the bottom, I resist the urge to place my hand against the small of her back. To protect her. But I can't. Now she's one of us, I can't protect her from anything.

I push open the door, revealing the glow of the room and the figures of the people within. Sophie smiles. Hans stands next to the duplicating machine, arms crossed. Alex is the first to rise and greet her.

"Well, if it isn't Father Christmas. Welcome." He grips her hand with a warm grin.

Annalise smiles. "Hello, Alex."

"Nein." He shakes his head. "Here, it's Shurik. My Russian name."

"Shurik." She tests the pronunciation. He chuckles and corrects her. She tries again, with more success. Sophie laughs.

"You'll be affixing stamps to envelopes." Hans's tone is curt, his eyes assessing. To her credit, Annalise doesn't shrink toward me but meets his gaze head on.

"Anything you want me to do, I'll do it."

Hans gives a brief nod. "I'll show you where to sit." He jerks a hand in the direction of the table. Annalise follows him, unbuttoning her coat. She places it over the back of the chair he motions her toward and takes a seat. Hans places his hand briefly on the back of her chair.

"Glad to have you with us." He gives a slight smile.

"Danke, Hans." Annalise turns and looks up at him. "I'm grateful to be here with all of you, helping. The leaflets are brilliant."

He shrugs. "We should have written them long before now."

The rest of us move to our various positions. Sophie to folding leaflets and placing them in envelopes, Alex to typing addresses, and Hans and me to the duplicating machine.

The motions of cranking the handle are now as familiar as breathing, and I can do my part with little mental effort. Hans demands speed and perfection, but that doesn't stop me from glancing up every so often to watch the group at the table. Annalise's head is bent over her work as she pastes stamps to envelopes. How earnest she is.

How deeply every glance entangles her in my heart. I must keep my guard up. Yet every time I'm with her, against all judgment and reason, my guard breaks down a little more.

We're leaving for Russia before the end of the month. There's little doubt that this will be the last leaflet before our departure. Hans and Alex labored to make it the boldest yet.

Every word that comes out of Hitler's mouth is a lie. When he says peace, he means war, and when he uses the name of the Almighty in the most sacrilegious way, he means the power of the evil one, of the fallen angel, of Satan.

Alex is eager to see his homeland. But I know what we'll encounter. The broken bodies we tend now at the hospital will seem like mere scratches compared to men fresh from the field of battle.

Still, go I must, and try to do what good I can. My friends will be with me; that's one consolation.

Several hours later, we finish for the night. Tomorrow, we'll mail the leaflets we've duplicated tonight in postboxes across Munich.

I pick up a stray leaflet and scan the words. Annalise comes up behind me. Her hair brushes my shoulder. Warmth and softness radiate from her body. Suddenly, I want nothing more than to lean into her, press her close, an antidote to my exhaustion.

When I glance at her, she's not looking at me, but at the leaflet in my hand. Then her eyes shine as they look into mine.

"What?" I can't help my smile.

She doesn't smile back, but takes the leaflet from my hand. Hans wipes a rag across the duplicating machine. Sophie shoves leaflets into her brother's satchel. Alex places the typewriter in its case.

"'We will not remain silent,'" she reads aloud. At her words, the others look up. Annalise's voice fills the air, the room, and each of us down to the marrow of our weary bones. "'We are your guilty conscience. The White Rose will not leave you in peace.'"

CHAPTER NINETEEN

Annalise
July 23, 1942

AS QUICKLY AS IT began, it ended. I've worked alongside Hans, Sophie, Alex, and Kirk for two fleeting weeks—barely enough time to draw a breath between trips to the post office, smiling at the clerk sweetly enough for him to hand over fifty stamps without asking why, and nights hunched over the table, sealing envelopes and pasting stamps. Despite the tension and exhaustion, for the first time I've known what it is to work for a cause that truly matters.

Now the men are off to the front, the girls to their homes, and the requisite armaments work required of females who want to continue their university studies.

I can't deny how empty the prospect makes me.

The morning air is damp, and I'm glad I wore a sweater over my cranberry polka dot dress. Munich's Ostbahnhof is packed with soldiers who look too young and families who look too scared. Gone are the parades and banners of the beginning of the war that lauded Hitler's soldiers as the gods of the twentieth century. In their place are men all too human.

Men who may not come back.

Our group lingers outside the freight yard, the men reluctant to enter the fenced enclosure separating the platform from the street. Linden trees bloom in a neat row, the morning air fragrant with their sweet honey scent. Sophie, Alex, and Hans sit in a huddle on a bench, heads bent in conversation. Christl, the only man in our group in civilian clothes, stands in front of them. Stationed with a Luftwaffe unit, he isn't being sent to the eastern front. Kirk and Willi—a new friend of Hans whom I met at last night's farewell party—chat quietly off to one side. Willi's arms are folded, his jaw set, though he gives a brief smile at something Kirk says. Kirk chuckles. His uniform fills his broad shoulders, cap set at a jaunty angle on his freshly cropped hair.

Jürgen Wittenstein, a friend of the Scholls also leaving for the front, mills around, taking photos. I raise my own camera to my eye and snap pictures, wind tangling my curls around my cheeks. I'm glad I thought to bring it. I want, need something to remember this moment by during the months apart. The faces of my friends on little squares of black and white. Noticing, Jürgen smiles at me in understanding. He knows what pictures mean, how a simple image can conjure a thousand memories.

I snap Sophie, Hans, and Christl. Christl jots something in a notepad, while Hans looks on. Sophie's forehead is creased in that familiar way, a daisy pinned to her dress, her sweater bulky around her shoulders. No one is smiling.

"Hey, Scholls!" I call. "Smile for the camera."

They look up. Christl shoves the notepad in his trouser pocket with a grin. "Let's get a picture before I go. The four of us."

A memory captured in time. Hans with his arm slung around Sophie, Christl on Sophie's other side, his hand on Alex's shoulder.

"Ready?" I focus the camera. Alex pulls a face, making Sophie laugh. "One, two, three."

They're smiling this time, Sophie's mouth open mid-laugh, Christl's eyes disappearing into slits, Hans glancing at Sophie and chuckling, Alex looking into the camera with a crooked grin. Brother, sister, and friends, arms around each other.

Snap.

"Perfect." I fiddle with the camera, preparing to take the next photo.

Christl grips Hans's hand and claps Alex on the back, bidding his friends farewell with quiet words. I watch him walk down the street, glancing back once more. For once, the light has left his eyes.

"Don't I get a picture?"

I spin. Kirk gazes at me, a faint smile playing across his lips. All around us, families say their goodbyes on the outskirts of the station. Desperation makes some heedless of German dignity, a knowing desperation that this goodbye may be the last. Men in uniform sweep up their children and cuddle them close, kiss wives and sweethearts full on the mouth. The display of affection spears me with longing.

I want a husband to kiss and call my own. Not as Vater wanted for me—brood mare to a virile stallion, reproducing little foals for the Reich. I want love.

I want . . . Kirk.

I nod, unable to form a reply.

"Alex, come here." Kirk waves. Alex jogs over.

"At your service, Hoffmann."

"Give him the camera."

I pass the camera into Alex's hands. "Do you know how to work this thing?"

"Of course." Alex rolls his eyes. "I've got one back home."

"It's time the photographer was in one of the pictures." Kirk turns to me.

"Ready?" Alex holds the camera to his eye, squinting. "Smile."

It happens so fast. I'm not even sure who started it. If he put his arm around me first, or if I put mine around him. We smile for the camera. The wind blows my curls into my eyes.

Snap.

When Kirk withdraws his arm from around my waist, I realize it's possible to mourn the lack of something one has only known for seconds.

The troop train slogs into the freight yard, belching smoke. Its high-pitched whistle pierces my ears. Its arrival means goodbye. I will our final moments together to stretch out, to last and last. For the parting not to come at all.

Foolish, wistful thoughts.

"We have to join our company," Hans calls.

Alex hands the camera back to me. I slide its strap around my neck, while I thank him.

"My pleasure." He walks toward Hans and Willi, and the group of uniformed men head toward the freight yard. Kirk turns away, leaving me standing on the cobblestones. Sophie and I follow as far as the gate. They salute and report to the officer stationed there, the gate opens, and the men are swallowed up. Stubborn, sudden tears press against my eyes.

No goodbyes. No . . . nothing.

"Come." Sophie tugs my hand. "This way."

Women and children gather on the other side of the gate, the more daring ones standing on a cement ledge which gives them a boost in height. Sweethearts hold hands through the iron slats, a little boy balanced on an elderly man's shoulders lifts a chubby hand and waves to a soldier on the other side. "Vati! Look at me!"

"Hey there, my little man." The child's grin widens as his vati waves back.

But the young soldier's smile doesn't reach his eyes.

Sophie and I wait in silence. Minutes pass. The freight yard is an undulating wave of Wehrmacht gray.

"Look."

I glance in the direction Sophie points. Our friends stride through the crowd, heading toward us. My gaze locks onto Kirk, walking between Alex and Hans, the picture of a dashing soldier. Yet the sight of him in uniform doesn't swell my heart with pride, but makes it ache with sorrow.

"We were worried you wouldn't wait for us," Hans says.

Sophie, standing on the cement slab, clinging to an iron spike with one hand, meets her brother's eyes. "You know I'd always wait for you, Hans."

Jürgen snaps more photos, and I watch absently. He captures Sophie, sweater-clad arms spread wide, satchel slung around a fence spike while the young men pose below.

"Look, Annalise," she calls. "I'm a bird!"

Jürgen laughs.

Snap.

Sophie, looking down at the boys from the other side of the gate. They talk and trade jokes. In one hand, she holds a daisy, clutching the spike with the other. She is no longer smiling.

She too knows time is running out.

Kirk climbs onto the cement slab, gazing down at me. "I wanted to say goodbye." His tone is quiet.

I hoist myself up, so we're almost eye-level, facing each other across the barrier, one hand wrapped around the damp, cold metal of the fence.

"I . . . I didn't think we'd get to." I raise my gaze to his, noticing the little things. The tiny scrape along his jaw as if he cut himself shaving. The faint line of freckles on the bridge of his nose. The amber of his eyes.

If only I had paper and pencils. After my hands sketched him, my heart would not forget. But it's too late for that. I'll only have the photos . . . and my memories.

"Will you write to me?" He reaches out. Our hands meet across the barrier, holding tight, his touch warm against my chilled fingers.

"*Ja.*" Surely, he wouldn't ask if he didn't care, just a little. "I'll write."

"Do you believe in God, Annalise?"

I laugh, startled by the change in topic. "Kirk Hoffmann, you really are the son of a pastor. Bringing up theology now, of all times."

"I didn't ask you about theology. I asked if you believed in God. We've never talked about that." His eyes are earnest.

I can't lie to him. I sigh. "I don't know."

"This morning, before I left, my mutter told me God goes with us everywhere. And that even if we aren't where we want to be, He can use us for good. I thought it might comfort you to know that as you return to Berlin."

The train whistle wails.

"Wiedersehen, Annalise." He reaches up and, ever so gently, tucks a tendril of hair behind my ear. Unbidden tears prick my eyes. I must not cry. Not now.

"Be safe, Kirk," I whisper. I want to sob and beg him to come back. Tell him that if he does I'll do anything, even listen to his talk about God.

I can't ask him that. It's a promise he cannot guarantee, much less vow to keep.

He nods. Smiles once more, sad and sweet. He climbs down and walks toward his comrades boarding the train, shoulders straight, Wehrmacht uniform pressed, boots gleaming. I keep my smile firmly pasted in place as we watch them go, Sophie and I. The train chugs out of the station, the forms of the men leaning out the windows passing all too quickly, their called-out last words lost in the wind and whistle-shrills and pluming smoke.

When all that's left of the train is tendrils of smoke and the dispersing groups of families and friends, Sophie turns to me. She hugs her arms across her chest, wisps of hair escaping from her bobby pin and falling around her face.

"After four years of war, you'd think saying goodbye would be easier." She gives a brittle smile.

I shake my head. "Some things never change."

Sophie
July 23, 1942

That evening, Annalise and I retreat to my apartment. Alex bequeathed us his remaining stash of Chianti, and I pour generous portions into teacups—the only clean glasses I can find. Annalise settles onto my sofa, stockinged feet tucked beneath her. I cross to Hans's record player, crouch down, and leaf through the stack of records before finding the one I want at the bottom of the pile.

"They're *not* telling us what we can listen to tonight." I place the needle on the record. Ethel Waters's rich voice crackles mournfully onto the air.

"Hear, hear!" Annalise lifts her cup.

We sip our drinks while Ethel sings "Stormy Weather." The words fit my mood. I pour Chianti into my cup, inhaling the subtle cherry fragrance. The liquid sloshes from the bottle, puddling on the low table in front of the sofa. I don't bother wiping it up.

Bidding farewell to my friends made me realize how much they mean to me. Those few final words with Hans, our summer in Munich as fleeting as a full moon. Even the anxiety accompanying our leaflet production could be borne as long as we were together. Alex, warmth in his gaze, promising to remember me in his prayers while in Russia. Shaking Willi's hand, his kind gaze and solid grip inspiring such trust (will there ever be an opportunity to ask him to join our work?). Posing for photos and trying to laugh, when all I wanted to do was curl up in a ball and cry.

I place my half-empty cup on the table and glance at Annalise. She stares into her cup. I didn't miss the way Kirk looked at her and she at him—like they wanted to imprint the image of the other on their memories with ink that will not fade. Will their parting dim or strengthen their feelings? That's always the question.

Ethel's sultry voice fades as the record crackles to an end. I stand and move to change it. Annalise sets her cup on the table. This time, I put on Schubert's *Trout* Quintet, one of my favorite classical pieces. One degenerate record is enough for tonight.

"So you're off to Ulm tomorrow?"

I nod.

"Oh, the joys of armaments work."

I don't respond with something light and sarcastic. My thoughts turn to Vater, soon to go on trial. In the blur of removing any trace of our leaflet operation from the studio, selling the duplicating machine as a safety measure, planning last night's farewell party, and today's hurried goodbyes, I've managed to put the fast-approaching date all but from my mind. I pick up my cup. Already, the wine is growing lukewarm and flat. The air is stifling, blackout curtains cloaking the windows like smothering hands. We sit in dingy semi-darkness.

"What is it?" Annalise touches my shoulder.

I face her. Despite her youthful face, a concern older than her years fills her gaze.

"My vater."

Annalise doesn't take her hand from my shoulder. Her touch, rather than her words, urges me to go on.

"He's standing trial for saying if Hitler doesn't end the war, the Russians will be in Berlin within two years. A scourge of humanity, he called the Führer. His secretary overheard and denounced him. I'm surprised she had enough brains to know what that meant." My tone is dry. "Of course, the authorities pounced on it. He spent the night in jail, before they let him go because he was in the middle of an accounting project for Ulm's Finance Department. His trial is August 3. Mutter's health is already weak, and with Hans and Werner gone . . . I'm scared, Annalise." Admitting it eases the fear gnawing inside me. At home, I'll have to be brave. A strong shoulder for others to lean on. But with Annalise, woman to woman, I can be honest.

Annalise's expression tightens. "I wish I could say there would be justice."

I shake my head. "I hold out no hope for that."

She stares at the opposite wall, as if turning something over in her mind. Then she faces me. Her forehead is moist from the heat, and she looks as tired as I feel. "Kirk said God will be with us wherever we are."

"That sounds like him." I smile. I believe God is with us, but it is so difficult to trust, to follow after Him wholeheartedly when every day brings its own weariness, a new shade of darkness. Faith is trusting through the darkness, but sometimes I ask *how* and come up empty.

"Let's take it one day at a time. Focus on making it back to Munich in the fall. We can produce new leaflets then. Work even harder. Every paragraph written, each leaflet sent is power. They might be able to imprison your vater, work us like slaves in their factories, but if we concentrate on coming back here, we can bear it. All of it."

I nod, the determination in her voice bolstering my resolve. Joining us has changed Annalise. She's no longer the uncertain girl I first met but a woman whose friendship I'm grateful for.

I pick up our cups and hand hers over. "To making it through, then?"

I meant it lightly, but Annalise looks as serious as if she's taking a vow. Glass clinks. Schubert plays. "To both of us making it through."

CHAPTER TWENTY

Kirk
July 26, 1942
Warsaw, Poland

THREE DAYS OF TRAIN travel passed as the cars bearing us to the eastern front left Germany and crossed Poland. Days of talking amongst ourselves, reading books, writing letters, and staring out the smudged glass at the scenery. Poland is a desolate landscape, wide and empty. Thatched farmhouses sit in groves of birch, and the fields bear the marks of plunder and neglect.

Finally we reach Warsaw. After being shown to our quarters, we've been given the evening off. Most of the Second Student Medical Company will likely seek out the nearest bar to sate their thirst with Polish vodka.

Hans, Alex, Willi, and I head for the center of the city to have a look around.

We walk through gray-hued streets, passing piles of rubble where buildings once stood. In our uniforms, the four of us walking side by side, the denizens of the city give us wide berth. Our boots make a harsh sound on the cobbled street. A woman holding two small children by their hands, dress lank on her shrunken frame, scuttles past without so much as a glance. Two boys dressed in dirty, too-large shirts crouch on the sidewalk as we pass, bony hands outstretched, calling out something in Polish. I don't recognize their words, but I understand the cadence of their cries and the look in their wide eyes—*food, please.*

Alex is already rummaging in his pockets. He pulls out his iron ration bar and hands it to the youngest of the two children. Terror shines in their eyes. They see our uniforms, not our souls. I fumble for something to give, and hand the other child a brown-paper wrapped piece of dried meat. Shaking, as if from fear, he takes the food, whispering something through cracked and bleeding lips. I nod, wishing I could do, offer more, but we move on.

On the next street, SS officers in pressed uniforms and women in furs

129

exit sleek motorcars and enter a three-story building that looks like a hotel. Sultry music spills out as the double doors open, revealing a glimpse of plush carpets and crystal chandeliers.

We walk on, encountering more beggars, Polish citizens with war-scarred expressions, bars with swinging doors and raucous music, and the shells of bombed-out buildings.

Warsaw is a city trampled by German jackboots.

I glance at Willi. Beneath his gray-green cap, his face is grim. Stationed in Poland before, he's no stranger to the destruction the German army has wreaked upon this country.

Up ahead, a massive brick wall looms high, crowned with barbed wire. SS guards stand rigid on either side of the entrance. The eerie quietness grows with every step as we draw closer.

Hans nudges me, pointing toward the gates. "What is that?"

I'm not sure. But I intend to find out. "Excuse me . . . *Ja*, I'm speaking to you." I hail a passing adolescent boy. His wrists and ankles stick out from his tattered clothes.

He skids to a stop, shoulders hunched, head bent.

I smile, trying to look unthreatening. "What's that?" I point to the wall. Even if he doesn't understand German, he'll at least follow my gestures.

He darts a glance toward the wall, then back down to his holey boots. His ears stick out from beneath a ragged cap. "*Getto*," he mumbles.

"Ghetto," I repeat. "Ghetto for whom?"

"*Żydzi*." His gaze flickers up.

"He says it's a ghetto for Jews," Alex says quietly.

"Oh." I swallow. "Here." I pull a few cigarettes from my pocket, part of my army ration. "For you." Even if he doesn't smoke, he can use them to trade.

The boy doesn't move.

"For you," I say again, pointing from the cigarettes back to him.

Recognition glimmers in his eyes. He inches out a grimy hand. I continue to hold out my palm, smiling. In a flash, the boy grabs the cigarettes and pockets them. He takes off down the street at a run. Not like a mischievous kid getting away, but as if he's used to running for his life, used to fearing being shot at.

The four of us draw closer. The stench is overpowering. Humidity, decaying garbage, and an odor like rotting meat. Bile rises in my throat. A few meters away, a corpse is sprawled on the street. An old man. Dried blood coats one side of his head. His clothes may have once given evidence of his identity, but they've since been stripped from him.

"Now what?" I whisper to Hans. We can't go in—the signs posted near the gates declare Authorized Personnel Only.

Before Hans can answer, the sound of tramping feet reaches my ears. We instinctively move away from the center of the street and onto the sidewalk, standing against an abandoned brick building on the Aryan side of the city. If there's anything we've learned, it's how to become invisible. To observe.

About forty men and women trudge toward the gates, herded by SS soldiers. Their clothes are tattered, their faces chalky from lack of sun and nourishment. They walk with eyes focused on the ground, shoulders stooped, bodies drawn into themselves. All wear armbands emblazoned with the Star of David.

A young woman near the middle of the queue catches my attention. Most of the women wear kerchiefs, but her shoulder-length curls are uncovered. Their color, that peculiar mix of gold and red, is the same shade as Annalise's. She turns slightly, her profile in view. Other than her hair, she looks nothing like Annalise. Her face is pinched and aged beyond her years. She stands in the queue, gaze down, hands folded over her waist, next to a man about the same age. The sun glints on her hair, making it shine.

The gates open, and each person passes a piece of paper to the guard, who gives a cursory glance before handing it back. Another guard searches them, a quick running of his hands down their bodies, before they move forward, swallowed by the gates and whatever is behind them.

"Jewish workers." Willi's gaze is riveted on the group. "They must be allowed to leave the ghetto for factory work or something like that."

"How long have they been kept here?" Hans asks.

"A couple of years, maybe. I imagine conditions behind the walls are indescribably awful."

We linger a few moments more as the queue grows shorter. "Let's go," Hans mutters.

We turn and head in the opposite direction.

A cry. A shot. I start. Spin around, heart thudding.

The woman with the reddish-gold hair lies in front of the ghetto in a spreading pool of blood. Beside her, in the blood, is something round and brown. A potato.

A scream builds inside of me. I force it back. Alex and Willi are pale. Hans's mouth is a tight line.

"Why?"

"She must've been smuggling food." Willi's eyes close for an instant, as if to wipe away the images.

"And that was enough to shoot her?" Alex's face matches how I feel. Frantic. Disbelieving.

"For them, *ja*" is all the reply Willi gives. What else is there to say? A Jewish life was taken. I don't need to see the inside of the ghetto to know many more lives are taken daily, and will continue to be.

Life, all life, is precious. A dull mourning I will not soon shake rises in my chest.

Just before we turn the corner, I glance back once more.

One of the guards drags the woman away by the feet, her head lolled back, exposing the pale skin of her throat. The ghetto wall rises high, an impenetrable force of brick. The queue shuffles forward.

We walk on.

CHAPTER TWENTY-ONE

Sophie
August 3, 1942
Ulm

THE HARD-BACKED CHAIR PRESSES into my spine. In the courtroom, the air is sticky and tinged with the odor of perspiration. A fly buzzes above the head of the balding man in the seat in front of me.

Beside me, Mutter's face is pale, her lips set in a thin line. I take her hand. It's clammy. Shaking. I squeeze hard, willing her to look at me and draw some courage from my gaze.

She stares straight ahead, eyes never leaving her husband, my vater, as we wait to hear his fate.

Fräulein Wilke stands in the witness box, wearing her BDM uniform, her hair in two long braids, though she's at least my age.

"What exactly did Herr Scholl say, Fräulein Wilke? Would you repeat it for the benefit of the court, please?" The district attorney's brow glistens with sweat, his rotund frame garbed in a black suit.

The presiding judge leans forward.

Fräulein Wilke turns slightly in the witness box, facing the judge, not Vater. Her chin lifts. "He said our Führer was a scourge of humanity." Her voice falters, as if she's unused to so many gazes on her.

A collective gasp of outrage filters through the courtroom.

"And that if the Führer did not end the war soon, the Russians would be in Berlin within two years." Fräulein Wilke dares a glance at Vater. He sits on a bench against the wall, flanked by two guards. His expression is blank, but I can tell he's fighting an internal battle. Vater is many good things, but an even-tempered man is not one of them.

"Then he dared . . . he actually *dared* to compare our Führer to Attila the Hun." Fräulein Wilke grips the witness stand, as if overcome.

Mutter turns to me. "How bad do you think it will be?" she whispers.

"Courage, Mutter." I squeeze her hand. "See how brave Vater is. He's not afraid, and neither should we be."

Mutter nods. She's wearing her nicest summer dress, a narrow-brimmed hat, graying hair pulled into a tidy bun. This morning, she straightened Vater's tie and made sure his suit was pressed and his mustache trimmed before we left for court. These two decent, ordinary people don't belong in a courtroom like common criminals. I inhale a sharp breath.

Vater's right. Hitler is like Attila the Hun. If only he'd restrained himself enough to wait until he was at home to say so, instead of in the hearing of his secretary, the loyal little Nazi.

The trial drags on. Vater is given a chance to defend himself, and he does his best to deflect Fräulein Wilke's statements.

I track the judge's expression. It remains unconvinced.

Finally, Vater is told to stand as his sentence is read. Between the two young guards, he looks stooped and old, dark hair threaded with gray, the skin around his jaw sagging and pasty. My heart thuds dully, matching the ache in my temples. Mutter squeezes my hand, her sweaty grip clenching my fingers.

Please, God . . .

The judge rises. "Robert Scholl, you are charged with malicious slander of the Führer and sentenced to four months imprisonment. You are also required to pay all court costs in full. You will be granted a three-week reprieve before serving your sentence to allow you time to sort out your business affairs. The court permits this leniency out of its regard for your service in the community." He drones on, but I scarcely hear him. Mutter exhales, some of the color returning to her cheeks.

I expected worse. But how will we manage with Vater imprisoned, our income gone?

A half hour later, the three of us walk home in the afternoon heat, through familiar streets. Children pedal by on bicycles, summer flowers decorate window boxes with splashes of color. The endlessly high spire of the grand Ulmer Münster rises skyward, tip piercing the heavens.

I look up at Vater, walking between us in the center of the cobbled street. He's said little since leaving the courthouse, only pressed Mutter close against his chest for a moment. I've always looked to my vater as a source of strength. Now his own is gone.

"What will you do, Robert?" Mutter peers up at him, as we turn down Münsterplatz.

Vater stops, taking Mutter's hands in both of his. I stand on the outskirts of their circle of two.

"I've already arranged for Eugen Grimminger to manage the business while I'm away." He says *away* as if he's leaving for a trip, not a prison sentence. "He and Inge will work together. We'll manage, Magdalena." His tone is firm, as if, by the resolve of his words, he can make them come to pass.

Mutter nods and gives a little smile, a vote of confidence. But I can tell she's shaken. Her health hasn't been strong in several years, fault of her heart condition. Without my brothers and now Vater, there will be no man for her to lean on. I must do all I can to take their places.

Hitler has tied all our hands. Because of him, Vater must go to prison and I must work in an armaments factory during summer vacation, laboring for the Reich, instead of helping my own family.

My chest burns.

"You're frowning, Sophie." Vater tweaks a strand of my hair. "Come now, chin up. Remember, *Allen—*"

"*Gewalten zum Trotz sich erhalten,*" we finish the Goethe quote together. *Despite all the powers, maintain yourself.* It's our family's equivalent of squaring one's shoulders and getting on with it. We've repeated the phrase to ourselves and each other over the years, until the words flow from our tongues as naturally as breathing.

I smile, to show him I'm all right. He wraps a solid arm around my shoulders, giving them a quick squeeze. Tears press against my eyes, but I blink them away. He slips Mutter's hand into the crook of his arm, and we move in the direction of our apartment.

When the labor service extends your term another six months: maintain yourself.

When your brother is arrested for belonging to an illegal youth organization: maintain yourself.

When you don't know if your closest friends will return from Russia on their own two legs or in a wooden box: maintain yourself.

When your vater is sentenced to prison: maintain yourself.

When you look around and all you see is evil and injustice . . .

"*Allen Gewalten zum Trotz sich erhalten,*" I whisper, squinting into the blindingly bright sky.

CHAPTER TWENTY-TWO

Kirk
August 14, 1942
Gzhatsk, Russia

THOUGH THE YOUNG SOLDIER'S blood never touched my skin, its imprint none-theless stains me. I strip my gloves from my hands, remove my mask, cap, and surgical apron. Carbolic soap stings my hands as I wash up in the anteroom.

I brace my fingers against the basin, head bent, taking slow breaths.

We laid him—Dieter was his name—beneath the harsh lights of the operating theater, abdomen a mess of shrapnel and chewed flesh. Eyes young and wide in his pale face, fingers clutching my sleeve as we prepared him for surgery.

"Am I going to die?"

Do you lie to your patient? Does telling them they have a chance bolster their body? Or is it merely false hope? It's the question asked by everyone dealing with the sick and wounded.

I chose the former with Dieter. Flashed him the kind of smile I'd give my younger brother—if I had one—and said: "Not on my watch."

We did our best. But too often our best isn't enough. We couldn't save Dieter. The third man to die on the table in as many hours.

I exit the hospital, surprised to realize it's mid-afternoon. Beneath the bright lights of the operating theater, it's impossible to tell what time of day it is.

I lean against a crude wooden fence, staring out across the plains, the clean wind whipping against my face. Bark scrapes my palms, raw from harsh soap.

We know painfully little about the men whose lives we hold in our hands. Our job is to patch them up, mend what's broken so they can be shipped out to fight for Führer and Fatherland again. Fed back into the ever-ravenous war machine.

My eyes sting. What a senseless waste it all is.

Laughter echoes, carried by the wind, as a group of personnel exits the doors of the makeshift hospital. I turn. Alex heads in my direction, lighting a cigarette.

"Fancy meeting you here." He flashes a grin, wind tousling his hair.

"Off duty too?"

He nods, settling himself beside me on the fence. Smoke clouds from the end of his cigarette. I don't know where his officer's cap went. His uniform coat is only half buttoned. If the chief medical officer sees that, he'll be in for a tongue-lashing.

"Busy morning?"

"The contagious diseases ward isn't a very exciting place. Spotted fever, that type of thing. Hans says he feels superfluous. I told him to wipe the frown off his face and stop using such big words."

"Three men died on the table today." I face Alex, seeing not my friend but Dieter. He probably had a family back home proud of him for serving the Fatherland, a mutter who fussed over how fine he looked in his uniform. But on the operating table, he was just a scared kid, battling for his life. "All of them, so young. The last one couldn't have been more than a few months over eighteen. He should've had his whole life ahead of him. And now, he's gone." I swallow. "Those songs about battles and glory and honor . . . they don't talk about what a man's insides look like when they've been chewed by bullets, or how limbs grow limp and heavy when there's no life in them. Or how eyes . . ."

Alex clamps a firm hand on my shoulder. "Kirk, come on. You know what this is like." His gaze radiates understanding though. "You're caring too much, and when we care too much, we can't do the job we were sent here to do."

I scrub my hand across my face. "You'd think it'd get easier. But the longer it goes on, the harder it is to accept. They just get younger and younger, the soldiers in those beds. Though I don't believe in what we're fighting for, I believe in the lives of each and every one of those men."

"Look." Alex snuffs his cigarette with the toe of his boot. "You need a rest. Tonight, you and Hans are going out with me."

"I don't know, Shurik—"

"Nothing doing." A grin teases his lips. "I'm going to show you Russia. My Russia. Besides, I want you to meet my friends."

"Your friends? Come on, what is this?"

He holds up his hands, eyes alight with boyish anticipation. "Wait and see."

Hours later, Hans and I follow Alex into the night. The air is crisp and cold, the sky above star studded. Our boots make squishing sounds on the moist earth. Tonight the sounds of thundering guns, the shudder of falling bombs are absent, though it's been almost constant during the past weeks as Russian artillery shelled Gzhatsk.

As we tramp through the woods, I hope Alex is as certain as he seems about where he's going. He walks fearlessly forward, as if a map of the country has been branded into him from birth.

A warm glow shines through the forest. We draw closer, and I glimpse a cottage nestled in the woods. Smoke curls from its chimney. Alex strides through the clearing, Hans and I following.

"Shurik, we can't just—"

But Alex is already at the door, lifting his fist to knock.

It hasn't escaped my notice he isn't wearing his uniform coat.

"He better know what he's doing," I mutter to Hans. Whatever ties Alex may have to Russia, we are still Wehrmacht soldiers. The Russians will see us as such.

The door opens with a groan. A bearded man stands on the threshold. A little girl, garbed in a colorful blouse and skirt, clings to his pant leg.

The man looks beyond Alex's shoulder to us. Fear flashes in his eyes. Alex says a few words to him in Russian. I can't make out what they're saying, except Alex is greeting him by name, and the man is calling him Shurik. The man opens the door, and Alex ducks inside, motioning Hans and me to follow.

The front room of the cottage is dim and smoky. A fire blazes in the hearth. A young woman sits in a chair by the fire, sewing in her lap, dressed in an embroidered blouse and skirt, a kerchief. The little girl scampers across the rough plank floor and climbs up on her lap.

Alex turns to Hans and me. "This is Yuri." He gestures to the man. "Vanja." He points to Hans, using the Russian form of his name. "Kirk," he says, pointing to me. "And Anya and Katya." He nods and smiles at the two girls. "These are my friends," he says in German to Hans and me. "I met them last week."

Burly arms folded, the man looks us over, gaze hovering on our uniforms. I know what he sees. Two men in the garb of the Wehrmacht, an army that has inflicted immeasurable suffering upon his homeland. He looks at Alex, who speaks to him again in Russian. From the expression on Alex's face and his gestures, I can tell he's convincing him we're not here to do harm.

Finally, the man nods and says something in Russian.

Alex turns to us. "He's welcoming you to his home. Say 'Spasibo.' It means thank you."

"*Spasibo*." I smile.

Yuri's weathered face splits wide with a grin. His teeth are yellowed, several missing.

Speaking in Russian, Alex sets the burlap sack he brought on the trestle table and dumps out the contents. Two chocolate bars, cans of tinned meat, and a packet of cigarettes roll onto the table.

Yuri reaches out and touches one of the tins gingerly. The young woman, Anya, and the little girl, Katya, lean forward. Yuri turns, addressing Anya with a few quick words. She answers and stands, lifting the little girl off her lap. Anya peers at us shyly, colorful skirts swaying.

We settle onto the bench pulled up to the trestle table, while Yuri and Alex talk in rapid-fire Russian, gesturing as they speak. Arms folded on the table, Hans watches with rapt interest. Anya stands near the table, staring wide-eyed at Alex and listening to the conversation. Katya lingers near the fireplace, hands bereft of any plaything. Every so often, she rises up on tiptoe and holds her hands above her head like a dancer. She can only maintain the position a few seconds before she wobbles and lands on two feet again. I smile. She blinks at me with dark eyes.

I walk toward her, the conversation a musical blur in the background. Slowly, so as not to scare her, I kneel. She remains still, hands clasped.

"Kirk." I point to myself, repeating my name.

"Katya." She lisps her name. One of her front teeth is missing.

What can I offer this child? I don't share her language. My countrymen are attempting to destroy hers. Because of Hitler's army, this small girl with glossy hair and pink cheeks has suffered war's devastation at an age when life should be at its most peaceful.

A boyhood trick comes to mind. I pull my handkerchief from my pocket and deftly twist the square into the shape of a rabbit. I place it in my cupped hand. A flick of my wrist.

The rabbit jumps. The first time, Katya starts back in surprise. I do it again, and she draws closer, eyes wide.

The third time, she giggles. I grin, laughing with her. The laughter of childhood is a casualty of war. Childhood itself is stolen by war's cruel hands. But tonight in this humble cottage, a little Russian girl laughs high and clear, the sweetest music I've heard since entering this country.

Anya sets a bottle and glasses demurely in front of Yuri. Yuri pours clear liquid into the glasses, and Alex calls me over. I hand my handkerchief to Katya.

"Katya keep." I say it a couple of times before she gets my meaning. She hugs the toy to her chest, smiling.

That night, we drink Russian vodka and listen to music both haunting and wild, played by Yuri on his balalaika. Alex takes Anya's hands and together, they dance in the center of the room, her skirts swirling, his feet stomping. Both are laughing, dark curls escaping Anya's kerchief, Alex's head thrown back. Katya claps along to the music, and by the end of the evening, she's climbed up on my lap and snuggled against my chest, falling fast asleep.

We walk back to the hospital, the air bitter, night a black cloak draping the landscape.

Alex turns to me. His hair falls into his eyes, mussed from dancing. "I'd stay here if I could," he says softly. "If there was any way . . . I'd stay here."

"There's more humanity in one of these so-called subhumans than in the entire chancellery of the Reich." Hans's jaw hardens.

I say nothing, walking alongside my friends, letting the night and stars wrap around me, the notes of Russian music lingering in my ears.

CHAPTER TWENTY-THREE

Sophie
August 28, 1942
Ulm

FACTORY WORK IS A soulless, loveless occupation. The din echoing off the high-ceilinged room rings in my ears long after the siren signals quitting time. I stand for ten hours a day, stuffing powder cartridges into ammunition shells. My back aches, and the knots in my neck refuse to release, no matter how long I soak in the bath at night.

I want to scream.

We're slaves who have appointed our own slave driver. Only we call him Führer.

Grease and grit blackens my hands. Shells roll past on the conveyor. Machines clatter. All around me, girls and women stand in long lines, our clothes long since gray-tinged.

I glance at Dina, the Russian prisoner working next to me. She looks up and smiles. She's rail-thin, face pinched and pale. All the Russian workers are. They're slaves, same as us, only we get to go home every night, while they live in barracks adjacent to the factory, fenced in by barbed wire.

A bread roll in my skirt pocket bumps against my thigh. I'll give it to Dina during the noon break. In the face of such hunger, it's the least I can do.

When the foreman is on the opposite side of the room, I attempt conversation. Dina has been teaching me words in Russian. Our secret rebellion, talking when we've been told to be silent.

I tap her on the shoulder, once and quick, before stuffing shells again. "Your earrings are pretty." The clanking of machines almost drowns my words.

Her forehead scrunches. Her blond hair is tucked beneath a kerchief, and freckles dust her delicate nose.

"Earrings." I point to my bare earlobe, then to hers, adorned with a set of bangles. Many of the Russian women wear jewelry, albeit cheap and tarnished, a nod to femininity despite their shapeless work dresses.

Her nose wrinkles as she laughs. She touches her earrings. "*Ser'gi.*"

"*Ser'gi.* Earrings."

"Ear-rings."

"Pretty. Like you." I point to her earrings and then to her. We giggle together, heads bent, hands still moving. Two girls who can barely understand each other, being simply . . . girls.

"You!" The foreman's voice booms from behind. I stiffen and keep working. Dina turns to glance at him, head tilted, wisps of hair curling around her cheeks. He jabs a finger into her face. "Lazy Russian *dummkopf. Schnell.*"

Dina laughs, not at all fazed. I resist the urge to laugh too. How is she supposed to understand him? She says something to him in Russian and giggles again. He glares at her, red-faced, and storms away.

What spirit these women have. Every night, as they walk toward the barracks, they talk softly together, as if the day's fatigue is already forgotten. We German girls trudge home in weary silence. I envy their camaraderie, remembering the way it was with Annalise.

I cough, the air hot and choking. Out of the corner of my eye, I glimpse Dina. Expression blank, she stuffs three shells, then leaves one empty. It slides past on the conveyor. She continues on with her work, as if nothing has happened.

My breath stills. My gaze follows the empty shell.

Sabotage . . . Prevent the smooth operation of the war machine.

When we wrote those words, did we actually consider their meaning? Sabotaging weapons means someone we care for could find themselves helpless in battle.

What if Fritz ends up with Dina's bullet? What if he's unable to fight back because of it?

I swallow, throat dry. I keep working by rote, a human machine for the Fatherland.

The words I recently penned in my diary fill my mind:

Mustn't we all, no matter what age we live in, be permanently prepared for God to call us to account from one moment to the next? How am I to know if I shall still be alive tomorrow? We could all be wiped out overnight by a bomb, and my guilt would be no less than if I perished in company with the earth and the stars . . .

"My guilt would be no less," I whisper. "None of ours would be."

My hands shake as I stuff the second-to-last shell in a group of four. I leave the fourth empty.

It slides down the conveyor, out of sight. I sense Dina watching me. I meet her gaze. Her eyes are wide, questioning. As if to ask, *How can you, a German, do this thing?*

I look away and bend to my work.

Even if we spoke the same language, I'm not sure I could find the words.

⌁

After cleansing the grime of the factory from my skin, and gulping down a hasty supper, I leave the table, grab my flute, and pedal down Münsterplatz on Inge's bicycle. A summer breeze wisps across my cheeks, pulling my hair back from my face. The tires bump across the cobblestones.

I ride as fast as I can, arriving at the grim brick building within minutes. I lean my bicycle against a tree and approach the prison, flute in hand. Craning my neck, I count the second-floor windows.

One. Two. Three. Four.

The fourth window. Vater's.

I don't know if he'll be waiting. Nor if he'll even see me. Against the reddish-hued building with its rows of black-barred windows, I'm small. A girl in a worn summer dress and lace-up shoes, staring up at her vater's prison window.

I place the flute against my lips. Slowly, I tease soft notes from the instrument, gaze never leaving the window. Oh, for him to see me and take courage from this. The forced confinement must be a torment. How he loved evening walks by the Danube, busy days at the office.

The tune stiches itself together in my mind. It isn't until I reach the second verse I realize what I'm playing. "Thoughts Are Free."

In an instant, I'm back in Eickemeyer's studio, working alongside Hans, Alex, and Kirk, exchanging shared smiles, the brave notes of the song emerging proud from our lungs.

> *Thoughts are free,*
> *Who can guess them? . . .*

I miss my friends, the purpose of our work in Munich. Then we stood united against this oppression. Now we're scattered like dandelion dust in the wind, forced to root ourselves to new, unyielding ground.

The music drifts onto the air as I play, the sun sinking lower and lower in the sky, a canvas of red and gold against the dirty brown of the prison.

Movement from the fourth window catches my eye. Lowering the flute, I stand on tiptoe, lifting one hand in a wave. Is it my imagination? Nein. A shadowy figure stands at the window, form all but hidden by the close-set bars. Yet it's Vater. I know it.

I wave again, my heart straining to reach beyond the confines between us. *I'm here*, I want to call. *Everything will be all right. Don't worry, Vater. Your Sophie won't let you down.*

Instead, I lift my flute, the notes of my song rising higher than before. Though I fear not high enough.

Annalise
September 22, 1942
Berlin

A letter from Kirk waits on the hall table when I arrive home from the factory where I work as a secretary. When Mutter first asked who "this Kirk" was, I told her "a friend from university" and left it at that. She hasn't asked since, perhaps because she too understands what it is to feel alone.

Settling onto my bed, I slit the envelope with my thumbnail and unfold the pages. The army post is sporadic at best, but Kirk and I still manage to correspond. Each letter, every line draws us closer together.

Dear Annalise,

I'm sitting on an overturned crate outside the hospital, paper in hand, thinking of you. If you knew how often this scene occurred, you'd laugh, perhaps. Or perhaps you'd understand. I don't deny I hope it's the latter.

Each day we discover something new of Russia. In spite of the shooting that goes on steadily in the distance, we venture out when not on duty to visit the town and walk the countryside. One morning, Hans and I procured a pair of horses and went riding through the high steppe grass. Exhilarating! Russia is a beautiful country, sweeping and boundless and startling. The sky is like a ribbon of silver blue unfurling across a limitless expanse. See how I'm trying to be poetic? I know the painter in you will appreciate my efforts. Those of us with cameras have snapped photographs. But black and white doesn't begin to do justice to the array of shades on display.

It's a strange kind of paradox, such a captivating land being the backdrop for the base act of kill or be killed. Last month, we were out walking when we came across the decomposing body of a dead Russian.

Alex suggested we bury him, so we did, nailing a Russian cross together and sticking it into the ground as a grave marker. Will you think me strange if I say it felt somehow symbolic?

Alex has been sick with diphtheria for several days, and Hans has a touch of something too. I think we've all given too much blood. There's so much need here that one cannot help doing what one can, but it does put a strain on the system. Thankfully, they're both on the mend now.

As for me, I've been prosaically healthy, which is a blessing, as I've been needed in surgery almost every day. Ten men die here every day—some days even more. Everyone takes it all very calmly. To do otherwise would be to fall to pieces on a regular basis, and that won't do anyone much good. It's difficult to witness suffering and be unable to alleviate it as much as one would wish. I suppose that would be the case for a doctor even in peacetime, but it seems much worse in war.

Some of your letters have reached me. Every day, during mail call, I hope for something from you. Alex teases me mercilessly about this. He says hello, by the by. He's looking out for a samovar to bring home. It makes the best tea, rich and hot. We drink cupfuls of it!

Now, Annalise, I want you to pretend we're walking side by side through the Englischer Garten and tell me of yourself. Can you tell I'm stealing a glance at you, wondering if I ought to take your hand?

In your last letter, you mentioned you'd cracked open your Bible. Well done! I wish I were there with you so we could discuss it. I've had plenty of practice, listening to Vater's sermons over the years. Knowing you, you probably have all sorts of questions.

But until that day comes, let me tell you this. In a world full of hate, there is a God of love. It's a love that, in spite of everything, still fills me anew each time I see fresh evidence of it. God loves you, Annalise Brandt. And His is a love that remains unshakable, no matter what storms may come. Because not only does He love, He is Love itself.

I have to report for duty, so I'll close now. My thoughts and prayers are with you.

Yours,
Kirk

I lower the sheets, fingertips still wrapped around their edges. I lie back on my bed, the paper resting against my chest, over my heart.

God loves you, Annalise Brandt.

If only I could believe it's true. If only it were. All my life, I've craved unconditional love. The kind that says: *You don't have to be the brightest or the most pleasing or perfect. I love you in spite of, and because of, your inadequacies. To me, you are perfect.* This longing to be known and understood, to be the giver and recipient of such love has never served me well. Mutter loves me in her own way, and my brothers do too. Even Vater would, I'm sure, call his desire to see me settled as the wife of a high-ranking officer a kind of love. But like a hungry youth who's never full, human love has always left me empty.

If God is love, then surely His is a better, higher love?

For years, I've ascribed to Vater's belief that God doesn't exist. While he called the Führer our savior, I chose to believe there was none.

But in the midst of the brokenness, I've begun to question again. To search for meaning in this life so easily snatched away. There has to be something beyond the world and its weary trappings.

There has to be *hope.*

And as I've paged through the Bible I purchased at a second-hand book-shop, reading long into the night, I've grasped for threads of it with a des-peration I didn't know I possessed.

I settle at the desk in the corner of my bedroom and reach into the top drawer. My hand trembles as I hold up a tiny square of black and white. It's of the two of us, smiling into the camera, arms around each other, my hair tangled around my cheeks, a laugh tugging his lips.

I swallow, loneliness overwhelming. Though alone, I must continue to form my own views and ideas in a world hostile to both.

I pick up my pen, imagine what I'd say to him if we were sitting side-by-side in my apartment or walking together across the university grounds. A droplet of ink hovers on the tip of my pen as I form the first words.

Dear Kirk . . .

Kirk
November 4, 1942
The Polish Border

"I will never wash the soil of Russia from my boots."

Alex spoke those words our last night in Gzhatsk. Now he sits beside me on the train taking us back to Germany, smoking moodily.

Leaving Russia is hardest for him. In the days before our departure, he disobeyed many an order. All of us got into a brawl with some Party officials at the tavern a few nights before we left. Hans and Alex had drunk too much schnapps and started singing a song the officials took offense at—probably because it was a parody of a popular Wehrmacht marching song. If it weren't for my and Willi's smooth talking, I doubt we'd have gotten ourselves out of that one. And instead of standing in line for delousing before boarding the train, Alex talked us into pooling our resources to purchase a packet of tea and our own samovar. Though we still have lice, we also have the richest, strongest black tea I've ever tasted.

The train jolts. I cup my hands together and blow, trying to get warmth into my stiff fingers. Bitter air seeps through cracks in the windows. Hans and Willi sit reading across from us, while Alex blows smoke rings into the air.

I reach into the pocket of the overcoat covering my uniform, brushing against the bundle of letters wrapped in twine. All from Annalise.

What will it be like when we're together in Munich again? Our letters have drawn us closer together, paper providing opportunity for conversations we haven't had time for in person.

There hasn't been a day I haven't thought of her, missed her, dreamed about her.

The train wheezes to a stop. A corporal strides down the crowded aisle, uniform pressed, boots gleaming black. In sharp contrast to us, dirty, unshaven, Alex's boots crusty with Russian mud. Not to mention the lice.

"You're free to disembark. We've a wait ahead of us." His tone is crisp.

The men begin to stir, and we file off the train. Outside, the sun is startlingly bright, the cold biting. I tug my collar up around my chin. Train tracks stretch across the flat landscape, endless as the sky.

"Look at them." Hans's voice catches my attention.

I turn. A group of ragged men, dirty and skeletal, are being herded away from the tracks, hammers and picks slung over their shoulders. Two German guards walk in their midst, goading them with rifle butts.

Behind me, Alex draws in a sharp breath.

One of the guards jabs a man with his rifle butt. He falls to the ground with an *oompf.*

Alex's unshaven jaw hardens. A pulse jumps below his eye.

"Get up, you Russian swine." The guard stands over him. Face pressed against the brown grass, the prisoner lets out a low moan. "I said, *get up!*"

It's almost physically painful to watch him struggle to rise. His shoulders protrude like wooden knobs from his loose gray shirt. His hair is patchy, his nose bent at an odd angle, as if recently broken. Another prisoner, a younger, dark-haired man, helps lift him to his feet, and they shuffle toward the shivering huddle of other prisoners, waiting for their next directive.

"I can't take any more!" Alex's eyes flash. "My countrymen . . ." He strides toward the prisoners.

Hans, Willi, and I exchange glances before following.

By the time we reach him, Alex stands beside the injured man, handing him a cigarette and helping him light it. He speaks quietly in Russian, while the man listens, face pale.

A few of the other prisoners cast longing gazes toward the lit cigarette. I walk over to one—the younger man who helped his friend stand—and pull a cigarette from my coat. I hold it out, an offering.

His eyes burn into me like coals. Breaths cloud from his cracked lips. I expect him to refuse. Then slowly, he reaches out.

I offer him a light, and he puts the cigarette to his lips with a slow inhale.

One of the guards marches over.

"What do you think you're doing?" His swarthy cheeks redden. Before I can answer, he rips the cigarette from the man's hand and stomps it out with his boot.

"Showing our gratitude for the repair of these tracks by sharing our cigarettes." I keep my tone even. As a sergeant, I outrank this corporal.

"Gratitude to a Russian prisoner of war? Or are you such a *dummkopf* you didn't realize what these were?"

"*Whom* these were, you mean." Alex comes toward us, tone edged in steel. "I believe you mean whom, Corporal."

"I can call these subhuman wretches *anything* I like." The corporal leans forward, teeth gritted. Spittle flies from his mouth and lands on my face. The prisoners watch, motionless, bodies shrunken into themselves.

"Subhuman!" Alex lunges forward. "I'll teach you—"

I have to stop him. This time, we might not be so lucky. The train wheels screech. "Sergeant Schmorell." My voice rises above the fray. I grab the back of Alex's coat, yanking him away from the corporal. "We have a train to catch."

He looks at me, panting, hair falling into his eyes. He nods, swallows. Giving the corporal one last look of disgust, he follows us toward the train. We swing aboard just as the wheels begin to move.

The clacking of the train's gears fills my ears as we move down the crowded aisle to our seats. Sweat slides down my back despite the cold air. Alex sits heavily beside me, refusing to meet my gaze. He'll thank me later.

I glance out the begrimed window at the group of prisoners still guarded by the corporal. They pass from view. I close my eyes, leaning my head against the hard back of the seat, willing rest to come. To pass the time in sleep until we reach Munich.

Munich, the word floats through my semi-consciousness as I drift off. Munich. And Annalise.

CHAPTER TWENTY-FOUR

Sophie
November 7, 1942
Ulm

ALL DAY, INGE, LISL, and I have been making ready for Hans's arrival. The heavenly aroma of sauerbraten wafts through the house, mingling with that of fresh-baked *kuchen*, ration coupons saved for just this occasion.

My stint at the armaments factory ended in late September, and in a few days, Hans and I will travel to Munich to move into a new apartment on Franz-Josef-Straße for the winter semester.

I should be overjoyed. Sometimes, I wonder what's wrong with me because I'm not. Vater was released from prison after serving half of his four-month sentence. Hans, Werner, and Fritz wrote clemency letters, which, coming from three Wehrmacht soldiers, impressed the authorities. Vater is thinner, gray threading his hair more liberally than before, but the external changes aren't the most startling. Despite how he puts up a front around Mutter, his spirit has been broken. Deemed politically unreliable, he's no longer able to run his business, and though he can still work as a bookkeeper, our financial situation looks bleak. Eugen Grimminger, Vater's close friend, did his best to manage the firm in his absence. But Eugen's wife is Jewish, and thus, their own future hangs under a cloud of uncertainty.

I continue to write to Fritz, the volume of our letters vacillating by will of the army post. It seems a lifetime since our time in Munich, ages since his lips last pressed against mine.

I can't put my feelings for Fritz in a box and label them. If only life were so simple. If only love were. It would be easier if the distance between us were spanned instead of yawning wider, if the secrets of resistance didn't lie between us.

I want to believe in something better, brighter for the two of us. Once I did. But hope has become something I no longer trust.

The news from the front grows grimmer with the approach of winter (where are our German victories now?). The battle for Stalingrad grinds on, and from the BBC, we've learned of Field Marshal Rommel's retreat in North Africa at El-Alamein. Fritz writes candidly of the horror he's witnessed, millions of soldiers on both sides consumed with mutually killing one another. War makes animals out of the best of men. I can't help but wonder who Fritz will have become if . . . when he comes home.

A knock sounds on the door to my bedroom.

"Come in." I call, doing up the buttons of my navy dress.

Inge pokes her head inside.

"We're all downstairs. Hans should be here any minute." A sparkle glimmers in her eyes, overtaking the weariness. With Mutter's ill health, capable Inge shoulders much of the household burdens.

"I'm just changing." I slide my arms into my gray cable knit sweater and follow Inge downstairs. The family is gathered in the parlor—Vater beside Mutter on the sofa, Lisl in the armchair opposite. I perch on the edge of Lisl's armchair, while Inge heads in the direction of the kitchen to check on the evening meal. The carved wall clock chips away the hour. Almost seven.

The final moments are always the hardest. Russia will have changed Hans. What course will our work with the leaflets take now? No matter what my brother decides, I can't return to the old ways of doing nothing.

A knock sounds on the front door. I jump up.

"I'll get it." I race into the hall, Vater's booming laughter in my wake. I unlock and throw open the door, bringing a gust of chilly air into the foyer.

Hans stands outside, wearing his uniform, the darkness a silhouette behind him. He drops his suitcases. I take him in, gaze seeking, anxious. A smile broadens his lips, bringing an answering one to mine.

He pulls me into an embrace, and I press my cheek against the cold wool of his jacket. I've missed him. Our late-night talks, his half grin when he's laughing at his own private joke, the strength of our shared ideals.

When I draw away, I read the answer to my question written in his eyes.

Once in Munich, our resistance will begin again.

Annalise
November 16, 1942
Munich

It's been 116 days since I bid farewell to Kirk at the Ostbahnhof—116 days of aching loneliness, questions winging through my mind (is he thinking of me as much as I'm thinking of him?), letters bridging the space between us, 116 days of wondering if my heart will still be as twined with his when the last one has elapsed. Now I find that it is so.

Standing on the corner of Franz-Josef-Straße, I check my reflection in my compact mirror. My hair hangs in soft curls, reaching to just above my shoulders. My eyes are wide in my pale face, and a hint of lipstick brushes my lips. I'm wearing a double-breasted black wool coat over a white blouse with tiny black polka dots and a burgundy skirt—clothes I purchased in Berlin.

I admit my sole purpose in buying new clothes was to look nice for him. Our intimacy has deepened through letters, but I can't help but think the Annalise of reality differs sadly from the Annalise of letters. In letters, it's easier to modulate oneself, control the picture presented. Reality is . . . well, reality. I don't know if I could endure the distance, the disappointment if the new dimensions to our relationship fail to carry over.

I tuck the compact in my satchel, heels clicking as I walk down the street. Air raids have scarred Munich, but Franz-Josef-Straße remains untouched. I go through the narrow alley, around back to the stucco garden house, and press the bell.

A few minutes later, the door opens. Sophie stands inside. She breaks into a smile, one that crinkles her eyes and lights up her whole face.

"Sophie!"

"How good it is to see you." She closes the door and pulls me into an embrace. I hug her tightly back.

"Someone's been shopping in Berlin." She grins, looking me up and down. Sophie is wearing her old cable knit sweater, paired with a brown skirt. Her hair is pinned as she always wears it, right side pulled back with a bobby pin, the rest hanging straight, brushing her jawbone. She looks as simple and sensible as always. Which reminds me . . .

I rummage through my satchel. "I brought you something." I pass over a parcel wrapped in brown paper. "An early Christmas present."

"Oh, Annalise." Sophie takes the package and unties the string. The wrapping falls to the floor, as she holds up a burgundy sweater. She gasps. "It's beautiful." She runs a hand over the soft knitted fabric.

"I thought the color would look nice on you. I hope it fits."

She holds the sweater to herself, hair falling into her face as she looks down at it. "It's perfect. Might even make me look fashionable." She smiles again. "Danke, Annalise."

Voices sound from somewhere in the house. My heart trips as I try to discern the cadences. "Is everyone else here?" I take off my coat and hang it on a hook alongside other coats and scarves. Two bicycles lean against the wall next to a standing hat rack.

"Hans, Alex, and Willi have been here for hours. I told them to make themselves sandwiches for dinner, because I certainly wasn't going to cook for them. I did enough of that in Ulm." She laughs, bending to pick up the wrapping paper.

"What about Kirk?" I try to sound casual, but a renegade flush rises in my cheeks.

"Not yet." Her knowing grin says she sees right through my subterfuge. "I don't know why. It's not like him"—the bell rings and both of our gazes swing to the door—"to be late." She pauses. "I'm going to join the others. Why don't you answer the door?" Then she's gone, the sweater in her arms, footsteps receding up the stairs.

The bell sounds again. I stare at the door, throat dry.

I'm not ready for this. For so long, I've waited for it. Now that it's here, I'm scared and unsure again. Will we disappoint each other? Will he find me changed since we last met, and if so, for the better?

I turn, about to call Sophie back.

Nein, Annalise. You can do this.

Squaring my shoulders, I close my fingers around the knob. The door opens.

Kirk stands on the stoop, wearing a brown overcoat, hair slicked back.

One look at him is all it takes. I can barely think, scarcely breathe, my thoughts reduced to three words. A single refrain.

Kirk is here. Kirk is here.

He smiles. It's a little crooked around the edges as if he's nervous too.

"Please, come in." I step aside, wincing at my too-polite words. He walks past me, and it's our first meeting at Hans's apartment all over again. I'm lost in the scents of clean soap, something masculine. His warmth radiates through me for a too-brief instant.

We face each other in the semi-lit entryway. My bare arms prickle in the lingering cold.

"You look . . . you look . . ." He clears his throat. A hint of red stains his cheekbones. "I've missed you, Annalise."

Longing seizes in my chest, his words all but my undoing. In this moment, my fiercest wish is for his arms to come around me, to lean into the solid strength of him. All the loneliness, the vacant weeks of missing him come flooding back. Every hour passed as if it were a day, every week, a lifetime. Now he's here, and all I want to do is hold him and be held by him.

"I've missed you too." I inhale through parted lips. Waiting. Hoping for him to take a step closer.

Is he battling the same emotions? There's only half a meter between us. How easy it would be for one of us to cross it.

He draws a sharp breath, runs a hand along his clean-shaven jaw. Looks away. I brush my damp palms against my skirt.

When he looks up, he's smiling again. "Come." He holds out his hand to me. I clasp mine in his, our fingers closing around each other's. "Let's join the others."

CHAPTER TWENTY-FIVE

Kirk
November 18, 1942

TWO NIGHTS AGO, WE talked and laughed, brimming with the effervesce of old friends coming together again. I tried and failed to keep from looking at Annalise, the light of her eyes, her softly curling hair, the wide abandonment of her smile as she laughed at one of Alex's stories.

Seeing her again made me realize how deeply and dangerously I've come to care for her. In the midst of a resistance more dangerous than war is not the time to give your heart away.

But the heart, in all its caprices, makes no allowances for time or place.

We reopen Eickemeyer's studio and settle in for long hours of discussion. Hans has invited Willi to join our work, and I'm glad of it. We need his quiet steadiness. He lent much of it in Russia, a tempering contrast to Hans and Alex.

"We must join forces with the wider resistance movement." Hans paces back and forth, gesturing with the cigarette in his right hand. Perched on a crate, Sophie looks up at her brother. "Mailing leaflets to random names out of a telephone directory is all well and good, but it isn't enough."

"We need to expand our reach to other cities." Willi props his chin in his hand. He sits at the scarred wood table, across from me. "I have friends in Saarbrücken and Bonn who might be willing to start a group of their own."

Hans nods. "That's a start. Come on, what else? Shurik, why don't you tell them?"

Beside me, Alex folds both arms on the table, leaning forward. "My friend Lilo says she can put us in touch with Falk Harnack."

"Arvid Harnack's brother?" While in Russia, we managed to listen to a few foreign broadcasts on Willi's portable radio. Over the crackling airwaves, we heard of Arvid Harnack's arrest, along with that of his wife Mildred, an American-born university lecturer. They, along with others, had been seized in a Gestapo action against the resistance group known as *Die Rote Kapelle.* The Red Orchestra. Hearing of the existence of a widespread resistance network thrilled us, especially Hans. One of the Red Orchestra's leaders was an oberleutnant in the Air Ministry, proof that others in Germany—even among the highest ranks of the military—believe in the overthrow of the Reich enough to risk their lives for it.

Alex nods. "Lilo's engaged to Falk. She says she can arrange a meeting. His unit is stationed at Chemnitz."

"Do you think Falk Harnack has contacts in the wider resistance?" Traute stands behind Sophie, arms folded.

"Lilo assures me he does," Alex replies. "She says he'll meet us, if we'll risk the journey."

Hans inhales a drag of his cigarette. "However much or little he knows, it's imperative we broaden our horizons if we hope to have any real effect. But the Gestapo and military police are cracking down, searching trains, and checking papers. We don't have passes or travel permits. If we're caught, we'll be charged with desertion."

His words sink into the room. Sophie's brow furrows. Annalise glances at me. Our eyes meet. I offer her a slight smile. She looks away without returning it.

Our work comes with risks too numerous to name. The opportunity to meet with a man like Falk Harnack may not come a second time.

"I'm willing to chance it," I say.

Alex nods. "You know I'm in."

"It's settled then." Hans looks between us. "Shurik, Kirk, and I will meet Harnack at Chemnitz. Shurik, you're in charge of making arrangements with Lilo and Harnack."

Alex nods.

Hans pinches the bridge of his nose, still pacing. "We'll need funds if we're to increase production. All of us can contribute, but our allowances won't cover everything."

"I've asked Fritz for a loan," Sophie says quietly. "I know he'll send me the money."

"I can write my vater." From her seat on a crate, Annalise looks to Hans. "I'll say I need it for living expenses."

Hans gives her a long look. Since she's joined us, slipping into our circle like she's always belonged, it's been easy to forget who her vater is.

Annalise, though, never forgets. The rest of us keep our work secret from our families for their safety, not because they'd disown us if they knew. In joining us, Annalise has turned aside from ever fully being a part of her family again. As well as accepting the danger to herself, she's dealt with this loss too. It makes me even prouder of her, the woman she's become.

"That's a good idea." I nod, smile. "Everything helps."

She gives me a grateful look.

"Traute?"

Traute's gaze meets Hans's.

"Didn't you say your uncle in Vienna is in the wholesale office supply business?"

She nods.

"We need a duplicating machine. A bigger one."

Traute doesn't hesitate. "I'll go to Vienna and see what I can do."

Hans looks at Traute, admiration in his eyes. "Danke."

"I'll give my aunt our leaflets too and take some to Hamburg when I'm there next. There are already groups in the city meeting at bookshops and cafés, discussing ways to take action. I've friends who regularly attend the meetings. They'd be eager to help."

"I'll rely on you to establish contact." Hans flashes Traute a quick smile. "Let me see, what else? We'll need someone in charge of our finances, recording amounts received and the names of those who make a donation, even if they don't know what they're donating to. That way, after this is all over, we can repay our debts."

"I can do that," Sophie says quickly.

"Great. After we talk to Harnack, we'll have a better idea of how to proceed." Hans's eyes glimmer as he looks at each of us. Willi watches him thoughtfully. Alex leans forward, collar unbuttoned, pipe in his mouth. "Harnack may doubt many things about us, but our determination won't be one of them."

Kirk
November 28, 1942
Chemnitz, Germany

"Do you see him?" I glance at Hans, voice cut to a whisper.

Hans shakes his head. "Not yet."

The three of us stand outside the gates cordoning off the barracks and military camp. Two sentries guard the entrance, and every so often, a uniformed soldier comes in or goes out. None of them is Falk Harnack.

I shove my hands into my pockets, fingers stiff with cold, every sense on alert. The trip was an agony, sitting motionless on the hard bench seat of the train, willing ourselves to be invisible, our faces blank as military police walked the aisle checking papers at random. Each time I thought: *This is it. We're going to be caught and charged with desertion.* But each time, by some miracle, they passed us by.

"How long should we wait?" Alex's cheeks are ruddy with cold. None of us are in uniform. That alone brings us, as men of military age, under suspicion.

Hans's jaw tightens. "As long as we have to."

The sky is winter gray. One of the sentries stomps booted feet, breath clouding like cigarette smoke from his pale lips.

The gates swing open. A tall man strides past the guards with the briefest of nods. A wool overcoat is slung over his uniformed shoulders like a cloak. His polished black boots crunch on the frozen ground as he heads toward us.

"Hans Scholl?"

"*Ja.*" Hans steps forward. "Corporal Harnack?"

The tall man nods.

"It's good to finally meet you."

"Likewise." The men grip hands. "Come." Harnack gestures toward the road. "I've reserved a room at the Sächsischer Hof."

We say little as we walk down the frosted road toward the city of Chemnitz. Harnack hails a taxi on the outskirts of the city, and we ride the rest of the way to the hotel. Crammed into the back seat, elbows and knees poking into each other, the four of us exchange cautious glances. The interior of the taxi is rank from its previous occupants, and the driver keeps sniffing and wiping a hand beneath his dripping nose.

Finally we pull up to the hotel and exit the taxi. Our boots sound staccato on the tile floor as we enter the lobby. Once the Sächsischer Hof must have been the epitome of nineteenth-century grandeur. Now the lobby's furnishing shows wear marks, and muddy footprints track across the checkered tile.

Harnack registers at the front desk (under an assumed name, of course). We climb carpeted stairs and walk down a deserted hall. At room 204, Harnack unlocks the door. One by one, we enter the darkened room.

Harnack flips on the light. The bulb flickers, then burns bright. Blackout curtains cover the only window. Harnack hangs his coat on a wall hook, then removes his cap and sets it on the low table in front of the sofa. One by one, he tugs off his gloves and places them next to the hat. The three of us stand clustered near the door.

Slowly, he turns. And for the first time really looks at us, pale blue gaze piercing.

"So you made it undetected." A slight smile flits across his chiseled face.

Hans nods. "We managed to escape detection, sir." Though only a few years older than us and beneath us in rank, Harnack commands respect.

"Clever evasion or beginner's luck?" Harnack shrugs. "Since I wasn't there, I couldn't say."

Hans stiffens.

Harnack withdraws a silver case from his pocket, pulls out a cigarette, and taps it against the edge of the case. He takes a seat on the sofa. A gilded mirror with a crack in it hangs on the wall above the sofa, capturing Harnack's reflection.

"Take off your things and have a seat." He gestures to the sofa. "I didn't expect you to bring a crowd, Scholl."

The three of us remove our outerwear and hang it on the wall hooks.

"Alexander Schmorell. Pleasure to make your acquaintance." Alex sticks out his hand, which Harnack shakes, cigarette in his mouth.

"Kirk Hoffmann. It's an honor to meet you." When Harnack grasps my hand, both his grip and gaze take my measure.

Alex and I move toward the sofa and sit on opposite ends, Harnack between us. Hans remains standing, hands in his pockets.

"All of you are involved in this leafleting campaign?"

We nod.

Harnack takes a slow drag of the cigarette.

"As for our leaflets, we thought you might take a look." Hans withdraws folded copies of our four leaflets from the inner pocket of his suit coat. He passes them to Harnack.

Harnack unfolds one and smooths it across his knee.

It takes twenty minutes for Harnack to read the leaflets. We watch him, collectively holding our breath. We've poured our lifeblood into those pages. They represent hours of sleepless nights, debates, probing for just the right word.

Hans flexes his fingers, gaze never leaving Harnack. I shift in my seat. Every so often, Harnack mutters something indistinct, scanning the words and smoking his cigarette, a deep furrow knitting his brow.

Finally, he looks up, cigarette long since burned to a nub, ashes scattering the rug.

"Well?" Alex leans forward.

Harnack spreads out the leaflets on the low table. "Their style is academic, philosophical, and too florid to have any impact on the general population. It's blatantly obvious this is the work of privileged intellectuals with little knowledge of how to influence the working man." He glances up. "The realities of resistance are much harder in practice than in theory. It's useless to approach any of it with idealism."

Alex frowns. "You think that's what we've done?"

"Not entirely. But you've a great deal to learn if you hope to have any effect beyond academic circles."

Harnack's words sting. But there's more at stake here than our pride. Harnack is right. We're middle-class university students. Our writing reflects that.

"Very well." Hans crosses to stand beside the sofa. "Please, go on."

For an hour, Harnack goes over the leaflets one by one. Not once does he mince words, but he does point to several sections where we've succeeded in conveying our point in a succinct and convincing way. We don't wince at his criticisms, nor beam at his praises. We simply listen and absorb.

"Do you think if we produce new material we have a chance?" Alex asks when Harnack has laid the fourth leaflet aside and lit a fresh cigarette.

"A chance at what, precisely?"

"At doing something of value for the resistance." I speak up, immediately regretting how eager I sound.

Harnack gives a soft laugh. "Perhaps it's time I told you something of the resistance."

"I wish you would." Hans's tone is terse, but there's no mistaking the flash of excitement in his eyes. Harnack gives a little smile, a shake of his head.

"I presume you know there's a wider movement in Germany."

"Vaguely," Hans says. "We've heard the foreign broadcasts about the Red Orchestra. The arrests of your brother and the others."

A shadow falls on Harnack's face. He puts the cigarette to his lips, inhales. "What we're seeking is a united force. Where all are of one accord, if not on everything, at least on our main aims and goals. If we're scattered, each smaller group with their own objectives, none of us will accomplish much of significance. Everyone must think of themselves as part of one group, not as Communists, or Social Democrats, or conservatives. Our aim must be threefold—assassinate Hitler, overthrow the government, and come to an agreement of peace with the Allies."

I draw in a sharp breath.

For so long, we've wondered about the resistance beyond our circle in Munich. Now, we have evidence it exists from the lips of a man who's part of it.

"A military group is making preparations for a coup."

"What can we do?" Hans sits on the edge of the low table, facing Harnack. "How can we make contact?"

Ash falls from Harnack's cigarette. A single set of footfalls sounds in the corridor. Harnack freezes, still until they fade.

"I can put you in touch with people in Berlin." He meets Hans's gaze. "It'll take time to arrange. When I know more, we'll schedule a meeting."

We talk long into the night, the hours flying by—midnight, one, two. We discuss what the new government might look like, the roles we might play.

"I intend to take up politics after the war." Hans props his elbows on his knees. "It's something I've been thinking about for a long time."

"We'll need good men like you," Harnack says, his brief nod greater affirmation than a string of words from someone else.

As we shrug into our coats to make the trek through the wintery streets to the station, I pull Harnack aside.

"Your brother and his wife?" Harnack's underlying darkness has not escaped my notice. He's not only a contact in the resistance, but a man fearing the fate of those he loves dearly. The mere act of meeting with us attests to his incredible bravery and his urgency for as many voices as possible to rise in protest so his family's sacrifice will not be in vain.

Harnack's face is pale and haggard in the dim light. "They're to stand trial in the next few weeks." He glances away, quick. "I wish I could say they can expect justice." He reaches out, clasps my hand, grip tight. No longer is his gaze that of an assured leader instructing those below him, but of a man cracking beneath unbearable strain. Throat jerking, Harnack swallows. "But I no longer delude myself."

CHAPTER TWENTY-SIX

Annalise
November 30, 1942
Munich

On a cold Monday evening, I answer a knock at my apartment door. Kirk stands outside.

"Hey." He gives a crooked grin.

"Hello." I try unsuccessfully to hide my answering smile. "Come in." Warmth blooms inside me that not even the winter air can dispel. I've just finished dinner and am in the process of washing the dishes. An apron covers my woolen dress, and my hair is damp from where I pushed it behind my ear with soapy hands. Schoolbooks clutter the table, and two of my blouses and some towels hang on a makeshift clothesline stretched across the room.

"Smells good in here." He takes off his overcoat and leaves his shoes by the door.

"It smells like potato pancakes." I head into the kitchen and plunge the remaining dishes into the rinse water. I'm so focused on cleaning the mess I don't see him approach until I look up and find him next to me, just behind my shoulder.

"I like potato pancakes."

"Maybe I'll make you some sometime." I pile clean silverware onto a towel.

A smile crinkles the corners of his eyes. "I'd like yours even more."

"Any particular reason you came over?" I decide to let the dishes air dry, and I wipe my damp hands on my apron, turning to face him. Kirk's presence in my kitchen makes the space shrink, becoming a little island of two. But instead of disquieting me, it makes me want to lean in. Draw nearer, shrinking the space all the more.

"I just missed you." We're standing close enough our feet almost touch. Close enough I can smell the fragrance of peppermint on his breath.

My heart skips a beat. Twice now, he's said, "I missed you." No one has ever told me that before. Mutter feels it, no doubt, but what she misses is the security and strength I bring, not me. Kirk's words are intimate, conjuring images of me standing on tiptoe, the worn fabric of his shirt fisted in my hands, his mouth slowly brushing mine. My cheeks warm. "Did Hans and Alex catch the train to Stuttgart?" My words are rushed, a cover-up for my thoughts.

He nods. "They're going to talk to Hans's friend Eugen Grimminger about our need for funds. After our meeting with Harnack, everything seems to be falling into place."

"It was really something, wasn't it?"

Kirk's gaze shines. "I wish you could've been there. Listening to him talk about plans for a new government . . . it made me believe it could really happen. Think of it. We could be proud of our leaders instead of ashamed. A restoration of democracy and equality. For everyone, not just so-called Aryans."

I smile into his eyes. "What office will you hold in this new government?"

"Something high-sounding, of course." He laughs. "With my own private study. You'll have to make an appointment to see me."

I cross my arms. "Oh, I will, will I?"

"Absolutely. No barging in unannounced."

"You mean like you just did?"

"That's called a friendly visit." We're teasing, laughing, the distance between us whittling down to almost nothing. How easy it would be to bridge it altogether, to take one step closer and wrap my arms around him, heartbeat to heartbeat.

His gaze darkens, looking into mine. His breath brushes my cheek.

A knock sounds on the door. We both start, putting space between us. I cross the room, heart a dull thudding in my ears.

I walk into the front room and open the door. My landlady stands outside. "Telephone, Fräulein Brandt."

"Danke." I glance at Kirk, now standing in the middle of the front room. My landlady looks between the two of us, gaze sharpening, as if we've been up to something disreputable.

If kissing is disreputable, give us another minute and we might have satisfied you.

Faint red tinges Kirk's cheekbones at her knowing look. "I should . . . um, be going too." He moves to grab his coat and shoes.

He may be a leader in our underground resistance, but give him a meddling old lady and he turns into the shy pastor's son. I bite back a smile.

"I'll be downstairs," I say. "This shouldn't take long."

Kirk nods. I follow her downstairs to the telephone and wait until she disappears into her apartment before picking it up.

"Hello." I cradle the mouthpiece beneath my chin, glancing over my shoulder. Kirk comes down the stairs.

"Annalise." Mutter's voice crackles across the line, followed by a heaving sound.

A twist of alarm starts in my stomach. "Mutter, are you there? Are you all right?"

Kirk stops on the bottom step. His gaze finds mine. Inexplicably, I cling to it.

More heaving, followed by muffled sobs.

My fingers tighten around the mouthpiece. "Mutter, can you hear me?" I make my voice firm. "I need you to tell me what's the matter. What's going on?"

"Your . . . brother . . ." Sobs garble her words.

God help me, I don't want to hear what comes next. I don't want to . . . I don't—

"We just . . . received word. Horst was killed in action."

⌐

December 9, 1942
Berlin

There is no memorial service for Horst Rudolf Brandt. Only a black cross next to his name in the newspaper serves to mark his death. Vater doesn't return from the front, nor does he do anything other than pen a letter to his wife: *Our son died honorably for a glorious cause. His death should make us proud and urge us onward in the work of obliterating all the Fatherland's enemies.*

I returned to Berlin to spend a week at home. Mutter scarcely leaves her room, intermittently weeping and staring out the window. Heinz has been sent away to a training camp for an elite branch of the Hitler Youth. Albert rarely speaks, attending school and Hitler Youth meetings as if in a daze, returning home and spending hours sitting on the upstairs landing, arms folded, eyes too serious for a boy so young. Loss is hard to reckon with at his age. At any age, even in a world where death announcements fill newspapers in endless lines of stark type. Each line, a life.

Snow spits upon Berlin with pelting flakes. I drift through the house, a boat unmoored, trying to coax Mutter into rallying, cooking her favorites, suggesting we visit friends, brushing her tangled hair and plaiting it into her usual upswept braids.

It's early morning, barely six, and I'm taking the train back to Munich today. I can't deny my relief. I sit upright in bed, propped against pillows, arms hugged around my knees. Blackout curtains wrap the room in darkness.

I miss my brother. Not the man he's been these past years, hardened under Vater's tutelage, breathing party ideology like air. Nein. That man has been dead to me a long time, his life leached out as "Das Lied der Deutschen" played.

I miss the big brother who called me Lisi and lifted me atop his wide shoulders so I could touch the sparkly star on top of our Christmas tree.

The freckles on his nose. His high laughter as he ran through the park with his new kite, me just behind, our steps faster and faster until the kite sailed airborne on the autumn wind. We both cheered. Those cheers, so full of innocent jubilance, echo in my ears even now.

They were to be the last.

Four months later, our laughter was replaced with a roar of *Sieg Heils* as Hitler became chancellor. Horst became obsessed with Germany's rising future and his place in it. There were no more kites, smiles, or Christmas-tree moments.

It's too late now. My brother's laughter is silenced.

Tears slide down my cheeks in the darkness, a long-held back release. I'm not like Sophie, with her loving family, nor Kirk with his. Alex has parents who adore him, and Christl's wife and children look at him as if his were the hands that hung the moon.

I'm alone. Empty, aching. Alone.

"God goes with us everywhere."

Oh, Kirk. I clamp my hand to my mouth, hot tightness knotting my throat. I wish I had faith like my friends. All of them seem to possess a steadfast strength outside themselves, to have, in spite of everything, hope.

During summer break, I paged through the Bible, my mind awakened to stories I'd never heard. While I read, I could never eliminate Vater's scoffing voice.

"The Bible is full of lies. God? There is none."

Then I remembered Kirk's letters.

God waits for us with arms outstretched. It's up to us to run into them and choose to remain there, through joys and hardships alike. His is a love great enough to encompass this life and the one to come. There's a future far outlasting earth in heaven, and it is free and beautiful and without pain.

Life is a fraying thread that could snap at any moment. I honestly don't know if this time next year I'll be alive. My brother's death—strong, invincible Horst—has painted this reality on a canvas of vivid color. Air raids decimate German cities weekly, leaving loss and destruction in their wake.

Loss. Always, so much loss.

I wish I felt something, a heavenly touch to affirm Kirk's words. Right now, though, I'm just broken and scared, facing an unknown future.

I don't want to be alone anymore. But how can I escape it? We are born, we live, and we die alone. Thus, I've always believed, Vater's words a reinforcing echo.

There has to be more. Or else, what is the purpose in this vain, mad thing called life? We thirst for happiness, yet so often are handed misery. If there's nothing beyond this earth, then what's the point in going on?

There is none.

What is faith, anyway? An emotion, a belief, a combination of the two? I wish I knew, but I don't. All I know is I don't want to live like this anymore, my own strength the only thing holding me up, the span of this life the measure of my existence.

With shaking fingers I form the sign of the cross. Somehow, though I'm not Catholic, it seems right to do in the moment.

"God." My voice is choked, wrested from the raw, desperate places inside. "If You're really there . . ." A sob shudders out. "I want to belong to You. I . . . don't want to be alone anymore. I'm sorry I've never believed in You. Please . . . save me . . ."

When I open my eyes, I draw in a long breath. Though I'm still bone-weary, the tension in my chest has lessened for the first time since Mutter's telephone call. Perhaps that in and of itself is a miracle.

I wash and dress, pick up my suitcase, and leave my bedroom. The house is cold and empty, my steps an echo. I pass my brothers' rooms, a row of three closed doors. Like their lives, cut off from mine.

I stop beside my parents' door and turn the knob. It creaks softly open.

Mutter sits by the window, clad in a nightdress and shawl, bare feet scarcely touching the floor. Both garments seem to swallow her, as if loss stole her flesh, along with her will. She stares out onto the street, the blackout curtain pulled away. The sky is pewter.

"Mutter." I set down my suitcase. "It's Annalise." I kneel beside her chair.

She turns, looking at me with eyes that seem a void in her pale face. "Annalise." The word emerges reedy from her cracked lips.

I shouldn't leave. But I can't bear to stay, to leave our work with the leaflets and the university behind. It will only be for a few more months anyway. Then the winter semester will end, signaling the close of my time in Munich, and I'll . . . what, return home for good? I don't know yet, but I'll find some way to care for Mutter regardless. In the meantime, our housekeeper is a capable woman, kind even. She can be trusted to care for Mutter in my absence.

"I'm leaving today." I try for an encouraging smile. "I have to go back to Munich to finish school."

She nods, but I'm not sure she really hears me.

"Will you be all right?"

Another nod.

"It won't be much longer. In a few months, I'll be home. I promise." I smile again. "We can go visit Tante Grete in the country. Would you like that?"

No response.

"You can call me anytime." I pull her into an embrace. As if my touch awakens something inside her, she puts her arms around me, hugging me with a strength that belies her brittle exterior. In that moment, she's my mutti again. Mutti, whose laughter used to echo through our little apartment before Vater's striving moved us away, who wiped my forehead with a cool cloth when I was feverish, whispering soothing words, and who, every day before I left for school, would always wrap me in a hug before I hurried out the door.

I pull away and look into her eyes, framing the side of her face with one hand. A spark flickers through her gaze.

"I love you." I press a kiss to her cheek. Her skin is like tissue paper. She doesn't respond.

I stand and turn toward the door, picking up my suitcase. There, I pause.

Framed by the gray light of dawn, gaze toward the window again, she looks old, tired, and very alone.

⌁

Kirk
December 11, 1942
Munich

Wrapped in coats and scarves, boots slipping on the slick cobblestones, Annalise and I walk toward her apartment, the sky a canvas of star-studded pitch. Annalise has her hands in her coat pockets, and she keeps her gaze on the frost-glossed cobblestones as if unsure of her footing.

I have so many questions I want to ask about her time in Berlin, her brother's loss and how she is bearing up beneath it, but broaching them doesn't seem right. So I wait and walk beside her, our shoulders almost brushing, my hand at the ready to steady her if she slips.

We reach an intersection just as a car drives past, headlights off. Our steps pause and my gaze follows the car. One can never be too cautious when traveling on foot in these days of blackout and frequent accidents.

"Look."

I turn. Annalise points at the sky, head tipped back.

"The stars. Look at them."

I look into the sky, cold air tingling my cheeks, the warmth of her shoulder brushing mine. Countless pinpricks of light, some brighter than others, are scattered across the darkness like little diamond chips. "Beautiful, aren't they?"

"We all see the same stars." Her words are so soft I almost don't catch them.

"What?"

She meets my eyes, face half shadowed. "We all see the same stars. It doesn't matter whether we're a servant of the Reich or an enemy, Jewish or Gentile. All of us look up at the same night sky and see the same stars."

"God's view of equality, right there."

"No matter how wrong the world is or how hard it is to live in it, if it's a clear night, we know there will be stars." She tilts her head. "Maybe that's faith. Knowing that no matter how dark it seems, God's light is there, even if we can't always see it."

Her words give me pause, but in a good way. She's spoken of faith in the months since summer vacation, but never with this note in her voice. Almost . . . peaceful.

Unable to resist, I slip an arm around her shoulders, and we continue down the street. "That doesn't sound like the Annalise I used to know."

She nods. "I know. Something's changed. Nein, not something." She leans closer into my side as we walk. "Everything. God is real, Kirk. He's real, and I believe in Him. I've given my life to Him." Her eyes shine as she looks up at me.

"What? Annalise . . ." My words trip over each other. "That's . . . that's the best news I've had in a very, very long time." A grin stretches my cheeks, matching the one on her lips. "How did it happen?"

"It started over the summer, with your letters." She laughs. "The whole thing is practically your fault." Then her expression turns serious. "I was miserable in Berlin. The family I used to have, even the family I thought I had six months ago, they're gone. Not just my brother, but all of them. I was lonely and scared and I thought a lot about life. The point of it all. I've been reading the Bible, and well, it has to be true. If it isn't, then there's no purpose in life at all. And I've never believed that." She lifts her face toward the sky as we walk. "If there's evil, there has to be good, somewhere. If there's hatred, there has to be love. If not from mortals, than surely from God."

I nod, her words sinking deep inside, overwhelmed by God's goodness. I've prayed for her salvation but knew that to push her beyond our letters and natural, not forced conversations, would only drive her away.

"There couldn't be a greater form of it than Christ's sacrifice on the cross." I meet her gaze. "My vater always says it's 'love too pure for human language to describe, a gift that begs to be encompassed by all mankind.'"

We reach her apartment and climb the steps. Her back pressed against the door, she faces me, cheeks pink with cold, her eyes sparkling like stars themselves. "I'd like to meet your vater."

"He'd like to meet you too." I smile, her sweet nearness warming me until I no longer notice the cold, the street around us, or anything except the woman before me.

Her eyes widen. "You really think so?"

"I know he would. He's said so."

She gasps. "You told him about me?"

I shrug, grinning. "How could I help but tell him about someone as wonderful as you?"

She looks down, lips pressed together as if to hide a smile. "If I had a family like yours, I'd tell them about you too." Her words are little more than a breath, all but stealing my restraint. A moment of her lips against mine. One soft, glorious kiss.

But tonight isn't the right time. Not on the steps of her apartment in the bitter night air, when any stranger could walk by. I would never kiss her without her consent, and I could not ask for it unless I followed with the right words. *I love you. Will you marry me?*

More than anything, I want to say them.

Yet I do not.

Reluctantly, I take a step back, putting distance between us, cold dousing me that has nothing to do with temperature. I make myself smile. "Well, I suppose I should say good night then."

A look of confusion, almost of disappointment, dawns on her features. "Good night," she says quietly, then turns and fumbles with the door.

I walk away, steps quick, head lowered against the cold. My steps have to be quick. If I delay, I might do something crazy. Like turn around, bound up the steps, pound on the door until she opens it, take her in my arms, and kiss her as hungrily as I've ached to do. Just the mental image is enough to make me walk faster.

In the opposite direction.

I should pray for her as she begins this new journey of faith, and I will. Both for her and for myself.

Because with the tension of our work digging below the surface of every move I make, the endless uncertainty of the war, and the near pain it is to be close to her and then leave her, I don't know how much longer I'll be able to do as I've just done and walk away.

CHAPTER TWENTY-SEVEN

Sophie
December 14, 1942
Munich

COAT BUTTONED TIGHT, HANDS shoved in my pockets, I walk briskly toward Lindwurmstraße. It's been snowing on and off all morning. A layer of dirty gray coats everything—the street, the buildings, the sky.

"Who is Gisela Schertling again?" Annalise walks beside me. I'm glad she's with me. I missed her while she was in Berlin, her earnest determination and steady presence at our meetings. Since her return, she's seemed different. Calmer and more driven than ever.

"A girl I know from the labor service. After I left, we exchanged letters on and off. Her vater is a prominent Nazi newspaperman. I wish I hadn't encouraged her when she suggested coming to Munich. I've no doubt she'll expect to be often in our company. She's studying art history, so you'll probably see her in classes."

"Try not to worry." Annalise loops her arm through mine. "We're nothing if not good at maintaining our cover. Besides, you know Hans. Remember how he tried to keep me out of things?"

I nod. We walk in silence for a few minutes.

"Have you had word from Fritz?"

I shake my head. Slush seeps through a hole in my shoe. "Anxiety is like hunger. The longer it gnaws at you, the more used to it you become, though it doesn't make enduring it any easier. He's still somewhere in Russia. You know as well as I how bad things are there."

"If only that little corporal would surrender and pull our boys out while some are still alive," Annalise mutters under her breath.

I nod. But conceding to defeat isn't something the Führer is known for.

"I wish I could tell you he's alive and well. That he hasn't written because he hasn't had time."

"I wish I could tell you I cared as much as I should." I close my cold, cracked hands into fists inside my thin pockets. "But without any word and with how busy we've been, it's easy to . . . forget. That makes me a horrible person, I know."

"The last thing you are is a horrible person, Sophie. You're tired. We all are. God watches over Fritz." Annalise meets my gaze. The startling blue-green of her eyes stands out in her cold-flushed face. "Over all of us."

I stop, facing her on the sidewalk. "Since when did you start talking so confidently of God?"

"Since Berlin." She smiles.

We reach Gisela's apartment and climb the steps. I press the bell. A few minutes later, the door opens. A striking blond wearing a green sweater that clings to her curves stands inside.

"Sophie!" Gisela gives a little laugh, shaking her curls. "How marvelous to see you. Come in, come in."

We hasten inside, stomping slush from our feet. I introduce Annalise, and the three of us make our way upstairs to Gisela's apartment. It's tastefully decorated and cleaner than any student rooms I've been in. Tea things lay spread out on a cloth-covered table. Gisela invites us to take a seat, before sliding into her chair.

"Now, tell me everything." Gisela pours tea into china cups. "You too, Fräulein Brandt. Say . . ." She tilts her head. "Brandt sounds familiar. Are you any relation to . . . ?"

"My vater." Annalise takes the cup Gisela offers her.

"Is that so?" Gisela laughs. "What a coincidence. I'll bet my vati knows yours." She pours her own cup and takes a dainty sip. "So what's it like here?" She leans forward. "It's absolutely terrific to finally be in Munich. You must have all sorts of fun."

"Not really." Warmth from the teacup radiates through my chilled fingers. "We study a lot and go to lectures. We attend concerts sometimes. There's one tomorrow night. You're welcome to join us." A concert. *Ja*, that will be safe. Let her think she's included, just a little. Otherwise, she might get angry, even suspicious.

"Will Hans be there?" Gisela stirs her tea.

"Maybe. His schedule is pretty erratic."

"I so enjoyed meeting him when I spent the weekend with your family." I shrug. "I doubt you'll be seeing him much."

"That's a pity." China clinks as Gisela sets her teacup down. "What are you studying at the university, Fräulein Brandt?"

Gisela and Annalise talk about art, while I sip my tea, half listening.

My life bears little resemblance to the days when Gisela and I met in labor service. Once, we were friends, but I can no longer view her as such.

Now she's yet another person from whom we must hide the true nature of our lives.

I press back a sigh, glancing at Gisela.

Secrets. So many secrets.

$\swarrow$

Kirk
December 15, 1942

Marry me, Annalise.

There is nothing I want more than to speak those words to the woman at my side. In them encompasses what my heart recognizes as truth.

I love her.

In the months we've known each other, I've gone from attraction to mistrust to friendship. During the months in Russia and our reunion in Munich, my feelings have deepened, until it's become as impossible to deny them as it would be to live without breathing.

Neither of us were in a concert-going mood, so she suggested she make good on her promise to cook for me. I sat on her sofa, alternately studying and watching her through the open kitchen door. Warmth from the stove burnished her cheeks, and she hummed softly as she prepared potato pancakes and ersatz meat—cooked rice patties fried in some kind of fat. I set the table while she put the finishing touches on the meal. The flicker of candles between us, we laughed and talked.

Watching her across the table, eyes alight as she laughed at one of my jokes, or chin propped thoughtfully in her palm as she shared about her time in Berlin, only served to seal the truth. One I've wrestled with in prayer, asking for my will to be aligned with His.

I want to marry her. Buy a house in the country after the war and watch our children grow—a girl with her reddish-gold hair and my smile and a boy with my eyes and her laugh. Grow old with her beside me, if the Lord wills we live that long.

How fragile life is. Yet with what tenacity the young cling to its threads.

Nothing is guaranteed. Not in war and not in life. I don't know what the months ahead will bring, if we'll both live to see the end of this war. In ordinary times, I'd court her slowly, savor every moment of the gentle unfolding of our love. These aren't ordinary times. If we don't reach for a future now, one or both of us might regret it later.

Let there be no regrets.

"Hey." I nudge her shoulder. We'd been studying, but somewhere along the way, the books had been laid aside and she fell asleep, head resting on my chest, hand curled beneath her chin. I sat, listening to the sounds of the city pass by as her chest rose and fell with even breaths, my arm around her shoulders.

I don't know how she can sleep. I'm never more wide-awake than when I'm with her.

"Kirk." She blinks sleepily and smiles. "You're still here. I must've fallen asleep." She yawns, her lips parted in an *o*.

"No *must have* about it." I grin, slipping my arm from around her shoulders. "I wanted to talk about Christmas."

She sits up straighter on the sofa, smoothing her hair behind her ears. The candles left on the table wreath the room and her face in a honey glow.

"Christmas? It's coming up, isn't it? I almost forgot." Her brow wrinkles. "Why do you want to talk about that?"

"Have you made plans to go to Berlin?" If she has, I won't press her to stay. Much as I'd miss her, it would be wrong of me to keep her from her family.

She shakes her head. "There will be little Christmas cheer at our house. I figured I'd spare the train fare and stay in Munich. Hans and Sophie, Shurik, everyone, I think, will be with their families. So I'll spend a restful day here with a few good books."

You don't have to spend Christmas alone, Annalise. Spend it with me.

Everything rational inside me says this is the wrong time. Our country is at war. We're resisting a government that will stop at nothing to annihilate its traitors. I have little to offer her in the way of worldly wealth.

This may be the wrong time, but could it somehow be the right one for us?

God help me, I have to try.

I stand, heart pounding and throat dry. While Annalise watches, wide-eyed, I get down on one knee in front of the sofa.

"Kirk . . . what's . . . what are you doing?"

"Spend Christmas with me. Spend every day with me." My voice catches a little as I look into her eyes. "We don't know what the future holds, you know that as well as I. And maybe this isn't the right time, and I'm being irrational. But there's one thing I'm sure of. I love you, Annalise. Marry me. Please. Marry me."

For a long moment, she stares at me. Is it the candlelight, or are those tears in her eyes? "Oh, Kirk." Her smile is sad. "You really are sweet."

I gaze up at her, the tightness in my chest making it hard to breathe. What if, while I've been dreaming of her, all she's been thinking about is our work for the resistance, seeing me as a friend and nothing more? The sudden thought punches me in the gut.

She exhales a long breath. "But this . . . us . . . it's impossible."

"Why?" My voice is hoarse. I gather every ounce of strength, because I want her in my life, however she wants to be, even if it's only as friends. The thought of that being all we ever share shreds me from the inside. I swallow, forcing out the words. "If you don't feel the same, that's . . . I understand. I know this is sudden and I couldn't expect you to—"

She shakes her head, swiping a hand beneath her eyes. "It's not that."

"What then?"

She turns her face away. "I'll always be my vater's daughter," she whispers the words in a voice so low it's scarcely audible.

"That isn't true." I reach for her hands, wrapping mine around them. "That's not all you are."

Slowly, she looks up, so I go on. "You're Annalise. The woman who sees the world in color, and paints the beauty in it. The woman who, whenever she laughs, makes you want to laugh too, just for the sheer joy of being near her. The woman whose heart breaks for her country enough to take action against it. You're kind and caring, and I've never known anyone more stubborn when you set your mind to something." At this, she gives a sound between a sob and a laugh. "Your vater, your family, we'll worry about them later." I pause, taking in her face, the crumpled expression there, as if she's waging an inner war. "I'm afraid too. But I want to spend every hour, every breath I've got, loving you."

She meets my gaze, tears shining on her cheeks. "Do you really mean it?"

"More than anything." I couldn't have spoken wedding vows with more fervency.

"Then *ja*, Kirk Hoffmann." A slow smile spreads across her tear-streaked face. "I would like to marry you. Really, really like to marry you."

"Are you sure?" My voice cracks.

She nods. "*Ja*." A laugh escapes. "I'm sure."

I stand, joining her on the sofa again. We look at each other, hands intertwined. Both of us wear hesitant smiles. Her lips part with gentle breaths.

I lean closer. Her gaze follows me. I cup her cheek. Her skin is so soft it steals my breath.

"May I"—I swallow hard—"kiss you now?"

Her smile deepens. "I was hoping you would."

Slowly, not wanting to hurt or scare or do anything but love her, I press my lips against hers.

Heaven must have dreamt up kissing because I can't imagine anything less ethereal could have conjured this sweetness. Our lips brushing, my hands tangled in the glorious silk of her curls, her hands clutching my shoulders. Tender. Knowing. Perfect.

Annalise.

How long we stay like this is anybody's guess. Love must lengthen time because these few minutes pass like hours.

When finally, regrettably, we draw away, she meets my gaze, hands still on my shoulders. Her eyes glow with joy, but there's a kind of sadness there too. The bitterness of war taints everything. Even something as new and wondrous as this.

"What is it?"

She only shakes her head before wrapping her arms around my shoulders, holding, almost crushing, me to herself, her whisper soft against my hair. "I love you too."

CHAPTER TWENTY-EIGHT

Kirk
December 17, 1942

THINK YOU CAN TAKE your mind off your girl long enough to focus on business?" Alex grins.

I shove his arm and he laughs. "Shut it, Schmorell."

I glance at Hans, expecting some response. But he's lost in thought today, taking long strides, slightly bent forward as if against the wind. Professor Huber has invited us for tea, a kind gesture toward students he also calls friends.

Doubtless he's completely unprepared for what Hans plans to ask him.

We walk faster to keep up with Hans, the cold penetrating our layered outerwear. I barely heed it, thoughts turning as they've done the past two days whenever I've not been occupied with classes, hospital shifts, and resistance work (and often even then), toward the wondrous truth.

In four days, Annalise will become my wife. In a simple civil ceremony, we'll speak vows that will bind us together, come what may.

It seems like a dream too incredible to be real.

But the preparations we've been making during every spare minute confirm how real it is. I'll pay off my lease and move into Annalise's apartment. Our marriage will remain a secret to everyone except my parents and our close circle of friends. Annalise is determined her family must not discover our marriage. "For now," she says. "We'll tell them when the time is right."

I won't argue with her. Though I'm uncomfortable with this concealment on top of everything else, she's doing what she feels she must.

We reach Huber's door, and Hans gives a brisk rap. For a distinguished intellectual, Huber lives in a rundown part of town. Buildings crumble with age, and the close-set street bears the marks of people struggling to make ends meet. A few children wearing clothes too small for their growing bodies play a game of tag amongst the puddles, taking advantage of the weak sunlight.

The door opens.

A girl of about twelve peeps out, regarding us with a curious gaze.

"Hello, Birgit. You remember me. Hans Scholl. I was here before."

She nods. Two long braids dangle down her pinafore. "Are you here to see Vater?"

"We are. He's expecting us."

"Won't you come in then?" She opens the door and shows us where to hang our coats.

We follow Birgit through the Hubers' apartment. The temperature varies only by a few degrees from outdoors until we reach a crowded sitting room where a coal fire crackles in a blackened hearth. Professor Huber sits near the blaze, turning the leaves of a book.

"Your guests are here, Vater." Birgit settles at a table covered with schoolbooks and bends to her work.

"Danke, Birgit." He gives her a fond smile, then rises to greet us, one hand leaning heavily on the back of his chair. "Ah, Hans, Alex, Kirk. Christmas greetings to you all. Please, sit down." He motions to a worn sofa and a kitchen chair that wobbles when I sit.

Frau Huber bustles into the room, little Wolfgang clinging to her apron. With the air of a gracious *hausfrau*, she pours tea and passes around a small plate of *lebkuchen* before leaving the room, Wolfgang in her arms.

I glance at Hans. He drums his fingers on his trouser leg. Slowly, testing, he and Huber begin to discuss politics, but it doesn't take long before their conversation turns into full-out debate. Birgit hunches over her textbooks, a pencil in hand, mouth moving in whispered recitation.

Hans pulls our first two leaflets from his pocket.

"Remember these, Herr Professor?" He passes the leaflets into Huber's hands.

Spectacles tilting over his nose, Huber turns over the pages. "*Ja.* I received these last summer. The leaflets of the White Rose."

"We wanted to speak with you about them."

"You know my thoughts already." Huber passes them back to Hans, hand twitching with a tremor. "Leaflets are all well and good, but there must be drastic action. Drastic action from within the Wehrmacht itself." His voice rises. "There's a limit to passive resistance. Unless blood is shed, it *will not work*!"

"We wrote the leaflets."

"What did you say?" Huber's gaze sharpens.

"We wrote the leaflets, Herr Professor." I speak up. Huber's attention swings in my direction. "All of them."

"We've come to solicit your support," Alex says. "We've long admired your lectures. Your intellect could be a great help to us."

Huber sighs, kneading the soft flesh of his chin. The skin beneath his eyes is baggy and waxen. Life under a dictatorial regime is a constant battle, and right now, Huber looks worn-out well and truly.

"Listen, Herr Professor." Hans lowers his voice. He flicks a glance at Birgit, dutifully studying, as if noticing her presence for the first time. "Could you send her out of the room?"

Huber nods. "Birgit." The girl looks up. "Go to your mutter. You've done enough studying for today."

Birgit clambers off her chair. "Wiedersehen, gentlemen," she calls with a smile.

"We're only heating two rooms. Our bedroom and this sitting room." Huber's fatherly smile vanishes after his daughter closes the door. "That's all we can afford."

I nod. "These are hard times."

"Continue, Hans," Huber says.

"We've recently met with a member of the resistance in Berlin. Several high-ranking officers are planning a coup. They intend to assassinate the Führer and rebuild the government."

The color drains from Huber's face. All except his eyes, which become brighter. "I don't believe it."

"It's true." Alex gives a faint smile. "I heard it myself."

Hans rushes ahead. "My plan is to form resistance cells at all major German universities and create a widespread network of contacts across Germany. Already, we have members in our group with connections to students in Hamburg and the Rhineland. We want you to join us. We've plans to produce a new leaflet after the holidays. You have a powerful way with words. We'd welcome your assistance."

For a long moment, Huber stares into his empty cup, chin dipped low. I've heard of people who think the future can be read in the pattern of the leaves. I don't believe that, and I doubt Huber does either, but to the three of us, casting glances back and forth, it seems he stares into the cup long enough to read a thousand futures.

For us, the decision grew organically, out of long discussions and months of debate. We're asking Huber, here and now, line drawn in the sand, to choose.

Only God knows what it will cost him. Only He knows what it will cost any of us.

Finally, Professor Huber looks up. He nods. "Well then, consider it yours."

Annalise
December 20, 1942

"This time tomorrow night you'll be a married woman. I say we celebrate. Chianti?" Sophie pops the cork on a bottle. "Pour please." She hands me the bottle, along with two dubiously washed glasses. "Duke Ellington, here we come."

I stifle a gasp. "Sophie . . . we could get into trouble." You couldn't be my vater's daughter and not hear his lectures on the *Swingjugend*, rebellious German youth who thrive on the sultry beat of American music and duck joining the Hitler Youth and BDM. Many have been arrested and sent to work camps. Swing is as dangerous as it is exhilarating.

Sophie shrugs. "Now that we live in the garden house, we're the only ones in earshot. Besides"—riffling through a stack of records, she looks over her shoulder and gives an impish grin—"it don't mean a thing if it ain't got that swing."

I laugh in spite of myself, pouring wine into the glasses from my seat on the sofa. The electrifying strains of swing crackles from the record player. In the center of the room, Sophie does a little twirl, singing along, her accented English blending with the deep voice on the gramophone. I cover my giggles with my hand.

"Come on!" She scampers across the room, pulling me up with her. We sway and sashay to the music, doing our best impression of swing (which I can only imagine since I've never seen it done). I spin her out, and she twirls, skirt spiraling. Her eyes crinkle as she laughs, and her hair swishes around her face. Round and round, we spin, the room, her face, the apartment blurring in a whirl of giddiness, laughter, and crackling music.

"Ah, I'm dizzy!" She gasps for breath. We collapse onto the sofa. I hand over her glass, and we sip our drinks. I glance at Sophie, who's still breathless, cheeks flushed and eyes sparkling. She smiles at me, a look of warmth and joy.

Friendship. A bond that brings two souls together, regardless of family and background. A rare gift indeed, to call someone a true friend. In Sophie Scholl, I've found the truest friend I've ever had.

Wherever our lives take us, I'll forever be glad to have had her in mine.

The music stops. Sophie moves to turn it off and stashes the record in a cupboard. We sit, legs tucked under ourselves on the sofa, facing each other in the lamplight, half-empty glasses in our hands.

"Where is everyone tonight?"

"Kirk and Alex went to see about a duplicating machine." Sophie sets her glass on the low table. "I don't know where Hans is. When I got home this afternoon, he was gone."

"I wouldn't be surprised if he went over to Willi's to talk over his trip to Saarbrücken."

"It's a good plan. I only hope Willi's friends are receptive. Telling someone new is always dangerous, but we haven't any choice if we want to expand our group beyond Munich." She sighs, all levity gone from her expression, then shakes her head as if to say *enough*. "Let's not talk about work tonight. It's the eve of your wedding. Looking forward to becoming Frau Annalise Hoffmann?"

The heat of a blush spreads across my cheeks. "Kirk is . . . he's everything I ever wanted but didn't know existed."

Sophie smiles, leaning her cheek against the back of the sofa. "He's a good man."

"I didn't think it was possible to love and be loved like this." I meet her gaze. "My parents . . . well, I can't remember affection between them, much less more."

"You haven't told them?"

I shake my head. "It's to be a secret. For now, at least."

"It's a beautiful thing, the love between the two of you. The culmination of that love in the vows you'll share. Sometimes"—her voice catches—"I think it won't ever happen for me."

I don't miss the pain in her gaze.

"What about Fritz?"

She presses her lips together, eyes falling shut for an instant. "I care for him. Truly I do. We've been engaged for such a long time. It's like everything's on hold until the war is over. Love. The future. Peace. That's why I'm happy for you and Kirk. You're not waiting. You're seizing the moment and living in the present." She smiles wistfully, eyes large and sad in her expressive face.

More than anyone I've met, Sophie Scholl, with her strong yet gentle spirit, deserves to love and be loved. My heart aches for her.

I place my hand on her shoulder. "The time will come for you too, Sophie. I know it."

She nods, but I sense it is less about affirmation and more to reassure me.

The door bursts open, bringing with it a gust of cold air and laughter. Hans and Gisela stagger in, windswept and out of breath.

Sophie rises. "Hans, you're home."

He unwinds his scarf, cheeks ruddy with cold. "Gisela and I went for a walk through the Englischer Garten."

"Ran, mostly. It started to snow." Gisela laughs, unbuttoning her coat.

"Take off your things and get warm. I'll walk you home in a little while." Hans and Gisela share a smile. "I'll be right back." He heads down the hall toward his room.

Running her fingers through her snow-damp curls, Gisela walks toward the sofa. "You know, Sophie, your brother can be quite charming." A smile tugs at her plush lips.

From my place on the sofa, I glance at Sophie. She doesn't seem to have heard Gisela's offhand remark. Instead, her gaze follows Hans.

And in her gaze lies fear.

CHAPTER TWENTY-NINE

Annalise
December 21, 1942

TODAY, KIRK HOFFMANN, I *become yours.*

Over and over, the words whisper through my mind, anchoring me to reality. Because the girl who walked through the door of the registrar's office this December morning on the arm of a man in a pressed suit who can't take his gaze from her face, can't stop smiling . . . can it truly be me?

Joy is like aged paper. It crumbles.

Who's to say this joy, this moment will hold fast? Outlast an hour? A year?

"You all right?" Kirk asks. We sit holding hands on a backless bench in the unheated corridor.

I nod, smiling, trying to convince myself and him that *ja*, I am all right, that everything will be. "Absolutely."

Kirk's parents sit on the bench opposite us, dressed in Sunday best—wool coats, a little navy hat atop Frau Hoffmann's graying hair. I can't help my shyness around them. We met once before, three days ago when Kirk introduced us at his apartment. The difference between them and my own parents rattles me—the way Kirk's vater clapped a hand to his son's back and congratulated us when we met outside the registrar's office, how his mutter smiled and kissed my cheek and called me *daughter.*

"Next," calls a male voice from inside.

The four of us rise, steps echoing on the worn hardwood. The cramped office smells of mothballs. Behind a desk sits a tired-looking man who eyes us from behind overlarge spectacles. A picture of the Führer hangs above the desk in a black frame. I force my gaze away from his unsmiling face.

First, we must produce paperwork: birth certificates, certificates of Aryan ancestry, our already-applied-for marriage license. My heart thuds like a kettledrum as we stand before the desk while he scans our papers.

Not in the way of a nervous bride, but out of fear that the registrar, who issued us the license a few days ago, might suddenly connect my name with Vater's and refuse to perform the ceremony. Though that likely wouldn't be legal, since I'm of age, I can't quash the fear that's dogged me most of my life, that of Vater's interference.

The registrar looks up, owlish gaze landing on me. "Let us begin."

The Hoffmanns sit on slat-backed chairs off to one side, their gazes on the two of us. On the other side of the desk, the man rubs a finger beneath his nose and flips through a small black book.

Kirk and I grab hands without being told to. He squeezes my damp fingers, twining them through his, his touch wordless reassurance.

It takes less than ten minutes. There are no sentimental readings or songs sung by warble-tongued sopranos. The vows are perfunctory, the tone of the man reading them, bored. Halfway through, he sneezes loudly into a handkerchief and stuffs it back into his pocket before continuing.

When I imagined my wedding, as little girls do, I envisioned a church with stained glass windows, a dress of flowing white, violin music for the processional. Not a freezing office with Hitler on the wall and a balding registrar whose nose drips.

One part matches my dreams, though. I imagined a man gazing at me with his heart in his eyes. Kirk is. I dreamed his voice would shake a little with emotion when he said, "I will." Kirk's does.

Ja, this moment, this man are everything I imagined and more.

There are no rings for either of us. Aside from the expense, we want no outward sign of our union. The registrar raises an eyebrow at this too, but Kirk only smiles, and whispers, "One day."

I nod and smile.

One day.

God willing, there will be a *one day* for us. Today I let myself believe it.

"I now pronounce you man and wife." The words linger in the air and in my heart.

Wife. Kirk Hoffmann's wife.

I can scarcely take in the fullness of it. How rich and true and right it is. For so long, I've been Standartenführer Brandt's daughter. Kirk has given me a gift today, the gift of new belonging.

I turn, fingers slipping from Kirk's, to greet the Hoffmanns. In an instant, Kirk's hand is on my waist, pulling me toward him. Our gazes mingle, and I ache from the sheer magnitude of love mirrored in his.

Hands framing my shoulders, he presses a soft kiss against my lips, vowing with his touch as much as he did with words. *I love you. No matter what happens, I love you.*

"There," he says when he draws away, a boyish grin teasing the corners of his mouth. "Now it's done properly."

The Hoffmanns surround us. Pastor Hoffmann clasps my hands in his warm calloused ones. His eyes are kind. "Welcome to our family."

Frau Hoffmann draws me close. She smells of rosewater and her embrace is strong, as if she has enough strength to transmit it to others without losing any herself. "My very dear daughter. I pray God's blessings on you and my son."

"Danke," I whisper, throat tightening. An ache for my own mutter pierces through me. If only she could have joined in the sacredness of today. But Vater would never have allowed it. I shiver at his fury if he knew what I'd just done.

It's too late, Vater. You don't own me anymore.

We sign the license and prepare to leave the office. Just before we exit, the registrar hands Kirk a thick black book, emblazoned with a gold eagle atop a swastika. The letters on the spine spell out *Mein Kampf*.

"A gift from the Reich. To get your family library started off right." He cracks a faint smile.

I stiffen. Kirk gives a tight nod. "Danke." He puts the book beneath his arm, and we leave the office.

Sunlight shines from the sky and the air is biting cold. The street bustles with pedestrians wrapped in coats and mufflers, hurrying with purpose in their steps. We pause outside the registrar's office.

"Well." Pastor Hoffmann rubs his hands together. "What now?"

Kirk and I exchange glances. We'd been so occupied with actually getting married, neither of us had thought about afterward. I hadn't gone to the market to buy anything for our dinner, which left us with the option of a cheap restaurant. Inwardly, I wince, then rebuke myself for it. What does it matter where we go or what we do, as long as we're together?

Frau Hoffmann smiles at the two of us. "We'll go to our house, *ja*? I'm making schnitzel and red cabbage. And Kirk's favorite *Gesundheitskuchen*."

My breakfast of dry toast was hours ago. Just thinking about a slice of rich, buttery *Gesundheitskuchen*—good health cake—makes my mouth water.

Kirk turns to me. "What do you think?"

I give Frau Hoffmann a grateful look. "I'd like that. As long as it wouldn't be too much trouble for you."

"No trouble at all. It's not every day your only son gets married, especially to such a pretty woman." Pastor Hoffmann's eyes twinkle. I glimpse Kirk in his vater's face, a mirror of what my husband will be at that age—broad shoulders a little stooped, face lined with creases, hair turned silver. The idea of Kirk as an old man fills me not with the distaste of youth for aging, but with intermingled dread and hope. Hope that such a day will find us. Gut-deep dread that it won't.

"It's settled then." Frau Hoffmann nods. "You come with us, and I'll cook for you."

Kirk chuckles. "There's one thing you'll learn quickly in our family, Annalise. Mutter always gets her way when she's set on something."

"You've finally caught on." Frau Hoffmann laughs. "My son has a pretty thick head for it to take him twenty-three years to reach this conclusion."

Laughing, the four of us move down the street. I look up at Kirk, and he slips an arm around my waist, pulling me toward his warmth. Our steps crunch on the frosted cobblestones. We smile, a wordless exchange meant for the two of us alone. I lift my face toward the warmth of the sun.

Today, if only for a little while, there are no clouds in the sky.

Kirk
December 21, 1942

I stand in the doorway of the bedroom, one hand propped against the frame. Earlier, as we unpacked my belongings, this room was ordinary. Now, lamplight softens the space in shadows, suddenly intimate.

Annalise stands near the window, back turned to me, fingers fumbling with a clasp. I cross the room, throat dry.

"Here," I whisper. "Let me help you."

I push her hair back, exposing her neck. She sucks in a breath. My fingers brush the softness of her skin, the wispy tendrils of her hair. I unhook the clasp of the simple silver pendant and place it on the desk.

"Danke," she breathes. Slowly, she turns to face me.

I look into her eyes. Her breath shudders. My heart thuds.

"I know I could never make you as happy as you've made me today." I swallow. "But I intend to spend the rest of my life trying."

She presses her fingers to my lips. "Don't you see, my darling?" A soft smile curves her mouth. "You already have."

I wrap my arms around her, overwhelmed that this woman, beautiful in body and spirit, is my wife, and there's nothing to keep us from loving each other. Our lips meet in a slow kiss. She sighs, the kiss deepening, my fingers twined in her hair, her hands on my shoulders.

A siren whines.

We start, jerking away. The shrill cuts through the air.

"Do you think it's a false alarm?" Annalise's eyes are wide, her hair tangled around her cheeks.

"I don't know. But we can't take any chances." I grab her hand, pulling her from the room. "Come on."

We hurry from the apartment, grabbing our coats, locking the door behind us. Our steps are loud as we race down the stairs, hand in hand, into the cold street. The sky is soot. People surge through the alley toward the air-raid shelter. Annalise and I are swept up in the frantic, jostling crowd. Footsteps pound. A baby wails. Sirens shriek.

A man stands at the shelter door, pushing people in. "Hurry now, hurry!"

Gripping hands, we descend the steep stairs. The light is murky. Men, women, children line the walls, some on benches, some crouched on the floor. There's no unity in their dress, a mix of coats, pajamas, business suits.

Their expressions, though, are the same. Resignation mixed with fear.

Annalise and I make our way to the back, walking through the narrowing pathway, as more and more bodies find their way into the bunker. There's a sliver of space at one end of a bench. Annalise sits, and I stand next to her, back pressed against the cold wall, hand on her shoulder.

A slam of finality as the shelter door shuts, dimming the sound of sirens. Trapping us.

Minutes pass. An explosion sounds, distant. Still, it trembles through the walls, reverberates through me. A clatter, like water trickling over tin, as a child uses the bucket in the corner, shielded by his mutter's skirt. The air is dank and smells of urine and stale cigarette smoke and too many bodies packed into one place.

Another boom. The light flickers. The shelter shudders. A child cries.

I keep my hands steady on Annalise's shoulders. "It'll be all right," I whisper.

She turns, looking up at me, face half hidden in the scant light. "We're together, at least." She gives a weak smile.

"There's no one I'd rather be stuck in a shelter with." I grin, but it comes out forced. I rub my thumb over the scratchy wool of her coat, tracing circles on her shoulder.

This is supposed to be the happiest night of our lives. We're supposed to have hours to love each other, fall asleep twined in the other's embrace.

Instead, there's no certainty we'll make it out of the raid alive. Everyone's heard the stories of people suffocating in bunkers from the heat of the bombs, walls caving in, burying them beneath layers of rubble. Sharp fear grinds inside my chest.

Love makes one want to live. It is its blessing and its curse.

An eerie silence falls over the bunker. Men stare at the ceiling, a woman rocks a bundled-up little girl in her arms. We're all waiting for the next one. The one that may not pass us by.

An hour later, the all-clear sounds, and we file out of the shelter.

If only Goebbels could see us now: cold, weary, trudging. It might give him a dose of reality, the true picture of the morale of the German people.

Our street is untouched. Wherever the bombs fell, it was nowhere in the direct vicinity. The crowd disperses. Annalise and I walk to the apartment in silence, our steps shuffling up the stairs. I unlock the door. She takes off her coat and hangs it on its hook. The light flickers as I turn it on.

It's late, we've spent over an hour in a shelter crammed with people and smells and must. Doubtless, the odor hangs on our own clothes.

This isn't a night to become lovers.

I rub a hand across the back of my neck, about to suggest (I don't really know what), when Annalise comes toward me, gaze meeting mine.

"This isn't how I imagined."

I nod, sighing. "I know."

"It was supposed to be candlelight and soft kisses and no interruptions." Her smile is a little sad.

"It will be." I brush a strand of hair behind her ear. "We have all the time in the world. Tomorrow, and—"

She shakes her head. "Nein, Kirk. We don't. We can't know that."

I say nothing. She's right. I can't promise my beloved forever. I cannot even promise her tomorrow.

Even if there wasn't a war, there would still be no certainties. But war is life magnified. What happens in life once, happens in war a thousand times over.

"We have right now." Her breath brushes my lips. "This moment. And I love you."

As her lips meet mine, the world fades away.

CHAPTER THIRTY

Sophie
December 24, 1942
Ulm

BEFORE THE WAR, I considered Christmas the one time of year when every-one put aside their differences. It was, after all, a celebration of unity, good tidings, and great joy.

Now I know better. War allows nothing. Christmas became a time when it was far too easy to focus on all one had lost in the year preceding rather than anything gained. Perhaps some people still mark the passage of the holidays with the hope that "maybe things will be good next year."

I know better than that too.

I stand outside, wrapped in my winter coat, facing darkness.

There are no windows with curtains thrown back so the light of Christ-mas tree candles might illuminate not only one's own house, but the dwell-ings of those around them. There are no carolers tramping door to door to beg a cup of something warm in exchange for a chorus of "O Tannen-baum." There's no childlike anticipation that tomorrow will bring a day of feasting and merriment.

There's only darkness, a scattering of stars in the blackness overhead, and the beating of my own heart.

I stare into the sky, frosted breath clouding from my lips, and try to pray. Something holy and fervent to commemorate this night. But all my brain can conjure is emptiness and a plea for help to be better than I am. All other words, as they so often do, drain out of me, leaving a void.

I turn my thoughts to our work, the one thing that fills me with a mea-sure of clarity. Before arriving in Ulm, Hans and I stopped in Stuttgart. He paid another visit to Eugen Grimminger, who'd needed time to consider Hans's request for funds. This time, Herr Grimminger wrote out a check for five hundred marks to finance our leafleting operation. Meanwhile,

Willi has gone to Saarbrücken and other towns in the Rhineland to speak to his like-minded friends about forming their own cells.

Even at Christmastime, our work goes on.

Footsteps crunch behind me. Vater walks toward me to stand at my side. I glimpse his face in profile. In the starlight, his sturdy frame appears shrunken. Breath plumes from his mustached lips.

For several minutes, we don't speak. Then his arm comes around my waist, and he pulls me against him. I lean my cheek into his scratchy overcoat and inhale his familiar scent.

"My little Sophie," he whispers. "What a mad world this is."

"Vater?" I glance up at him. "What do you mean?"

His chest lifts with a sigh. "All I ever wanted was to provide a good life for my children. Give them everything they desired, all possible advantages. And now that demon Hitler has robbed me of the ability to do that." Under his breath, he curses Hitler. His body tenses. "I found your mutter upstairs weeping because we couldn't afford a Christmas tree this year."

"None of us care about that." I pull away to look into his face. "That's not what Christmas is about."

"Nein?" He shakes his head and laughs softly. "Then tell me, the wisest of my women, what *is* it about? I haven't heard from my youngest son in weeks. For all I know, our Werner could be . . ." He pauses as if searching for the word.

The word I don't want him to say. I have to believe my youngest brother is out there, somewhere, alive. He was never more fully Werner than at Christmas. He used to pester Inge and me to distraction: "How much longer till we can see the tree?" I wanted to box his ears from exasperation.

Now I just wish I could hug him.

"Never coming back." Vater's voice is gruff with emotion. "My daughters wear careworn looks, my wife is more ill than she lets on, our home has been overrun with borders, and Hans seems not himself. I find little to celebrate this year."

"We're together, Vater." My whisper is fierce. "This year, let's celebrate that. And God is still with us."

"Is He? I wonder." Vater gazes off into the distance. "Sometimes it seems as if He has abandoned Germany altogether. Abandoned it to murderers and tyrants."

I say nothing. It would do little good to say how often I've agreed.

"Vater, Sophie." A shawl held over her head, Inge approaches. She looks between the two of us. "Mutter is asking for you. We're going to sing carols."

Vater's mask falls into place. He would not dare show such unguarded emotion in front of his frail wife. He turns to me with a smile, a gesture of bravery. Of *Allen Gewalten zum Trotz sich erhalten.*

"What do you say, Sophie?" His tone is bright, like he's trying too hard. "Shall we sing carols?"

We return to the house to find the family gathered in the parlor, along with the married couple and their adolescent daughter who rent our upstairs rooms. Lisl sits at the piano, turning over some music. Hans sits on the sofa next to Mutter, looking half-asleep, but he rises and lets Vater take his place, coming to stand next to Inge and me in front of the piano. Gently Lisl presses down on the glossy keys, the first bars of "Stille Nacht" rising onto the air.

Our voices fill the Christmas treeless room with song. Our favorite carols, followed by ersatz *kaffee* and stollen without raisins that crumbles because it doesn't have enough butter.

Despite all the powers, we maintain ourselves.

Later, when the rest of the family has gone to bed, I linger in the parlor, a sheet of paper in my lap, a single lamp my only light.

Christmases past fill my mind, wreathed in a glow of gold. Vater heaping our plates with sliced goose; Hans, fork in mid-air, laughing at one of Inge's jokes; Fritz sitting beside me, our shoulders brushing, sneaking glances at me over our glasses of currant wine.

Ah, Fritz. Where does this Christmas Eve find you?

I imagine him somewhere in the great white expanse of Russian winter, one among thousands of men. Doubtless there will be little to remind him of Christmas this year. Will his thoughts turn, as mine do, to the holidays we've spent together? Impromptu snowball fights, weaving Advent wreaths, stealing kisses when no one was looking.

I close my eyes in an attempt to lose myself in a sweet memory, a gift to myself this Christmas Eve. My mind scrambles for details and sensations, but . . . none come.

My hands ball into fists. I press them hard against my eyes as hot tears trail my cheeks.

I can't remember the touch and taste of his lips against mine. I know I once felt it, but the memories are wrapped in a fog I can't push past.

Panic soaks through me. What more have I forgotten? If our kisses, then what else?

How to love him? Have I forgotten that?

My breath comes quick and sharp.

Nein. Not that. Never.

Fingers shaking, I lift my pen. Wondering, as I form the words, if the man I pen them to is even among the living.

> *I'm thinking of you this Christmas Eve, wherever you are. Tonight we sang all the old carols while Lisl played the piano. I hope your heart is free from cares tonight and that you are remembering our Christmases together, as I am.*
>
> *The first Christmas was an unlikely one: the Christ Child laid in a humble manger. Yet everything about that night was a miracle. Let us trust one will come for us too.*
>
> *Until then, know my prayers are with you, as is my love.*
>
> *Yours,*
> *Sophie*

CHAPTER THIRTY-ONE

Annalise
January 13, 1943
Munich

THE AUDITORIUM OF THE Deutsches Museum echoes with the sounds of students shuffling to find a seat, muffled coughing, and muted chatter. Students and faculty have been ordered to attend an address by Paul Giesler, the Party leader of Munich and Upper Bavaria, to commemorate the 470th anniversary of the founding of Ludwig Maximilian University.

Kirk, Hans, Alex, and Sophie have vowed to boycott Nazi-sponsored assemblies. They're at Hans and Sophie's apartment talking over leaflets.

I'd rather be with them. But I've a bland curiosity to hear what Giesler has to say. Perhaps it will be worth a mention in our next leaflet.

I settle onto a bench in the middle of the balcony. Below me, in the main auditorium, sit row upon row of uniformed men—soldier-students and high-ranking Wehrmacht and SS officers, along with faculty garbed in ceremonial robes.

Seated on the swastika-draped platform on both sides of the podium, along with invited dignitaries, are leaders of the National Socialist Student Association. They turn their gazes expectantly to the podium, waiting for the speech to begin.

We don't have long to wait. Giesler strides from a side entrance. Thunderous applause echoes as he mounts the platform, dressed in a brown uniform with a swastika armband. I hide my hands in my lap and don't clap.

Giesler looks across the packed auditorium like a king assessing his subjects. His coarse face dons a satisfied look, and he lifts a hand for the applause to cease.

"I greet you, officers, students, faculty." His voice echoes off the high ceiling. "This year marks the 470th anniversary of the founding of Ludwig Maximilian University, and it is indeed a great occasion. The university is an integral part of National Socialist society, and in a short time, you, the students, will be standing on the command bridges of German life."

As the minutes pass, my eyelids grow heavy. His voice may be booming, but he's no orator.

I snap out of my daze, blinking. Giesler is bellowing now.

"Twisted intellects and falsely clever minds are unacceptable and are not an expression of real life. Real life is transmitted to us only by Adolf Hitler, with his light, joyful, and life-affirming teachings." He pauses, as if expecting a torrent of applause to drown his next words. Receiving none, he goes on, congratulating students who are recently returned, or are about to leave for the front, adding a nod to those performing factory work. "But many—" He sweeps his arms in an expansive gesture. "Many in this very room, without talent or seriousness of purpose, are expending valuable time and resources that would be better used for the greater victory. Their presence here is nothing less than waste. Waste!" He spits out the word like a bad piece of cabbage. "The university is not a rescue station for well-bred daughters shirking their duties for Führer and Fatherland."

I suck in a breath, cheeks flushing. How dare he make judgments about the female students. Around me, students whisper amongst themselves, shifting in their seats.

"Insolent cad!" comes a feminine cry from the back of the balcony.

"How dare you," a red-haired woman calls, leaning over the balcony.

Giesler cranes his neck, looking up at the students in the balcony, face reddening, posture like an angry bull about to charge. I sit, hands tight in my lap, every nerve thrumming with vindication. They're actually shouting back. I want to shout with them. Yet I don't dare draw attention to myself.

"A woman's place is not at the university, but with her family, at the side of her husband!" Giesler volleys the words up at the balcony.

Young men stamp their feet and boo. A few loose earsplitting whistles. Girls get up from their seats, surging toward the exits in a flurry of skirts, satchels, and outraged voices.

"Women!" Giesler shouts, shaking his fist. "Women should present the Führer not with a diploma, but with a child every year. And if any of you aren't sufficiently attractive to catch your own man, I'd be happy to lend you one of my adjutants." He grins, leering up at the remaining girls. "I can promise you *that* would be a thoroughly enjoyable experience."

"Enough!" A young officer bursts from his seat below. "Students, will we stand for insults to ourselves and our women?"

A uniformed veteran with only one leg raises his crutch. "Nein!"

The cry is taken up. I join the refrain, calling out along with the rest. Shouting at Giesler, his depravity and chauvinistic dominance.

For a glorious moment, I don't think of the danger or who might be watching. I hurl insults down at Giesler, and for fleeting seconds, it's as exhilarating as champagne. Giesler may be the one we shout at, but embodied in him is everything the Nazis stand for. In those seconds, the cry feels universal.

Around me, students are pushing and shoving, storming out of the balcony. Boots stomp. SS guards race into the balcony, herding us with shouts of "Out, out, out!" I rise, caught in the middle of the crowd. An elbow jabs my ribs. I grip my satchel close to my chest. Within are fifty stamps I purchased at the post office before coming to the assembly.

"They've arrested some of the girls who left in the middle of the speech," exclaims a brunette as we're shoved toward the door by the roiling crowd. I glance over the side of the balcony.

On the stage and in the auditorium, male students brawl with National Socialist Student Association leaders. Blood spurts from the nose of one as two young men in Wehrmacht uniform pummel him, while others shout for the release of the women. The cause of it all—Giesler—is nowhere in sight.

Revolt. The word rises in my mind. *The students are revolting.*

We clatter down the stairs and into the lobby. Shouts. Fists hitting flesh. The shrill of police whistles. Never have I seen such a thing, such tumult. Boots pound the marble floor as just-arrived commando squads grapple to restore order.

I slip through the surging crowd, heart pounding not with fear, but with elation, pushing my way outside into cold air and weak sunlight. Students pour down the steps, flooding past me, forming groups and linking arms. Heads held high, they march toward the bridge linking the island with the rest of Munich.

They're singing. Like victorious soldiers, their proud voices rise into the air.

Visitors en-route to the museum stop on the sidewalk, pointing and gesturing. The students march past them, steps high and arms linked.

I long to join their ranks. But I remember the leaflets and Sophie and Kirk. I can't risk getting caught. This demonstration can't last forever. Sooner or later, they'll disperse or be forcibly broken up. Likely, the latter.

I hurry to Franz-Josef-Straße, lungs burning, shoes slipping on slick cobblestones, taking a streetcar part of the way. When I reach the garden house, I'm hot and panting, hair disheveled and cheeks stinging from the wind. Alex answers the door. "Back already? How was it?"

"Let me in, and I'll tell you." I move past him, shrug out of my coat, and hang it on a hook. Inside the Scholls' rooms, Sophie, Kirk, and Hans sit around a table littered with scraps of paper. Their gazes swing in my direction. Alex comes in behind me.

Kirk rises, taking in my disheveled state. "Annalise? What's happened?"

I gulp in a few breaths. It's still unimaginable, such a thing actually taking place. For so long, we've all been afraid to so much as open our mouths. Now this, a visible protest in broad daylight. Among the students, no less.

Facing the group, I outline what I witnessed. Their expressions transform from disbelief to astonishment to the giddy exhilaration still purling through my veins.

Sophie speaks first. "Our leaflets. They must have spurred this on."

"We haven't produced a leaflet since the end of July," Hans says. But his eyes shine too.

"We wanted to make people think, generate a feeling of unrest instead of accepting whatever edict handed them." Kirk's tone is musing. "Sophie's right."

My hands itch to grip the handle of the duplicating machine. To sweat and sacrifice and work to open the eyes of those around us. "What happened today can only be the first of such protests. Demonstrations to the government that the people, especially the students, are not automatons bending to their every whim. Today they proved we still have a voice. We must work harder."

Sophie's eyes flash, her slim jaw jutting forward. "*Ja*. There is no time to waste."

CHAPTER THIRTY-TWO

Sophie
January 15, 1943

No LONGER DO WE head our leaflets with the ambiguous title the White Rose. Now, our fifth pamphlet reads *Leaflets of the Resistance Movement in Germany: A Call to All Germans!* Who would guess a group of students is behind those formidable words? In them, we sound like someone who ought to be listened to, given heed. I'm proud to own the title.

Professor Huber isn't fond of our new name, but Hans and Alex overruled his objections. The addition of Professor Huber has brought with it a good many heated arguments. Hans and Alex each wrote drafts of the fifth leaflet to be combined into one, as they'd done before. But Professor Huber flatly rejected Alex's contribution. "He sounds like a raving Communist," he stated. "Absolutely unacceptable."

Alex is not a Communist. Nor is he merely Professor Huber's student to be given a passing or failing mark. In the resistance, there must be equality. We're all taking risks, we students more than Professor Huber. In the end, the fifth leaflet was a compilation of Hans's draft with a few select portions from Alex. Kirk, Willi, Annalise, and I gave editorial feedback.

Annalise and I hurry down the street after a run for envelopes between morning and afternoon classes. Little has changed since Annalise became Frau Hoffmann except that, at the end of our meetings, she and Kirk walk home together instead of parting ways.

We're all walking a thin line, balancing lectures and studying with our work on the leaflets. The men have the added burden of shifts at the hospital and roll call, although they've taken to skipping the latter and getting friends to cover for them.

All of us are running on too-little sleep and pent-up nerves, rushing to gather supplies. With the first four leaflets, we averaged one hundred copies per edition.

This time, we aim for thousands. The tide of the war is turning in favor of the Allies on both the western and eastern fronts. Our army has been surrounded at Stalingrad for months. They can't hold out forever. "Victory at any price," Hitler says, while his people pay bitterly for it. While countless die. While Fritz . . .

"You look thoughtful," Annalise remarks. "Close call in there, wasn't it?"

"I suppose." I shrug as we turn down Ludwigstraße. We got fifty envelopes each and dodged the clerk's questions as to why we needed so many. "But what else is new?"

Two boys in Hitler Youth uniforms stand on the corner of Ludwigstraße, jangling red collection cans.

"Give to the winter relief fund, so none shall starve or freeze," one calls to us, breath pluming from his lips. His companion jangles the can in his mittened fist.

Annalise pauses and reaches into her coat pocket, but I grab her wrist. Her gaze flashes to mine.

"Don't you dare," I whisper.

"Give to the winter relief fund to support our glorious soldiers!"

A woman stops and opens her handbag, praising the boys for their service. I duck my head and hurry past, Annalise following.

"What was that about?" she asks, when we're halfway down Ludwigstraße.

"So none shall starve or freeze?" I fight to keep my voice from escalating. "You mean so our soldiers won't? What about the people in the Polish ghettos, the forced laborers here in Germany? No one seems to care about them. But aren't their lives just as important? We can't support this cause, not even by giving a few marks. Even if . . ." I swallow, Fritz's face filling my mind. "Even if it means the soldiers we know will suffer because of it. We must make no concessions."

"You're really something, Sophie Scholl." Awe emanates from Annalise's gaze.

"I'm not something. I'm just fed up." A mix of sleet and rain pelts from the sky, landing on our hair and coats. "The other night, Hans and Willi were discussing what they'd do if they found a way to gain close proximity to the Führer. Hans told Willi about that pistol he brought back from Russia and said he'd have no hesitation using it. Willi said he didn't know if he could. I was in the kitchen doing dishes, but you know what I wanted to say?"

The lower half of her face partially hidden by the collar of her coat, Annalise shakes her head.

"If I had the chance, if Hitler walked by right now and I had a pistol, I'd shoot. If a man can't or won't, a woman must. You have to do something to avoid being guilty yourself."

Annalise nods, though her eyes grow wide.

Hitler has caused the death of hundreds of thousands, likely more than we realize at this moment. If it takes his death for the madness to stop, then is it wrong to support assassination? Greater minds than mine could argue both sides of this case. All I know is he's worse than a murderer, and there is no court of justice in Germany today, except the people themselves.

We approach the main university building, its stone-colored exterior blending with the dirty-gray sky.

"You'd die though." Annalise's voice is quiet. "If you shot Hitler at close range, you'd be shot right back."

I stop, turning to face her. She looks at me, her curls a flame of color amid the gray. "Does that really matter?" A strange cold feeling that has nothing to do with the elements sweeps through my body. "So many have died in support of the regime. It's high time someone died against it. How can we expect righteousness to prevail if there is hardly anyone willing to sacrifice themselves for a righteous cause?"

Annalise says nothing other than a soft, "I know."

We walk through the doors and into the echoing Lichthof. Annalise says no more about our conversation, but the finality of my words echo in my ears the remainder of that long, winter day.

⟿

Kirk
January 18, 1943

"I can't believe you left her there. What if she wakes up?"

"Sophie . . ." Hans sounds placating.

Unbuttoning our coats in the entryway of Eickemeyer's studio, Annalise and I exchange glances. Hans and Sophie stand at the bottom of the basement steps, Sophie's arms crossed over her chest.

"What's the matter?" I keep my voice light. With our fifth leaflet finalized and enough supplies gathered, we have many a late night ahead. Whatever Hans and Sophie are arguing about, we've no time for.

They turn. "Hans left Gisela asleep in my room at our apartment. They were listening to records, and she asked to spend the night." Sophie's tone is flat.

Hans blows out a sigh. "She won't wake up. If she does, I'll tell her I had to work a late shift at the hospital, and you were with Annalise."

"That's not the point, Hans. Don't you see—"

"Why are you so opposed to Gisela, anyway?"

"Opposed—"

I hold up a hand. "All right, you two. Let's get to work. No sense wasting time."

Sophie presses her lips together but follows the rest of us into the basement. Alex hunches over a typewriter, a pile of envelopes to one side. Willi sits in a chair next to him, chin propped in one hand, reading over a copy of the leaflet.

Hans and I take charge of the duplicating machine. Sophie, Annalise, and Willi fold leaflets, affix stamps, and seal them into envelopes, while Alex types addresses. I don't ask Hans about his relationship with Gisela. His fascination with that beguiling blond is one thing about him I don't understand. Sophie has told me Gisela shows no signs of negativity toward National Socialism. In fact, somewhat the opposite. Hans seems to trust her. The rest of us keep our distance.

Hours pass. The work is grueling—turning the crank hundreds of times, hunching over the table to affix stamps and seal envelopes. My shoulders burn. We trade shifts often, but it's a constant battle to keep my eyes open, my mind clear. I keep a close eye on Annalise. Though she's a willing member of our group, she's also my wife. I can't help but want to protect her.

I type addresses, while Alex works with Hans. This time, we're using directories from outside Munich, addressing leaflets to residents of Augsburg, Stuttgart, Ulm, Salzburg, Vienna, and Frankfurt. The fine line of type in the worn address book blurs. I blink fiercely. *Focus.*

At the duplicating machine, Hans curses. He stops cranking. Swears again.

"What's the matter?" I mumble around the pencil between my teeth, fingers poised above the typewriter keys.

"Something broke." Shirtsleeves rolled to his elbows, hands covered with ink, Hans fiddles with the duplicating machine, taking it apart. Alex watches over his shoulder. After a few minutes, Hans holds up a ratty piece of ink-coated fabric. "Blasted belt tore."

I yank the pencil from my teeth, resisting the urge to sink my head into my hands.

"Too bad Traute's uncle couldn't get her anything. One night in, and this machine's already giving us problems," Alex mutters with a look of disgust.

"You're the one who bought it. Why couldn't you have gotten something decent, instead of this second-hand piece of garbage?" Hans slams his fist on the table. "We don't have time for delays. The rest of you don't seem to realize *we don't have time*!"

"Don't shout at me, Hans Scholl." Alex's nostrils flare. "You're the one who's been cranking too fast. That's likely what broke it. That shopkeeper was nothing but a liar, telling me it had hardly been used."

"What do we need to fix it?" Annalise's voice is weary but firm. From her seat beside Annalise, Sophie eyes the two men with a look of growing unrest.

"A piece of fine silk fabric." Willi walks over and picks up the strip with two fingers. "About this size."

"I could take off my shirt." Alex grins at his own lame joke. No one joins him. If the machine breaks down, our work is kaput. Finished.

Fine fabric . . .

I stand so quickly my chair almost tips over. "Don't do anything. I'll be right back."

"Kirk, where—" Annalise calls after me, but I'm already halfway up the stairs, grabbing my coat and opening the door. After hours in the musty basement, the night air hits my face like a clarifying breath. I pull my coat tighter around myself and stand on the stoop. The street is still.

I give myself no time for second-guessing and start walking, my footfalls on the cobblestones and my quick breaths the only sounds.

In less than five minutes, I'm standing in front of a brick house two streets down.

My pulse quickens.

Two swastika flags hang limp, one from each front window.

Fine fabric indeed.

Heat floods over me despite the cold, sweat trailing down my back. Crouching low, I creep across the lawn. My heart thuds. Not a single light shines from the two-story building—no doubt the residence of some wealthy Nazi.

Five steps away.

Four.

Three.

My shoe slips on the frost-slick grass. I grind my jaw, steady myself, taking the final steps to the window.

Blood pounds in my ears. I glance both ways. Nothing.

The fabric flutters slightly, as if stirred by a breath. My fingers are centimeters away.

I reach out. Grab hold. A tug. Another.

In an instant, the flag is in my hands, fabric chilled and moist. I ball it in my pocket and force myself to retreat as quietly as I came. With each crunch of my shoes on the frozen ground, I expect footsteps pounding behind me, voices shouting *halt*!

I barely breathe until I'm well away from the house. I run then, light on my feet, flattening myself against buildings whenever I hear a sound.

I let myself back into Eickemeyer's. Everyone sits around the table, slumped and defeated. Alex smokes. The typewriter and pile after pile of sealed envelopes clutter the tabletop.

"Salute the flag, proud German youth!" I pull out the flag, brandishing it high.

"Where did you get that?"

"Do you think it will work?"

"Give it here, and we'll see."

We cluster around, breathless, as Hans and Willi bend over the machine, measuring the fabric, cutting it to size. Annalise slips to my side and takes my hand in hers, her slim, warm fingers squeezing mine. For several minutes, they work to put the machine back together, voices low, movements quick in the flickering light. Hans takes a fresh piece of paper, feeds it into the tray. No one speaks. Willi turns the handle.

Clack-clack.

Sophie lifts the newly inked page, holding it up for us to see. "It worked." Her voice is a little breathless.

"Führer, we thank you." Alex says in a perfect impression of Goebbels.

We laugh together, a wave of release.

When our laughter dies down, Hans turns to the machine. "Back to work."

Three hours later, shortly after 4:00 a.m., we finish.

"What's our final count?" Hans wipes his brow with a handkerchief.

"Almost two thousand." Annalise adds a stack of envelopes to the pile.

"That's great." A little smile plays across the edges of Hans's mouth. "Excellent. For tonight, at least. We'll do another batch tomorrow. As far as distribution, I'm covering Salzburg. Shurik's taking Vienna and Linz. Sophie, Augsburg and Stuttgart. Willi is heading to Cologne, Bonn, Freiburg, and—"

"Saarbrücken." Out of all of us, Willi looks the least sleep-deprived. Despite Hans and Sophie's favorite "maintain yourself" quote, it's quiet Willi who embodies its meaning. "I got hold of a duplicating machine a few days ago."

"You what?" Hans stops latching the typewriter case.

"A friend in Munich had a contact. I got another machine. I'm taking it to Saarbrücken with some leaflets."

"To your friend Bollinger?"

Willi nods, strands of blond hair falling over his broad forehead.

"Over Christmas, your friends weren't interested."

"Heinz and Willi Bollinger were. They're forming a circle in the Saarbrücken area. Willi Bollinger said he was willing to print and distribute our leaflets if he had supplies. I'm bringing them."

"Let me get this right." Annalise, hands tucked in the pockets of her bulky sweater, stands next to the massive pile of envelopes. "You're going to transport leaflets to those cities?"

"To give the impression of a wider network," Hans says. "If leaflets start appearing, postmarked beyond Munich, it will make it look like a far-reaching organization is behind them."

"You'll have to take trains. Don't you know what they're doing on trains these days? They're searching luggage, checking papers, looking for black market food and deserting soldiers." Annalise's voice escalates. "You're young men, not in uniform, traveling alone. If you're searched and caught with the leaflets, you'll be arrested and interrogated. What will happen to us then?"

"I've already thought of that." Alex massages the stem of his pipe. "When we board the train, we'll stow our luggage in the baggage rack of one compartment, then take seats in a different one. If our cases are searched, there'll be less of a chance of tracing them back to us." He'd answered Annalise's question as if she'd a right to ask it. Hans, on the other hand, looks up from beneath a wayward shock of hair, as if annoyed someone would dare question his plans.

"None of you have passes?"

"Alex and I have forged travel papers," Hans says. "Willi doesn't though."

I look to Willi. His features are steady and impassive. "You're going without travel papers?"

Willi shrugs. "I don't have much of a choice, do I?"

"What if you get caught?" Sophie's voice is quiet.

Hans glances at her. "It's the nature of passive resistance not to get caught."

"Tell that to the Gestapo," Alex mutters.

"What's our part?" Annalise turns to Hans.

"I'm leaving the duplicating machine and studio keys in Kirk's care. The two of you will run off as many leaflets as you can while the rest of us are away." Hans shoves envelopes into two canvas rucksacks.

I already knew Hans wanted Annalise and me to stay behind. I can't deny the prospect chafes. I'd rather be boarding a late-night train along with the others, spreading our resistance movement beyond Munich. I can't help but think he's protecting me—us—now that we're married. As he protects Christl.

I look around the room at the haggard faces of my friends stowing our supplies, so we can trudge home through the cold and dark, to equally cold and dark apartments to catch a few hours' sleep, before getting up to do it all over again.

This time, I'll let myself be protected. For Annalise's sake. Were she not my wife, I'd insist on helping with the transportation of leaflets. Without travel papers, if need be.

But next time, I won't be left behind.

CHAPTER THIRTY-THREE

Sophie
January 27, 1943
En Route to Stuttgart

BITING AIR WHISTLES IN from a crack in the train compartment. I sit motionless on the hard bench seat, fingers folded atop the handbag in my lap.

My head aches from the sheer effort of keeping my features calm, my mind alert. I can't remember the last time I slept more than four or five hours straight. Over Christmas, probably.

The train is dingy and dimly lit, crowded with civilians, soldiers. Their heads loll as they sleep, or try to, nodding and jerking back to wakefulness at intervals. The air smells of unwashed wool and stale smoke. Somewhere in the compartment, a baby fusses.

I keep my gaze on my handbag. Not once do I look in the direction of the next compartment, where, wedged between a battered black suitcase and a green duffel bag, I stowed my rucksack, seven hundred envelopes within.

It's three hours from Munich to Stuttgart. Once there, I must retrieve my rucksack, exit the train, and deposit the leaflets in mailboxes across the dark city. Laid out in basic language, it sounds straightforward.

It's anything but.

I've already done the same, two days ago in Augsburg. Two hundred leaflets, a hundred without stamps. I bought the stamps at the post office near the train station, then shut myself in a stall in the station's lavatory. The cramped stall stank of urine, and I crouched on my haunches on the cracked linoleum, affixing stamps to envelopes as fast as my fingers could fly. Thankfully, mailing them was a straightforward process, and I arrived in Munich late that same night. I lay awake for hours, exhausted but sleepless.

Beneath my coat, my stomach gurgles. I packed a slice of bread in my handbag, but hunger is a luxury I can't afford. Along with fear, sleep, or any similarly inconvenient human need.

Like Fritz. Thinking about Fritz is a human need. Worrying about whether he is safe. Or sick. Or dead. News from Stalingrad is fed out in scraps. As if nobody really wants to say how bad it is. That alone coils dread inside me. The press never hesitates when it comes to declarations of victory.

Over an hour later, the train lurches to a stop. I wait until the narrow aisle is crowded with passengers, before rising. A Gestapo officer in a leather trench coat makes his way through the crowd, stopping at random to check papers. My throat goes dry.

The officer opens the suitcase of an elderly couple, who watch with looks of undisguised fear. The Gestapo is on the lookout for smugglers of black market food. Not subversive printed material.

I weave my way through the crush of passengers, toward the next compartment. My ankle gives a painful twist, but I keep moving beneath the murky light.

Almost there. The baggage rack is two rows ahead.

Two soldiers block my path.

"Pardon me." I force a demure smile. Dressed in my drab brown coat, I can't play the pretty fräulein card. Still, the men move aside.

I reach the overhead baggage rack and grasp the rucksack, pulling it down, shoving my handbag inside, and securing the straps to my shoulders. The officer is still checking luggage and asking questions. I keep my gaze straight ahead as I wait in line. Sweat trickles down my back despite the drafts of cold air leaking through the doors.

Almost to the exit. Following two soldiers, as if I'm part of their group, I descend the train steps and leave the station behind.

A sharp wind buffets the air and scrapes my lungs. Groping darkness stretches before me, save for the milky light of the half moon. A burgeoning glow in the sky, ethereal.

The streets are empty. I try to convince myself the hard part is over, that all I have to do now is locate a few mailboxes and dump the leaflets. But the exhaustion weighing me down doesn't dull my nerves. It heightens them.

God, please. Protect me.

I wing the desperate prayer heavenward and walk on, a solitary girl through empty streets. Darkness is an echo, magnifying everything. My own rhythmic footsteps, the rasp of each breath. Allied bombings have scarred Stuttgart, and I pass blackened shells of destroyed buildings. In the moonlight, the holes and gaps in their exteriors are skeletal eye sockets.

I spy a postbox up ahead and walk toward it. I glance in every direction before pulling the rucksack off my shoulders. My chilled fingers fumble to undo the buckles. A lock of hair dangles in front of my face. I shove it behind my ear. With one hand, I pull out a pile of envelopes. With the other, I lift the cold metal handle, the chipped paint pressing into my fingers as I feed the envelopes in. They fall from my hands, hitting the bottom with little thudding sounds.

Support the resistance movement—distribute these leaflets!

The final line of our leaflet pushes me onward.

Securing the rucksack to my back again, I hurry to the next postbox. Slush seeps through a hole in the bottom of my shoe. My eyes have adjusted to the darkness, and I find my way easier now. In two hours, I've located three more mailboxes and gotten rid of half the leaflets.

The mail slot clanks closed. I'll finish the job tomorrow, taking a streetcar to the outskirts of the city and depositing the rest in postboxes there, so too many don't appear in one place.

Footsteps. Behind me. My throat clenches.

I slide the straps of my rucksack over my shoulders and turn slowly, as if I've every right to be out in the middle of the night mailing a letter.

A policeman walks toward me, his shadow looming large behind him. I pretend not to see him and walk crisply away from the mailbox.

"Halt!"

Every inch of me goes cold.

Always innocent.

My brother's voice echoes in my ears.

I stand still and wait for the policeman to approach. A breeze blows hair into my face. I school my features, making them a blank slate.

When he stops in front of me, I look directly at him.

"Papers, please."

I reach into my pocket and pull out my wrinkled identification papers. He takes and scans them, gaze hidden by the black brim of his cap.

He looks up, eyes two beady pebbles in a lumpy face.

"What are you doing out so late?"

"Mailing a letter." It's always best to stick as close to the truth as possible.

"What letter could be so important that it couldn't have waited until morning?"

The straps of my rucksack dig into my shoulders.

The rucksack that still contains three hundred leaflets.

"It was to my fiancé." *Oh, please let him not have seen me put more than one envelope into the mailbox.* "I'm so busy during the day, I don't have time to write until late at night. But I know how hearing from me lifts his spirits." I put a bit of Annalise into my words, her flair for drama.

The policeman nods, as if accepting that here is no dissident, just a young woman sending letters to her soldier boyfriend. "Take care, fräulein. The streets aren't safe at night."

I nod, smile. "Of course. Danke." I walk past him before he can wonder why I needed a rucksack to mail just one letter.

I return to the train station and sink onto a metal bench in a corner of the third-class waiting room, rucksack on my lap. Across from me, a solitary man finishes his cigarette, its blackened stub glowing. My heartbeat slows, though my temples throb with a driving ache.

I was lucky. That's all. The policeman could have kept asking questions, searched my rucksack. Personal business is a thing of the past. Privacy, nonexistent.

I remember my prayer. Perhaps it wasn't luck but a divine hand keeping me from danger.

I stare at the window covered in blackout paper, waiting the interminable hours until dawn, not daring to open my handbag to pull out the bread or to close my eyes even a moment. I'm not sure I could sleep even if I wanted to.

What about next time?

Is each act of daring, every risk only another on the road to the final one? Where our luck will run out and nothing will be able to save us.

⟿

Annalise
January 28, 1943
Munich

"Are you sure?" Kirk touches my arm as we stand in Eickemeyer's studio.

I meet his gaze. "Sophie and Alex aren't back yet. The three of you can't do this alone. I can help."

He swallows. There are circles beneath his eyes, his jaw shadowed with stubble. Raw fear and love war in his gaze, as if he wants to pull me into his arms and keep me there. I steel myself against it, fighting weakness. If I surrender to it now, it will shatter me.

Finally, he nods. "All right. She's in, Hans," he calls. "Give her a route."

Hans pushes past Willi to come toward us.

"Cover the area from Karl-Theodor-Straße down to Schleißheimer Straße. From there, go home, not to the studio. Each rucksack contains roughly a thousand leaflets. Don't bring any back, unless you absolutely must. Questions?" In that moment, this lanky youth with the curling brown hair and handsome face is nothing so much as a general commanding his troops. His tone is terse, his gaze glittering with a strange tension.

I shake my head, trying to stand tall, to ignore the thrum of fear beating inside my chest. "I understand."

We wrap ourselves in winter woolens, stash leaflets in satchels and rucksacks.

"Let's get moving. It's after eleven." Hans claps his hands.

Willi drops his cigarette butt into an empty *kaffee* cup and pulls a dark cap over his hair. We gather our bags and make our way up the stairs into the dark entryway. Hans opens the door, peers out, glances both ways. The weight of my satchel digs into my palm. Mittens would make my fingers unwieldy. Soon, they'll be freezing. Beside me, Kirk stands perfectly still. His coat smells of ink and the spice from his shaving lotion. I inhale, the band of tightness around my lungs loosening a centimeter.

Hans turns. Nods.

We exit the building. Hans locks the door. Willi's solitary shadow vanishes into the blackness. Kirk lingers a moment. His gaze holds mine—my husband who encircled me in his strong arms only this morning as dawn crested the city.

I offer a slight smile, then resolutely turn and walk away.

It's bitterly cold—"too cold for anyone to want to be anywhere but their beds," Hans had said. "The streets will be ours."

A half moon shines like a silver thumbnail. I imagine bombers cutting through the blackness, loosing fire upon the streets of Munich. Unexposed, in the open, there would be little time to make it to a shelter.

God—the shaky prayer fills my heart—*protect us all this night.*

I keep a brisk pace, alert for footsteps, voices, movement. Doubtless, policemen and block wardens are still on the prowl. My steps echo in my ears, and my breath comes in short pants. Time blurs. The cold air dries the roof of my mouth and burns my lungs.

I turn onto Karl-Theodor-Straße, remembering Hans's instructions.

"Parked cars. Telephone booths. Sides of buildings. Doorsteps."

I fumble in my satchel and pull out two or three leaflets—a flash of white in the blue-black darkness. A grocer's, desolate at this hour, is on my right. I place a leaflet on the stoop, wedge one in a crack of the shop window. It takes only seconds.

I hurry onward, leaving leaflets in my wake. Darkened houses. Shops. Benches. On the window of parked cars. Inside telephone booths.

A propaganda poster, sun-bleached and ragged with age, depicts the

Führer with an arm raised in victory, a crowd of adoring troops in his wake. The image of a lie. How cruelly we've all been lied to.

I rip a small piece from the roll of tape in my pocket and secure the leaflet. Right over the Führer's face.

Opposition can be cathartic. Tonight, I taste its force.

Head bent, I stride on, flitting in and out of doorways, scattering leaflets. Bending up and down, leaving our words behind.

Tear off the mantel of indifference with which you shroud your heart! Cast your decision before it is too late!

In the distance, a car rumbles. My breath seizes as its outline turns down the street. Headlights doused due to blackout regulations, it drives slowly toward me. Seconds before it passes, I press myself into a doorway, my shoe leaving a muddy print against the leaflet I just placed.

I scarcely dare to breathe until it passes. My legs shake as I step into the open. For the moment, undetected.

I look up, down, all around. In the middle of this black and empty street, I'm completely alone. Defenseless. I grit my teeth and keep walking, doggedly leaving the leaflets. Gone is my former exhilaration. Now it's just cold and dark and frightening.

Faster. Hurry. I leave two leaflets on an iron bench. The pages flutter as I drop them.

I pass familiar landmarks rising out of the shadows—the Church of St. Ursula, its spire a narrow finger pointed toward the sky. In the clutch of night, it looks nothing like Kandinsky's painted rendition, geometric strokes depicting a landscape of bold color.

There is no color in this world of darkness.

I force myself to empty the satchel. My wristwatch is hidden by the sleeve of my coat, but I figure I've been out three hours. A lifetime.

I trudge through the night to our apartment. With frozen, shaking fingers, I unlock the door and let myself inside. The front room is scattered with books and unwashed clothes and dirty dishes. Legs aching, I shuffle into the bedroom.

I take off my winter coat and scarf, exchanging my clothes for a flannel nightgown and woolen socks. Kirk hasn't returned. My stomach gurgles, but I can't summon the strength to prepare food. Not that we've much to prepare. I crawl beneath the covers and pull them over my head, trying to get warm, to stop the shaking.

I press my cheek into the pillow and close my eyes, but I can't slow the thudding of my heart, much less sleep.

An hour later, the door rattles, and footsteps come into the bedroom.

Kirk undresses and climbs into bed beside me. In that murky space between wakefulness and sleep, I lean into the heat of his body. He wraps his arms around me, his chin against the top of my head. Minutes pass. His breaths begin to even, and I place my hand over his heart, letting each beat radiate through my fingers.

Kirk
January 31, 1943

Women and babies. Some things never change. The moment Christl steps into the Scholls' apartment, Sophie and Annalise crowd around him, peppering him with questions.

"What color eyes does she have?"

"How do the boys like their baby sister?"

"Does she favor you or Herta?"

Christl smiles and laughs and answers their questions, but his bearing is tense, his laughter slightly hollow. He unwinds his scarf and shrugs out of his coat. Alex takes both and invites him to sit, clapping him on the shoulder. Hans and I are already in the front room, where we've spent the past hour studying. We see Christl rarely these days, as he spends what little free time he has with his wife and children.

I rise to let him have my seat, and he sinks onto the sofa, opposite Hans. Alex pulls up a dining-room chair, and Sophie and Annalise hasten to the kitchen to bring tea.

"What is it, Christl?" Alex frowns with concern.

Christl kneads a hand across his forehead. "Herta's unwell. Puerperal fever."

Hans looks up. "Is it a serious case?" For centuries, puerperal fever has robbed countless newborns of their mutters. But we have better medical treatment now. And Christl, as a physician in training, should be able to see his wife gets the best care.

"Moderately." Though Christl hasn't participated in our leafleting activities, he looks as tired as the rest of us. "With the other two, she was fine. No complications. Just a healthy baby." He meets Alex's gaze. "And now—"

Alex refuses to let him finish that sentence. "How are her spirits?"

"She tells me not to worry. 'I'll soon be up and about again,' she says. But she's so pale, so small in that hospital bed . . ." A sheen films his eyes. "Thank goodness the boys are staying with my stepmother. I've been given

so little leave, and with my studies . . . it's terrible I can't be with her more."
His features are haggard, bereft of his usual winning smile.

We all have something that gives life its purpose, makes each breath
worth the taking. In this mad world, Christl clings to his family. I can't
bear to think what it would do to him if he lost any of them, especially
Herta. He adores her. Though they've been married three years, they still
look at each other with the tender awe of newlyweds.

Sophie and Annalise stand in the doorway between the kitchen and
front room. Their gazes radiate concern. Sophie crosses to Christl's side.
She crouches in front of him, face lifted to his. Afternoon sunlight falls on
her pale face, illuminating the two of them, a swirl of dust motes in the air.

"We'll pray for Herta," she whispers, gripping his hands. "God will hear
us, and He will have mercy on her. You must believe it, Christl."

Christl nods, ducking his head. "Danke, Sophie." His voice cracks. They
look at each other for a long moment, as if through Sophie's gaze, Christl
pulls in strength.

He clears his throat. "I didn't come to make you all sorry for me." He
smiles, a shadow of the old Christl, the one whose quiet grin could make
you believe in goodness. "Something smells great. Is that for us?"

"Of course." Sophie rises, and in a few minutes, we're clustered around
the table, eating toasted bread and drinking tea amid the clutter of the
apartment. Annalise settles beside me, her shoulder brushing mine. She's
become so pale, faint bruises beneath her eyes. But she smiles at me, a
look between lovers. Such moments are sunlight, and in spite of it all, with
Annalise, I find its brightness still.

"So . . . the leaflets?" Christl pushes aside his empty plate.

"We're in full operation." Hans replies, tone vague.

"I figured that. People are talking, you know. The other day, I heard
someone in the barracks mentioning their uncle found a bunch outside his
shop. I wouldn't be surprised if the Gestapo are already on the hunt."

"I know they are." Hans takes a bite off the corner of his toast. When
he sets it down, his hand isn't completely steady. "Why wouldn't they be?
We're causing a stir." A shadow of a defiant smile edges his lips.

"Tell me you're being careful. That you're taking every precaution."

"Don't worry about us." Hans's gaze flickers to Christl, then back to his
plate. "You've got enough on your mind."

"What are you really doing, Sophie?" Christl leans forward, eyes earnest. Pleading. Sophie sits across from him, hair tucked behind her ears,
fingers wrapped around her cup of tea.

"What we believe to be right." She gives a slight smile.

"You're taking greater risks. I know it. I fear for you all. The Nazis are still in power. If they discover someone is succeeding at opposition, they'll stop at nothing to hunt them down. We've all heard the stories. The sentences are harsher. Once a casual joke at the Führer's expense got you imprisoned. Now . . . you're executed. And you are undertaking much more than casual remarks." He pulls out his pipe, but instead of lighting it, he places it on the table and stares at it. Then he looks up, meeting our gazes. "I believe with all my heart in this cause. Perhaps if I'd no one but myself to care for, my life would hold less value, and I'd be the first in line to sacrifice it. But I don't want to die at their hands, and I don't want any of my friends to either. Maybe that's wrong. Maybe I'm a coward. But there it is."

"We have no aims of martyrdom." Hans's jaw tightens. "But we're not stopping."

For a long moment, no one speaks, each lost in his own thoughts. I admire Christl. I don't admire him any less for wanting to stay alive for the sake of his family. To daily anticipate, to wish for death, one would first have to surrender hope.

Is clinging to hope in spite of everything an act of bravery or naivety?

Finally, Christl meets Hans's eyes. "Would you let me write something for your leaflets? You don't have to print it if you don't like it."

Hans sighs, shaking his head. "Christl . . ."

"I want to do it. In that way, at least, I could work alongside you. What is it that British author said? 'The pen is mightier than the sword.' Please, Hans. Let me use mine."

Sophie turns an inquiring gaze on Hans. In the stillness of the Scholl apartment, Hans regards Christl. It's an easy matter to risk oneself. To gamble with the future of a friend gives any good man pause. Despite his complexities, Hans Scholl is, at heart, a good man.

At last, he nods. "*Ja*, Christl. Take your time, and when you're satisfied, give me a draft to look over."

"Danke." Christl's gaze, though still weary, is alight with new determination.

"Don't thank us," Sophie says. "We would be honored to print your words."

CHAPTER THIRTY-FOUR

Kirk
February 3, 1943
Munich

ANNALISE—HALF DRESSED, MUSSED, getting ready for classes—hums in the kitchen. I inhale the crisp, brown scent of toasting bread and blow on my steaming ersatz, then get up from the table and cross to our Volksemp-fänger radio, one of Annalise's contributions to our married home. With an extra antenna and a lot of tinkering, we've been able to pick up the evening BBC broadcast. "Take that, Herr Goebbels," Annalise had said with a laugh, looking over my shoulder as I rigged up the antenna over the Christmas holiday. I smile, remembering those golden honeymoon days.

"Breakfast is ready." Annalise carries in two plates of toast—the barest hint of butter, no jam. Like all couples, we've settled on a division of labor. I get up before her and make *kaffee*, while she does the toast. Routine, one of the stabilizing normalcies in a married life that's anything but.

I fiddle with the dial on the radio, fighting a yawn. A clatter as Annalise sets the plates on the table. Static crackles from the radio, turned to an "approved" station. Then low notes of mournful music.

"That's the second movement of Beethoven's Fifth." Annalise's cup clinks on its saucer.

The music dies away. A male voice begins to speak.

"The battle for Stalingrad is over. True, with their last breath, to their oath to their flag, the Sixth Army, under the inspirational leadership of General Field Marshal von Paulus, has been defeated . . ."

My breath seizes.

Over 330,000 German soldiers fought at Stalingrad.

I turn to Annalise. Her hand is pressed to her lips, and her face is ashen. Is her vater among those saved? Or those lost? What of Sophie's Fritz? My schoolmates from boyhood? How many?

So many.

I go to Annalise, sit beside her, and take her hand in mine. She leans against my shoulder. Neither of us speak. The announcer's voice echoes in the air, his final words filling the apartment.

"They died so that Germany may live."

After the defeat at Stalingrad, the time is ripe for action. A move bolder than any we've made yet.

When Alex first mentioned his plan, the idea got pushed aside in favor of printing more leaflets. Still he persisted.

"Our leaflets can only go so far. Anyone can ball them up after a second's scrutiny. We need something impossible to ignore. Imagine! Truth written in the sky for everyone to see. Only we can't write it in the sky. So we'll write it on buildings . . . with tar paint."

Alex has paint and a few handmade stencils, crafted out of lightweight tin. Hans, a loaded pistol.

This is too risky to tell the others about. Especially Sophie or Annalise. We gave the excuse of working a late shift at the women's clinic due to a complicated childbirth case. Instead, we wait at Eickemeyer's studio until eleven. Hans paces. The aromatic scent of Alex's pipe whelms the basement room. Chin in hand, Willi looks lost in thought. I don't blame him. Since the announcement, I've been unable to stop thinking about Stalingrad. The men who died. The ones still trapped there.

All day, frantic men and women packed the streets, clamoring to buy papers, desperate for news. It was piteous to see their expressions. Grief. Shock. There wasn't one who didn't look crushed, trodden upon. For many, the defeat at Stalingrad is the first time they have questioned the Führer at the helm of our country, considered victory something we might not actually achieve. Tomorrow morning, they'll have something else to question.

If we succeed.

After eleven, we leave the studio, our supplies in canvas bags slung over our shoulders. Due to the three days of national mourning imposed by Goebbels, everything has been shut down for hours: cinemas, restaurants, concert halls. The street is black and silent. Moonless. A light rain mists from the sky, slicking the cobblestones.

I shiver and pull my collar up around my chin. Hans and Alex are flushed with pent-up energy. Their stride is quick, like they can't contain themselves another second. Willi and I follow behind, constantly on guard.

Have I been entrenched in danger so long it makes me feel nothing?

Three months ago, my heart would have raced, my stomach knotted with sick suspense. Now I'm careful, but no longer afraid.

The night, after all, is the friend of the free.

Alex is definite about his choice of buildings, those with prestige that will attract notice. We approach the National Theatre, a towering edifice of gray stone.

Willi stands as lookout, Hans's loaded pistol at the ready.

Breathing hard, Alex unfurls the stencil. I wrench open the can of black paint. Chemicals and tar burn my nostrils. Its surface shimmers like a millpond in the night. Hans and I each grab a side of the stencil and hold it flat against the cool, damp stone of the building. Alex dips his brush into the paint and slaps it across the stencil, filling in the outline.

"Hurry." Hans glances toward where Willi stands a few meters away, the hand holding the pistol concealed in the folds of his coat as he scans the street.

We pull away the stencil. Some of the paint drips off, coating our hands.

DOWN WITH HITLER

In glistening black letters for all to see.

"One more thing." Alex grins a wicked smile. In quick strokes, he draws a swastika beside the words.

"Hold this." He pries open a can of red, hands it to me. Dips his brush. He slashes the red in a bold *x* over the swastika.

Then we move on. Willi and I trade places, and I serve as lookout while they work, scanning the streets, pistol clenched in my grip. At any moment, air-raid sirens could sound. Or we could be caught by a policeman or an innocent passerby.

With the evidence streaked across our hands, it would all be over.

Street by street, building by building, we deface over twenty structures with HITLER THE MASS MURDERER! and DOWN WITH HITLER.

Hans and Alex are drunk on exhilaration, drawing swastikas with a flourish and covering them with ugly gashes of red before racing onward. Paint dribbles down pale stone. My hands are sticky with it, the stench heavy in the misty air.

"The university!" Alex's eyes dance. "We mustn't leave them out."

Up ahead are the familiar gates with high stone walls on either side. Seized with inspiration, infected by the giddiness of my friends, I grab Alex's paintbrush and dip it in glistening black. In broad strokes, I paint a single word. One that has ceased to have meaning in Germany today.

FREEDOM

Over and over, we daub the word onto the entrance to the university.

Alex slaps paint across the *DOWN WITH HITLER* stencil. Hans yanks it away, revealing the words. They gleam in the darkness. Paint trails onto the cobblestones.

My shirt is drenched with sweat, my coat with drizzling rain. In the distance, the university buildings we've come to know so well stretch out in sleeping silence.

FREEDOM

Willi jogs over. "We've got to get out of here." His face and hair are eerily pale in the faint light.

Alex rolls up the stencil. I grab the can of half-empty paint.

We leave the university behind, walking quickly on the rain-slick cobblestones. Hans says something about a bottle of wine in his apartment, but I only want to get home to Annalise. To wash the paint from my hands and hold her close and cherish the moments of calm.

Though even in those moments, wrapped in her embrace, the tightness in my chest never dissipates. Not really. I lie awake, staring at the ceiling, exhausted but sleepless.

The tension of the day magnified by the silence of the night.

CHAPTER THIRTY-FIVE

Sophie
February 4, 1943

FRITZ IS ALIVE. FOR two days, I've carried the unbelievable truth with me. I thought him dead. Lost, along with thousands of other men and boys stolen by Stalingrad. By some miracle, he made it out on one of the last planes evacuated. From the military hospital in Lemberg, he got word to his parents, and they phoned me in Munich.

War leaves none of us as we once were. Fritz lost two of his fingers to frostbite. Never again will he play his beloved piano or fasten his own tie.

But he is alive. He will come back to me.

Should that make me long to live too? In light of our work with the leaflets, taking his silence to mean the worst, I'd begun to think of my own life as something expendable. Now I have more than myself to lose, to regret. With Fritz's return, a spark has caught tinder inside me, warming the frozen places.

I want to preserve myself for the fiancé who needs me more than ever, to give what we once had another chance. To be Fritz and Sophie again, changed perhaps, but with the hope of a future together still before us. To let the possibility of loss bind the cracks in our fractured love.

But I can't stop. We're in too deep. And if I stopped, I'd never be able to meet my own eyes in the mirror again.

I walk with my sister Lisl in the direction of the university beneath a gray morning sky. She's taken a break from her teaching duties to visit Hans and me. Of course, she knows nothing about our leaflets, which has curtailed my own activities somewhat. I sense a barrier between my sister and me, built by the work that encompasses so much of my time and thoughts, yet about which I cannot say a word. Still, it's been a pleasant visit. Hans and Alex returned from the hospital well after one in the morning, flushed and exultant. They opened a bottle of wine and sat at the table with us talking for hours about everything and nothing. Strangely, they said not a word about their urgent childbirth case.

"Tell me about Mutter." I turn to my sister. "Is she really as ill as Inge says?"

"It's true, she's poorly." A little fur cap frames Lisl's face, her dark hair hanging in loose curls around her shoulders. "Her energy is low, and she spends most of the day resting."

A newsboy hawks papers on the corner, stamping booted feet in the cold. The newspaper is bordered in black. As we pass, I catch a glimpse of the headline.

Tragic, Heroic Defeat!

I don't need to buy a paper to get my fill of defeat. We've been defeated for years. Many are just now waking up to it.

"I should go home. For a week or so, anyway. I can help around the house and see to Mutter myself." I've neglected my family more than I care to admit these past months. They need me. And truthfully, I need them.

Lisl nods, cheeks red with cold. "It would do Mutter a world of good to see you."

We turn down Ludwigstraße. "We'd better hurry. Professor Huber is lecturing, and I'm sure no one will object if you sit in."

A smile brightens Lisl's face. I mull over travel plans as we walk until her voice breaks into my thoughts.

"What's that crowd doing there?"

A group is gathered in front of the university entrance. A few whisper and gesture. Most stare silently, before ducking their heads and walking on. We stop on the fringes, and I crane my neck to peer around the man in front of me.

Two women wearing kerchiefs and ragged dresses plunge sponges into buckets of soapy water, vigorously rubbing the stone exterior.

My heart gives a little kick.

FREEDOM. DOWN WITH HITLER. The words are nearly a meter high, rendered in thick, black strokes.

A guard barks at the women. "*Schnell*! This should have been finished by now."

One of the women stops scrubbing. Her hands are red and chapped, and she wipes a strand of hair out of tired eyes. "It will not come off," she says in broken German. "The paint . . . it sticks."

"Well, it better come off," the guard mutters. "The university rector is furious."

I take in the words hungrily. Written resistance. What a glorious sight. Whoever did this believes as we do, enough to court the dangers of detection.

Then I remember. Hans and Alex waking me last night. A strange odor hung about their clothing. I figured it was something they used at the hospital.

They couldn't have . . . couldn't be behind this graffiti?

Of course. What other reason would they have to be out so late? They were at the university and likely elsewhere in the city, plastering buildings with words that no one dares utter. Alex is behind this. It was his idea. I'd wager it.

How reckless. How . . . effective.

Next time, I'll ask them to take me along.

Lisl stares at the scrubbing women, the painted words scarcely diminished by their attempts to remove them. Her brown eyes are wide. They'd be all the wider if she knew her own brother was behind it.

"Come." I tug her arm, and we walk on. I glance over my shoulder, flinging one last look at the women's vain efforts to erase the handiwork as the crowd continues to gather.

I hope it never comes off.

⌁

Annalise
February 8, 1943

Let the shadows stay outside, just for a little while. Let there be peace, if only for a moment.

The refrain is prayer and plea both as Kirk and I lie together in the darkness. My head rests against his warm chest, his arm encircling me, an anchor of protection. His eyes are closed, but I sense he's awake. His even intakes of breath brush my ear, and I listen to their steady cadence.

How deeply I've grown to love him. I, who for years never trusted, never let anyone in, have given myself fully to this man. Daily, I marvel at his gentle kindness, steadfast strength, and determination to see darkness made light. The beauty of our love steals my breath. Could I truly have gained such a husband—I, Annalise Brandt, whose fate was to wed a high-ranking officer to breed babies for the Fatherland? It seems a porcelain reality.

One I fear will shatter at the slightest jolt.

How long can we go on living as students by day, cranking out leaflets by night, the weight of exhaustion an endless pressure on our eyelids, constantly looking over our shoulders, fraught with tension, uncertainty, dread? How long before our resistance is discovered and we must pay the penalty meted out to traitors of the Reich?

I want nothing more than to cling to Kirk and safety. But I cannot. We cannot stop what has been put in motion, only move forward and pray for guidance.

Kirk stirs. His fingers trail my shoulder, their warmth penetrating through the fabric of my nightgown.

"I have to go out."

I look up. "Now? Why?"

He sighs, his face shadowed in the dimness of our room. A lock of hair curls over his forehead, brushing the place I kissed not half an hour ago, my lips against salty sweat and smooth skin. He doesn't answer.

"You're going to do it again, aren't you?" I sit up in bed, swiping my tangled curls back from my face. "More graffiti?"

He nods.

"They'll be on alert, you know. Munich was in an uproar last time."

He nods again. Rises, swinging his long legs over the edge of the bed. In the darkness, he begins to dress, pulling his shirt over his broad shoulders. I watch him, the covers pulled around me, my heartbeat a raw taste in my throat.

Dressed in a woolen coat, a low-brimmed cap, he turns to me, leaning over the bed.

"Annalise." My name is a husky whisper on his lips.

"*Ja?*"

"Promise me . . ." He swallows. "Promise me if the worst comes, you'll do all in your power to save yourself. If something happens to me, I can endure it. But I couldn't endure, knowing you . . ." Something broken and anguished lives in his face as he looks down at me in the darkness. "I need you to promise to fight for yourself, whatever it takes. I've got to know one of us, at least, will survive."

I shake my head, throat hot and tight. "Don't talk like that."

"I have to." His voice is firm. "Please, Annalise. Promise me."

In the moment, those who ask for such promises cannot know what it will require to keep them. And those who make vows cannot foresee what honoring them will demand. But in all our raw, human frailty, we seek and give words that, in truth, are as weightless as a summer wind.

Still, I nod, sensing Kirk needs this from me. "I promise."

He takes my face in his hands, framing my cheeks. He presses a kiss to the top of my head, then brushes his lips against mine. My eyes burn with tears.

Don't go.

"I'll be back in a few hours." He gazes down at me, expression torn.

Then turns and leaves the room, his footsteps reverberating through the apartment. The door shuts.

Bring them safely home.

Sometimes I wonder how long God will keep answering that prayer.

I sit in the darkness, taking slow breaths through my nose, until the knot in my throat lessens and tears no longer threaten.

I should have gone with him. But Hans and Kirk would never allow it. Sophie told me she offered to take part, and Hans refused, telling her it's too dangerous. She's in Ulm now, helping her family. I'm glad she wasn't here to witness this afternoon.

Falk Harnack, our liaison with the resistance in Berlin, met with us at the Scholls' apartment. He praised our last leaflet and arranged the promised meeting for Hans, Alex, and Kirk in Berlin on February 25. "I'll introduce you to my contacts," he had said. "Then we can proceed as a united force."

Only this afternoon I sat in the same room with a man embroiled in the wider resistance movement. Following the arrangements for the meeting, Harnack went on at great length about the government after the war and how everyone must work together, regardless of prior political views, for the cause of obliterating Nazism.

After Harnack left, Professor Huber spoke up. "I won't remain in the same organization as someone who suggests we work with Communists. You should cancel the meeting." Hans and Alex refused. Then Hans took exception to a line Professor Huber had written in the leaflet he'd drafted, about the students supporting our glorious Wehrmacht. Alex said he wouldn't print it—"the Wehrmacht is little better than the Nazis." Huber left furious.

Sans the offending line, we still plan to print Professor Huber's leaflet, addressed simply to *Fellow Students*, detailing the horrors of Stalingrad, urging the students of Germany to rise up against those holding them in political bondage.

I hope Sophie rests while at home. She confided in me that she's been having splitting headaches, and she rarely smiles these days, lost in a world of her own.

As for my own family, I can't help missing Mutter and my younger brothers. When Mutter called last week, she said Vater made it out of Stalingrad and is returning to Berlin to recuperate from a shoulder wound. She asked if I wanted to come home and see him. I didn't give an answer.

I hug my arms against my chest, staring at the blackout-covered window.

Kirk is out there somewhere, running through the darkness, leaving the imprint of truth on the buildings of Munich.

Kirk, Sophie, Alex, Willi, Christl, Hans. Mutter and Vater Hoffmann. My true family.

For them, I would do anything.

CHAPTER THIRTY-SIX

Sophie
February 15, 1943

I STAND ON THE threshold of my brother's room. Hans sits at his desk, head resting against the back of the chair, staring into nothing. Scraps of paper and two sheets of eight-pfennig stamps litter the desktop.

I rest my hand on his shoulder. "Hans?"

He starts, body jolting in an involuntary response. Then his gaze focuses. "Oh, Sophie." He clears his throat. "All unpacked?"

I nod. "I put the jam Mutter sent in the kitchen cupboard. I can tell you about our visit."

He pinches the bridge of his nose, like he does when he has a headache. "Some other time. I'll be going out in a bit."

"Where?" My fingers close around the worn woolen edges of my gray sweater.

He doesn't answer. He and Gisela picked me up at the Hauptbahnhof, and the three of us went out for an early dinner. With Gisela there, I spoke only of inconsequentials, asking nothing about the leaflets.

"Where are you going, Hans?"

He turns in his chair, facing me. For a long moment, he eyes me. "We're going to graffiti the Feldherrnhalle."

I suck in a breath. The Feldherrnhalle, once a monument to the Bavarian army, is famous as the site of Hitler's failed 1923 putsch. After he assumed power, Hitler immortalized the fallen "martyrs of the movement" with a bronze plaque and SS guard of honor who stand in ceremony day and night. All who pass the site are required to perform the Hitler salute or risk being stopped and questioned.

If Hans succeeds, it will be a gesture of blatant defiance that could feed the unrest brewing since Stalingrad. But if he's caught . . .

"Not tonight, Hans." I swallow. "Please."

"I've already arranged to meet the others."

"Unarrange it then!"

He doesn't reply. Just sits there, face grim and determined.

I must make him see. Graffiti is one thing, but the guarded Feldherrnhalle . . . Maybe if he'd suggested this two weeks ago, I'd be begging to go along. But our work has taken its toll, and right now it threatens to break me. Each uncalculated risk heightens the likelihood of our carefully constructed house of cards collapsing, scattering us all.

"Vater found one of our leaflets," I say softly. "I must have accidently left it in a book I brought home. He came to me. I've rarely seen him so grave. 'Sophie,' he said. 'I hope you two don't have anything to do with this.'"

Some of the hardness in Hans's face fades, making him look young and boyish. And suddenly, as afraid as me. "What did you tell him?"

"I told him we were too . . ." My voice shakes. "We were too smart to involve ourselves with something like that. I lied to him, Hans." My eyes fall closed, tears pressing against the edges. My head aches. Exhaustion ebbs through my body. Will there ever come a day when the weight of so much concealment will cease to crush me?

Hans's arms come around me. I lean into his chest, the musk of pipe smoke and the worn cotton of his shirt enfolding me. I let myself linger in the comfort of being held. Of being, for a moment, the one who isn't strong.

"How much longer?" His words whisper against my hair.

"Until what?"

Against my cheek, his chest lifts in a sigh. "Until it ends."

$\swarrow$

February 16, 1943

"What are these for?"

Hans and Alex look up. Stacks of leaflets cover the table—roughly two thousand copies. Hans must have brought them from Eickemeyer's.

"These?" Hans gestures to the piles.

"*Ja.* These." I fold my arms across my sweater-clad chest, leaning against the doorframe of the kitchen.

Alex looks away. Hans rises, lanky frame filling the low-ceilinged room. For a long moment, he stares at me. Is he contemplating his next words, or has his mind wandered in another direction? Circles ring his eyes, and his skin is pale. He's jittery, gaze darting to and fro with a glittery sheen. This morning, I found a half-empty bottle of pills in his room, drugs he's using to keep himself alert.

He needs rest. We all do. I didn't fall asleep until he returned home after defacing the Feldherrnhalle, somehow managing to escape detection. When I finally did, it was fitful, dream-laced, and I awoke more exhausted than when I'd gone to bed.

"I'm taking them to the university."

"The university?"

Hans nods, absently picking up a stray copy and scanning the words.

I want to shake him. *Snap out of your haze and talk to me.*

"You're going to leave them outside at night?"

He shakes his head. His gaze meets mine. "I'm going to scatter them in the Lichthof during the day."

"During the . . . you can't be serious, Hans." I take a step closer. "That's foolishness. You'll be caught for sure. Shurik, tell him it's too dangerous."

Alex scrubs a hand across his jaw, posture defeated. "I've tried, Sophie. Believe me."

"It's a simple operation. Go in when morning classes are in session, scatter the leaflets, and leave before lectures let out. The Lichthof will be empty. It'll take less than ten minutes." Hans's tone is pressing, convincing.

"And if you're caught?"

"I won't get caught. It's no different than anything else we've done. Think of the flame it could light among the student body if they read Huber's words. 'The day of reckoning has come, the reckoning of the German youth against the most heinous tyranny our nation ever had to suffer. In the name of all German youth, we demand of Adolf Hitler's state the return of personal freedom, the most precious good of the German people, of which he has cheated us in the most wretched manner.'"

Hans recites the words like an orator, the impact of each sentence filling the air. My gaze has fallen on the typed lines dozens of times as we duplicated, folded, sealed them into envelopes, working most of today to crank out thousands of copies. Yet they still stir something inside me. Despite the exhaustion, the tension, the aching in my head, I sense . . . life. If we can rouse the student body to action, it could lead to widespread uprising. The Führer can't rule Germany without the support of the people, especially the young.

This could make a difference.

I turn to Alex. "Are you going with him?"

"He said he wouldn't," Hans cuts in.

"It's too risky. We're going to Berlin next week. Once we meet with Harnack's group, we can determine our next steps."

Hans turns back to the leaflets. "I won't force you, Alex. I'll go by myself."

"I'll go with you." I speak the words without fully contemplating them.

But . . . *ja*. With me at his side, surely we can escape detection. It will be like he says. Walk in, scatter the leaflets, and leave. I can't count the times I've walked the streets of Munich, leaving a trail of leaflets. Even in broad daylight. It's surprisingly easy, as long as one is fearless.

"Nein." Alex stands, chair legs scraping the floor. Shadows darken his blue-gray eyes, eyes once so alight with life and love of it. "Take them at night, if you must. Leave them outside."

Hans barely gives him a glance. He strides toward me, placing his hands on my shoulders. He smells of pipe smoke, and his hair is boyishly tousled. "Sophie, are you sure?"

I nod, meeting his eyes with a steady look.

A smile eases across his lips. He trusts me now. When I first came to Munich, I had to prove myself to him. Now he trusts me.

I won't let him down.

I won't let any of us down.

"Sophie. Please. Both of you, think about this."

"It'll be all right, Shurik." I smile, trying to reassure both him and myself. "Really."

"We won't do it tomorrow," Hans says, voice absent. "We'll wait until Thursday."

"There's no reasoning with either of you." Alex's voice is deflated, like he knows this is a battle he can't win.

"You needn't stay. Sophie and I can finish up."

Hans didn't mean it to be a dismissal; he cares too much about Alex for that. But it echoes like one nonetheless.

Alex hesitates, looking torn. Then he walks toward the door, picks up his coat off the back of the sofa, and shrugs it on. At the door, he pauses, gaze falling on us. His throat jerks. I look back at him, lips pressed together. Reflected in his eyes is the bravery and despair of the resistance we've undertaken. My heart aches to see it now.

With one final glance, Alex turns away. The door clicks shut.

By the table, Hans scans a piece of paper. He holds it up, two creased pages covered in cramped handwriting. "Christl's leaflet. He gave it to me finally. It's brilliant. I want to begin distribution as soon as possible."

I smile. "Christl always did have a way with words."

A knock sounds. "It's Gisela." Hans refolds Christl's leaflet and places it in the pocket of his trousers as he strides toward the door. "I asked her to come over."

I scan the apartment. Leaflets are piled on the table, along with stamps and stacks of envelopes. Panic vises my chest. "Hans, wait!"

He turns, hand on the knob.

"We can't let her in here. Look at the place."

"She already knows, Sophie," is all he says before opening the door.

I stand next to the sofa, arms hugged across my chest. Gisela steps inside. In seconds, Hans has her in his arms. Their lips meet in a hungry kiss.

Gisela knows.

I shouldn't be surprised. She's been at our apartment often enough during the past weeks, she'd be an idiot if she didn't suspect. How can Hans trust her so much?

I press my hand to my churning stomach.

I don't. Not the way I trust Annalise or Traute. Gisela isn't one of us, and it's obvious she still holds National Socialist views. If we're caught and Gisela's connection with Hans is discovered, would she hold back during an interrogation? Or betray us all?

They stand by the door, still kissing, Hans's fingers tangled in Gisela's hair.

Squaring my shoulders, I turn and walk down the corridor to my bedroom, leaving them alone. Once in my room, I close the door behind me and curl up on my narrow bed, squeezing my eyes shut.

You're the bravest person I've ever known, Sophie Scholl.

Fritz's voice. There it was, filled with laughter, as my seventeen-year-old self snuck into his barracks, blatantly violating the no visitors rule. Now I would never take risks for something so foolish, and the girl who once had is someone I no longer recognize.

If he knew what I was doing now, would he still call me brave?

The question rises, lingers.

It will be weeks before he's released from the hospital. We need time together, unscarred by war's demands. To sit in some sun-dappled spot overlooking the Danube with our arms around each other, to say what cannot be conveyed through empty pen and paper.

To somehow find a new beginning.

"I miss us, Fritz," I whisper into my pillow, a tear sliding down my cheek. "I miss you."

CHAPTER THIRTY-SEVEN

Sophie
February 18, 1943

I DRESS TO BE inconspicuous. A gray skirt, the burgundy sweater Annalise gave me, and my brown, button-down coat. Anyone who saw Hans and me walking across the university grounds toward the Lichthof would think us two ordinary students on our way to classes. It's a spring-like day, unusually warm, sun scattering its rays with a liberal hand.

In ten minutes, it will be over and done. In and out. Just like Hans said. I'll be on a train to Ulm in a couple of hours, leaving Munich and its cares for another long weekend at home.

I glance at Hans as we approach the wide front entrance. He looks at me and gives a little smile. Both of us slept until nine this morning, and his gaze is clearer than I've seen it in weeks.

In and out.

In my left hand, I carry my suitcase. Seventeen hundred copies of our sixth leaflet are within. No fear drums inside my chest. Only purpose. In ten minutes, we'll be long gone, the leaflets left behind. Our ideas scattered for our fellow students to read.

Read . . . and act.

Hans pushes the door open. Our footsteps echo on the stone floor. We turn left.

The clatter of footsteps breaks the quiet. I start. Beside me, Hans tenses. Traute and Willi hurry down the stairs, carrying their satchels. I blink at the sight of our friends. Traute wears a blue spring jacket. A red scarf wraps Willi's neck, the ends showing through his open coat.

"Hello, Traute, Willi." Hans greets them as if this were any ordinary morning at the university.

"We left Huber's lecture early. We don't want to be late getting to the neurology department." Willi's gaze lands on the suitcase in my hand. Questioning. "Coming with us, Hans?"

"Not today. We'll meet later."

"All right." Willi and Traute move past us. Traute. I forgot to tell her . . . Quickly, I glance over my shoulder.

"The ski boots you wanted to borrow are on the back stairwell. Just go in and get them, in case I'm not home this afternoon."

She turns, black curls brushing her cheeks. She smiles. "Danke, Sophie."

Then they're gone, disappearing through the swinging front doors.

Hans and I exchange a quick glance. Time is running out. We race up a flight of stairs. As we enter the Lichthof, I lift my gaze to the high-vaulted ceiling. Sun sparkles through the glass dome. The Lichthof is marble and echoing. Vast. And empty.

Our footsteps pound in time with my heart. We hurry two flights up to the third floor. Flashing a glance over my shoulder, I crouch beside a pillar, unlatch the suitcase, yank an armful of leaflets from the top. Hans grabs several stacks, his satchel in one hand, the leaflets in the other.

We part ways. I dart down the hall, bending down, placing piles of leaflets at intervals. On the opposite side, Hans does the same.

Bend.

Place.

Bend. Place.

Half running, I scatter leaflets outside of classrooms, on stair steps. My heart hammers. My breath heaves in and out. There's no time to stop. To think. By the time classes release—which can't be more than seven minutes away—our bags must be empty.

I skid, nearly tripping on the slick surface. Pausing for a second, one hand lighting on the balustrade, I glance at the far-away floor below. Two marble statues flank the grand main staircase. Their cold, white eyes are empty. Watching.

I retrieve the suitcase, flit down the stairs to the second floor. My hair bumps my cheeks. Sweat slides down my back beneath my coat. Hans's footsteps are loud beside me, his breathing heavy.

We scatter leaflets in front of classroom doorways, along the row of square marble pillars on both sides of the first floor. Hans fills his arms and races across the empty room to the other side.

Bend. A stack of leaflets in front of each pillar. The pillars are massive, hiding me as I place the leaflets. I rush forward, into the open. Exposed.

Papers fall from my fingertips, skating across the floor. I kneel on the stone tiles to grab another stack.

"Hurry." Hans grasps my arm, pulling me to my feet. "We have to go."

We half run toward a side entrance. The door to the outside is straight ahead. I pause, pulse racing, ears attuned for footfalls, voices. Hans looks down at me. "Sophie. Come on."

"The suitcase isn't empty," I whisper, the realization striking me suddenly. "There are still some left."

"What?" he gasps.

"Let's go. Back to the third floor." I start running before he can answer, toward the stairs, back up. My legs burn.

The world blurs, time suspended. Breath pants from my dry lips. Sun streams from the glass ceiling, blinding. I set the suitcase down. It falls open. Grabbing a handful of the remaining leaflets, I scatter stacks along the edge of the balcony, on the floor.

Almost finished.

Hans grabs the last pile from the suitcase, placing it on the edge of the marble balustrade.

"We have to go," he whispers. His eyes are dilated, his jaw tense. "Now."

I grab the suitcase. "Coming."

In a flash, I glimpse the stack on the balustrade. My fingers are a touch away.

The German name will remain defiled forever unless the German youth at last stand up, avenge and make atonement . . .

In a single movement, I reach out, push. The leaflets rain downward, into the void. A cascade of paper and sunlight.

For an instant, I watch their fall, mesmerized.

The bell shrills. Students pour out of classrooms, books in their arms, satchels swinging. Hans and I slow our steps, blending into the crowd.

"You there!"

My heart jolts. I fling a glance at Hans. His face is impassive.

"Halt!" The male voice echoes from below.

My breath seizes. It can't break free. The world closes in, time slowing down.

Eickemeyer's studio key. In my pocket. I have to get rid of it. The frantic thought blares above the numbness. I glimpse an open door nearby. A women's restroom. I dart into the empty, white-tiled room. A faded ottoman sits by the door. Grasping the key from my pocket, I shove it beneath the cushion and race back out. It took only a few seconds. Hans stands where I left him, utterly still, almost catatonic.

Perhaps they weren't calling to us. Perhaps . . .

Of one accord, we join the throng of students spilling into the halls. Several pick up leaflets, scanning them, passing them around. Murmured voices rise and ebb. Casually, unhurriedly, we make our way down the stairs.

Surely there are so many of us. Surely he didn't see our faces . . .

A stocky man in workman's overalls shoves through the crowd, pushing students aside. "You there. Halt!"

Heads down, Hans and I keep walking. Toward the doors.

Toward escape.

Don't look up. Ignore him. Ignore—

"Stand still!" The man grabs hold of Hans's arm. Hans jerks back. "Come with me. You're under arrest."

I stand perfectly still next to my brother. All around, students stop and stare.

"Whatever for?" Hans's tone is even.

"I saw you." The man's voice is sharp and guttural, his face inches from Hans's. "You scattered the leaflets. You're under arrest."

"That's absurd. It's an effrontery to take someone into custody at the university." Hans glares, jaw jutted forward.

"You threw leaflets over the balustrade."

I swallow. *He saw us.* There's no way out. We're surrounded.

Trapped.

In a split second, I make a decision. "Nein. I did."

The man turns to me, as if noticing me for the first time. Of course, he wouldn't notice me first. I'm only a girl, after all. A nobody.

I stare straight back at him.

His pudgy face contorts in a gleeful sneer. "Both of you. Come with me. We'll see what the rector has to say about this." He grips Hans's arm with one hand, mine with the other. His fingers pinch into my flesh. As he leads us up the stairs, I keep my gaze straight ahead.

This is a test. Just a test. All I have to do is pass.

Stay calm. I drill the order into my brain.

Stay. Calm.

We sit on straight-backed chairs against the wall of Rector Wüst's office. Light streams through the windows, a pattern on the floor. Rector Wüst sits behind a massive oak desk. He eyes us with misgiving. On his desk sits a stack of the leaflets.

A single knock.

The door opens. Hans and I look up. Three men in trench coats and low fedoras enter the room. The shortest of the group advances toward Rector Wüst, who rises from his desk.

"Inspector Mohr?"

The man nods. "Heil Hitler." He raises his arm in a perfunctory greeting, which Rector Wüst echoes.

"Here are the persons in question." Rector Wüst gestures to us.

Inspector Mohr looks in our direction. I do not stiffen my shoulders under his gaze, neither do I slump them. I school my features into perfect calm.

You are an ordinary college student. You know nothing of leaflets. You are innocent.

The man who apprehended us—a janitor called Schmid jabbers at Mohr's elbow. "I saw them throw the leaflets over the balustrade. Beyond a doubt, I know it was them." He picks up one of the leaflets from the desk and hands it to Mohr. "Here. Read their sedition for yourself."

Mohr scans the leaflet, muttering the words to himself.

"'Our nation stands shattered by the demise of our men at Stalingrad. The ingenious strategy of the Great War corporal senselessly and irresponsibly rushed three hundred thirty thousand German men into death and doom. Führer, we thank you!'"

He stops. Looks up. His eyes meet mine. Beneath the brim of his fedora, his gaze is penetrating. Other than the sharp gaze, he has an ordinary face. Squarish and middle-aged.

With measured steps, he crosses the room.

"Papers." He holds out his hand for Hans's identification. Hans opens his leather wallet and withdraws them. Mohr gives a compulsory scan, then turns to me. I reach into my coat pocket and hand over my folded identification papers. Our fingertips brush. He looks over the small booklet. The back of my neck begins to itch.

"Are these yours?" He gestures to the suitcase and satchel sitting beside me on the floor.

I nod. Mohr picks up the suitcase and satchel and carries them to the desk. A soft click as he unlatches the suitcase.

Out of the corner of my eye, I glance at Hans. He's sitting with his elbows on his knees. He shifts, shoulder bumping mine. His gaze flickers imperceptibly.

What is he doing?

"The suitcase is empty." Mohr turns back around. "What were you doing carrying an empty suitcase?"

"I was going to visit my parents in Ulm this afternoon." My answer is swift. "I needed the suitcase for clean laundry."

Rector Wüst, Mohr's men, and Schmid stand near the desk. All gazes level on us. Beside me, Hans shifts again. Alarm curls through me. I don't dare glance in his direction.

"There!" One of Mohr's men dashes over. "He's hiding something."

I do look now. He jerks Hans's hands from between his knees, clawing his fingers open. Hans struggles. The man yanks something free, holding up a crumpled piece of paper. It's ripped in half, the tear jagged.

My heart accelerates. What was Hans trying to destroy?

Mohr comes over, stride unhurried. He takes the half-ripped paper and scans its contents. His brow creases.

Mohr looks up, gaze narrowing. "Where did you get this?"

"A student gave it to me." My brother's voice is steady. "I don't know who. I've never seen him before."

Mohr frowns. "Why did you tear it up?"

"I didn't know what it was. I didn't want it to incriminate me. I haven't even read the thing."

One of Mohr's men crouches on the floor, gathering the remaining pieces from beneath Hans's chair. Then it dawns on me. Christl's draft. The one Hans showed me and then shoved back in his trouser pocket. He's wearing the same trousers today.

I let none of this show on my face. Another knock. More men in uniform stride in, carrying stacks of leaflets.

"This is all of them, Inspector," one of them says, adding to the pile on the desk.

"So many." Mohr lifts a brow. With methodical movements, he places the leaflets into my open suitcase.

My mouth goes dry.

Mohr latches the suitcase, faces us. "A perfect fit."

Of course it would be.

I push the thought away. I must think as if I'm innocent, or it will all be useless.

Mohr turns to the men with him. "Let's get going."

One of the officers grabs my arm and pulls me to my feet. He wrenches my hands behind my back. I still as the cold metal handcuffs noose my wrists. I fix my gaze on Hans, being given the same treatment. My brother stands proud, his expression fearless. A slant of sunlight falls upon his strong, handsome face.

I am not afraid. I am not afraid.

But I am.

They march us from the office and down the stairs. Students crowd the Lichthof, almost as if they're being kept there. I don't dare look at any of them. To show recognition would bring that student also under suspicion. In case any of our group is among them, I keep my eyes down. The metal cuffs bite into the tender skin of my inner wrists.

Dear God, this can't be happening.

Behind me, I hear Hans call out to someone, but I can't make out his words.

Out we go into the sunlit afternoon. Spring air wafts across my face.

We're herded into separate black cars. One of Mohr's men crowds into the back seat beside me. The door slams.

The motor starts, and we drive away, the university disappearing from view.

At one time, Wittelsbacher Palace housed Bavarian monarchy. Its towering exterior of weathered stone still looks the part with ornate windows and Gothic carvings. A castle. A fortress.

Now Gestapo headquarters.

I'm led, still handcuffed, into the bowels of the building, through a warren of narrow, echoing corridors. The car holding Hans drove on ahead of mine. I don't know where in this maze of a building my brother is, or if he's here at all.

My arm is numb from the grip of the guard. The gazes of those we pass—men in severe uniforms and dark suits—eye me with accusation. As if I'm a criminal in prison garb, instead of a slim girl in a brown coat.

Allen Gewalten zum Trotz sich erhalten.

I run the timeworn words through my mind.

Help me, dear Lord.

We enter an office lined with cabinets—the beveled letters on the door read "Reception Department." Two uniformed guards sit at desks, turning over papers, telephones at their elbows. A woman stands behind a taller desk, bent over a clipboard. The man holding my arm removes my handcuffs and gives me a little push toward the desk.

The woman looks up. She's slim, brown hair knotted in a tight bun. Probably in her thirties.

"Name." Her tone is businesslike.

"Sophia Magdalena Scholl." I rub my wrists where the cuffs bit into them. My shoulders ache.

Her pen scratches. "Date and place of birth."

"May 9, 1921. Forchtenberg."

"Residence."

"Number 13 Franz-Josef-Straße."

She notes it on her clipboard, then glances up. "Empty your pockets. Remove all jewelry and valuables."

I unfasten my simple leather wristwatch and pass it across the desk. The woman places it in a labeled box, followed by my coin purse, a box of matches, a handkerchief. I have nothing else. She finishes her notations and strides from behind the desk, clipboard in hand.

"This way."

I follow her down the hall and into an anteroom. She closes the door. The bare-walled room is lit by a bright overhead light. A low wooden table sits in the center.

"Remove your clothes and give them to me."

I take off my coat and lay it on the table, followed by my sweater. My roughened fingertips catch on the soft material. I remember Annalise's smile when she gave it to me. "It's perfect."

Annalise. Was she at the university? Did she see us being led away?

What about the rest of our friends—Alex, Willi, Kirk? Do they know we've been arrested? Are they planning escape? We never talked about what to do if something like this happened. We should have.

It's too late now.

My fingers tremble as I unbutton my blouse. I draw in a deep breath through my nose. I must be calm.

God, help me.

I stand in my underthings beneath the harsh lights. My arms prickle with cold. She's searching my clothes. Finished, she turns to me. Her hands run along my body. I stand still as she frisks me, staring at the dirty gray wall opposite.

She looks up. Her pale blue gaze finds mine, tinged with something beyond businesslike coolness.

"If you have anything incriminating, give it to me and I'll get rid of it. I'm an inmate too," she whispers.

I smile at the irony. Just where would she think I'd be hiding something? I'm practically naked, and she's already searched my clothes.

"There isn't anything."

"Admit nothing. The interrogators are a canny bunch. You must be careful."

"I have nothing to hide." Is this a Gestapo trap, putting me in close proximity with a sympathetic woman? If so, I won't fall for it.

"I'm Else Gebel." The woman offers a little smile.

"Sophie Scholl." I say, then realize she already knows that.

"You can get dressed. You'll go back out to be fingerprinted and photo-graphed, and then they'll take you for questioning, I suppose."

I reach for my clothes, their comforting warmth sliding over me. Comb-ing my fingers through my hair, I follow Else from the room.

"Inspector Mohr" reads the black letters on the door. I'm led inside by a broad-faced man wearing a gray suit and swastika armband. He motions to a bench against the wall. I sit, grateful for a momentary respite. The ante-room looks like an ordinary office. Desk, typewriter, and telephone. The man who led me inside thumbs through a stack of papers, barely looking at me. On the opposite end of the room is a closed brown door.

I swallow, my mouth unbearably dry. Am I prepared for interrogation? Of course we always knew it was a possibility. But there's a difference between knowing something is possible and facing it. Today was supposed to be an in-and-out operation. In spite of the risk, I was sure I'd be going home this afternoon.

What will they do to me? Hans told me they tortured Falk Harnack's brother. If they torture me, will I be strong enough to stand it?

My stomach cramps.

A red light flashes above the door, making a low humming sound.

"He's ready for you." The man opens the door.

I stand and smooth my hands across my skirt.

"*Schnell*, Fräulein. He doesn't have all day."

My legs tremble, and I put all my concentration into taking slow, even steps. I step through the open door without a glance back. It closes behind me. Inspector Mohr sits at a polished desk.

He looks up. "Sit down."

I walk toward the chair, sensing Mohr studying my every move. A falter, the slightest show of fear, could add fuel to my implication.

The room's furnishings look filched from the palace's prior occupants—dark wood and rich carpet. Burgundy velvet drapes with gold tassels cloak the two windows. Afternoon sunlight filters in, landing on the desk. A secretary sits at a small table off to the right. She looks away, lips pursed, when I glance at her.

Mohr pulls out a sheet of paper and places it in front of him. His dark hair is sparse and thinning, his hairline receding. He steeples his fingers beneath his chin and regards me for a long moment.

I meet his gaze. An innocent person has nothing to fear. So I shall be innocent.

"Well, Fräulein Scholl. Shall we begin?"

⟶

"If you were traveling to Ulm this afternoon, then why were you at the university?"

"Because I'd made plans to have lunch with a friend the previous day and wanted to tell her I couldn't make it."

"Your friend's name is?"

"Fräulein Gisela Schertling." In the tapestry of truth and lies, it's best to weave in as much truth as possible and make up only what is necessary. It's easier to slip up with an invented story than an established fact.

Mohr jots down the name.

"And where was Fräulein Schertling?"

"At Professor Huber's lecture Introduction to Philosophy. I knew the lecture would be getting out around 11:00 a.m."

"Herr Schmid said you were on the third-floor gallery at 11:00 a.m. Professor Huber's lecture room is on the second floor. Why were you upstairs?"

The party pin on Mohr's lapel glints in the sunlight. My lips are dry. I force myself not to moisten them with my tongue. "When we passed the second floor, the lecture hadn't let out. To pass the time, I decided to show my brother the psychology department, where I often attend lectures. That is upstairs."

"Can you describe the location of the leaflets?" Mohr's gaze never leaves my face. Even when taking notes, it still seems like he's watching me.

I shrug. "My brother and I had already noticed the leaflets at the entrance to the second floor. They were scattered around, stacked in piles. It was the same on the third floor, except there was a pile on the balustrade."

"Did you read them?"

"Briefly."

"What was your reaction?"

"My brother laughed at the leaflet. He stuck a copy in his pocket."

"I didn't ask about your brother's reaction, did I, Fräulein Scholl?"

I take a deep breath.

"Nein." I give a little smile. *That's right, look embarrassed, abashed.* "I'm sorry. I saw them so briefly, I didn't have time to form an opinion. As I said before, I'm apolitical. There were a lot of them though. Whoever scattered them must have worked quickly."

"Herr Schmid said he saw you push the leaflets off the balustrade into the Lichthof. Why did you do that?"

Beneath the desk, my hands are damp with sweat. My neck aches from sitting so stiffly. I swallow. "It was a foolish act, with no premeditated thought behind it. I have a playful nature and like to play pranks. I realize it was a stupid mistake, which I now regret."

Mohr ponders this for a moment. He reaches into his coat and extracts a silver case. He opens the case and takes out a cigarette. Taps it against the edge of the case.

"Why were you carrying an empty suitcase?"

He already asked me this. He must be trying to trip me up. Mohr is not an interrogator for nothing.

"I've already told you. I intended to fill it with laundry I dropped off when I visited my parents in Ulm from February 6 through February 14."

He reaches into his desk and retrieves a lighter. "Train fare is at least fifteen marks. That's a lot of expense, just for clean laundry." He flips the lighter with the pad of his thumb. A flame glows. He touches the tip of the cigarette to the flame. Not once does he take his gaze from me.

"It wasn't just for laundry. I planned to visit a friend who's recently had a baby." That too isn't a complete lie. I did plan to visit Ruth Düsenberg, an unwed girl my parents have been helping during her pregnancy.

"You were in Ulm last week. Why didn't you visit her then?"

A pulsing ache starts in my temples. "I wanted to see her and the baby again, since she's leaving for Hamburg soon. I'd already told my parents I was coming on Friday to spend the weekend at home. I only pushed my trip up one day to visit Fräulein Düsenberg. My sister Inge's boyfriend, Otto Aicher, is on furlough, and we intended to travel to Ulm together. He was getting in on the 11:30 train. I'd arranged to meet him at the Holzkirchner station."

Mohr sets his cigarette in an ashtray, jotting notes. Tendrils of smoke curl upward. I swipe a strand of hair away from my face.

Mohr lays down his pen.

The interrogation continues.

CHAPTER THIRTY-EIGHT

Annalise
February 18, 1943

POUNDING.

I sit up on the sofa and blink, groggy with sleep. What time is it? My joints ache and my body is hot with fever. A glance at the table pulled next to the sofa reveals an empty breakfast tray and several wadded-up handkerchiefs, bringing back foggy memories of this morning, when I woke with a sore throat, too feverish to attend my scheduled classes. The room is shadowed. Dim.

More pounding.

I stand on shaky legs and cross the room, leaving my blanket on the sofa. I'm still in my nightdress, feet clad in woolen socks.

I open the door.

Two men in fedoras and trench coats stand outside. I glimpse a flash of my landlady's face behind them before she vanishes from view.

"Gestapo." The single word is clipped. It slams against my fever-fogged mind.

"What can I—"

"We're looking for Kirk Hoffmann. Is he here?"

"Nein." I shake my head, pulling the collar of my nightgown closed.

They push past me, boots tracking muddy prints across the floor. The narrow-faced one in front strides through the apartment, throwing open doors, tearing through cupboards. Clatters. Crashes. Our dignity tossed aside with our belongings.

I stand in the center of the room, while the other officer leans against the wall. His tall frame knocks a picture crooked—one of my paintings.

The first officer finishes his search and comes back into the room.

"Where is Kirk Hoffmann?"

They've discovered something. The realization filters through my feverish mind.

Kirk was supposed to be on duty at the hospital today; the reason why he couldn't stay home and take care of me. Performing the work of a doctor's assistant, not scattering leaflets or painting graffiti.

The officer strides forward, right up to me. "Answer the question." He shoves his face close to mine. His breath reeks. My mind whirls.

"How should I know? I'm not his keeper." My voice emerges raspy. Whatever happens, I can't lead them to Kirk. But I don't know where he is, where *not* to lead them.

"Who are you then?"

My throat is raw and dry. My legs waver. I need to sit down. But the officer blocks my path to the sofa, gaze drilling into me.

I draw myself up with the dignity of a standartenführer's daughter. "Pardon me, gentlemen. I've been ill. I'll go into the kitchen and fetch a glass of water, then return and answer your questions." I move to sweep past him, but he grasps my forearm.

"You'll answer our questions now. Who are you and what is your relationship to Kirk Hoffmann?" His grip tightens, crushing my arm. I'm thirsty . . . so thirsty . . .

"I'm . . . Frau Annalise Hoffmann. His wife." The moment the words are out, I wonder if I've said the right thing. In our two months of marriage, I've remained Annalise Brandt to all but a few. Perhaps giving my name as Annalise Brandt, daughter of the great standartenführer would have made them show me some respect in whatever awaits us.

But nein. Kirk is my husband. I won't deny him like Peter in the courtyard.

"Is this his residence?"

"This is our apartment. Tell me, what did my husband do? We live very dull lives, I'm afraid. We're students at the university." A cough wracks my body. I press my hand to my mouth. My lungs and chest ache.

He ignores my question. And my coughing. "When is your husband expected to be home?"

I wipe my hand against the back of my mouth. If it didn't hurt so much, I'd have tried to keep coughing. Anything to avoid his questions.

"I don't know," I murmur. The other officer smokes, leaning against the wall, letting the ashes fall onto the rug.

"Don't worry. We'll wait. Sit down." He gives me a shove in the direction of the sofa. I stumble.

"Let me at least get dressed." I turn my gaze away from my interrogator and toward the officer with the cigarette. He's younger, his posture suggesting a lack of zeal for the job. Perhaps he might take pity on a sick young woman in her nightgown.

He stares at me, cigarette trailing smoke. "Very well."

"Go with her," the other officer says. "Watch her."

I move toward the bedroom, the young officer at my heels. My gaze takes in the unmade bed where Kirk and I lay only hours ago, the indentation in his pillow, his volume of Rilke on the bedside table.

What is happening to us, my love?

The officer leans against the doorframe, watching as I pull a woolen skirt and sweater from the armoire. I give him a searing glance. He flushes and looks down at his boots. I force myself to pull my nightgown over my head and dress in the clothing. I run a brush through my hair and sit on the edge of my bed to pull on my stockings and lace up my shoes.

He follows me to the kitchen, in chaos after the search. I turn on the tap and fill a tumbler with water. The cool trickle down my throat eases the rawness. We return to the front room, and I sit on the edge of the sofa. Time drags, but my mind races.

What's happening? It's an ordinary Thursday. What could have gone wrong?

An hour (or is it longer?) passes. Then footsteps, a key in the lock. My heart pounds.

Dear God, let it be someone else, anyone else . . .

Kirk opens the door. I watch helplessly from the sofa as he takes in the two officers. A flicker of shock and alarm flashes through his eyes, before he schools his features into a hard, blank stare.

"Kirk Hoffmann?" The officer in charge unfolds himself from his seat.

"*Ja.*" Kirk meets his gaze square on.

"You and your wife will come with us. You're to be taken in for questioning."

"On what grounds?" In his uniform, Kirk is the image of a perfect German soldier. Perhaps they'll realize they've made a mistake. They aren't here for us after all.

"No questions."

"You can't just—"

The officer takes a step toward Kirk. "No questions."

In seconds, he's pulling Kirk's arms behind him, snapping on handcuffs. The younger officer comes toward me. For a moment, apology fills his eyes, before he hauls me to my feet. Cool metal closes around my wrists, chafing. Panic slides sharp talons around my throat. I try and wriggle my wrists, but I can't move.

Dear God, this can't be happening . . .

I meet Kirk's gaze, clinging to it like a drowning woman, as the men lead us from the apartment and into the night.

Sophie
February 19, 1943

It's been ten hours since the start of my second interrogation. Still the questions come.

Bright white light from a desk lamp glares directly into my eyes. Across the desk, Mohr is a shadowy figure, blurred by the light. His distinguishing characteristic is his voice, rising and falling depending on the question and my answer.

I'm slipping. Hour after hour, I've tried to hang on, to parry the questions, to stay alert. But I'm weakening. Deep in the pit of my stomach, I sense it.

Mohr reaches into a drawer of his desk. Deliberately, he pulls out a pistol, placing it between us.

"A .08-pistol. Found in our search of your apartment."

They'd searched our apartment. My chest tightens. We'd become careless out of exhaustion over the past weeks. *Stupid. Stupid.*

What else had they found? Leaflets? The typewriter?

I envision our front room, as we'd left it before going to the university. What had Hans done with the typewriter? Was it at Eickemeyer's?

The table. Toast crumbs. A cup with half-drunk tea. The typewriter in its case. Shock punches the breath from my lungs.

Dear heaven, had we left leaflets lying about too?

My gaze falls on the pistol. Mohr waits for my answer, likely wondering at my pause. "It belongs to my brother. Hans is an officer. He served in Russia during the break between summer and winter semesters."

"If the pistol was to be used for the purpose of fulfilling his duties in the Wehrmacht, why keep it in his personal quarters?"

Stop. I want to scream. *Just stop.*

Instead, I face Mohr, eyes stinging in the light. "I couldn't say."

"Know how to use it?"

I shake my head.

"A total of 186 9-mm caliber bullets were found in your desk. What were they doing there?"

"Hans must have put them there." That much is true. I'd make up a reason why, but if Hans has given another explanation and our stories don't match, it would bring our innocence under more doubt.

"You don't know the purpose of bullets stored in your own desk? You're not an idiot, Fräulein Scholl."

"It isn't a crime to own a weapon."

"It is to conceal information." Mohr withdraws several sheets of stamps. He passes them across the desk.

I press my lips together, keeping my face blank. Four sheets. One hundred eight-pfennig stamps. The Führer's profile glowers up at me from each one.

Oh, Hans.

"Care to explain their purpose?" Mohr leans forward, arms folded on the desk.

"I've never seen them before."

"You're lying, Fräulein Scholl. You said you'd purchased stamps a week ago."

"I purchased fifteen stamps of various denominations. Not these."

"Eight-pfennig. The same kind used to mail the leaflets."

"As I said, I know nothing about them."

"There are one hundred stamps here. Found in your brother's desk. All of them could not have been purchased at the same post office without suspicion. Someone had to go to a great deal of trouble in order to obtain them. This is proof"—he stabs his finger against the sheet of stamps, voice rising—"proof your brother is part of a treasonous organization against the German government."

"It proves nothing except that he likes to write letters. My brother is a medical student, a soldier. He is not the person you're looking for." I dig my nails into my palm.

Stay. Alert.

"What about this?" The desk drawer creaks as Mohr opens it again. He holds up a little notebook. Tightness spirals through my body.

A notebook with a faded blue cover. The record of expenses incurred during the leafleting operation, along with lists of those who donated and the amounts given.

I know every line in it.

"It's in your handwriting." Mohr licks the tip of his thumb and leafs through the pages. "An expense record, perhaps? For materials purchased to produce leaflets." He sets the notebook on the desk.

"It is a record of expenses," I say. "Some friends have loaned me money for living expenses in Munich—"

"You're lying!" Mohr slams his fist onto the desktop. "I ordered you to tell the truth, and you are blatantly defying that order."

"Nein." My voice escalates. "I'm answering your questions to the best of my ability."

The door opens. "Inspector Mohr?" A male voice. "A moment, if you will."

Mohr rises without a word to me. The man at the door comes into the room. Mohr exits. The door clicks shut.

I blink against the light, turning my gaze from it. I close my eyes. A kaleidoscope of spots dance before me. A minute passes.

I open my eyes, focusing. The clock on the wall reads 5:00 a.m. My eyes are gritty. The secretary is long gone, leaving Mohr and me alone for the past several hours.

Only a door separates my brother and me. Hans, in the next room, also being interrogated. How is he holding up? Is he evading the questions? Or breaking beneath them?

Earlier I seemed momentarily distracted, and Mohr asked what was wrong. I ventured to voice my concerns about Hans's welfare, saying I knew it was often the case to use force during interrogation. Mohr gave me an almost fatherly smile, got up, and opened the connecting door. For a moment, I glimpsed my brother's face—deathly pale in the eerie light. Our gazes met. Then the door shut.

"See," Mohr had said. "I told you he was all right. We're not the monsters you believe us to be, Fräulein Scholl. Just good citizens of the Fatherland, doing our jobs."

Hans isn't all right. He's pale and exhausted.

But Mohr was right about one thing. Those employed within these walls are "good citizens." Following orders. Doing their jobs.

Model German patriots.

I resist the urge to let my face fall into my hands.

How long can it go on?

For a moment, I let my posture relax. Crumple. Almost. Tension knots my neck muscles. My sweater is damp at the armpits.

The door opens. Mohr steps inside, and the other man exits. Leather creaks as Mohr takes his seat. For a long moment, he regards me, features shadowy in the unrelenting light.

"It's no use, Fräulein Scholl. We have your brother's confession."

Everything within me stills. This is just another trick. Hans wouldn't have . . .

Mohr picks up a sheet of paper. "'Because I—as a citizen of Germany—wish not to show indifference toward the fate of my nation and its people,

I resolved to act upon my convictions and print the truth that has been denied to my countrymen. That is how I came upon the idea of writing and producing leaflets.'" Mohr lowers the page. "Your brother takes the blame for everything. Read his statement for yourself." He slides the paper across the desk.

Beneath the glaring light, I take it in—typed words against white paper.

At the bottom of the page is my brother's signature. Unmistakable.

A slow heat rises inside me. I raise my eyes from the paper to Inspector Mohr.

"There's no point in lying." He leans forward, voice low. "You took part in your brother's activities. Come now, Fräulein Scholl. Admit the truth. Who else is responsible for writing and distributing the leaflets?"

My hands are shaking from stress and fatigue. The light burns my eyes.

I'm not ashamed of what I did, not one single piece of it. I would do it again without hesitation. I clear my throat, gathering the words from deep inside. After I voice them, there will be no taking them back. I meet Mohr's gaze—what a weak, misguided man—without flinching.

"I am."

Mohr stares at me without speaking. He draws in a long breath, a sigh. I confessed. He should be elated.

I confessed.

God, help me.

"Our scientific report specifically states the author of the leaflets is a man."

Sudden energy rallies through my body. I have a cause now. I must forget about everything but fighting for it. No one but the two of us will bear this blame. Someone must remain to continue the work when this is all over.

For we will not be.

"Then your scientific report is wrong. I participated as much as my brother. In everything." I'm strong again and the words flow seamlessly. "In the summer of 1942, we resolved to act on our convictions that Germany has lost the war and every life sacrificed on the altar of victory is a life sacrificed in vain. The decision to produce leaflets as a form of passive resistance was made by both of us."

I pause. A heavy weariness possesses my body.

Dear God, I don't have the strength to go on.

"May I be allowed to rest now?" My voice cracks.

Mohr nods, some of the steel in his eyes softening. "*Ja.* In a little while, you may rest." He switches off the bright light, faces me. "Twenty-one years old. A mere girl." His voice is distant, musing. "Such a waste." He rubs a hand across his eyes.

I turn my gaze away, too tired to contemplate his words or the expression in his eyes. A minute passes.

He picks up the phone on his desk with a click. "Stenographer. We have a confession."

Sophie
February 20, 1943

My third interrogation. In the hours of endless questions, Mohr has drilled me on every aspect of our activities, probing for new information. He maintains it's impossible the two of us accomplished so much alone. Over and over, I give evidence to the contrary, listing dates and numbers of leaflets, casting blame upon ourselves with the same fervency I once deflected it.

I mentioned Alex though. At first, it was a slip of the tongue in the blur of questions. But Mohr pushed relentlessly until I admitted Alex was our accomplice. I played down his involvement as much as I could.

Still I betrayed him.

A cold sickness soaks through me, to my core. Have I ever known such soul-crushing regret? So many regrets.

How many will pay because of them?

Mohr sits back in his chair and lights a cigarette. It's late morning, five hours since we began. The curtains are pulled back. Sunlight weak as broth filters into the room.

"It fascinates me that you, a young woman who has enjoyed every advantage and educational opportunity, would be so blatantly misguided. All the Führer has done has been for people like you, the next generation. And you repay his generosity with this?" Mohr picks up one of the leaflets, tosses it back onto the desk. "Sedition! Treason!"

He seems to want to argue with me. Why, I have no idea. What does it matter to him to convince me he's right and I'm wrong? It seems our philosophy, as well as our actions, are now on the dock.

Yet the words pull at me, begging for release. My beliefs are worth defending. Even if, in doing so, I alter no one's opinion.

I face him across the desk. "If the Führer keeps on, there will be no next generation. They'll all be dead. Tens of thousands of German lives were lost at Stalingrad. And all for what? Victory? That word has no meaning."

"It has great meaning! It means Germany will again be able to hold its head high after the abominations of the Great War and the Treaty of

Versailles." Mohr leans forward, cigarette smoldering between his fingers. "It means we, the German people, will be able to take pride in ourselves because we have, at long last, a leader to be proud of."

My words won't save me. Nor, I doubt, will they change this man. But still I say them. If I don't defend truth when it's most difficult, who am I to have defended it in the first place?

"Are you really proud, Herr Mohr? Are you proud of a country that sends thousands of innocent men, women, and children to their deaths because of their race? Because they are not 'pure' enough for you. How can anyone take pride in knowing many have been killed, even German citizens, because their physical health deemed them unfit to live? By whose standards? Who are we to judge who dies and who lives? We are not God."

Mohr opens his mouth, but I rush on.

"You speak of victory. It is a lie. The worst kind of lie, because too many people have been forced to believe it out of fear of what will happen to themselves and their families if they speak their true feelings."

Mohr's lip curls. "You would have done well to have nurtured some of that fear yourself. I hope, at least, you see that now."

I shake my head. "I don't regret my conduct. I believe I've done the best I could for my country and my conscience. I'm ready to stand before God only with the regret I didn't do more."

"God." Mohr spits the word. "He cannot save you now."

A slow smile spreads across my lips. "He is the only one that can. If not in this life, then in the one to come." Conviction, pure and warm, seeps through me.

For a long moment, Mohr stares at me. He puts the cigarette to his lips, the tip glowing orange. Inhales. "Such passion," he says softly, blowing the words out with the smoke. "So misguided. Work with us, Fräulein Scholl. Surely you see now how you were swayed by your brother's actions. You looked to him for guidance, and he led you astray. The court would be sympathetic to such a statement made by a young woman."

For one shameful instant, the idea lures me. All I have to do is say the words. It would mean a lessening of the blow to my parents. A chance. Life.

But what kind? One lived with the knowledge that at the last minute, I turned my back on my conscience? That would make me little better than Hitler and his generals.

That is no life.

I turn my gaze toward the window. Even here, in such a place as this, the sun shines.

I swallow. "You're asking me to let my brother take all the blame? To go against all I believe in order to save myself?" I shake my head, my voice strong. "Nein, Herr Mohr. My brother and I should receive the same sentence. If what we have done is a crime, we are equally guilty."

Snuffing the cigarette in an ashtray, Mohr rises. His broad chest lifts in a sigh. The party pin on his lapel glints up at me. "Very well then." He pulls a handkerchief from his pocket and wipes it across his palms. "I'll ring for someone to return you to your cell." He doesn't look at me. "I have nothing further to say to you."

CHAPTER THIRTY-NINE

Kirk
February 20, 1943

"TELL US ABOUT YOUR connection to Hans Scholl." The voice on the other side of the light is knife-point sharp.

"Scholl and I are both part of the Second Student Medical Company. It was only natural we would know each other."

"Gisela Schertling stated you and Scholl spent a great deal of time together. What did you do?" Inspector Kruger is a shadow. At first, the light was mild. Kruger has since turned it up. My eyes water.

"We share similar interests in literature and philosophy. We're fond of Goethe."

"You're telling me you and Scholl got together and talked about Goethe?" I shrug. "Why not?"

"Not a word about treasonous printed matter? Like this?" He passes a sheet of paper across the desk. I recognize the bold heading of our leaflet. *Fellow Students!*

"Never seen it before."

"Even though almost two thousand copies of these leaflets were scattered in the university Lichthof just two days ago?"

"I wasn't at the university. I was working at the hospital where LMU medical students assist the physicians. I've already told you this." My mouth is dry. My stomach, hollow.

Why didn't Hans tell me his plans? I could've stopped him. Or gone with him.

Why did you do this, my bold, reckless friend?

"Don't tell me during your conversations about literature and philosophy, Scholl didn't mention his own literary attempts," Kruger says the last with a sneer. "You were good friends. You must have suspected something."

"In the course of my friendship with Hans Scholl, he gave the impression of being fully dedicated to German victory. In our service together at the front, I found him a perfect soldier, desirous to do his duty for the Fatherland. I'm shocked to discover he would be behind something so defamatory. It's not like him at all." Perhaps it's not customary for a Christian to pray he will be a convincing liar. But today I pray that prayer and mean it with all my heart.

"Scholl himself mentioned you procured stamps for him in January. Stamps used for the distribution of leaflets."

The Gestapo will do anything to get information, even give false evidence. What has Hans told them? Beneath the desk, I wipe damp hands across my trouser legs.

"It's true I purchased a quantity of stamps for Scholl, at his request. He said he needed them to send letters to his family and comrades on active duty. This seemed to me a reasonable request. Scholl promised to reimburse me at a later date, since he said he was short on funds."

"And did he?"

"Nein. It was such a small matter between friends. I'd forgotten all about it until now. Scholl was always performing little kindnesses for those in his circle. I was happy to return the favor."

"Those in his circle? Like Schmorell? We have a reward for a thousand marks posted, to be granted to anyone with information regarding his whereabouts. Both Scholl and his sister Sophie have detailed Schmorell's participation in full."

I draw in a shallow breath. They incriminated Alex? Or was the interrogator just telling me this so I would affirm it?

My head pounds. Though they put me in a cell with a cot, I didn't sleep last night. Worry for the Scholls and Annalise kept me awake, staring at the cracks in the ceiling, panic a vise around my throat.

"Schmorell was part of Hans Scholl's circle of friends. But I never knew him to be involved in anything untoward. Alex is an artistic type. Always sculpting or making music. Between you and me, he's got more imagination than brains." I try to sound like I'm playing along with the interrogator, leaning forward, adding a chuckle at the end.

"Artistic, you say? Have you heard of the 'artwork' appearing around Munich? 'Freedom. Down With Hitler.'"

"I've seen the graffiti, ja. Who in Munich hasn't? But I doubt Alex would waste good paint on something like that. It's too expensive."

"Enough! Admit you knew Scholl and Schmorell were involved in high treason. Christoph Probst was their accomplice."

Christl? This is the first his name has been mentioned. What does he have to do with it? Except . . .

Hadn't Hans mentioned Christl had written a leaflet draft?

"You guys are crazy." I laugh, hoping Kruger didn't notice my momentary pause. "Probst? He's too busy having brats. Three children in as many years of marriage. He hasn't got time for anything else." Never would I have spoken such about these, my dearest friends, if not to protect them. Out of all of us, Christl must be kept safe.

"What about you then? Your wife is in custody too, you know. It will fare better for both of you if you tell us everything."

Annalise. Her name hits me like a fist to the gut. The look in her eyes as we were led to the Gestapo car hasn't stopped haunting me. The way her body shook next to mine on the seat, her eyes filled with fear, her face flushed with fever.

I force thoughts of her away. If I let them in, they'll be my undoing.

"Annalise is the daughter of an SS officer. Do you honestly think we would have any part in activities, which, as you've said, are equal to high treason?"

"Your wife herself admitted your marriage was a secret. She stated her *vater* had no knowledge of it."

"That has nothing to do with the case at hand."

"While you are in our custody, Herr Hoffmann, *everything* is relevant." Kruger rises. He switches off the light. I blink, vision blurred by blotches of white. "We will find out the truth about each and every one of you." He leans forward. "And then you will pay the price."

Sophie
February 20, 1943

The cell door creaks open. I turn from where I've been standing at the window, staring out at the canvas of blue sky from behind black iron bars.

Else—my cellmate since arriving at the Wittelsbacher Palace—hastens past the guard. The door groans closed, the key scraping in the lock. A smile lights up her pale features.

"Did you have a good rest?"

I nod. "*Ja.* Danke."

"I have news." She sits on the edge of her cot, folding her hands in front of her. "It's about the prisoner brought in earlier today."

"It's Alex Schmorell, isn't it?" A shudder passes through me. Alex, so handsome and fine, inside this place, dragged into the undertow along with us. Could I have somehow shielded him?

The question is a painful echo.

Else shakes her head. "It's a man called Christoph Probst."

Breath leaches from my lungs. I cling to the cold cell wall, legs weak beneath me.

"Nein." I press my lips together, hot tears choking my throat. "Nein."

"Sophie, what?"

Else's face is a blur through my tears. "Christl is innocent. He has a family. A wife and two little boys. A baby daughter, just born." I press my hand to my mouth, droplets of salt and water sliding over my fingers. "He's so . . . good, Else. So good. He doesn't deserve this. All he did was write a few words. That's all."

"I'm sorry," Else whispers.

I swipe my hand across my cheek, gulping back a sob. "He has the most . . . radiant smile. To look at it is to watch the sun rise."

Memories. Christl laughing as he lifted his little Michael onto his shoulders, a look of pure joy on his face. Christl, passionately declaring only action could provide our absolution. Never have I seen such love in anyone's eyes as when he spoke of his wife.

"My Herta. The best and dearest of women."

All he wanted was to live in a loving world, to give love to those around him. An ordinary man who saw darkness and sought to eradicate it.

"Surely he will receive a lighter sentence." I gather myself, drawing in a long breath. "Imprisonment only. And the war will be over soon."

One miracle. Christl's release. Would that be too much to ask?

I sink onto the edge of my cot, head bent, aware of Else's gaze upon me.

In such a world as this, there are no miracles.

February 21, 1943

Do you know what you are being charged with? the gaze of the prosecutor seems to ask. He passes a stack of papers across the desk.

"In accordance with regulations, here is a copy of the indictment. Your trial will take place tomorrow at 10:00 a.m. at the People's Court in Munich. The president of the People's Court, Judge Freisler, will preside." He pauses, as if expecting some reaction from me. I don't give him the satisfaction of one. "You've been charged with high treason," he adds.

I only stare at him, hands limp at my sides.

"If you will sign this, stating you are in receipt of the indictment." He sets a piece of paper before me, along with a pen. I bend over the desk and slowly form my name. Hair falls into my face. I must have left my bobby pin back in the cell.

The pen clicks against the desk as I set it down. I pick up the indictment, the three-page document weightless in my fingers. Only words. My life is one long lesson in their power.

"Take her away." The prosecutor opens a leather binder, as if I'm no longer in the room. The guard grasps my arm and leads me out of the office, into the maze of corridors.

Where are they taking me now?

Physically, I'm in their control. Only my spirit remains my own.

Footsteps meet my ears. A guard comes down the other side of the corridor, holding onto the arm of a woman.

Annalise. Pale, her hair a flame around her face. She walks erect, shoulders back.

Our eyes meet.

Those who have never been denied underestimate the power of a single look. In the moment our gazes meet, much is said that words cannot convey. Perhaps more than has ever been said in the course of our friendship. Neither of us beg for strength. We both give it to each other, like a cord from which heat flows. It makes me brave to look at her, remembering all that's passed between us. The conversations and shared secrets. Laughing and sipping Chianti. Working late into the night, bolstering each other onward. She smiles softly, and I recall the moment I first saw that smile, when she bid me goodbye after I caught her reading Heine.

We were girls then. Experience, not time, has made us women.

We pass each other. I don't dare look behind me.

The guard unlocks the cell, and I step inside, carrying my indictment papers. Else sits on a chair next to the wooden table, rubbing a spot on a shoe with a piece of cloth. The door groans shut.

I slowly scan the typed words of the indictment. In emotionless legalese, the three of us—Hans, me, and Christl—are charged with high treason, conspiracy, of having attempted during a time of war to give aid to the enemy against the Reich, and of demoralization of the armed forces.

My hand begins to shake. I set the indictment on the table.

"Our trial is tomorrow," I say softly.

Else nods.

"Will you get into trouble if you read the indictment?" Suddenly, I want the comfort of other eyes besides mine upon these cold, final words.

She shakes her head and picks up the pages. As she reads, her face turns pale, her eyes, afraid.

When I first stepped through the doors of Wittelsbacher Palace, I thought I might be able to escape the worst. This indictment has laid bare my illusions for what they were. Illusions.

My footsteps are loud in the tiny cell as I cross to the single, barred window. I close my eyes and lift my face up, letting the sun warm it. How I've always loved the sun. As a child, I never tired of lying on a blanket, falling asleep caressed by its rays.

I'll never lie on a blanket beneath the sun again.

My chest tightens. I don't fear death, but I mourn the loss of the life I might have lived. I'll never again listen to the soaring notes of a violin or run barefoot across warm grass. Never again feel the pleasant burn in my legs from climbing the Alps, reaching the top breathless and windblown, the world spread before me, close and faraway all at once.

Fritz and I will never marry. I'll never hold the soft warmth of a newborn child in my arms. Feel a lover's kiss against my lips, his hands around mine as we circle the room in dance.

I cannot help my longing for those things any more than I can help my need for breath. I've always thought life a joyful thing, the world a gift. In spite of bombs and war, the insanity of hatred, the darkness crushing all around me.

Now that very darkness will destroy me too.

I draw in a breath, imagining myself drinking in sweet mountain air instead of the dank must of the cell.

Turning, I glimpse Else lying on her cot, the indictment beside her on the gray blanket. Sadness fills her eyes. As if she too realizes there are no more illusions.

I smile a little. "Such a fine, sunny day," I whisper. "Isn't it?"

Else nods.

"And I have to go. But so many die every day on the battlefields, all those promising young men. What will my death matter if, because of our actions, thousands will be awakened and stirred to truth. Surely, the students will revolt when they hear what has been done to us."

"I'm sure of it," is all Else says. She looks at me with a strange kind of wonder, her cheek against the faded pillow slip.

"I could just as easily die of a disease. But there would be no purpose in such a death." I straighten my shoulders. "My only regret is that I didn't do more, that I've sold my life too cheaply."

"You don't know what the sentence will be." Else sits up, arms wrapped around her knees. "It might be a long imprisonment."

I shake my head. "If Hans is sentenced to death, I must not get a lighter sentence. I'm as guilty as he is." I sit on the edge of my cot. I'm calm again. Numb, maybe, but in control of myself.

"At the very least, everyone receives ninety-nine days before execution. The war might be over by then," Else says. "It won't be long before the Allies invade."

I suppose it's possible. But what is the point, really, in letting myself clutch at another illusion?

A knock sounds on the door. Else and I look up. A man in a suit steps inside the cell.

"Sophia Magdalena Scholl?"

I rise.

"I am Attorney Klein, your defense." A wisp of a mustache frames his thin upper lip. "Do you have any questions?"

"Can you confirm my brother is entitled to a firing squad? Since he's a veteran of the war." My voice is steady. At the very least, Hans should not have to die a humiliating death.

Klein takes a step back, shock evident in his gaze. He fiddles with the rim of the hat in his hands. "I . . . I believe your brother has been stripped of all rights as a soldier."

"And what of me? Will there be a public hanging?"

I must ask these things. I must know.

Klein's face blanches. He coughs. "I'm not certain."

"Can you at least tell me what will happen to my family?" I close my hands into fists at my sides. "Will they be arrested too?" I well know the government protocol of *Sippenhaft*—collective responsibility. When one sins, all suffer.

"I have no influence in the matter."

"What kind of lawyer are you?" I no longer care what any of them think of me. Nothing I say will change tomorrow's outcome. My voice rises. "I've asked you three questions. You haven't answered one."

His face reddens. "You dare insult me! You should expect no mercy tomorrow. The People's Court will uphold justice, and you will get what you deserve."

"I have no further questions." I grit out the words, turning away.

Seconds later, the door shuts.

CHAPTER FORTY

Annalise
February 21, 1943

MY CELLMATE SNORES SOFTLY, though it's only afternoon. Here there is little to do but sleep and wait to be summoned. Here humans are chattel, moved at will.

I lie on my cot, spent from the cough that's shredded my lungs, the headache pounding against my temples. I've asked to be treated by a physician. Thus far, none has been sent.

I'm permitted to rest, for now. But it's only a matter of time before they come for me again.

I've been interrogated twice. Both times, I managed to hold my own against the questions, playing up the fact that I was a bored university student. My secret marriage to Kirk Hoffmann? Well, wasn't that just like a film? Treasonous leaflets? Oh, I'd seen one of them. It had been sent to me in the mail. But I burned it as soon as I read it. Sophie Scholl? My friend, who talked with me about art and theology. "I'm sure you must be mistaken. She has no interest in politics."

All the while, my insides knotted with fear for my friends. For Kirk. I suspect others have been arrested and interrogated. My cellmate told me Willi Graf is in custody. Beneath Willi's mild exterior is a sharp mind. I know he'll stay one step ahead of them.

I saw Sophie this afternoon. We passed in the corridor as I was on the way to my cell after interrogation. She looked tired and rumpled, the sweater I'd given her half buttoned, her eyes large in her pale face. But the expression in them assured me she'd not lost her fighting spirit. Our shared look of solidarity strengthened me more than anything has since arriving in this place of locked doors and endless voices and loud footsteps.

A set of footsteps comes down the corridor now. I tilt my head and listen, holding my breath, waiting for whomever it is to pass. Instead, the steps slow and stop. In front of my door.

My mouth goes dry.

A rattle as the key turns. The door moans on its hinges.

"Frau Hoffmann?"

I nod, rising.

"Come with me. You have a visitor."

"A visitor? Who?" The question escapes, a remnant of the outside world, where questions are answered. Here everything is veiled, prisoners kept in a state of perpetual uncertainty.

Leaving my cellmate still asleep, I follow the guard, every step making my head throb worse. Surprisingly, he doesn't seize my arm but lets me walk beside him. I tuck a piece of hair behind my ear, smoothing back the tangled strands.

As we pass rows of cells, I strain my ears for a familiar voice, looking down every corridor for a glimpse—just one—of Kirk. As before, nothing.

We stop in front of a door, and the guard fumbles with a set of keys. I wait, apprehension a patter in my chest. I thought visitors weren't allowed since we're in interrogative custody.

The guard gives me a push inside. The room is dim, a single light hanging above a scarred wood table. A man stands in front of the barred window, his back to me.

Vater. Even before he turns, I recognize him. I would know those broad shoulders, that always perfectly Aryan bearing anywhere.

It was May when I saw him last. The day I left for university. The past ten months have aged me more than just days. Then, deep down, I still craved something from him, though I'd never have admitted it. Approval. A parent's love.

I've grown stronger since. Sure of myself and what I believe and secure in God. Has it died then? The craving?

I don't know.

"Hello, Vater."

He turns. I'm struck by how the months have changed him. His face bears new lines, gray threading his close-cropped blond hair. A white sling stands out against his uniform, cradling his injured arm.

"Annalise." His tone is curt.

I pull my sweater tighter around myself, folding my arms across my chest. "What are you doing here?"

"I might ask you the same thing." Weak light from the window bathes his features.

"How did you find me?"

"One of my colleagues phoned. An acquaintance from Munich." He takes a step closer. "I've never been so humiliated." The words are a hiss from between gritted teeth. "A daughter of mine entangled in treason against the Reich—"

My chin juts forward. "I know of no treason."

"So you've nothing to do with the leaflets? The graffiti, slurs against the Führer plastered all over Munich?"

I do not answer. Nor do I break my stare.

"They tell me your husband's here too. You're married."

"I am."

"We had an agreement, Annalise. You broke it."

"I fell in love." My words are fierce. And the truest ones I've spoken in the past three days.

"With a traitor."

"My husband is no traitor. He's a good man." *A much better man than you will ever be.*

"A good man is one I would've chosen for you. An officer to do your family and the Fatherland proud." He blows out a husk of a sigh. "Why, Daughter?"

"What?" I whisper, caught by the word. Daughter. He hasn't called me that since I was a child. Then it was his address to me, the closest thing to an endearment I've ever heard from his lips.

"Why did you do this? You were always a good girl. A bit unruly perhaps, but an obedient, loyal child."

I press my fingers into my palm, the pain anchoring me.

A good girl. An obedient, loyal child. Since when did he ever show by word or deed that I was those things to him? Not in years. If ever, they are lost to my memory. I was always hungry for words telling me he loved me, something to show I was enough.

They never came.

"I've done nothing to be ashamed of."

"You're involved with these students, these rabble-rousers. Scattering leaflets, defacing buildings with treason." He takes a step toward me, almost as if he would place both hands on my shoulders, as he did when I was little and he wanted to tell me something important. "Tell me you knew nothing about their activities." His gaze is almost pleading. "Tell me your friends are guilty, and you are innocent." He holds the words out to me, an offering almost. Denounce my comrades to save myself. I can lie on behalf of us all, but I cannot, will not do this.

"We are *all* innocent of any crime. The Scholls are ordinary young people. Hans is a sergeant, a medical student. He was at the front last summer. Sophie spent years in the labor service."

"They are the perpetrators behind this outrage of dissent!" His words are a crescendo. "Judge Freisler will deal with them accordingly."

The very name of the infamous People's Court judge makes my limbs weak.

Silence hangs between us. "How is Mutter?" I venture to ask.

"She's sick. Since hearing of your arrest, she went into a decline."

I see Mutter's face as it looked when I left her. So pale and gray. She wanted me to stay. If I had, I'd still be in Berlin, away from this prison and the fate of my friends.

I don't regret being here. We did what needed—demanded—to be done. But I do regret causing her pain.

"Tell her I love her." My whisper is a broken thing. When was the last time I let myself break before him? But I'm breaking now, for my mutter and my brothers and the family I lost. "Will you . . . do that for me?"

His nod is almost imperceptible. "Auf Wiedersehen, Annalise." He moves past me and knocks on the cell door.

My eyes fall closed. There's no use in echoing a goodbye that will not be heeded. But something inside makes me murmur one anyway, my whispered words drowned by the key in the lock and the step of the guard.

Two hours after Vater leaves, a physician enters my cell. Apparently concessions are made after one receives a standartenführer as a visitor. Likely the only good his rank will ever do me. The thought makes my lips curve in an ironic smile.

The cold metal of the stethoscope presses against my chest as the doctor listens to my breathing. I sit on the edge of my cot, body shaking. With fever? Stress? Exhaustion? All three and so much more.

The doctor draws the stethoscope away. "You have acute bronchitis, which could turn into pneumonia." He pauses, shifting on the low wooden chair. "Have you suffered from any lung conditions in the past?"

I shake my head.

"I'll leave you with something for your cough and aspirin for your headache. Were you not here . . ." He looks away. "I'd recommend further treatment. But they won't permit your release."

I nod.

"If you grow worse, don't hesitate to ask for me again."

"Who should I ask for?" My voice is as limp and wrung-out as my body.

"My name is Dr. Friedrich Voigt." He rests a hand against my knee. The briefest of touches. His eyes are gentle. Compassionate, almost. As if he understands how powerless one truly is in this place. Our gazes hold.

"I'm Annalise," I murmur.

He gives a faint smile and reaches into his bag, withdrawing a bottle and a paper packet.

The door opens. "Time's up." The guard's voice is brusque.

Dr. Voigt flicks a glance at the guard. "I'm instructing the patient as to her treatment. You'll permit me a moment more." Yet when he turns to me and explains the medicine and dosage, his voice is cool, his words perfunctory. He leaves within minutes, bag in hand.

After pouring a dose of the medicine onto a spoon and swallowing the syrupy-sweet liquid, I lie down on my cot, hands folded across my middle, staring at the ceiling. Images flicker through my mind. Alex grinning, strumming his balalaika, tossing it aside and grabbing my hands, whirling me in a dance. Sophie hurrying down the street to buy envelopes, pausing beside a horse and cart stopped near the curb. Laughing as she patted the horse's neck, before stepping into the shop.

Kirk pressing a kiss against my lips as his mutter carried in the *Gesundheitskuchen* amid smiles and sunlight and the sweetest of joy.

I squeeze my eyes shut.

Dear God, what will become of us?

⌁

Sophie
February 21, 1943

He is the last person I expect to see when the cell door opens.

"Fräulein Scholl." Inspector Mohr comes inside. My gaze lands on the parcel in his hand. He sets it on the table. From her seat on her cot, Else watches him warily.

"*Ja?*" I rise from my cot.

"I thought . . . you might like some fruit. Apples." He gestures to the paper-wrapped parcel. "A packet of cookies as well."

I've had answers and retorts to his every question, but I don't know what to say to this. This Gestapo interrogator showing me a kindness? It baffles me. What place do small kindnesses have when he and his kind are working to send us to our deaths?

I regard his face in the dim light. In a different world, would he have been a better man, one who stood by morality and conscience? The question tugs at me, but I do not entertain it. Everyone, regardless of circumstances, breeding, or time, always has a choice.

And Mohr has chosen to bring me fruit.

He clears his throat, obviously expecting a response.

I nod. "Danke, Herr Mohr." I expect him to leave, but he lingers, shifting in the cramped, gray-walled space, looking out of place in his tailored overcoat and hat.

"There is something else."

I wait for him to continue.

"Your family." He pauses. "I've included paper, envelopes, and a pencil in the parcel. You ought to write to them tonight. At Stadelheim, they will only permit a short note."

He means for me to write farewell letters. Now, while there's still time.

Again, I nod. "I will."

"Good." Mohr is visibly relieved. He moves toward the door and knocks.

Before being escorted out by the guard, Mohr turns. Framed in the doorway of the cell, one might think him a proud, important man.

But in his delusion, he is poorer than the humblest prisoner.

I watch him go. Should I hate or pity him? Right now, I don't have the energy for either emotion.

Else has opened the parcel and spread the contents out on the table. Two apples and a packet of butter cookies. Several sheets of writing paper and envelopes.

"Do you want anything?"

I shake my head. "Maybe later." I manage a faint smile. "I'd best get started on these."

She nods.

I pull my chair up to the table and pick up the pencil. Getting on with things, Vater would call it. "Don't hesitate, but take up the task at hand," he would say. His voice, that rumbling baritone, over my shoulder as I sat at the kitchen table with a pile of dreaded homework. "The task at hand, Sophie."

Ja, Vater. The task at hand.

The page stares up at me in all its blank whiteness. My breath shudders when I draw it in.

God, how? How am I to do this?

The plea encompasses not only the letters but every step of the journey that lies ahead.

Gracious God, You have shown Yourself strong before. Please, do not fail me now.

Slowly, the words come. How faltering and small they seem. How ill-equipped to convey my heart. My pencil stumbles, and several times I have to put it down and take long breaths until I can go on. A letter to my parents. Then one to Inge.

Lastly, to Fritz.

> When you hear what has happened, I pray you will understand. I beg you, do not worry about me. My faith lies in God, and I am not afraid. I do not have to ask myself the question, Would I do it again? The answer is already before me. There's freedom in such clarity.
>
> Be strong in the life ahead of you. Never compromise, no matter what others around you do. I know you will become a man I would be proud of. I've seen you grow into such a man in the years we've spent together, and I'm already so very, very proud.
>
> Please do not let anything stop you from living fully and loving without reserve. We are granted many gifts in this life. Love is perhaps the greatest of them. Hold it tight.
>
> You are in my heart as you have always been, and I will think of you until the last as I have always done.
>
> Yours always,
> Sophie

I fold the letter and slip it into the envelope, address the front, then lay it on top of the other two. I've done all I can.

Outside, the light is fading. I move slowly toward my cot, leaving the three white envelopes in a pile on the table. The bulb in the cell switches on, illuminating the room in penetrating brightness. I look up at it, as does Else.

Neither of us say a word.

I lay down on my cot, turning onto my side to face Else. We exchange a smile. I'm glad she can still smile at me. It makes me braver than I might have been if I were alone.

After a pause, she says, "Tell me about your family."

So I do. Several times, we laugh over incidents from my childhood. Hans has always been a leader, I tell her. Often he led us into mischief-making, like swimming in the Danube in the middle of winter. How cold we got, and what a scolding Vater gave us when we came home drenched and shivering.

"How will your parents take it, when they find out what has happened?" There's kindness in Else's gaze as she asks.

I swallow, throat suddenly tight. "I worry most about Mutter. Her health is not strong, and to lose two children at once . . . I pray she'll be granted the strength to bear it, that it will not completely shatter her. Werner is on the Russian front, and she already worries for him so. But Vater is different. He will understand better what we have done. He always taught us to think for ourselves." I tuck my hand beneath my chin. "Vater will be proud of us."

"You're fortunate to have grown up in such a family."

"*Ja*," I whisper too softly for Else to hear. "I've been very fortunate."

Else rises and readies herself for bed, then we bid each other good night. The light shines in a steady gleam, as it will shine all night, but I close my eyes anyway, the thin blanket tucked around my shoulders.

I must think only of this moment. Not tomorrow.

Oh, God. Be with me. My heart is weak and feeble, but You are my strength.

As clear as a whisper in my ear, the truth fills my mind. I don't have to do this alone. I am not alone. I am His. And He will walk beside me. Through everything.

For years I've wondered if my love for Him was enough, questioned my worthiness to enter His presence. Tonight, I question no longer. Holy peace floods through me, inexplicable, but present.

And with peace, comes sleep.

CHAPTER FORTY-ONE

Sophie
February 22, 1943

I OPEN MY EYES. Else stands over me, already dressed, hair loose around her shoulders.

"Time to get up," she says softly. "I'll help you get ready."

I rise from the narrow cot. Else hands me a cake of soap, and I go to the sink in the corner of the room and splash water over my face. Its coolness trickles down my cheeks. How refreshing I've always found these morning rituals. Cleaning oneself to start the day.

Else beckons me to sit at the table. She takes up her own hairbrush and works it through my limp strands with gentle strokes. As if she stands in for the mutter who is not here today.

"I had a strange dream last night." I fix my gaze on the window, morning sunlight filtering through the bars. "I was carrying a baby up a steep mountainside to a little church to be baptized. The baby wore a long, white gown, and I held it fast in my arms, like keeping it safe was the most important thing in the world to me. Suddenly a crevasse opened in the mountain, right over where I stood. I had just enough time to lay the child on the side of safety before I fell into the abyss." I turn in my chair, looking up at Else. "It's a sign. The child represents our idea. It will survive, but we must die because of it." The dream was so vivid, and vivid still is the warm glow of hope it brought.

She smooths her hand across the crown of my head and lays the brush aside. Her face is pale, dark shadows beneath her eyes as if she spent a sleepless night.

Else, Else, more afraid for me than I am for myself. How kind you've been.

An hour passes. Breakfast arrives, and we eat the squares of brown bread and sip the cups of tepid ersatz. The warmth soothes my throat, and I hold the tin cup up to my nose, inhaling the fragrance, imagining real *kaffee*.

The indictment still sits on the table, along with my letter-writing pencil. While Else pins up her hair, I slowly form letters, tracing a single word onto the back of the page in the hope that, like our graffiti, it will embolden others with a courage beyond what they think they possess.

Freiheit.

Freedom.

A knock sounds. We both rise. I take Else's hands firmly in both of mine, looking into her eyes.

"Promise me that someday you will go to my parents and tell them of our time together."

Else nods. "I promise."

She helps me on with my coat. The door opens. A guard stands outside. "Prisoner Scholl."

Before the guard takes hold of me, I turn, looking one last time at the woman who has been a companion, almost a friend in these few short days. "God bless you, Else."

Else looks on with a kind, steadfast gaze. "God bless you, Sophie."

I will see Hans today. The thought fills me with a kind of gladness during the ride to the Palace of Justice, crammed between two guards. How I've missed my brother during these four days apart.

We pull up before the massive, gray stone building, and I am hauled out. Handcuffs bite into my wrists. They hurry me inside, through a vast foyer of grand pillars, our shoes an echo on the marble floor. We ascend a set of stairs. Sun filters through a high glass cupola. A swastika hangs from the balustrade, an emblem of bloodstained red.

We enter an anteroom. To my relief, they remove the handcuffs. I barely have time to rub at the chafing on my wrists before they take hold of me again, and we march through a pair of doors.

I sense the gazes of everyone in the room turn to me, the low hum of murmurs escalating. I take it all in with a glance—uniformed SS and Wehrmacht officers interspersed with men in dark suits. They sit in rows of straight-backed chairs, the black-robed lawyers at their table along the side. Large, picture windows let in morning sunlight. A bronze bust of Hitler sits on a pedestal behind the empty bench. I yank my gaze away from it and from the swastika on the wall.

The room teems with men, not a woman in sight. Their stony faces regard me with open disgust.

I catch a glimpse of Hans. My heart leaps. They push me toward a bench where he and Christl sit with guards between them. I slide onto the end and look past the guard, toward them both. Hans smiles slightly. He looks well, thank God. Pale and tired, but still my strong, brave brother. On the far end sits Christl. Our eyes meet, and I wish I could take his hands in mine and squeeze them tight.

In the past four days, we've fought alone against the opposing forces. Now, we're together again. No matter that this is a show trial where the word justice is a farce, the three of us won't go down like silent lambs. Surely, we'll be permitted to speak.

They'll have no choice but to listen.

"Hans," I whisper.

"No talking." The guard roughly shushes me.

The undertone of conversation dwindles to a halt. A man enters the room. Freisler. In his bloodred robe and cap, he looks like an actor in a Shakespearian drama. Thin, almost gaunt, robe aswirl about him, he strides to his chair at the front of the room behind the oak bench. A cadre of assistant judges follow at his heels.

Freisler pauses before taking his seat. Chairs scrape as everyone rises. We stand too, forced up by the guards. A second passes. In a single movement, everyone raises their right arms.

"Heil Hitler!" The roar of voices fills the room.

I press my lips tight together, my arm at my side. Out of the corner of my eye, I see Hans and Christl also do not salute.

No concessions.

It's one of Hans's favorite phrases. Until the last, we'll make none.

We resume our seats. Freisler removes his cap. His balding pate adds to his hawkish air.

He turns his gaze on us. Hatred glimmers from his eyes. I sit still and straight, hands in my lap, refusing to flinch.

"The proceedings of the People's Court will now begin in the case against Hans Fritz Scholl of Munich, Sophia Magdalena Scholl of Munich, and Christoph Hermann Probst of Aldrans near Innsbruck." Freisler pauses. "These three are charged with traitorous aiding and abetting of the enemy, preparations for high treason, and demoralization of the armed forces." His voice escalates with every charge.

"Call Christoph Hermann Probst."

One of the guards leads Christl to stand in front of Freisler's bench. His voice is quiet as he answers the initial questions about his birthplace, age, and marital status.

"Speak up!" Freisler shouts. "You cowering idiot!"

"I wish to say a few words in my defense." Christl folds his hands in front of him. His shoulders are stooped. Already, he looks crushed. Freisler's court is no place for this gentle, pure-hearted man. "Namely that I didn't know what I was doing when I wrote the leaflet—"

"What's this? Not know what you were doing? You expect the court to believe you composed the leaflet in your sleep?"

"That is not what I mean to say." Christl lowers his gaze. "I suffer from psychotic depression—"

"Psychotic depression! And that is your excuse for treason against the Reich? I suppose every man should be allowed to suit himself then, hmm? Psychotic depression!"

I cringe as he calls Christl a horrible name. Hans's face is taut, his lips pressed in a thin line.

"I've admitted fully to my actions and retracted all statements. The leaflet I wrote was not a final copy—"

"Then you mean you planned to add more to this outrage of sedition?" Freisler picks up a piece of paper, Christl's pieced-together leaflet draft. "More along the lines of 'Roosevelt, the most powerful man in the world.' That cripple! The man cannot even walk. He is not fit to run a country. Yet you elevate him above the Führer, the greatest leader this world has ever known."

"I did not know what I was doing. I'm apolitical—"

"Apolitical." Freisler's body shakes. To look at him, one would think he's having a seizure. "You are a subhuman! No better than the lowest of Jews."

"Please, Herr President. My children—"

"No German child should be raised by a vater like you. You whimpering parasite. End of questioning."

Christl keeps his gaze down as the guards take hold of him. He looks up for an instant as he slides into his seat. His jaw is tight, and a slow burning fills his eyes.

He wouldn't have pleaded for himself if not for Herta, Michael, Vincent. Baby Katja. To him, those four are more than life, than anything. My chest aches. Freisler was moved by none of it. Christl humiliated himself for nothing.

"Call Hans Fritz Scholl."

Two guards lead Hans forward. My brother faces Freisler, hands clasped in front of him, his bearing proud. A comma of hair falls slightly over his forehead. It makes him look young.

We're all so young.

"Aha! The ringleader." Freisler ignores the preliminary personal details. "We have here before us an example of German youth. He has been given every advantage in being permitted to study at Ludwig Maximilian University for the purpose of becoming a physician. But how does he repay us?" Freisler waves a piece of paper in his clenched fist. "By writing and producing this seditious trash."

"It is not trash." Hans's tone is even, his gaze direct. "It is what I believe. And it is true."

"You call this truth? Stating our Führer is insane? That our glorious cause is fought for nothing?" His face purples. "Do you admit to writing these leaflets?"

"*Ja.*" Hans nods.

"Then you admit to stating the war is a farce?" Freisler leans forward. "That the German people will be defeated?"

"It is only a matter of time." Hans's voice rises. "Hitler has led the German people down a road which can only lead to ultimate defeat. Anyone who comprehends military strategy cannot help but realize this. Every life lost in this bloodbath is a life lost in vain."

"How dare you—"

Hans continues. "Germany will have to give account for its actions when the war is over. Then you will be standing where we stand now. The slaughter of innocent Jews, the destruction in Poland. As a soldier—"

"As a soldier!" Freisler shrieks. "You are not a soldier. You are a disgrace to Germany and to manhood."

Sweat trickles down my back. Hans defends himself and his actions without flinching. Finally Freisler shouts that his ears can no longer take being assaulted with such poison, and Hans is led away. Our gazes lock as he passes by me on the way to his seat. I nod.

If only Vater could see you today. He would be so very proud.

"Call Sophia Magdalena Scholl."

I rise before the guard can haul me to my feet. He grasps my arm and walks me to stand before the bench where Freisler and the assistant judges sit. Freisler's face glistens with sweat. The black-robed judges stare at me solemn-faced.

My legs shake. I draw in a steadying breath. I have no need to fear him. He can only do the worst to me, and I am already prepared for that.

"The little sister of that defeatist swine. What do you have to say for yourself?" He leans forward, pinning me with a glare.

Standing before Freisler, I'm alone and exposed, a girl in a room of men who see me as evil. I lift my gaze briefly to the ceiling.

Nein. Not alone. God is with me, and He is my strength.

My mouth is dry. I clear my throat. "I fully admit to having participated in the writing and distribution of the leaflets." Thank God my voice is strong and doesn't waver or shake.

"Your brother's puppet?"

I will fight back. And I will speak truth as long as I can. This may be my last chance to do both. "Nein. I did it of my own free will. And I would do it again. We wrote the leaflets to proclaim the truth to the German people about the evil around them. The horror you and everyone would see if you looked beyond the propaganda being—"

"Shut your mouth, you impudent *dummkopf*—"

I raise my voice and keep talking. "The propaganda being blasted throughout Germany, blinding the eyes of German citizens to the truth. To thinking for themselves. To morality."

"You dare to speak of morality! I suppose you think calling for sabotage in factories producing weapons for the war effort a moral action?"

"All we did was toward the aim of shortening the war and saving lives that are being lost by the thousands in a vain pursuit of total victory. What we said and wrote is what many people believe. They just don't dare say it out loud. Somebody, after all, had to make a start." My hands form fists at my sides. I look at Freisler, the other judges, then turn slightly and fix my eyes upon the audience. Pride shines from my brother's eyes.

"You vile girl. You . . . you disgrace to German womanhood!" Freisler rages.

The rest of the room is strangely quiet. Not one in the audience of men meets my gaze.

"You may do what you like with us today." I turn back to Freisler, my voice echoing through the silent courtroom. "You have that power now. But someday, all of us must stand before God and give account for our actions. Before Him, no one will be able to hide. Not even you."

Let them hear it. Let someone, one person, be stirred by our words.

"Shut up!" Freisler slams his fist on the table. "This courtroom has heard enough pollution. Take her away."

I keep my head high as I'm led away from the bench. Hans and I exchange glances as I slip into my seat.

We succeeded.

Despite Freisler, despite it all, they heard the truth.

After a brief recess, the court gathers to hear the verdict. I draw in a deep breath. My stomach clenches.

Everyone in this room already knows the outcome, even us. What will happen next is simply a formality.

Someone coughs. A commotion sounds outside the courtroom. Raised voices. Heavy footsteps. I start. Vater fights his way through the courtroom, while a guard grapples to restrain him. Following Vater is our mutter. And Werner, holding onto her protectively.

My eyes burn. My parents. My brother. My precious family.

Here. For us.

I want to go to them, to hold them, embrace Vater and Werner and hug my mutter close. They are only steps away. But I am trapped.

Red-faced and panting, Vater works his way toward the defense attorney's table. The guard releases him, and he bends down and whispers something in my lawyer's ear. Abruptly, Klein stands and walks over to Freisler.

"The vater is here and wishes to speak in defense of his children," Klein says.

"Remove him from court!" Freisler shouts, slashing his arm up and down for emphasis. "All of them. *Schnell*!"

The guards grasp hold of my parents and herd them from the room. I glimpse my mutter's pale, scared face looking back at me as the guard drags her away. My throat swells.

"One day there will be another kind of justice." Vater turns at the door, fighting against the guards. "They will go down in history!"

The doors slam, drowning his voice.

For a moment, all is utter silence. Freisler gathers himself and asks for closing statements. The three of us are ordered to stand. My head spins. I can still see Mutter's anguished eyes.

In spite of my outward bravery, I'm still just a girl who'd give anything to feel her mutter's arms around her.

"My only desire has been to end this bloodbath and spare Germany the agony of new Stalingrads." Christl swallows. "I ask for clemency on behalf of my wife and children."

"Scholl, Hans."

"I request all punishment be given to me, and that Christoph and Sophie be spared." My brother's voice is strong, his gaze firm as he faces Freisler.
Oh, Hans.

"If you have nothing to say in your own defense, keep silent." Hands folded on the table, Freisler fixes his unblinking stare on me. "Scholl, Sophia."

I say nothing. What's the point?

Freisler dons his cap. Chairs scrape as the court rises.

"In the name of the German people . . ."

I barely listen as Freisler reads the verdict aloud. It's as if I'm existing in a haze of fog, floating upon clouds. Floating far, far away . . .

"They are to be punished by death. Their honor and rights as citizens are forfeited for all time."

The words cut through the haze. My eyes fall closed.

"Today you hang us," Hans calls out. "Tomorrow it will be your turn!"

"Remove them from this courtroom!"

Guards hurry us from the room and out the double doors. My heart thuds dully. The corridor is a mass of people and voices.

In the midst of it, Werner shoves toward us. I drink in the sight of him, his frantic efforts to reach us. The crowd lets him pass, this young man in Wehrmacht uniform. He reaches our side. Hans clutches his hand. Tears fill Werner's eyes.

Not since childhood have I seen him cry.

"Stay strong, little brother. No compromises," Hans whispers, his words a benediction. His own eyes are moist.

I fight back a sob. I will not cry here.

Werner nods, face crumpled. I reach out to him, our hands clasping, clinging. Impatient, the guards push us onward. Outside, two black cars sit parked near a back entrance. White sunlight streams from behind feathered clouds. I breathe in fresh air through the tightness in my lungs.

Christl and my brother are shoved into one car. I rivet my gaze on them, barely heeding the roughness as I'm prodded into the second, along with a guard. The engine starts, and the driver backs up and turns, leaving the courtyard of the Palace of Justice behind.

Where we go, I know not. Only what will happen there.

"Ninety-nine days," I whisper. "Ninety-nine days."

CHAPTER FORTY-TWO

Sophie
February 22, 1943

I STAND MOTIONLESS IN front of the barred window of a cell in Stadelheim Prison. Long days stretch ahead of me, one after the other. How will I fill them? Do they even have meaning in view of what awaits me at their expiration?

Sunlight bathes my face. Eyes closed, I bask in its rays, my quiet breaths the only sound in the sparse gray cell.

"Dear God." Those two words encompass my prayer. I can conjure no others. "Dear God."

A knock, then the cell door opens. I turn. A female prison warden comes inside. Her face is a map of hardened-over miseries.

"Fräulein Scholl, come with me. You've been summoned to the prison office."

I follow. Only mild curiosity penetrates the fog in my brain. We walk dingy corridors, footsteps echoing. Pausing before a half-open door, the woman nods.

"They're expecting you."

Hands at my sides, I cross the threshold. The chief prosecutor sits behind a desk in a dimly lit office, flanked by two guards. I stand before him.

"Sophia Magdalena Scholl." His tone is granite.

I nod.

"In his decree of February 22, 1943, the Reich Minister of Justice has chosen not to grant clemency, but to let justice take its course. At 5:00 p.m. today, the execution will be carried out."

I can't move. I can't breathe. My mind is a screaming, writhing thing. My heart stammers, everything inside of me shaking.

"You're dismissed."

I force myself to turn and walk out of the room. The woman warden waits for me outside. She takes my arm. In minutes, I'm back in my cell, the door locked behind me.

I stand in the middle of the cell, heart pounding, nausea churning through my body in thick, hot waves.

"Ninety-nine days," I whisper into the emptiness.

My legs give out. I collapse to the ground, arms wrapped around my knees. I rock back and forth, choking sobs shaking me to the core.

I have less than an hour left.

My breath comes in heaving gasps. I'm being smothered, suffocated by a crushing hand. Air. I need to breathe.

There isn't air. There's only the four walls of this cell, closing in on me.

Calm. I must calm down. Gain control, somehow.

How?

"God . . . God, help me." A keening, guttural cry, wrenched from deep inside. "Do . . . not . . . forsake . . . me . . ."

I curl my body into itself, head bent, trying to take deep breaths.

Somehow I pick myself up off the floor. Smooth my fingers through my limp hair.

I resume my place by the window. A knock comes again, followed by the face of the same woman warden.

"You have visitors." Her tone is softer this time, as if she too has learned what will happen. "Come with me."

Again a walk through more corridors. The unbolting of another door. The woman nods, bidding me enter. I do, uncertain of what awaits me.

I do not expect to see my parents on the other side of the barrier. I drink in the sight of them, familiar, well-loved faces that have shaped my life.

"Mutter?" I blink, afraid they will disappear, be taken from me.

"Sophie. My Sophie." Both of us reach across the barrier and clasp hands. Her touch is strong and warm.

"My own mutti." Almost beyond my control, I smile.

Mutter pulls away and rummages in her worn handbag. She pulls out two pieces of chocolate candy—my favorite—and holds them out to me. "Would you like some?"

Heat rises in my throat. Nothing has changed. Whenever she would visit me during labor service, she always brought along my favorite chocolate. I would always smile and take it.

I'll do no differently today. "Danke." I take the wrapped pieces from her hands and place them in the pocket of my sweater. "I haven't had any lunch."

Vater stands beside her, his frame large in the tiny cell. "My brave daughter." He runs a gentle hand along my cheek. "I'm so proud of you both."

"We took responsibility for everything. That will fan the flames. People will rise up when they hear what has been done to us." My voice is strong.

Mutter takes my hands again, clinging to them. Tears glisten in her eyes. "You'll never walk through our door again. How I always loved to see you come home. You brought the sun with you."

Her words tear my heart in two. Still I keep my smile in place. "Oh, Mutter. These few short years . . ."

"Time's up," comes the woman warden's voice.

Seconds left. Only seconds with these who have given me life. Who taught me to live it well.

God, why did it have to come to this?

Vater pulls me into his arms, and we embrace across the barrier. I lean into the strong chest that has brought me comfort so many times, drawing in his scent. Countless childhood sorrows were cried out in the shelter of his arms.

But this final time, I will not leave him with the memory of my tears.

Next, I hug my mutter, clinging to her with all of my strength. If only I could relive a day, an hour of my girlhood, how differently I'd do things. I would listen more and love her better. Now it is too late.

She takes my face in her soft hands, her gaze urgent as she looks into my eyes. "Remember, Sophie. Jesus."

I swallow. Her touch is breaking me apart. I can't hold back the tears much longer. "*Ja*. And you must remember Him too." I turn away, knowing I must. At the door, I pause and smile again, wanting their final picture of me to be brave and serene. Standing on the other side of the barrier, they look old and worn. Shattered.

God be with you, my own beloved parents.

The woman warden closes the door. Its click is harsh and final. Heedless of her presence, hot tears slide down my cheeks. I can control them no longer.

God, I know I will see You soon, but this thing You ask of me is hard. So very hard.

"Fräulein Scholl?" A voice draws my gaze up. Inspector Mohr stands to one side of the corridor, carrying a briefcase.

"Herr Mohr." I swipe a hand across my cheeks. "I've just said goodbye to my mutter and vater." My voice cracks.

He nods, gaze somber. His mouth opens as if he wants to speak, then just as abruptly he closes it again. He did well not to speak. His words can offer me no solace.

The woman warden pulls at my arm and leads me away.

Soon the waiting will be at an end, and I will be free. Finally free from everything. I sit alone in my cell after the prison chaplain's visit, hands listless in my lap, body empty of tears.

The familiar grinding of the key in the lock, the groan of the door. A man stands outside, another prison warden.

"Fräulein Scholl, it's time." His voice is not unkind.

I rise. My legs no longer tremble as I follow him down the corridor. He pauses before a barred door and turns a key. He looks back at me. Compassion fills his weathered face.

"This isn't customary. You have a few moments." He hands me a cigarette, a match. Uncertainly, I take both.

I walk through the open door. Inside an empty cell stand Hans and Christl. Both are wearing prison uniforms, but their faces remain unchanged. My brother's eyes glow with a kind of radiance. Christl smiles, gentle and crooked.

I pass the cigarette and match to Hans, and he strikes it against the wall. A flame flares to life in the dim room. He lights the cigarette and shakes out the match. Puts it to his lips and inhales, then passes it to Christl, who does the same, then passes it to me.

We've already received communion of the sacred kind. But this moment together is nearly as hallowed. A communion of souls. Friendship and ideals have bound the three of us together.

As we have begun, so we will end.

I let the cigarette fall to the floor. Then turn to Christl and put my arms around him. He embraces me. Hans pulls me close, and I hold on to my brother, my friend. He's always been both to me.

We stand in a circle of three in the center of the cell.

"In a few minutes, we'll be together again," Christl says.

"In eternity," I whisper.

The door opens. Two men enter the room. Both are dressed in black.

"Sophia Scholl."

I let them take hold of my hands and bind them with handcuffs. My gaze clings to Hans and Christl. I need no courage from them. I only want to look at their faces as long as I can.

The men take hold of my arms, one on each side. I pause and look over my shoulder.

"*Freiheit*," I breathe.

Outside, sun streams from behind clouds. A breeze stirs my hair. Our footfalls echo as we walk across an open courtyard.

There is purpose in this. In death, as in life. Someday perhaps my story will be told, and others will remember. That to witness wrong and stay silent is as much a crime as committing evil oneself. That youth does not exempt one from responsibility. That freedom is a gift.

I pray they will remember. For I will not be here to tell them.

The span of my life flashes through my mind. All of its joys and sorrows, moments of hope and heartache. I have been blessed. With family, friends, the love of a good man, and a yearning to do what is right. All of those things have made me who I am. And every experience has brought me to this place now.

We stop before a small brick building, and the door opens.

A memory rises up. Of swimming in the Danube on a summer's day, floating on the expanse of glittering blue water. Of joy and laughter and surrender.

I was at peace then.

And I am free now.

CHAPTER FORTY-THREE

Annalise
February 26, 1943

"THEY'VE BEEN EXECUTED." INGRID, my cellmate, crouches next to my cot, voice at a whisper. "I heard two of the guards as I was scrubbing the floor."

They're just words. Letters and syllables. But they slam into me with visceral intensity.

"All of them?"

Ingrid nods. "The very day of the trial. There were three. One called Probst. And a brother and sister by the name of Scholl."

I swallow, pressing my hand to my midsection. *Nein. Please God, nein.*

My eyes fall closed. Christl, with his earnest gaze and gentle heart. Hans, the leader I always sought to impress, Sophie's big brother.

Sophie . . .

My brown-eyed friend with her passion and ideals and smile that crinkled her eyes. I remember her wistful sigh as she spoke of girlish dreams of love, the flash in her gaze as she argued with Hans, the determined set to her jaw as she cranked the duplicating machine, dark hair a curtain around her cheeks. She'd shown me the meaning of courage.

She was the truest friend I ever had.

How quickly they stole her from this world. As if she, a twenty-one-year-old student, possessed a power the highest echelons of the Reich feared. They should have been given ninety-nine days for clemency appeals . . . for the verdict to be amended . . . for the war to end. Ninety-nine days.

They'd tried and executed her in less than one.

Dear God . . .

A touch on my arm.

"Someone's knocking. Compose yourself. Quickly."

I draw in a long breath and steel my features as the door opens.

"Come, Frau Hoffmann." The guard jerks his hand toward the door.

Ingrid doesn't look at him. I heed her example and keep my eyes down as I follow the guard into the corridor. Dr. Voigt's medicine has eased my cough and the ache in my head. Yet I'd gladly exchange the ache now possessing my heart for mere physical symptoms.

"*Schnell.*" The guard snaps the word. "Inspector Krämer is waiting."

Another interrogation. Sitting in the glare of white light as a thousand questions fire at me one after the other, sometimes the same ones every hour in an attempt to catch me giving different answers. It would be easier to confess, just to get them to shut up and leave me in peace. The temptation is undeniable. Right now, I'm exhausted enough to succumb to it. It would be easy . . . so easy . . .

But there are still those alive to save. Alex. Kirk. Willi. I will fight and I will live, and when this is all over, I will tell the world the story of my friends.

I keep my shoulders straight as I'm led inside Inspector Krämer's office. I know it well, every contour of the hard-backed chair, the meticulous desk. Behind the desk sits Krämer. He eyes me with his sharp gray gaze while he cracks his knuckles. I grit my teeth.

"Sit."

I do, smoothing my hair back from my face. Krämer flicks on the light and points it in my eyes. I wince. Krämer's nose is large and flat like a spatula. Dully, I wonder if his mutter dropped him on it as a baby and that's what made him so emotionless.

"Now then, Frau Hoffmann. We've conducted another search of your apartment."

Bile rises in my throat. I imagine Vater's face, shrewd and impassive, and try to make mine a mirror of his. What could they have found? Kirk was always careful, more than the Scholls. He destroyed all his draft contributions to the leaflets.

But amid the pressures of exhaustion and frenetic activity, it's easy to let something slip.

Krämer passes a piece of wrinkled paper across the table. The heading of our fifth leaflet stares up at me in the glow of light.

"Ever seen this before?"

"Nein." My answer is immediate.

"It was in your apartment."

I try to appear flustered, giving a little gasp. "Are you sure? Where?" That's right. Play the stupid little *hausfrau.*

"In the pocket of this." Krämer opens the drawer of his desk. He holds up a piece of cloth, unfolding it like a flag.

A gray winter skirt. Mine.

Sweat trickles down my back. I blink against the light. A frantic clamor rises inside me.

Think, Annalise.

"You've been lying, Frau Hoffmann. When you've been admonished to tell the truth. You thought you had me fooled, didn't you?" He leans forward, sour breath wafting over me. "I would not advise further deception." His tone is low. Lethal. A shiver spiders up my neck. He steeples his slender fingers atop the desk. "Now, I will repeat the question, and you will answer truthfully. Have you seen this before?"

My lungs are tight, but I don't allow myself to take more than shallow breaths.

I can still play the game. Nothing can be proved by my possessing a leaflet. I nod.

"Where did you get it?"

Forgive me, my brave, my dearest friend.

"Sophie Scholl gave it to me."

"When?"

"A few weeks ago, I think. She said she thought I might find it interesting."

They don't know I know about the Scholls. Now that they're . . . oh, I must think it . . . gone, they can be implicated without harm. Perhaps if I wasn't so desperate, I'd find another way. But there isn't time.

"And did you?"

I shake my head. "I only glanced at it. Political literature bores me. I must have shoved it in my skirt pocket and forgotten about it until now."

"Did you not think to turn it in to the Gestapo? That leaflet is crawling with treason. As a loyal citizen of the Reich, it is your duty."

"I told you I only glanced at it. I was busy that day—"

"Too busy for loyalty to the Führer?"

"Of course not. I would have reported the leaflet had I remembered it. The life of a university student is arduous. I simply forgot. As I said, I'm not interested in political matters."

"But your husband is?"

I rub damp palms across the fabric of my skirt. My clothes are rank with the scent of my own sweat. "I've already told you. My husband is apolitical. He's a serious medical student. Most evenings, it's difficult for me to pry him away from his books long enough to eat a decent dinner." I laugh, but it sounds tinny.

"Your husband has confessed his participation in the leaflet production and distribution." The words are measured.

Don't pause. To pause is to equate guilt.

"My husband would never have confessed—"

"He did. This morning." Krämer riffles through a stack of papers, picks up one. "Listen to this: 'My disgust at the atrocities perpetrated by our country in the name of German victory led me to produce and distribute leaflets during the summer of 1942.'"

Had Kirk actually said that? Or was it a lie to get me to admit guilt? "Kirk would never have said such a thing."

"Are you accusing us of presenting you with false evidence?" Krämer shoves the paper across the desk. "There. His signature." He jabs a finger toward the bottom of the page. My breath seizes.

Kirk Hoffmann

I recognize the script. The sloppy *H* that blends into the *o*.

The world tilts like a swirling top.

How had they gotten him to confess? The painful truth is Hans and Sophie can now be blamed for everything. Unless . . . Kirk didn't know they'd been executed.

"Now, do you believe us?"

I nod, body ebbing of energy.

"Are you prepared to make a full confession?"

Again, I nod.

"Well, then?"

I need you to promise to fight for yourself, whatever it takes. I've got to know one of us, at least, will survive . . .

I should forget Kirk ever spoke those words. Make a full confession and join my husband in whatever fate awaits us. It would be easier than fighting to survive.

I'm so tired of fighting.

If I confessed, maybe they'd let me see Kirk one last time. We could hold each other and say goodbye and forget everything else.

If something happens to me, I can endure it. But I couldn't endure, knowing you . . .

Kirk didn't ask. He begged. His pleading gaze brands itself in my mind.

If I confess, I'll be breaking both my promise and Kirk's heart. He only has so much strength, and it would shatter him if I broke down, simply to join him in the conflagration consuming us all.

For him to be strong, I must be too. I must maintain the facade. For him. Not for me.

I swallow, my throat like parchment. The words I must utter feel like a betrayal. Shaming me down to my core.

My lips part. "I had nothing to do with my husband's activities."

CHAPTER FORTY-FOUR

Kirk
April 19, 1943

BENEATH A RADIANT MORNING sky, the green police van trundles through the streets of Munich. I sit on the hard bench that wraps the interior of the vehicle, Alex on my right.

The space to my left is empty. I don't know what has become of my wife, my Annalise. Daily, hourly I pray she's somehow been freed. But in case the opposite is true, I want only her by my side in the short moments before we reach the Palace of Justice.

The van lurches to a stop. It's windowless, the faces of the men around me lined in shadows. The few minutes we stood in the courtyard, waiting to be loaded into the van, gave me the first breath of fresh air that's touched my face in weeks. The sky is radiant because I beheld it once, not because I see it now.

Similar thoughts have formed the basis of the almost two months I've spent in prison. Months marked by endless interrogations and an ever-growing certainty as to what awaits me. After my fifth interrogation, I finally confessed, shouldering the blame, insisting mine was the voice behind every one of the six leaflets. It wasn't until it was too late that I learned of Hans, Sophie, and Christl's trial and deaths. I'd already marked myself as guilty enough to merit the same fate. Which, if what we'd done is criminal, is the truth.

At the beginning of April, the trial date was set. Like the trial which sealed the fate of the three before us, our presence is merely a formality (though I'm sure Freisler will thoroughly relish shrieking at us). The verdict is already predetermined, like most of those meted out in the so-called People's Court, an ironic name for a system that rarely considers the people and esteems itself as the highest form of law.

The back doors of the van open. A guard hands a dark-haired woman inside. Traute takes in our group with a little smile before taking her seat. Gisela Schertling follows, her pretty features drawn and pale. Strange she hasn't been released yet. She tries to take the seat next to me, but I shake my head. She squeezes beside Professor Huber instead, who stares down at the floor, hands in his lap.

A muted voice says, "Danke." I glimpse Annalise, hair falling over her face, being helped into the van. She looks up, brushing back her hair.

Our eyes meet.

My wife, my love. Months apart have left me starved for the sight of her face, the cadence of her voice.

A wave of pain washes over me. All my fervent prayers were for her and my friends.

God, it doesn't matter what happens to me. But please. Spare my Annalise.

She squeezes between the row of knees and hunched shoulders to the back of the van. A final woman—Katharina Schüddekopf—also climbs aboard before the doors slam.

Annalise slides beside me. I gather the sight of her and press it into the folds of memory. Her face is pale and thin, making her hair appear darker. She grasps my hands and pulls them into her lap without taking her gaze from me. Her hands are cold, but her grip is strong.

"Kirk." My name on her lips is fragile, almost disbelieving. Her eyes seem to encompass every part of me.

"My darling, how are you?"

"Well." A little smile flits across her cracked lips. "And you?"

"I'm all right." I mean it. Right now, hands intertwined with hers, I am.

"You look thin. Are you getting enough to eat?" Her brow creases. How often I once kissed her there, in just that place.

Poets say love forgets nothing. We like to agree with them.

But circumstances prove how naive we are. I know I once felt her skin against my lips, but the memories have faded, withering in the weeks apart. There were moments when, God help me, I tried and failed to remember her smile, her voice, the curve of her cheek.

She's here now. I let the reality fill me like a refrain. *She's here now.*

"I'm fine." I lean closer. In minutes, we'll arrive at our destination. I have only minutes to do what I can to protect her. "Fight for yourself," I whisper. "Promise me you will."

She nods, lips pressed together. I inhale her fragrance, tainted by the grime of prison, but still distinctly Annalise. "I'll try. But what about you—"

"Hey, you two," the guard barks from across the aisle. "Shut it, and don't make me ask twice."

We fall silent, still clasping hands. Alex shoots me a sympathetic glance. Prison has worn him down, his fine suit torn and wrinkled, his hair falling into his eyes and in need of a trim. But his eyes haven't lost their essence, that blend of charm and fierce-heartedness that's signature Shurik.

All too soon, the wheels grind to a halt. The doors are opened, bringing spring breezes wafting into the stuffy van. As the guards unload us, I glimpse the brownish-gray stone of an immense structure rising skyward in faded Gothic splendor.

Next in line, I clamber out of the van, feet hitting the cobblestoned courtyard. Munich's Palace of Justice.

A palace it may be. But I'm no fool.

No justice awaits us here.

It lasted fourteen hours. Decked in scarlet robes trimmed in gold, Freisler rampaged and relished every moment. Our defense attorneys sat like useless puppets. As the day wore on, our stomachs cramped and growled. While everyone went for lunch during the afternoon recess, the sixteen of us remained on our hard-backed benches. During the dinner break, we were put in a cell and offered bowls of congealed porridge. No one ate much.

We all tried to defend ourselves. Only Willi was exempt from Freisler's attacks, perhaps because he was blond and stoic, blue eyes emotionless beneath Freisler's fury. "You almost got away with it," Freisler said in a half-jesting tone. "But we were smarter than you in the end."

Falk Harnack, who had somehow been implicated, put his training as an actor to good use and declared that after the executions of his brother and sister-in-law, how could anyone think he'd become involved in a petty, childish prank like producing leaflets? Apparently, we'd all managed to conceal Harnack's plans to introduce us to the resistance in Berlin.

Huber came armed with copious notes and tried to use reason, as if he addressed a lecture hall of students instead of a courtroom of handpicked Nazis. His words did us proud as he stated his goal had always been "a return to our own basic values, to a state based on legality, a return of trust between man and man."

Freisler called him a bum.

Alex attempted to explain what led him to take action against the regime, but every time he started to speak, Freisler cut him off, shrieking at him mercilessly for being part Russian. When Alex declared he'd no more readily shoot a Russian than a German, I thought Freisler would collapse from the force of his rage.

I held my own against Freisler and refused to shirk neither responsibility nor the reasons for my actions. Freisler flung curses and slurs, but I turned a little and fixed my eyes on Annalise. What did I care what that maniac said?

The judges believed Annalise knew vaguely about our activities, but her participation extended to procuring envelopes per the request of Sophie and myself. She didn't flinch when Freisler called her "Hoffmann's slut." I wanted to bash his brains out.

A shuffling as the doors open and the judges reenter the courtroom. The sixteen of us are seated on benches, flanked by guards. Blackout curtains cover the windows. Outside, the sky must be pitch. As the judges enter, everyone rises.

Perspiration slides clammy fingers down my armpits. Two seats down, Alex's face is gray.

Annalise, Lord. Let it be well with her.

With ceremonial flair (did the man never weary?), Freisler dons his cap. While the other judges look bored or muffle yawns, Freisler sweeps his icy gaze over us.

"In the name of the German people . . ." Our names are read one after the other. Someone coughs.

My empty stomach cramps. From where I sit, I can't glimpse Annalise. One look at her would give me strength. Right now, worn-down with fatigue, I have little left.

"That during a time of war, Alexander Schmorell, Kurt Huber, Wilhelm Graf, and Kirk Hoffmann . . ."

A strange rushing fills my ears, Freisler's voice an overarching echo.

"Used leaflets to call for sabotage of armaments and for the overthrow of National Socialism. They have propagated defeatism and maligned the Führer in a highly reprehensible manner, thereby aiding and abetting the enemies of the Reich and demoralizing our troops. They are therefore sentenced to death. They have forfeited their honor as citizens forever."

The words barely penetrate. I want to shout at him to hurry and get to the fate of the others. After pausing a moment to let the verdict sink in, Freisler continues.

Eugen Grimminger, who gave financial support to the Scholls, is sentenced to ten years. The other young men—friends of Hans and Willi—receive between seven years to eighteen months. Falk Harnack is surprisingly acquitted, doubtless due to some ulterior motive on Freisler's part.

Traute, Gisela, and Katharina receive one year each.

"Annalise Hoffmann"—every nerve in my body tenses—"also a student and part of the group centered around the Scholls, as well as being the wife of that traitor Hoffmann. Like Lafrenz and Schüddekopf, she was present at meetings where discussions took place about the best manner to act in opposition to National Socialism. Frau Hoffmann was also in possession of a leaflet, which she did not turn in or destroy. However, there's no evidence she had knowledge of the treason undertaken by the Scholls and the afore-mentioned others. She is therefore sentenced to two years imprisonment."

I release a long exhale as Freisler moves on. I don't dare turn and search for Annalise's face among the defendants. Tangible relief drains through my body. Two years. That's all. Two years is bearable. By then, the war may even be over.

She'll go free. She'll survive.

Right now, nothing else matters.

CHAPTER FORTY-FIVE

Annalise
April 19, 1943

FOR KIRK, I MUST *be brave.*

That thought alone pushes through the haze. We'll be together again in the police wagon. He must only see my strength.

An unbroken woman by his side for however long we're given together.

When we're herded aboard the wagon and freed of our guards, I push through the crowd to the back, arriving before him. The atmosphere is charged, electric after the tension of the trial. The men sentenced to imprisonment and the girls talk and pass around cigarettes as they settle in their seats. Professor Huber takes a place in the corner. His shoulders are hunched, his features shrunken and tired in the semi-darkness. I watch as he pulls something from his pocket—a photograph, maybe—and fixes his gaze upon it.

Head ducked low, Kirk makes his way toward me.

"I saved you a seat," I say softly.

"So you did." He smiles a little as he sits beside me. His face is pale, lines of fatigue aging his features.

The motor rumbles. The van rocks back and forth as we begin to move, turning down the street and leaving the Palace of Justice behind. I turn, angling my body so I'm facing him in the cramped space. He reaches for my hands. I hold on tight.

"My darling Annalise." He shakes his head as if in wonderment. "You're so beautiful."

My throat knots, but I smile through it. "Not really."

"When we first met, I remember thinking I'd never seen a smile quite like yours." He reaches up, and traces his fingers across my jaw. His touch is sweet agony, breaking me apart. "I fell in love with you that night, and the only thing that's changed is with every passing day, I love you even more."

I blink fiercely. In the darkness of the van, he looks at me with a sad smile. "It's going to be all right."

Leaning into his touch, I nod, trying to stay strong. "I know."

"Nein, Annalise. I mean it. It really will be. You'll be all right. And I will be too, knowing you are. God answered my prayer. I asked Him to save you, and He did."

He didn't answer mine.

Tears press against my eyes. But I don't speak those words aloud. They would do neither of us any good.

"Promise me something else. When you're released, I want you to go live with my parents. They'll take care of you, and . . . you can take care of them." His voice falters. "They love you so much. Will you do that for me?"

I nod, vowing with everything in me to do as he asks. "They're my family too. I'll stay with them always, and they'll never want for anything."

"Thank God I have you." He pulls my head down to rest on his chest and wraps his arm around me. Voices murmur and the van sways and we hold each other in the darkness. His chest rises and falls with every breath. My eyes slide shut.

Let me forget everything else and remember you. Let me leave not a drop remaining of this moment, but draw it in and keep it close. Let our minutes last a lifetime.

All too soon, the van stops. Bright white light flashes through the open back doors. One by one, we exit. Kirk and I cling to each other as long as we can. His lips brush my hair.

"Everybody out," comes the brusque voice of the guard. "Move along."

I press my lips against Kirk's in a frantic, searching kiss. He tastes of salt—my tears or his? He crushes me against him, and I wrap my arms around him as tightly as I can.

We've shared so many kisses. Our first, when he proposed by candlelight. And again, the tentative passion of our wedding night when we became lovers for the first time. Sleepy early morning moments stolen on the way to classes, and lingering ones late at night when we forgot the fatigue of the day and loved each other through touch.

Is this to be the last?

I must not think of that now.

"Move along." A hand grabs the back of my collar and jerks me away. I stumble after the guard and land hard on the ground, the impact jarring my body. We stand in the courtyard of a large gray prison building, the eerily bright flashlights of the guards the only light.

"Annalise." I turn at the voice near my elbow and look into Alex's face. He gazes down at me with a soft smile.

"Shurik." I make myself smile at him, heart breaking at the gallantry and kindness still evident in his eyes.

Kirk comes up beside us. He clasps Alex's hand in both of his. "God be with you, my friend." His face is steadfast in the white light.

"And you." Alex looks to me. "Both of you."

"Those sentenced to death on the right side, those to prison, on the left!" a guard shouts.

Farewells are broken apart as the guards marshal us into lines. My body is numb as I stand next to Traute. Cold air needles my cheeks. On the other side, Kirk stands beside Alex. Tall and proud, shoulders thrown back. A guard hurries them onward, toward the doors of the prison. Kirk turns.

Our gazes lock.

"I love you," I whisper, words caught by the wind. Hot moisture slides down my cheeks.

He stops, smiling a brave and broken smile. "I love you." His lips form the words I cannot hear. "I love you, Annalise."

I swipe the tears from my eyes with the back of my hand.

When I look up, he is gone.

CHAPTER FORTY-SIX

Friedrich
May 18, 1943

I WALK THE ECHOING halls of Stadelheim Prison, a clipboard beneath my arm, a black bag in my other hand. Passing guards give curt nods of deference. I imagine what they see—a middle-aged man with dark hair and an angular face, wearing a white coat and striding with purpose in his step. In this place of so much death, I—Dr. Friedrich Voigt—am here to bring healing.

The macabre irony has not escaped me.

My rounds at the prison sick bay take an hour to complete. Commonplace cases. Many of these patients hope to use their ailments as fuel to petition for shortened sentences. They rarely succeed.

According to the orderly, I have one more stop to make. One of the "death row prisoners" is showing symptoms of possible typhus. Having worked part-time at Stadelheim, along with Dr. Winter, for almost two years, I have access to all areas of the prison, permitted to come and go at will.

The row of cells reserved for those sentenced to death is outwardly little different than the rest of the prison. Same gray walls with closed doors at intervals. Same spick-and-span cement floor. Same scent of staleness, as if even the building struggles to breathe freely.

Only the placards on each door—Death Sentence—provide insight into the fates of those behind them. These prisoners occupy the cells for ninety-nine days—some less, some more—before they're led through the courtyard and to the shed in back of the prison, their earthly miseries ended. A day, a week later, another wretched soul takes their place and the cycle begins again.

"Right here, Dr. Voigt." The guard inserts a key into the lock. The door grinds open.

"Danke." I give a crisp nod before entering. The guard shuts the door. He'll wait outside until I knock to tell him I'm through.

The cell is small, as they all are, especially the death cells. Cot. Table. Chair. Bucket. A barred window high on the wall lets in a feeble stream of afternoon light.

My gaze falls on the young man lying on the cot. Dressed in a standard-issue prison uniform, in his early twenties. His brown hair is sticky with sweat, and stubble darkens his jaw.

I set my bag and clipboard on the table. A metal dish of congealed porridge and a tin cup of murky water sit on the table, both untouched. A Bible rests on one edge (despite our country's adherence to the Führer as our only god, they continue the practice of stocking every cell with a copy). A few bits of paper are stuck between the thin pages.

After spreading out my supplies and consulting my clipboard, I approach the cot with a stethoscope and thermometer. My knees creak as I kneel on the cold floor.

Kirk Hoffmann's eyes are closed. He shifts restlessly on the cot, turning and twisting. The rank odor of vomit and sweat stings my nostrils.

"Kirk, can you hear me? I'm a doctor. I'm here to help you."

A low groan issues from his lips. I insert the thermometer and, while I wait for the reading, undo the buttons of his shirt. A blotchy red rash covers his torso. Typhus. And a fever of—I hold the thermometer to the light—40.6 Celsius.

Kirk shivers, teeth chattering. I listen to his heartbeat and breathing before redoing the buttons and covering him with his blanket. Both the man and his cell need a thorough cleaning, though I doubt anyone will volunteer. Typhus is a feared disease. Curiously, German genetics are more susceptible than people of other countries. In this, we so-called Aryans are inferior.

Kirk continues to toss. His head lolls back, and he moans something indistinguishable.

"I didn't hear you." I place my hand on his arm. "What is it?"

"My love." The words emerge like a cry. "I'm sorry, my love. I'm so sorry." A dry cough racks his broad shoulders.

Kirk Hoffmann is a political prisoner, not a murderer. Once upon a time, old Dr. Winter told me, murderers were usually all one saw in the death cells. Now so-named political prisoners are executed right and left.

I know this because I've been called upon to witness the executions. To ascertain how long it takes for life to ebb from a decapitated body. I always fortify myself with a glass of something strong beforehand. Even with it, it's all I can do to stay steely during those moments.

Even now, the thought of what I've seen makes me want to retch.

The young man is one of those tried in April, part of the group who scattered leaflets and painted the sides of buildings with slogans defaming the Führer. I remember walking from my home to my private practice and seeing the graffiti, treason encapsulated in tar-based paint.

For those crimes, this young man who cries out for his love will die.

A cold, sick feeling drenches me to the core.

I remember the girl named Annalise, whom I was called to treat at the Wittelsbacher Palace. She too was one of the students. When I saw her in prison, she didn't look like a revolutionary, a dangerous threat to the Reich. Just a painfully young woman, a schoolgirl, really. As always, I could do little for her.

What kind of country punishes its youth who have committed no crime?

Kirk's eyes crack open. He blinks, looking at me with an unfocused gaze. "Thirsty," he croaks.

I hasten to the table and return with the tin cup and a packet of aspirin powder. I pour some of the powder into the water, then lift his head and hold the cup to his lips. He drinks, then lays back down. "Danke," he whispers. He stares at me a moment longer. "Are you . . . here to . . . interrogate me?" His body tenses.

I shake my head. "I'm a doctor. You're ill. I'm here to take care of you."

"They won't let up . . . keep trying to get . . . more information. I wish they'd . . . get it over with."

I look down at him, saying nothing. Doubtless that is the reason any attention is being given this man at all. They won't do away with him until they're through pumping him, and they're not through yet.

I rise. This man should be in a hospital, where he can be deloused, given a hot bath, put in a clean room, and served nutritious food. Of course, in solitary confinement and on death row, little of that will happen, but I'll speak to the guards anyway and leave them some packets of aspirin powder to administer. "I'm leaving now, Kirk. But I'll come back soon and check on you."

I'm not scheduled to work at Stadelheim for the next two days. I have private patients to attend to.

Good Aryans, not convicted political prisoners.

But when gratitude flickers across Kirk's pale face, I know instinctively I will keep my promise. Not that it will make a difference.

It is a greater kindness to the wretches within these walls to aid them in a speedy death.

And here I am, trying to save lives.

I jolt awake, drenched in sweat. Katrin leans over me, shaking my shoulder, long blond hair flowing around her face. Darkness etches the room.

"Friedrich." Her tone is soft, soothing.

"I'm fine."

"You're not." Concern mars her features. "You were having a nightmare. You were shouting Eli's name."

My body sags into the mattress. "Was I?" I sigh, rubbing a hand across my eyes.

She rests her head on the pillow beside me, her palm on my chest. "You haven't had a nightmare in years. Why now? Why Eli?"

"I don't want to talk about Eli." My tone is rougher than I intended. "Go back to sleep, Katrin."

"I can't." She sits up in bed, sheets tangled around her. Her jaw is set in a stubborn line. I know better than to refuse my wife when she wears that look. In our five years of marriage, I've learned this the hard way.

I sigh again.

"Eli was your best friend. Our best friend. He died in a horrific way. Something like that can't just be pushed aside."

"Eli was *Jewish*." Killed the night of Kristallnacht by a group of overzealous thugs two months before Katrin and I married. Eli, Katrin, and me. We'd been inseparable. A steadfast and true friendship, Eli my little brother at heart if not in blood, Katrin at our center. We were supposed to be indestructible.

Until the Nazis, we were.

I sit up, leaning against the headboard. Scrub my hands across my face. "They're murdering Jews, Katrin. Hundreds of thousands of them. I've read *Mein Kampf*. It was his plan all along." I look at her. "And I work for them, the criminals."

"You work at Stadelheim but only a couple of days a week."

"I witness executions."

Her face turns ashen. "You . . . you never told me that."

"I never told you because it's too horrible to talk about. I still can't talk about it." Not without being sick. Not without seeing every one of their faces, starting with the first.

"Then why tell me now?" To her credit, she doesn't linger on the fact that I've been keeping something from her. Katrin is a much better wife than I deserve.

"I met a young man today. A patient. He has typhus. Remember those students who were tried by the People's Court?"

Katrin nods.

"He was one of them. He's in a death cell, and he says he's still being interrogated. He looked . . . how can I describe it? He looked haunted. The worst part about it was . . . he was nice. Ordinary. About Eli's age when he . . ." I draw in a long breath, throat tightening. "When I told him I'd come back soon, he gave me this grateful smile. Like I'd offered him the moon."

"Can nothing be done for him?"

"If he has family, they'll petition for clemency. Will they succeed? I doubt it. Not in a case like that. The court is determined to make examples out of all of them."

"So he dies." Her voice trembles a little.

"They all die."

We sit in silence, our bedroom cloaked in blackout curtains and unspoken thoughts. If there were only some way . . .

The sentence hangs unfinished in my mind.

If there was, would I take the risk? Would I gamble with my life, the life of my wife, to save a stranger?

"What an indifferent world this is," Katrin says softly.

"Which is worse, I wonder. Indifference or hate?"

"It takes effort to feel hate. Indifference is easy." Katrin rubs a strand of hair between her fingers. The war has exacted its toll from us both. Stalingrad stole her brother. An air raid, my cousin from Cologne.

"And yet we're all guilty of indifference." I sigh again. "Except for a few, those students among them." I meet her eyes, searching them. "If an opportunity presented itself, would you risk your own life to save another? On the unlikely chance you'd actually succeed." An incredulous smile tugs at my lips. What I'm thinking . . . it's madness.

Katrin hesitates, then nods. "If we hope for a different world, then must we not begin now to do our part to make it so? If we don't, then who will?"

I lift my gaze to the ceiling, sending a prayer heavenward. "Who, indeed?"

CHAPTER FORTY-SEVEN

Kirk
May 20, 1943

FLAMES LAP AT MY body with reddish-orange tongues. I'm on fire. I have to be.

Water. What I wouldn't give to have someone pour it over me and douse the flames. I open my eyes. The gray walls around me dance and weave. My stomach heaves, only there's nothing left to retch out. Every joint in my body aches.

"Kirk." The voice sounds far away. I've heard it before. Where? I can't remember. It takes too much effort to remember.

"Go 'way," I try to mumble. My lips feel thick and unwieldy. "Leavemebe. No . . . more . . . questions . . ."

"I'm not going to hurt you, Kirk. I'm here to help. But you have to trust me. Do you trust me?" Something shadowy hovers above me. The source of the voice?

"Yeah," I manage. But I don't. I don't trust anybody. All they do is lie.

I want Annalise. She'll keep me safe. She'll make them go away.

She's not here. The voice belongs to someone else. A man.

And I'm supposed to be keeping her safe. I've failed.

"Failure." The little boy holding the teddy bear looks at me with glassy eyes. His frame is skeletal. Ghostly.

"Failure!" Hans shouts, his face anguished. I try to reach out to him, but he's too far away.

"Failure." Tears trickle down Annalise's cheeks. "You failed, Kirk."

"I'm sorry," I moan. "I'm so sorry."

"Shh. There now. It's all right." Slow soothing words. I let myself be lulled by them, swept away. A heavy sleepiness purls through my veins, silencing the voices.

The world goes dark.

Friedrich
May 20, 1943

Kirk lies motionless and stiff on his cot.

There's no time for deliberation. I've done it, and I must act quickly. I stow the supplies I've gambled everything on in the inner pocket of my bag. Syringe, needle, the vial of drugs. I draw in a breath of acrid air—it's only gotten worse since I was last here—and marshal my features into an appropriate expression of mild shock (it would never do to show too much emotion over a death row patient).

I cast a glance at Kirk. The drugs have lowered his breathing and heart rate to the point that a casual observer, like the guard, will think him actually dead. It would take a trained medical eye to detect otherwise.

This will work. It has to.

I rap hard on the cell door. At first, nothing. Then footsteps and a key in the lock.

"Finished?" The guard reeks of fresh cigarette smoke.

Smoking on duty, were you, my man?

"Not exactly." I pause for effect. My heartbeat fills my ears. Everything depends on my convincing performance during the next few minutes. "The man is dead. When I entered the cell, he was gasping out his last breaths. I did all in my power to save him." *Ja*, that's right. A little regretful, but then, medicine can't work miracles.

"Well, that'll cheat the executioner one."

"He had typhus. A serious case." A moderate one, actually. "He needs to be removed from the premises as quickly as possible. Only those who've been inoculated are allowed to move him." I ramble about typhus and its grim fatalities, watching the guard's eyes grow wider. He slowly backs away from the cell. "Is there a coffin about?"

The guard nods.

"See that it's fetched. One of you can help me clear the cell of the body." I shoot a look of disgust toward the door.

Another nod.

"The kommandant should be informed, and there's paperwork to be completed. I'll make a recommendation the corpse be released immediately to the Anatomical Institute. They'll find some use for it in their dissection laboratory."

"We'll begin preparations straightaway." The guard turns smartly, leaving me standing in the solitary corridor. Placards reading Death Sentence stare back at me.

I steady myself for a moment, drawing in calm. I must go to the prison office and complete my portion of the paperwork. Often the corpses of those executed are sent directly to one of the anatomical institutes, leaving the families no time to request the body for private burial. A practice begun after the families, quite naturally, tried to do so, robbing the institutes of dissection material.

I blow out a breath. I'm a doctor, not a man of quick words and cunning intellect.

But I must use my title as the first and conjure the qualities of the second if I'm to talk my way into the Anatomical Institute.

Two hours later, I'm en route to the Anatomical Institute. With the assistance of the guard, I lifted Kirk into the wooden crate they're using for coffins these days. Cheaply made, there are plenty of cracks to let in air. Yet unease filled me nonetheless as the lid slammed shut.

Once the institute gets word of a shipment, they're quick to send a truck over for pickup. During my own studies, I often participated in dissections. Of course then corpses were fewer and farther between. If any came from prisons, they were of convicted murderers, not random individuals who distributed leaflets or were caught tuning in to the BBC.

These days, the institutes have more bodies than they have time.

Soon I'm climbing broad stone steps and making my way through white-tiled hallways that smell of antiseptic and lime. None of the men striding purposefully through the corridors pay me any heed. I stop before a frosted-glass door, raised black lettering declaring this the office of Dr. Hermann Wagner. There's no guarantee the eminent anatomist will be in or that he'll even see me.

God didn't save Eli. Only silence answered my pleas then.

Is it too much to ask for a miracle on behalf of Kirk Hoffmann?

I send up a silent prayer anyway, as I raise my fist to knock.

A moment later, the door opens. White-coated and balding, Dr. Wagner takes my measure. His narrow eyes are cushioned in a face grown doughier since I sat under his tutelage.

"Dr. Wagner." I hold out my hand. He doesn't take it.

"Do I know you?"

"Once. My name is Dr. Friedrich Voigt. I studied under you years ago." I try for an "old times' sake" smile.

"I don't recall. Is there some reason you wish to see me?"

I nod. "Might I come in? It'll only take a moment."

The little eyes flicker with annoyance. Wagner opens his mouth. He's going to refuse.

"Only a moment, Dr. Wagner."

"Very well." Wagner steps aside and walks toward his desk. He motions for me to take a seat across from him.

"Speak fast, Voigt. I'm a busy man." Wagner leans back in the leather chair.

"Along with my private practice, I'm also on staff at Stadelheim Prison. As you know, our two facilities have been doing a good deal of business together as of late."

"That's an understatement." Wagner issues a gruff laugh. "Seditious rebels."

I lean forward, folding my hands atop the desk. "As you say, sir. However, there's a particular cadaver that should be arriving here any time now that I have a special interest in."

"Special interest in a cadaver?"

"It's rather an unhappy circumstance. You see, I happen to know the family of the young man. Kirk Hoffmann is his name. He died quite suddenly of an infectious disease. I know it's not standard practice, but I would like the body to be released to the family and given a proper burial."

"You're saying you wish me to bend the rules to retrieve the corpse of an old friend?" Wagner's bushy eyebrows twitch.

I nod, swallowing through the dryness in my throat. "I'm willing to take all responsibility upon myself if there are any issues. And . . ." I pause. "Make it well-worth your while."

Wagner may be a deft hand with a scalpel, but he'd never make it in a game of cards. I can read the greedy light in his eyes far too readily.

"So will there be any . . . difficulties?"

Wagner tilts his head, considering. "Not for, shall we say, five hundred marks. Then I'm sure any difficulties could be done away with without issue."

"Good. Once the body is in my possession, I'll see to it you receive compensation in full." I rise. "I'll come around with a van and take delivery in an hour, if that's convenient."

"Fine."

I turn and make my way toward the door.

"Say, what was his crime?" Wagner's words give me pause.

"Oh, one of those pathetic resistance situations. You know how they are." I keep my tone light. "I pity the family though. He was their only son."

Wagner chuckles. "At least he cheated the guillotine."

I place my hand on the doorknob, letting myself out.

Indeed, he may have.

⤝

Kirk
May 21, 1943

Cracking my eyes open feels like lifting cement bricks. When I do, everything is blurry and unfocused. My limbs are strangely heavy, but that doesn't stop them from aching. The back of my throat is dry and swollen.

My eyes ache with the effort of looking down. I'm covered in something white. Whatever I'm lying on is cushioned like a mattress. Around me are various crates and objects draped in cloth.

Where am I?

A rhythmic thumping. Footsteps? A figure emerges from the shadows. He's tall, dark-haired. Panic tears through me. It all comes back in a rush. Interrogators. A prison cell. A courtroom and judge in red robes spewing vile names. A girl with tears in her eyes . . . Annalise.

I arch forward, trying to sit, but the man presses me down.

"Steady now." His tone is quiet. "It's all right. Lie back."

Another figure appears behind the man. A blond woman. "He's awake," she says in an awed voice.

"Water, Katrin. Quickly."

The woman hastens forward, kneeling. She holds a glass in her hands. The man lifts my head, and the woman pours a trickle of coolness down my throat. I want to gulp every drop of the soothing water, but the woman takes the glass away after I've finished half.

"That's enough for now." She has a gentle voice. Like Annalise's, only softer.

"Where am I?" My words are old-man gravelly.

"You must rest." The man has my wrist in his grip. A familiar recollection from what seems like another life crosses my mind. Is he taking my pulse?

I shake my head, grimacing. "Nein. I need to know." Something isn't right. I'm not in a prison cell anymore. Again a rush of panic cramps my empty stomach. My head pounds.

The man lowers my hand onto the blanket and surveys me a moment more. "I'm Dr. Friedrich Voigt. This is my wife, Katrin." He gestures to the woman. She smiles. "You're in our home. Our attic, to be precise."

I rub a hand across gritty eyes. "I don't understand. Why . . . why am I in your attic?" This isn't real. I'm hallucinating. Didn't I once tend a patient who experienced similar symptoms? Did I ever even *have* patients?

"You had typhus. Still have, I'm afraid."

Typhus. Fever. Headache. Cough. Rash. In Russia, I treated men with the disease. That much I believe. "I was . . . wasn't I in Stadelheim?"

Katrin nods. "Your being here at all is a miracle." She pulls her sweater tighter around herself. "My husband helped you escape from the prison."

"Escape?" My voice is a weak echo.

Dr. Voigt smiles faintly. "I know it's a lot to take in. I'm one of the doctors at Stadelheim. I visited you while you were ill. Two days later, I gave you an injection which had the effect of making you appear stiff and unresponsive. In short, as if you'd died of the disease. I assisted in preparing you for transport and signed off on the necessary paperwork. I then went to the Anatomical Institute where I purchased your corpse under the guise of returning it to your family for burial. You were transported here yesterday in a delivery van belonging to Katrin's uncle. You woke briefly when we gave you a disinfecting bath, but you probably don't remember. Since then, you've been sleeping off the drugs—and the typhus, I expect."

"What? That's . . . that's . . ." It's insane. Drugged, smuggled out of the prison, my body purchased from the Anatomical Institute . . .

"It's true." Katrin smooths cool fingers across my forehead. "You're safe now. As far as your prison record is concerned, you've ceased to exist. We're making arrangements for false papers so you can travel to Switzerland as soon as you're recovered."

"Switzerland," I breathe. Memories of the time I spent in prison after the trial float back. My endless prayers, the weighty resignation that I would soon die. The farewell letters I wrote to my parents. My parents . . . "Does anyone else know I'm here?"

Dr. Voigt shakes his head. "Nein. And it must remain that way. You must contact no one while you are here. Not the slightest whiff of suspicion must come beneath the noses of the Gestapo, or they'll search for you without delay." His eyes are grave. "If you value your life and ours, you'll follow our instructions to the letter."

I sag into the mattress, body aching, mind drained. Turning my head, I look into Dr. Voigt's face. "Why?" My voice cracks. "Why would you go to such lengths to save me? We don't even know each other."

Dr. Voigt lowers his gaze to his hands resting on his bent knees. Turns them palm up, then back over again. He gives a quick glance into my eyes. I recognize the look there. Pain glossed over by time's veneer. "True, *ja*. Though in the scheme of things, does that really matter? All of us are fellow travelers along the same path. Should we not stop for the stranger, as well as the friend?" He touches my shoulder. "We'll bring up some soup. You need to rest and regain your strength."

The mention of food makes saliva rush to my throat. I swallow. "I . . . I don't know how to thank you."

An enigmatic smile touches the man's lips. "I didn't do it for gratitude."

"Then why?" I didn't ask him to, nor did I offer him anything of monetary value. In the months I spent in prison, I never once encountered anyone like this. Heaven help me, I'd begun to lose all faith in goodness, in and of itself, a long time ago.

"I did it to cease being a cog in the machine our country has become. A machine that makes men mad, turns them into animals." Dr. Voigt draws in a long breath. "Perhaps to prove to myself I hadn't become one too. And I did it for a friend. Now rest. We'll be back in a few moments." He and his wife turn away, footsteps soft against the floorboards.

I close my eyes, not knowing what I should think or feel. I cannot fully grasp what has happened to me. I expect it will be a long while until I'm able to do so.

Katrin returns and spoons hot chicken broth past my cracked lips, her voice and touch gentle. I'm too weary to ask more questions. She fluffs my pillows and smooths a hand across my forehead.

Minutes later, sleep comes.

CHAPTER FORTY-EIGHT

Kirk
June 10, 1943

THREE WEEKS LATER, I'M pronounced well enough to travel. I've spent the past weeks in the Voigts' attic, permitted downstairs only after the black-out curtains have been drawn. I've gained weight, the typhus rash fading. I've been given new clothes and a pair of wire-rimmed spectacles, my brown hair dyed black, after which Katrin took my photograph for my identity papers. Friedrich gave me a set of false papers (where he got them, he wouldn't reveal) and has spent the past weeks drilling me.

Kirk Hoffmann died at Stadelheim. You are Franz Beck, twenty-four years old, an orphan from Munich. You're unable to serve in the Wehrmacht due to a heart condition and are visiting relatives in Switzerland to work in their butcher shop in Bremgarten. Their names are Ernst and Waltrud Keller. Do not give any of this information unless asked. You are an Aryan. You do not need to answer to anyone. You will succeed. You will survive this war.

Friedrich has repeated this so often, I've almost started to believe him. Unfortunately, there are no Ernst and Waltrud Keller of Bremgarten. I'll be on my own in Switzerland. Vater's Confessing Church friend Rudolf Ganz lives in the countryside, caring for Jewish refugees who managed to escape while they still could. I pray I can find him and, after I tell him my story, he'll be willing to take me in.

I check my reflection in a handheld mirror. The young man with dark hair and glasses bears little resemblance to the Kirk Hoffmann I remember. I expect it's just as well. I place the mirror atop my neatly folded blankets on the mattress, then pick up my rucksack and descend the stairs for the final time.

Friedrich and Katrin wait for me at the bottom. Sunlight streams through the house, across the polished floors and cream wallpaper. Katrin holds a parcel wrapped in brown paper.

"There's sausage sandwiches and a few apples. This will last you on the train." She passes the parcel into my hands.

"Danke, Katrin." I stuff the parcel in my rucksack, then set my bag on the floor. "For everything." I pull the petite woman into my arms. Katrin Voigt has held a bucket while I vomited after eating too quickly, made endless trips up and down the attic stairs to care for me, and played game after game of chess to help me pass the time. Besides my own mutter, she's taken care of me more than anyone I've known.

Katrin hugs me back long and tightly. When she steps away, tears mist her eyes. "You take care of yourself now." She lifts her chin. "I don't want you getting thin again."

I smile. "Don't worry. I will."

"Go with God, Kirk," she says softly, then ducks her head and hurries toward the kitchen. Friedrich shakes his head at her departure.

"She doesn't want you to see her cry. You've become very dear to her."

At this, I swallow hard. "She's a fine woman. You're blessed to have her as your wife. I was blessed to know her."

"Do you have everything you need?" Friedrich glances at my rucksack.

"Ask yourself." I grin. "You're the one who packed the thing."

Friedrich chuckles. "Well then." He faces me. "Your train leaves in less than an hour."

"*Ja*." I pause, unsure how to continue. During my recovery, I had plenty of time to think through every aspect of what happened to me. Over and over I asked myself, Should I take this chance? Why had it been handed to me and not Hans, Alex, or Willi? Dr. Voigt assured me the executions of those tried in April had yet to be carried out. But the Nazis won't keep them alive forever.

My friends will die.

I will live.

I see no justice in it. Nor can I forget the fact that I'm leaving Annalise in prison, while I escape to freedom. My beloved Annalise. She'll think me dead, and I can do nothing to prove her wrong.

"It's the only way." Friedrich places his hand on my shoulder. A healer's hand. Friedrich assured me he'd continue to do what he could for the inmates of Stadelheim, though he doubted an escape like mine could be attempted again. I alone have been given a chance so many deserve.

"I know." I meet his gaze. "After the war is over, I'll come back as soon as I can. And you promise once it's safe to do so, you'll get word to my wife and parents?"

"As soon as it's safe. I have the address you gave me."

"There's no way I'll ever be able to repay you . . ."

"You're wrong there. You've repaid me in full." He looks away toward the front door of his home. "Years ago, I lost a friend because men in their cruelty deemed his life of no value. Eli was my best friend. In spite of his death, I still went right ahead and worked for men with their same brand of cruelty. I became a victim. Saving you has changed that. But it will never be enough." Emotion fills his gaze. "I couldn't save Eli."

"Maybe not," I say quietly. "Yet you did something."

Friedrich nods. He holds out his hand, clasping mine in a firm grip. "God be with you, Kirk Hoffmann."

"I only pray He makes me worthy of what you've given me."

"Don't worry." Friedrich gives a slight half smile. "He will."

I pick up my rucksack and head for the door. I turn, looking one last time at Friedrich Voigt. He watches me as I go, gaze firm and reassuring.

I open the door and let myself outside. It's a glorious summer day, the air fresh and warm. I stare up at the sky in wonder. How beautiful it is. How precious life is. Maybe it takes coming as close to the end of it as I did to realize its value. By some miracle I cannot find the sense in, while others have been robbed of life, I've been given it back again.

I still don't understand.

But for Friedrich and Katrin, and my friends wherever they may be, I will honor them by grabbing hold of this chance.

↙

Annalise
June 30, 1943

A letter rests beside the bowls of porridge and cups of ersatz on the breakfast tray. I carry the tray into the cell and place it on the wooden table. Cato, my cellmate, hastens to claim her cup and bowl and pulls her chair up to the table. Standing by the table, I pick up the letter, turning it over in my hands. The white envelope is addressed to me, the flap obviously ripped and resealed by the censor.

We're forbidden to sit on our cots during the day, so I lower myself to the rickety wooden chair. Cato's spoon scrapes the sides of her metal bowl.

My fingers tremble as I slit the envelope and slide out a single piece of folded paper. I hesitate before unfolding it. Since arriving at Rothenfeld Women's Prison, my place of residence for the next two years, I've received no mail. In prison, one has a tumultuous relationship with news from the outside, simultaneously craving and fearing it.

"Aren't you going to read it?" Cato asks between gulps. My cellmate is a thief, not a political prisoner. The first day I set foot in our shared cell, she announced our system of rules, the only way she said we'd be able to live civilly together. One of those rules was no prying into personal business. I'd remind her she's breaking it, but staring at the letter has rattled me more than I want to admit.

I force myself to take a deep breath and unfold the paper. Small, even script fills the sheet.

My dearest Annalise,

I do not know whether this letter will reach you, nor if any of the others we sent have done so. But I must write. There's no way to say this gently. Kirk has died. According to the letter we received from the prison, he died of typhus.

Both Paul and I are thankful his end came this way. Our efforts to claim his body were met with refusal, so we do not know where or if he has been buried. This is very difficult for me to write, and I know it will be harder still for you to read. Paul and I are comforted to know he is with the Lord now, in our glorious, eternal home. I pray you too will be able to find peace. Peace, I have learned, is a choice, not a feeling. I don't believe I fully understood this until the trials of these past months.

We will try and send a parcel to the prison. Please write and let us know what we can do for you. A letter from you would bring us much joy. You are our daughter now, Annalise. Paul and I pray for you daily and send with this all of our love.

God bless you,
Mutter Hoffmann

The letter falls from my hands, onto the floor. I stare at the gray wall, unwilling, unable to comprehend the words I just read.

Kirk is dead.

My body begins to shake uncontrollably.

How does one grasp such finality? Such emptiness? Outside, in the world beyond prison walls, people go on. Life goes on. While Kirk's . . . does not. The Nazis didn't even care enough to return his earthly remains to his family. My husband will never have a resting place. A grave in some shaded spot to put flowers on, to visit on Sundays.

I curse them for that. Not because they arrested us or tried us in a court of law that was a farce, but because they didn't even have the decency to let Kirk be buried by his family.

I bend double in my chair, hands fisted, head bent. Each breath is a shuddering gasp. My stomach churns with a wave of nausea. I clamp my lips together to keep from screaming. If I start, I know I won't be able to stop.

"Annalise?" Cato's voice sounds far away.

I look up. "My husband is dead." The words are brittle and empty. All I can think about is the way Kirk's eyes crinkled when he smiled at me and how I'll never see his smile again. My hands go limp against the threadbare fabric of my prison dress.

Cato's hand settles on my shoulder. She crouches beside my chair. "I'm sorry, Annalise. Really, I am. Was he . . . executed?"

I shake my head. "Typhus." A choked laugh escapes. "They were going to execute him anyway. I guess he saved them the trouble." The enormity of it, of this loss, swamps me uncontrollably. Tears slide down my cheeks, and I press my fist hard against my mouth, rocking back and forth. Cato rubs my shoulder, and I can tell she's trying to say something soothing, but my wracking sobs drown her words.

I don't know how long I cry. Hours? Centuries? I didn't know one could shed so many tears and yet they'd still keep coming.

Finally, Cato helps me to my cot and covers me with a blanket, muttering something about rules and where the guards can stuff them. I lie on my back, staring at the ceiling, lifeless and spent.

How am I supposed to go on? To keep breathing? To keep living? More than that, how am I supposed to want to do any of those things in a world without Kirk?

My gaze falls on the Bible on the table between our cots. I've read it nearly every day, clutching it against my chest, lips moving with prayers for a miracle for my friends, for my husband. Clinging to hope that the God who hears my prayers would actually answer me with one. Trying to have faith, to keep praying, to not give up in spite of everything.

And even now I'm supposed to keep doing that?

It's a bitter prayer, if it could even be called one at all.

I can do all things through Christ which strengtheneth me.

The verse I read weeks ago fills my mind like an echo.

All things? Surely some, but all? This? When I have nothing? Less than nothing?

"I can't," I whisper in a voice raw from weeping. "I can't."

He can.

Where it came from, I don't know, but the truth is there regardless. I don't believe it right now, don't even come close, but it gives me the strength to say in a tone more accusing than not. "Do it then, God. Do it through me."

CHAPTER FORTY-NINE

Annalise
April 24, 1944

BOMBS SHAKE THE PRISON. In the air-raid shelter, dozens of women huddle beneath a single flickering lightbulb, listening to distant shrieking, casting anxious glances at the ceiling as if one more blast will bring it down upon our heads.

I sit on a crate in the corner, hands between my knees, shivering in the chill night. Munich has been battered all afternoon, and after a respite, we're being hit again. My eyes fall closed as another explosion tremors through the building with its *crushing, crushing, falling* sound.

I no longer pray for God's protection. Who am I to seek it when thousands are daily added to the casualties of war? Now I pray for strength to face the next moment and, if I am to die, a painless death.

The women's prison is also a detention facility for juveniles, and last month, fifteen-year-old Hella Hahn replaced my former cellmate who'd been released. A year's sentence for telling a schoolmate Hitler's war is one big lie. She's lucky—these days many are losing their heads for less.

Hella sits next to me, her bony shoulder pressed against mine. She clings to me like a child, her wide eyes and heart-shaped face making her look thirteen rather than fifteen. Now she rests her head against my shoulder, and I stroke her soft, thin hair with work-roughened fingers.

It's astonishing how easily one can acclimate to a new routine, until it seems the landscape of life has never consisted of anything else. The routine of prison has driven itself into my bones. Sometimes I wonder if the girl named Annalise Brandt, who grew up in Berlin and studied in Munich, is someone else entirely, and the woman in the shapeless gray dress who responds automatically to commands and labors endless hours hunched over a table assembling electrical parts has been me all along. All those from our circle have left this prison—Traute, Giesla, and Katharina, released after a year. I'm the only one left.

"It's getting worse," an older woman moans.

"Be lucky you're down here and not out there," another says sharply. "This hole can't hold all of us. Some are still in their cells. The next hit might blow them to bits."

Hella shudders. I wrap my arm around her shoulders.

"Shut up. You're making it worse," a ginger-haired girl retorts. "We've got enough bad news of our own. We don't need to hear yours."

The guard assigned to our shelter squints at the crumbling ceiling grimly, ignoring the quarrel.

"Who asked your opinion?"

"I'm entitled to one, aren't I?"

"Not here, you're not." A bitter laugh.

Ka-boom.

Plaster rains from the low ceiling, landing on the heads of the women like snow. The air smells of urine from the bucket in the corner.

"We'll be dead in an hour, so what does it matter anyway?"

Hella whimpers. "Ignore them," I whisper, pressing my lips against her hair. "They don't know what they're talking about."

The insults and retorts fly back and forth, ragged nerves giving way.

If Kirk were here, what would he do?

How often I've asked myself that question. Thinking through his eyes has given me a clarity I would have otherwise lacked. Enabling me to be strong for others when I wanted to fall apart myself.

It's time for me to be strong again. Unlike the others, I don't fear death by the next bomb. I'd welcome it actually. To be with the Lord and with Kirk sounds like bliss. An end to these days of ceaseless misery.

Until then, if *then* indeed comes, I'm determined not to give up. When I prayed that prayer on my cot, drowning in sorrow after Kirk's death, I didn't really expect God to answer. When He did, it wasn't to take away the core-deep emptiness or erase all fear. He simply provided the strength to keep going another minute, another hour. It's humbling, this daily, child-like reliance, but faith has given me courage outside of myself. Peace, like Mutter Hoffmann says, is a choice, not a feeling.

Putting Hella gently from me, I stand and walk through the crowd. Ignoring the bickering, I turn to some of the onlookers who watch the disagreement with bland interest.

I take a deep breath. "Come ladies, gather 'round."

"What for?" Martha, the lanky woman I sit across from in the munitions workroom, hugs her arms against herself.

"We're going to pray. I think now would be a good time, don't you?"

Martha shrugs.

"Tell your friends. Let's get in a circle." I beckon Hella toward me.

Another blast jitters the shelter walls, reverberates through my body. The light sputters. Surprisingly, Martha walks away and speaks to some of her friends. After a few words, several follow her.

We form a circle of about thirty in the middle of the shelter. The others stand on the fringes, arms crossed, determined to have none of it. I expect the guard to protest, but he remains at his post near the shelter door, puffing on a cigarette.

"All right, everyone. Join hands." I grab Hella and Martha's hands. I've never prayed in a group before. I haven't even attended a church service since I was a little girl. What am I thinking, leading something like this?

But in this desperate place and time, while the world around us turns to rubble and not a one of us knows if we will survive this night, none of that matters. High-flung words won't impress a single woman here.

Faith, though, now that's something else altogether.

I look into the faces in our circle, flickering light illuminating them in a glow of shadows. Each gaze bears the marks of a different kind of suffering. The war has stolen more than we bargained for from all of us.

In and of myself, I can offer them nothing.

He can.

I hear Kirk's voice, see his soft smile urging me on.

"God is with us." My voice is strong. "He is always with us."

"Even in prison?" the ginger-haired girl asks with a jut of her chin. She stands on the outskirts, hands in her pockets.

"*Ja*, even here." My hand in Hella's is damp. "Especially here. In the worst places of this world, He is in those places. He sees every injustice—"

"Then why doesn't He stop them?" Nods and murmurs of agreement echo the ginger-haired girl's question.

I sigh. "I've wondered that too. I don't think we're supposed to have all the answers. Only to know that no matter how dark it becomes around us, there's always a flicker of light. His light." I swallow. "I've made the choice to trust Him. Not because I'm hoping for miracles, but because His love is the miracle." I pause. "Shall we pray together?"

Head bent, the ginger-haired girl slips into the circle. I smile at her. Some women cross themselves. Some bow their heads. Others stand stiffly, unsure.

The words come, faltering at first, but growing in strength. Hella squeezes my hand. Martha wipes away a tear.

And as the shelter convulses and sirens whine and we wait for dawn, our hearts rise toward heaven.

1

Kirk
May 7, 1945
Switzerland

"It's over." Rudolf Ganz bursts into the classroom. The students look up from their lessons with eager eyes at the sight of the white-haired man standing in the doorway of the sunlit schoolroom.

"What's over?" From my place at the blackboard, I give Rudolf a stern glance. It's a warm day, and the May air has been a lure all morning. I've had enough trouble keeping everyone on task without his interruption.

"The war. It's over! Germany has officially surrendered. I just heard it on the BBC."

I brace my hand against the blackboard to steady myself, drawing in deep breaths of chalk-laden air. We've known it was coming for weeks. Now it has come. The surrender. The end of six long years of untold heartache.

It's over.

I turn to face my classroom of students—German-Jewish orphans all. They stare at me utterly still, hands folded on their desks, eyes wide and far older than their years. For many of these children, their first memories are of the war. They don't remember a time before constant fear and rationed food and the deaths of their families. In Switzerland, they've lived in comparative safety, but they still bear the burden of memories. Child or adult, some experiences stay with one for a lifetime.

Making a solemn speech won't bring their families back or blot out the past. What these children need is simply to be children.

"What would you all say to leaving mathematics until tomorrow and playing outside instead?"

The children clap and cheer, their faces lighting up. War, for the moment, is forgotten.

"All right." I laugh. "Outside we go."

They make a mad dash for the door, jostling and laughing. Rudolf and I follow as they spill down the hall and into the sunshine. The grassy grounds are soon filled with games of tag and *fußball*, shouts and giggles carried on the breeze. We watch them, the brick manor house that has become a refuge for these children, and indeed for me, in the background.

"It's really over." I turn and look into Rudolf's weathered face.

"Hard to believe, I know." From the very first day I arrived at his door, still weak and tense from the strain of the journey, Rudolf Ganz welcomed me as if I were an orphan myself. The first night, I told him who I really was. He promised to keep my secret and gave me a job in the orphanage school. The years here have been good. During the day, there was always something to do, always the worry about having enough food and clothes to keep us in operation, always a child in need of love and care.

Only at night did thoughts of my family and Annalise press through the barrier and reduce me to a man frantic with fear, broken by agony. Germany has suffered much since I left it. More lives have been extinguished than I expect we realize.

I may return to find my loved ones vanished without a trace. I may never know what happened.

Both are very real possibilities.

I push my spectacles higher onto the bridge of my nose. Though I haven't continued to dye my hair, I still wear the spectacles to match the photo in my identity papers. Everyone knows me as Franz Beck. I've grown used to it; if someone called me Kirk Hoffmann, it would take me a moment to connect myself with the name.

"You're thinking about going back."

I nod, gaze fixed absently on the children. Hair streaming in the wind, lips parted in laughter, they look so innocent. These children, all children, are our future.

"When will you leave?"

I meet Rudolf's clear blue gaze. "As soon as I can."

"Travel won't be easy. Everyone will be trying to go somewhere, find someone."

"I know. But I've got to. To see . . ." I can't finish the sentence.

"Who is left," Rudolf says it for me. He knows as little as I about the fate of my family. I've forbidden him from writing to my parents. I wanted nothing to connect us, to put those I love in danger.

Through every day, Annalise's face is a shadow in the back of my mind. Our final moments together when she kissed me in the police van, whispering her love with tear-stained lips. At night, when the desperation became too much to bear, I let myself imagine seeing her again. My mind never allowed itself to conjure details besides looking into her eyes and taking her face in my hands. Pressing our foreheads together and holding each other with a strength that will never again part us.

My imaginings always left me where I started. Empty and alone and praying worn-out prayers for a miracle that may not come.

I left her. I left my friends. I heard on the BBC that Alex, Willi, and Professor Huber lost their lives at Stadelheim during the summer and autumn of 1943. I'll never again see the faces of my comrades. How young and fearless we were, typing our leaflets in the dark of night, breathing the air of revolution. We'd been so full of plans and dreams. So golden with promise.

None of it came to pass. We wrote six leaflets, defaced a few buildings, dreamed of contacting the Berlin resistance. Was it in vain? The sacrifice of these good, brave people?

I draw in a long breath.

I have to believe it wasn't. That their lives will count for something. That God has a plan in spite of the madness of man and the desecration of war.

I have to believe.

CHAPTER FIFTY

Annalise
May 30, 1945
Berlin

STANDING ON A SIDEWALK littered with rubble, I stare up at the brick edifice of the place I once called home. How is it even possible, when I've passed street after street leveled to ruins, that it remains untouched?

Berlin is a wasteland of gray. Buildings once proud are charred shells. Ragged children wander aimlessly. Everywhere, families stumble through the streets, hauling bundles of whatever remains of their worldly goods. Where they are going is a mystery, even to them it seems. Soviet troops stand on street corners, smoking German cigarettes, uniforms stark against the colorless landscape. Defeat shows on every dirty, ravaged face.

The Annalise of before would be shaking after the nightmare trip from Munich to Berlin. It took days to find a truck to take me, and I spent the trip with my arms wrapped around my knees, staring out a grimy window, pressed against the bodies of other desperate men and women trying to get to the city. Not knowing if, once I made it in, I'd be able to find a way out.

But I had to come back. To see what, if anything, remains of my family.

I climb the steps, sidestepping piles of broken glass and debris. I raise my fist and knock.

I've spent the weeks since being released from prison in Munich with the Hoffmanns. We waited out the bombings with our arms around each other, prayers on our lips. At the end of April, American troops marched into the city. Our liberators. How young they are beneath their stern helmets. They treat us with mistrust and occasionally derision. I can't say I blame them. I've talked with a few, and when asked, told them of my imprisonment. A particularly young soldier with wheat-blond hair and a farm-boy grin gave me a pack of Lucky Strikes and a tin of some strange meat-like substance called Spam. With food shortages rife and meat nonexistent, the Hoffmanns and I enjoyed it immensely.

Minutes pass. Silence greets my knocks. I'm about to turn away when I glimpse a curtain lift in a downstairs window. It falls again, and I wait uncertainly a few moments more, hands clasped at my waist.

The door opens a cautious crack.

"Annalise?" My vater's voice is a papery-thin whisper. He opens the door wider.

"Vater." I swallow hard at the sight of him. He's scarecrow thin, a threadbare suit coat hanging sack-like on his shoulders. His eyes are lifeless hollows in a gaunt face.

He steps aside to let me pass. Our once grand foyer is stripped bare. Glass litters the marble floor and dust hangs in the air.

We regard each other silently. I'm sure he's thinking the same about me. Prison turned me into a wisp with eyes too large for my thin face. I now wear my hair pinned in a loose knot at my nape, and I'm dressed in a navy skirt and cream blouse of Mutter Hoffmann's that she made over to fit me. The apartment Kirk and I shared was razed by bombs. Nothing of my own is left anymore. My clothes, my paintings, Kirk's books, our marriage license. All destroyed.

"How are you?" Thank God I no longer look at him with fear or even anger. The only emotion I can summon is a detached kind of pity. His beloved Reich is in ruins. It is said power makes small men great. I would add that the lack of it makes great men weak.

"Well." He draws himself up, as if trying to gather the fragments of who he once was. "And you?" His voice is toneless, the way one would answer a stranger.

"I'm fine." Once, I might've added, *No thanks to you*, but not anymore. What's the point? I cannot change the past. "Where's Mutter?" I made the trip to Berlin mostly to see her.

"She's dead. She died this past February. The letter the hospital sent said it was pneumonia."

After so much loss, it would seem I'd be immune to the pain of it.

"Was anyone with her?" Tears burn my eyes as I remember my mutter's face, gray in the light of dawn, when I bid her goodbye. She didn't want me to return to Munich. I left her, wanting to be with my friends and with Kirk.

I left her.

"I was at the front. I don't know." Vater draws in a long breath.

She died alone. The woman who spent her years in the shadow of her husband ended her life as she lived it. Desolate. I wasn't even there to hold her hand. My throat aches.

"And Heinz and Albert?" I look toward the stairs, expecting to see my brothers coming down to greet me.

Vater looks away. "Heinz was killed in an air raid in January. Albert died defending the city against the Russians. A hero of the Fatherland."

"He was sixteen. A child." My voice is choked. A million little memories rush over me at once. Heinz's laughter as he spun me in a dance in front of the Christmas tree. Holding Albert's soft warm body in my arms an hour after he was born, vowing to always be the best big sister. Sitting next to him on the parlor sofa while he sounded out words, my arm around his shoulders, inhaling his little boy scent. He'd look up at me with a sparkle in his eyes and a gap-toothed smile. "I did good, Annalise. Didn't I?"

Both of them. Gone.

"He was a hero." Vater's tone is firm. As if he's clinging to the only thing he has left to believe in. "All my children were. Except you."

I wish I could say I'd hardened enough for his words to have no effect on me. Oh, how I wish that could be true. I force myself to meet his eyes. "You are free to feel whatever you want toward me. I can't alter your hatred of me, any more than I can bring back the family we once had. But you don't define me. I pity you because I see the worthless foundation you built your life upon—"

"I don't want your pity." Something broken enters his gaze for an instant, swiftly replaced by ice. "Get out. This is no longer your home."

The finality of his words hits me like a slap.

I'm worthless to him. As I have always been.

My body shakes, going hot and cold by turns. I look at him once more, a tired old man standing in the shambles of an era that will never be again. "Auf Wiedersehen, Vater," I say softly.

He stands motionless.

I turn away, letting myself out of the house. The door clicks shut behind me. I stand poised on the steps of a place I once lived, in a city once glorious, now destroyed. Jagged breaths fall from my lips, and I brace my hand against the side of the building, fingers pressing into the brick to steady myself.

Dear God, You have always been my vater. And You have given me the Hoffmanns. Bring me safely back to them, to my true home and family.

Shoulders straight, I walk on, heels clicking with each step I take. A truth settles inside me, making me turn at the corner for one last look at my girlhood home.

I will never see it, or him, again.

/

Kirk
June 3, 1945

I dare not hope. Dare not allow myself even the slightest flicker of expectancy my journey will have a happy ending. War is not a storybook. Its cruelties don't end with treaties signed or dictatorships crushed. They reach beyond into the lives of those left in its wake.

Munich, the companion of my youth, is a city of ghosts. Architectural splendor has turned to heaps of ashes. Everywhere there is fresh evidence of poverty, destruction, and devastating loss. Her pride, her Führer, reduced her to this.

I walk slowly down the sidewalk, rucksack over my shoulder. How well I remember every house on our street—Frau Adler with her blue shutters and begonias, the Bergmann's next door, whose daughter my six-year-old self delighted in teasing because of her pigtails.

Next to that . . .

My heart falters.

Home.

Hope flares suddenly, stubbornly within my chest. It still stands. The yard is weed-ridden and the gate sags on its hinges, its latch broken. In disrepair, but undestroyed. It's more than I let myself hope for.

The gate creaks as I open it. My shoes crunch on the graveled path, late-afternoon sun warm on my face.

After two years, I'm home. Only . . . what does home mean after all this? Any imaginings that everything will be as before hold no weight. We're all scarred. Changed. To them, I'm a dead man.

I pause in the middle of the path, breath coming fast, almost angry at myself. Haven't I dreamed of this, envisioned it in my mind like a reel of film I can't stop watching? Now it's before me, and I can't make myself move. I should be running inside, into the arms of my family, if they are there.

The realization pulls the breath from my lungs.

I'm scared. Out here, I can imagine them as they have been in my dreams, alive and well. Taking those remaining steps and knocking on the front door will put an end to the illusion. I want that. I need that.

And I fear it.

Almighty God, give me strength.

The front door opens with a groan. A woman with a kerchief around her hair and a covered basket in her hand closes the door behind her. She makes her way down the steps, gaze on the ground.

Her slim frame, the set of her shoulders . . .

For so long, she's been lost to me, an ethereal dream, not flesh-and-blood reality. My beloved wife, heart of my heart, part of me body and soul. She starts down the path.

"Annalise." My voice is a serrated whisper.

She looks up. Our gazes lock. Her eyes widen, her face turns pale. The basket falls from her hand, contents spilling to the ground. She stands motionless, shaking her head back and forth.

I stride toward her until I'm a breath away. My rucksack falls at my feet. She hasn't moved, standing in the path, coils of hair escaping a brown kerchief, her frame painfully thin, gaze pinned to me as she shakes her head over and over.

"Annalise," I repeat. I ache to reach out and touch her, put my arms around her shoulders. But she looks at me as if I can't possibly be there. Tears shimmer in her eyes. My own well up.

"I'm here," I whisper, gently reaching out and running my thumb along her cheek, her tears embedding themselves into my skin. "I came back to you."

—

Annalise
June 3, 1945

I don't want to go crazy. I must not. The man in front of me is the product of my overwrought imagination. A mirage.

Kirk Hoffmann is dead. Not standing in front of me, whispering my name with a broken voice and tears in his eyes.

He touches my face, trailing a calloused thumb against my skin.

And says my name again.

My lungs squeeze as if they're caving in on me. I can hardly breathe, my gaze melded to his face. A face that has haunted me in dreams wrested from the deepest parts of my soul.

My legs buckle. He catches me before I fall, gathering me against his chest. "I'm here, my love." His arms are strong around me. "I'm here."

"This isn't true . . . this isn't happening." A cry falls from my lips, a tearless sob.

"Shh." He breathes, rubbing my back. "It's all right. I'm right here."

"I thought you were dead." I press the side of my face into his chest. "They said you were."

"He didn't send you word?"

"Who? Nein . . . We received nothing."

"It doesn't matter now," he whispers.

I lift my face and look into his. I'm not dreaming. The warmth of his arms around me, the creases around his eyes as he smiles are too real to be a dream.

"I never stopped loving you." I wrap my arms around his waist. "There wasn't a day I didn't dream, didn't think—"

Our lips meet in a hungry kiss. His hands tunnel through my hair, my kerchief falling to the ground. It's a kiss born of love that stays steadfast and of loss that shapes us. We're no longer Kirk and Annalise, the boy and girl once so young and golden, but a man and a woman who know what it is to come to the end of oneself and still keep going.

We've lived through a war that extinguished millions, borne witness to a darkness that engulfed the lives of our closest friends, suffered mentally and physically in ways ten years ago we would have called impossible.

Somehow, we survived.

We break the kiss. Our gazes meet. Sunlight streams from behind the clouds.

"I'll never stop living for them, Annalise." His gaze is fierce. "With you and God as my witness, I'll never stop."

Footsteps sound behind us. We turn. The Hoffmanns come slowly down the steps. I see it in their eyes, the battle of emotions, the fear and grief and disbelief. Finally, the joy. Mutter Hoffmann breaks away from her husband, and mutter and son run toward each other. I watch as he engulfs her in his arms, as they laugh and cry and hold each other.

"Thank God." Her voice rises onto the air. "Thank God."

Heart swelling, I smile as Kirk embraces Vater Hoffmann, emotion overwhelming the two men.

In the homes of the Scholls and so many others, families grieve in silence and try to go on living in spite of the empty places at the table and the aching spaces in their souls.

Should we ask why? Ought we to rationalize the seeming unfairness in this world? The temptation is great, no matter which side of the coin one finds oneself on.

Vater Hoffmann's choked voice, Mutter Hoffmann's streaming eyes and beaming lips, Kirk's bent shoulders as he tries to hold them both at once.

They stand in a circle of three, arms entwined, while sunlight falls in soft shadows and rays.

I shake my head.

Some answers we will never receive this side of eternity. It is enough to know God is present in all of our moments. Our greatest triumphs and deepest tragedies. Our beginnings and our ends.

Kirk holds out his hand to me, smiling, and I join my family. They make room for me in the circle, and I slip my arm around Kirk, Mutter Hoffmann's strong hand on my back.

The world around us may not showcase good. Evil may continue to flourish. Darkness may, in fact, choke us like never before.

A smile softens my lips, as I gaze at each beloved face and remember those faces lost to all but memory. Hans. Willi. Christl. Alex. Sophie.

Even the greatest darkness can be breached by the flame of a single candle.

My friends who once were. My family who are here now. My husband who has been restored to me.

Candles, all.

ACKNOWLEDGMENTS

SHARING THE STORY OF the White Rose was a labor of love in the truest sense of the word and one I could not have completed alone. I am profoundly grateful to those who came alongside me and devoted time and love to this project.

To Ann, thank you for translating Sophie's correspondence with Fritz Hartnagel. Your willingness to give of your time to help this English-speaking author glean from materials only available in German is a gift that contributed much to the writing of this novel.

To Heinz, for sharing his memories of growing up in WWII Germany. The afternoon I spent with you and your wife is one I will never forget. Thank you for your vulnerability and generosity in sharing this part of your past. I am humbled and grateful.

To Schuyler McConkey, for coming to my rescue and helping me brainstorm a tricky scene in this novel. To say you are amazing is an understatement!

To the dear friends who lift up me and my stories in prayer. For each and every one of those prayers, thank you. They are gifts beyond compare.

To my wonderful agent, Rachel Kent, for your encouragement, support, and ceaseless championing of my stories.

To the folks at Kregel Publications, I'm still pinching myself that I'm privileged to partner with such a talented and gracious team. You all are outstanding!

To my brilliant editors, Janyre Tromp and Becky Durost Fish. Janyre, thank you for refining this story and giving so generously of your wisdom and encouragement. Working with you is a gift. Becky, your keen editorial eye made this story sparkle. Thank you!

To my dad, thank you for your love and support as I've pursued my dream of writing. I'm so thankful to be your daughter.

To my mom, thank you for walking with me as I brought this story to life. You encouraged and prayed for me on the hard days, sacrificed countless hours to offer feedback on this novel, and continue to support me unconditionally. It is because of your influence on my life that I am a writer today. I love you!

To Sara, cherished sister and best friend. Thank you for encouraging me to write this story, for reading it a billion times and helping me to make it stronger, for sharing my heart for the students of the White Rose, for classic movie nights and endless conversations. Thank you for loving your (sometimes crazy) writer sis. We will always and forever be the Inklings 2.0.

To my readers, thank you for opening your hearts to the stories that hold so much of mine. Your encouraging emails and messages never cease to bless me.

And above all to Jesus, for giving me the gift of story. For Your grace, strength, and unfailing love. May the life I live and the words I write bring glory to Your name.

AUTHOR'S NOTE

"KEEP A GOOD MEMORY of me," Willi Graf wrote in his final letter to his family before his execution on October 12, 1943. I believe all who lost their lives at the hands of the Nazi regime would echo Willi's request to be remembered. I pray my novel has, in some small way, honored the men and women who never sought heroism but, through quietly following their convictions, earned the title nonetheless.

While Sophie and Hans Scholl, Willi Graf, Alexander Schmorell, Christoph Probst, Professor Kurt Huber, and their families are real individuals, Kirk Hoffmann and Annalise Brandt and their families are fictional characters. Annalise is, in part, inspired by an interview by Traudl Junge, Hitler's secretary during the waning days of World War II. Following the war, Traudl was tempted to blame her involvement with Hitler on youth and naivety, until she passed a plaque commemorating the Scholls. She realized Sophie, though a year younger, had clearly seen the criminal regime around her, and Traudl knew she no longer had an excuse for her inaction. I pondered the idea of creating a young woman as entrenched in National Socialism as Traudl was but who, through her friendship with Sophie Scholl, would open her eyes and take action. Kirk Hoffmann is inspired by others who worked in various degrees with the White Rose, including Jürgen Wittenstein. But while Jürgen was on the fringes of the student resistance, I placed Kirk in the center of it. Due to the large cast of characters this story presented, I was unable to detail the participation of several who were on the outskirts of the White Rose, including students Hans Hirzel, Susanne Hirzel, and Franz Müller, who helped distribute leaflets in Stuttgart and Ulm.

Although this is a work of fiction, my desire was to stay as close to the historical time line as possible, thus many of the scenes depicted in this novel are based on actual events as portrayed by biographers and historians whose works on the White Rose and its members I studied extensively, as well as on transcripts from the White Rose interrogations and letters and diaries written by the students and their families. The quote from Sophie's diary, as well as passages from the leaflets, are actual excerpts. I drew inspiration for thoughts and dialogue from studying the letters and diaries of the students, as well as from memoirs and recorded interviews by family and friends. In my portrayal, I've done my best to capture the essence of these extraordinary individuals and their beliefs.

To this day, many details regarding the White Rose remain unknown. There are conflicting accounts of when and how Sophie became an active participant in the leaflet operation. After the war, her fiancé, Fritz Hartnagel, said that in May 1942 Sophie asked him to get a requisition form for a duplicating machine officially stamped. This, supported by Elisabeth Scholl's statement that Sophie was involved from beginning to end, leads many to believe she was part of the group early on. Other mysteries include how the name White Rose came about and why the decision was made to scatter leaflets in the university's atrium.

For those interested in the fate of key players, I've included a brief summary below.

Hans and Sophie Scholl were executed on February 22, 1943, four hours after their trial ended. Seconds before the blade fell, Hans shouted a final cry of resistance, "Long live freedom!" He was twenty-four years old. Sophie was twenty-one. The Scholls and Christoph Probst are buried in the Perlacher Forest near Stadelheim Prison. To this day, visitors from all over the world come to honor them, many leaving white roses on their graves.

Christoph Probst was executed on the same day as the Scholls, leaving behind a young wife, two little boys, and a month-old daughter. He was twenty-three years old.

Alexander Schmorell attempted escape once he got word of the Scholls' arrest. Despite being sought throughout Germany as a criminal, with a one-thousand-marks reward, he evaded capture until February 24, when he was arrested after a young woman in an air-raid shelter inadvertently gave him away. During his interrogation, with no knowledge of the fate of his friends, he courageously took full responsibility upon himself in the hope of saving the others. He and **Professor Kurt Huber** were executed on July 13, 1943. In his last letter to his parents, Alex reaffirmed that he was dying with the "knowledge that I have served my deepest conviction and the truth." He was twenty-five years old.

In an attempt to extract information about the resistance, especially about trips to recruit new members, the Gestapo kept **Willi Graf** alive until October 12, 1943. Willi steadfastly refused to reveal the names of anyone involved and spent the last seven months of his imprisonment in solitary confinement. He died at the age of twenty-five.

Robert and Magdalena Scholl left Stadelheim Prison believing they had ninety-nine days to file clemency petitions and fight for an overthrow of the verdicts. They were crushed when they discovered their children had been executed an hour after they left the prison. The Scholl family was soon taken into custody under the Gestapo protocol of clan arrest. Robert Scholl was released after two years. Following the war, he became mayor of Ulm. **Werner Scholl**, the only member of the family not arrested, was reported missing in action in Russia, and his date of death remains unknown. Imprisonment and the loss of her children proved too much for Magdalena Scholl's weak health. She died not long after the end of the war, a broken woman in many ways. Following the war, **Inge Scholl** worked to preserve the legacy of her siblings, publishing an account of their story, *Die Weiße Rose (The White Rose: Munich, 1942–1943)* in 1952.

Fritz Hartnagel survived the war. After Sophie's death, he grew close to her older sister, **Elisabeth Scholl**. They married and had four children. Sophie's influence had a defining impact on Fritz's life, and he became a judge and an advisor to youthful conscientious objectors. Elisabeth passed away on February 28, 2020, one day after her one-hundredth birthday.

The Legacy of the White Rose

On June 27, 1943, the exiled German novelist Thomas Mann gave a speech over the BBC dedicated to the White Rose. "Good, splendid young people! You shall not have died in vain; you shall not be forgotten." Mann's words indeed came true, beginning days after the execution of Hans and Sophie Scholl and Christoph Probst when a young man named Hans Leipelt and his girlfriend Marie-Luise Jahn circulated a new version of the sixth leaflet with the heading "Despite everything, their spirit lives on!" Hans Leipelt and Marie-Luise Jahn were later arrested after attempting to take up a collection to support Professor Huber's widow and children. Hans was executed on January 29, 1945, at Stadelheim Prison.

In the summer of 1943, a member of the German resistance, Helmuth James Graf von Moltke, smuggled a copy of the sixth leaflet out of Germany and into Great Britain. Millions of copies were reprinted and dropped over German cities by the RAF with the title *Manifesto of the Munich Students*. Word of the White Rose reached as far as concentration camps, including Dachau, Buchenwald, and Auschwitz. One inmate recalled, "When we heard what was happening in Munich, we embraced each other and applauded. There were, after all, still human beings in Germany!"

Today the story of the student resistance continues to impact young and old with its legacy of defending truth in the midst of overwhelming darkness. In 2000, four million readers of the German magazine *Brigitte* named Sophie Scholl as the most significant woman of the twentieth century. In 2003, the German TV channel ZDF polled viewers nationwide for a series called *Greatest Germans*. Hans and Sophie Scholl took fourth place, above Bach, Goethe, and Albert Einstein. There are hundreds of schools and streets in Germany named after the members of the White Rose, and Ludwig Maximilian University has both a Geschwister-Scholl-Platz (Scholl Siblings Plaza) and a Professor-Huber-Platz. There is also a museum dedicated to the White Rose inside the university. Miniature copies of the leaflets and photos of the group's members (as seen on the cover of this book) are embedded on the cobblestones outside, a reminder to all who pass.

Yet there are still those who do not know their story.

When I first heard about the White Rose, I was profoundly moved by these young people's legacy. Hans and Sophie Scholl, Alexander Schmorell, Christoph Probst, and Willi Graf did not think of themselves as extraordinary. They were ordinary young people who loved nature, reading, and music. They had families, friends, and complicated love lives. All of them possessed a deep faith in God but struggled at times to reckon His goodness with the evil around them. Their flaws and frailties do not dim their sacrifice. They enhance it, because we realize they were not so very different from ourselves.

Writing this novel has been a rich and convicting experience, often opening my eyes to my own complacency, as I asked myself, "What would I have done?" In hindsight, it's easy to say we would have stood against Nazism, but the true answer requires a depth of soul-searching that extends to our own day-to-day lives. All of us can point to darkness in our world. We each have a voice. A ripple can become a flood—a single flame, a fire.

To Sophie, Hans, Alex, Willi, Christl, Professor Huber, and the many others who refused to remain complicit and so, by their actions, sacrificed their lives . . . thank you.

For you and for generations to come, we will not be silent.

For further reading, I highly recommend the following:

At the Heart of the White Rose: Letters and Diaries of Hans and Sophie Scholl edited by Inge Jens

Sophie Scholl and the White Rose by Annette Dumbach and Jud Newborn

We Will Not Be Silent: The White Rose Student Resistance Movement That Defied Adolf Hitler by Russell Freedman

A Noble Treason: The Story of Sophie Scholl and the White Rose Revolt Against Hitler by Richard Hanser

Alexander Schmorell: Saint of the German Resistance by Elena Perekrestov

The Short Life of Sophie Scholl by Hermann Vinke and Hedwig Pachter

NOTES

p. 37, **Nothing is more unworthy:** All quotations from the White Rose's leaflets were translated by Gerlinde Armstrong from Die Weiße Rose, *Flugblatter der Weißen Rose* (Public Domain, 2013), Kindle.

p. 41, **If everyone waits:** *Flugblatter.*

p. 42, **But now my years:** St. Augustine, *Confessions* (London: Penguin Classics, 1961), 278–79.

p. 80, **Nothing is more unworthy:** *Flugblatter.*

p. 81, **Who among us can guess:** *Flugblatter.*

p. 81, **If everyone waits:** *Flugblatter.*

p. 81, **Offer passive resistance:** *Flugblatter.*

p. 81, **Now I meet my brave ones:** *Flugblatter.*

p. 91, **Offer passive resistance:** *Flugblatter.*

p. 98, **Nothing is more unworthy:** *Flugblatter.*

p. 99, **Here we see the most terrible crime:** *Flugblatter.*

p. 100, **Thoughts are free:** "Die Gedanken sind frei," circa 1780. Translated by the author from the original German text.

p. 102, **One cannot grapple:** *Flugblatter.*

p. 103, **We ask you to make:** *Flugblatter.*

p. 112, **In this struggle for the preservation:** *Flugblatter.*

p. 120, **Every word that comes out:** *Flugblatter.*

p. 121, **We will not remain silent:** *Flugblatter.*

p. 142, **Sabotage . . . Prevent the smooth operation:** *Flugblatter.*

p. 142, **Mustn't we all, no matter what:** Inge Jens, ed., *At the Heart of the White Rose: Letters and Diaries of Hans and Sophie Scholl*, trans. J. Maxwell Brownjohn (Walden, NY: Plough, 2017), 230.

p. 207, **Support the resistance:** *Flugblatter.*

p. 210, **Tear off the mantel:** *Flugblatter.*

p. 226, **The day of reckoning:** *Flugblatter.*

p. 231, **The German name will remain:** *Flugblatter.*

p. 233, **Our nation stands shattered:** *Flugblatter.*

Don't miss this powerful story of a staggering love illuminating the dark corners of a Nazi prison from the masterful pen of Amanda Barratt

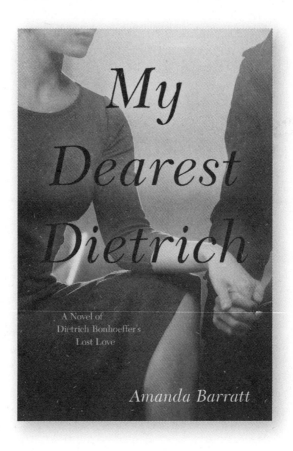

"[A] gripping historical romance . . . both dramatic and tragic."
—*Publishers Weekly*

"Humanizes the famous theologian [Dietrich Bonhoeffer], showing his devotion to one woman, his fellow man, and above all, his God."
—*World*

"In this richly researched novel, Amanda Barratt beautifully captures the story of Bonhoeffer's love for young Maria von Wedemeyer. . . . A true, heart-wrenching love story, *My Dearest Dietrich* is a must-read for fans of Bonhoeffer or World War II romance."
—*CRA Today*